Dacia Wolf
& the Dragon Lord

A magical coming of age fantasy adventure novel

Dacia Wolf

AND THE
DRAGON LORD

Book 2

Visit Mandi Oyster online at
www.MandiOyster.com

Facebook: https://www.facebook.com/MandiOysterAuthor
Instagram: https://www.instagram.com/MandiOyster/

This book is dedicated to the Princess and the Monster.
May your dreams become your realities.

Chapter 1

Scorched Pajamas

Trees crash to the ground, exploding into slivers.

Leaning over my horse's neck, I breathe in his fear. We speed up the mountain, ducking under aspen and pine branches, leaping boulders, and splashing through streams.

"Come on, Sherman, faster." I kick my feet into his sides.

A tree falls to my left, and I jerk the reins to the right. Sherman's footing is sure. He gallops faster than ever until …

Silence.

Sherman slows to a trot, and I sit back. The forest remains eerily still, not a bird sings nor cricket chirps. Sunlight filters through the canopy, casting moving shadows.

We climb an outcrop. Shattered trees litter the mountain-side, a path of tornado-like destruction, but Mother Nature can't be blamed for this devastation. What caused this is much worse.

Sherman lifts his head, flattening his ears. He skitters back.

I follow his gaze. Blackened talons rise over a rocky ridge. A red dragon crests the cliff, standing on a pile of downed trees. They creak and groan under the beast's weight. Its fierce, black eyes glare at me as smoke rolls out of its nostrils.

The dragon roars, and fire bursts between the trees. I rein Sherman to the side. Flames sting my arm, and Sherman rears. Thrown from the saddle, I land on my back. The air is forced from my body. I gasp, sucking desperately, but my lungs refuse to expand. The corners of my vision darken. I fight the panic building within me. A small breath sneaks through. Then another. My sight clears.

The earth trembles as the dragon advances. It stands as tall as an elephant. Folded wings run the length of its body. Its tail swishes from side to side, felling mature trees and bending saplings to the ground before they spring back up.

Fire blasts from the dragon's jaws.

I throw my hands out, and ice flows from my fingertips. Sizzling against the flames as they struggle to overcome it, and in the end, the ice swallows the fire.

The dragon roars. Branches and leaves vibrate free, falling all around me. I lower my arms, readying myself to stand.

The dragon charges.

My heart pounds against my ribcage, fighting to free itself. There's no way for me to move fast enough to stop the monster.

Between one breath and the next, a tingling sensation runs the length of my body, and I disappear. I push myself back on my elbows, scrabbling for a place to hide.

The dragon stops. Sniffing the air, it lowers its horned head and stalks forward. With every step, I can see hatred grow in its eyes.

"Show yourself, coward!" The beast's voice sounds like the low rumbling of timpani drums.

I close my eyes and will myself back into my dorm room.

When I opened them again, I lay in bed staring up at the ceiling. My pajama shirt was ruined, and my burned arm throbbed.

Over the last couple of weeks, my nightmares had become more frequent. In each dream, a different dragon hunted me. The first time, I had been flying through the air on a pegasus when a black dragon attacked. It was followed by purple, blue, green, and white dragons, each fiercer than the last. Even though red dragons had appeared in my dreams before, this one was different, more ferocious, and more persistent than the others.

I descended from my loft, changed my pajamas, and snagged a bottle of water from the fridge. I grabbed Glacier, my teddy bear, and asked her, "Why can't I be like everyone else?"

Chapter 2

Written In The Stars

*M*y first year of college raced to the finish. One week left. I pulled my duffle bag out of the closet and tossed a few things into it.

Why did the dreams have to come back? Leaning my head against the wall, I pinched my eyes shut. *Would I be able to hide them from Mom and Dad?*

Since learning to control my powers, I had been looking forward to going home. For once, I wouldn't be an embarrassment to my parents. They wouldn't have to fear me or be ashamed of me. I had thought that we could move on as a family. But now, who knew what would happen?

Rolling my neck from shoulder to shoulder, I sat up.

"Don't think about it right now. Cody'll only be a couple miles away." I stuffed another stack of shirts into my bag.

The edges fell in, and I looked at the remaining clothes in my closet. My wardrobe had decreased drastically since I had started living my nightmares.

Would Mom and Dad notice me coming home with fewer bags?

Hoping hearing my voice would stop this train of thoughts, I said, "You won't be alone."

I might've found comfort in that thought, but since I'd kept my dreams hidden, I couldn't expect him to be there for me. I exhaled a long, drawn-out sigh. I was going to have to tell him, but as soon as I did, everything would change.

The door opened, and I shoved my bag into the closet.

"Hey, Dacia, are you ready to go?" Samantha walked into the room wearing a red sundress. The color brought out her brown hair and eyes. Her high heels made her almost as tall as me.

"You look stunning," I said as I smoothed my dress down. "Dan's eyes are going to pop out of his head when he sees you."

Samantha shot me an approving smile. "Cody'll feel the same about you."

"Are you sure? I don't know if I should pull my hair up or leave it loose. I thought about scrapping this and putting on jeans."

Samantha laughed. "You look great." She turned me around so we were facing the mirror. "This dress is perfect. Green makes your eyes bright and contrasts your red hair. If I had curls like that, I would never pull them back."

I crinkled my nose at my reflection. "If only I could do something with the freckles."

She waved her arm. "There's a certain sweetness about them."

"That's easy for you to say. They're not all over your face." Admiring myself in the mirror, I had to admit this year had been pretty good to me. I had always been skinny, but after defeating Nefarious, I'd started working out. If I was going to be fighting monsters, I needed to be in shape. My months spent at the gym were starting to show—I looked toned.

"Yeah, I guess I'll wear this." I walked over to the window and looked out over the parking lot toward the men's dorm. I could just make out Dracaena Hall through the trees. "I figured Cody and Dan would be here by now."

"Did Cody give you any idea where we're going?" Samantha asked. "Dan won't say a word."

"No, I don't know what they're planning."

Samantha huffed as she plopped down in Big Bird, our yellow fluffy chair. "They're probably going to take us bowling or something like that." She folded her arms over her chest in mock severity and grinned at me.

"You know, I could actually see them doing that to us." I giggled. "If they do, we'll find a way to get even."

I gave up on packing, deciding it could wait until tomorrow. Samantha and I wouldn't have too many more opportunities to sit around gabbing. "So, do you ever get used to Dan's smile?"

"It's a great smile. Isn't it?" Her eyes glazed over, and she stared at nothing. I imagined she was picturing him. "I love how it brightens his face, and his dimples are so cute."

"Cody winces when I say he's cute." I folded my dress under me and sat in Cookie Monster, our blue, fuzzy chair, crossing my legs. "It's like it's an insult."

"I know, right." She shook her head. "I don't get it, but Dan doesn't like it either. He says little kids and puppies are cute. I guess he wants to be handsome or hot or sexy."

"I'm glad you two got together. You're such a cute …" I put my hand over my mouth and laughed. "Oops, I didn't mean cute. You make a great couple. You look like a little pixie next to him, and it's nice to hang out with you two."

At five o'clock, there was a knock on the door. I padded across the floor and looked out through the peephole. "They're not wearing jeans," I said as I turned the knob.

Dan stepped in first. He was dressed all in black, giving his auburn hair a redder cast. As soon as he saw Samantha, an angel's smile brightened his face. "Dacia." He nodded as he walked by me.

My breath caught in my throat when I saw Cody. The blue button-down shirt he wore made his eyes sparkle like sapphire pools. I gazed into them, getting lost in their bottomless depths.

His knuckles brushed over my cheek, snapping me out of my trance. I grabbed his black tie and pulled him toward me. "You look amazing."

"You sound surprised." He chuckled.

I dropped his tie, smoothing it down, feeling the hard muscles of his chest beneath my fingertips. "I forgot how good you look when you're dressed up."

"Thanks." His eyes softened. "And you're beautiful." He held my face in his hands, caressing my cheeks with his thumbs. He leaned down, and when he pressed his lips against mine, I melted into him. He slid his arms around my waist, pulling my body against his, keeping me from falling when my knees weakened.

He ended the kiss before I was ready and looked down at me with so much love that a blush crept up my neck and spread over my cheeks. With his hand on my hip, he turned me toward our friends.

Samantha bounced up and down on the balls of her feet. "So, where are you taking us?"

"Well—" Dan shot Samantha one of his famed smiles "—we were going to go for a walk, but since the two of you are wearing heels, I don't know now."

"But where are we going?" Samantha asked again.

"You'll see. Just relax." Dan wrapped his arm around her shoulders. "You are way too beautiful to be so impatient."

"I'm not sure if that was a compliment"—Samantha snaked her arm around his waist—"but thanks. You look pretty good yourself."

"Grab jackets." Cody walked toward the door. "Might get chilly."

Cody's Camaro was pulled up to the front of the dorm. The four of us piled into the car. Conversation was light as Cody navigated the winding mountain roads. About an hour later, he pulled into a parking lot at Cougar Lake.

I reached for the door handle, but Cody said, "Wait." He and Dan grabbed our jackets out of the trunk. Then Cody opened my door.

಄8಄

"Very chivalrous," I said as he took hold of my hand. Once I was out, Dan leaned the seat forward and extended his hand to Samantha.

"This way." Cody offered his arm to me. We walked to the boat dock and onto *The River Otter*. Once on board, we climbed the stairs to the open deck where a table was set for four. For a small-town girl like me, it looked like a scene straight out of a movie with its white linen tablecloth, sterling silver place settings, crystal glasses, and two dozen roses. Pink rose petals were scattered over the tablecloth and deck.

"Wow." Samantha's eyes widened, and a smile lit up her face. "This is really nice." She wrapped her arms around Dan's neck.

"It really is." I squeezed Cody's hand.

"I hope you enjoy it. It's for you." He gazed into my eyes, pulling me toward him. He tucked a loose curl behind my ear, letting his fingers linger against my skin. My face tingled, and shivers ran the length of my body. "We need to find the captain and let him know we're ready."

The four of us headed back down the steps to the pilot-house in search of Captain Matt Shepherd. We didn't have to go far before we found him sitting in the main salon. He was a familiar-looking man around six feet tall with a stocky build and a pleasant smile.

"Hello," he said getting to his feet and reaching his hand out to shake Cody's. As he took mine, recognition dawned in his eyes. "Hello, Little Sister."

As soon as he spoke, I recognized him. "Hello, nice EMT."

"So, this must be your brother." He lifted his eyebrow and looked at Cody. "You look much better than last time I saw you. I was one of the EMTs that took you to the hospital." Matt returned his attention to me. "Are you sure he's not your boyfriend?"

My face flushed. I glanced at Dan, hoping Matt wouldn't say anything else about Cody's injuries. "Well … he wasn't, but he is now. I'm Dacia by the way. This is Cody, and these are our friends, Dan and Samantha." I pointed to each of them.

"Nice to meet you," Samantha said while Dan nodded in agreement.

"The pleasure's mine. I'm Captain Shepherd, but call me Matt. A little history about myself, I served in the Navy for six years, and when I got out, I decided it would be nice to run shoreline cruises. *The River Otter* does four cruises a day in the summer, and in my spare time, I'm a volunteer EMT, as you know." He started to walk away. "Shall we get started?"

I looked around. "Nobody else is coming?"

"Nope, these two booked the entire cruise for you." Matt winked at me. "The staff will serve you on the open deck. Since this is a dinner cruise, it will last about three and a half hours. Enjoy yourselves!"

"Thanks." Cody grabbed my hand, and the four of us headed back to the open deck.

When *The River Otter* departed, soft music began playing. Dan and Samantha headed off to take their seats, but Cody and I stood at the railing and looked out at Cougar Lake. The sun hovered just above the mountains, but it would be a couple of hours before it set. Gentle ripples ran across the smooth surface of the lake as the boat left the dock.

"This is really beautiful," I said.

He brushed his thumb across my cheek. "Pales in comparison."

Warmth spread from my neck up onto my face. Even the tips of my ears were on fire. "I'm glad Matt didn't say anything else." Most people, Dan included, thought Cody had gone to the hospital for a kidney stone, but in reality, Cody'd been beaten for trying to keep me safe. He'd had two broken ribs, an injured knee, a concussion, and numerous bruises and cuts. His eyes had swelled shut. Since he'd healed in just a matter of hours, thanks to my powers, not many people knew the truth.

"Yeah." His face darkened, and the gentleness left his voice. "I didn't recognize him. I couldn't open my eyes." His fists clenched and unclenched. "I was supposed to protect you."

I wrapped my arms around his waist. "I know, Cody, but you're all right, and we're together now. Let's not think about it tonight." I nodded toward the table. "You have a wonderful evening planned for us. Let's enjoy ourselves."

After a few tense moments, Cody relaxed. "You're right. It's over."

A chill crept up my spine. *Is it, though?*

With his arm around my shoulders, we headed over to the table where Samantha was reading the card from her roses. As soon as we sat down, Cody handed me mine.

I took it out and read the sweetest words. "Dacia, loving you is like breathing. It comes naturally, and I couldn't live without you. Yours Always, Cody."

Tears welled in my eyes. "Thanks, Cody. I don't think I'll ever forget this night. Everything's so perfect." I took his hand in mine and gazed into his eyes.

The moment was interrupted by the arrival of our waiter. "Can I get you something to drink?" he asked as he handed us menus.

After ordering drinks and appetizers, we tried to decide what sounded best. After a lot of suggestions from everyone else, I settled on a New York strip. Cody ordered a bigger one. Samantha opted for ginger-crusted salmon, and Dan ordered a bacon-stuffed chicken breast.

"This is perfect, guys." Samantha fiddled with the hem of her dress. "To be honest with you, I figured you were going to take us bowling or to a movie or something like that. This is really, really nice."

"Why would we make you get dressed up to go bowling?" Dan's eyebrows pinched together, and he shook his head. "That doesn't make sense."

Samantha's cheeks turned red. "I thought maybe you just wanted to see if we'd do it."

"And, you?" Cody shot me an accusatory glance.

I shrugged. "Well, I never expected anything like this. That's for sure." After a moment's pause, I added, "I had no idea either of you was this romantic. Sam's right. This is nice … unexpected."

"Glad you like it," Dan said. "A little hurt about the bowling thing, but glad nonetheless." He flashed Samantha a charming smile.

Samantha grinned back at him. "As much as we like bowling, this is much nicer."

Our onion rings and cheese sticks were delivered. They were among the best I'd ever had, but I only ate a couple in anticipation of the main course. While eating, I watched Dan's ease with Samantha and wondered how he'd feel if he knew what I was capable of. Would he hang out with me if he knew I could shoot a fireball from my fingertips?

I closed my eyes and drew in a long breath. If my dreams kept up, Dan was bound to find out more about me, and I wasn't sure if I was ready.

"Dacia?" Cody waved his hand in front of my face. "Anybody home?"

"Oh, I'm sorry." I blinked my eyes several times, trying to orient myself. "What?"

Samantha lifted a slender eyebrow. "Dan asked if the four of us would be able to get together over the summer."

"Sorry. I was lost in the mountains." I pointed at the view. "I don't see why not. How far away are you from Sam? I can't remember."

Dan pointed at his mouth, then held his finger up. After he swallowed his food, he said, "I live about two hours from Sweetspire. So, that puts me five hours from you two."

"In Mimosa?" I asked in an attempt to keep my mind from wandering again.

Dan nodded his reply since his mouth was full again.

The waiter returned with our dinner. He set our plates in front of us and said, "Enjoy!"

My mouth watered at the delicious aroma. The steak was tender and cooked to perfection. Conversation quieted while we savored our food.

I'd eaten a little over half when I pushed my plate away. "I can't eat another bite. That was really good."

Cody stood up and reached his hand down to me. "May I have this dance?"

I placed my hand in his and let him escort me onto the deck. Dan and Samantha soon followed Cody's lead.

"This is great." I clasped my hands around his neck, and we swayed to the music. "I'll never forget this evening or our first dance."

He pulled me closer and whispered in my ear. "Me either."

I laid my head on his chest, and we danced to several more songs. I felt safe and warm in his arms and knew there was nowhere else I'd rather be.

The next time I opened my eyes, the clouds were pink, red, purple, orange, and yellow. "Let's watch the sunset." I pointed to the railing. "You don't see a view like this every day."

"Sure." With his hand on my lower back, he led me to the side.

I shivered.

"Cold?" Cody rubbed my arms. "I can get your jacket."

"No. I'm fine." I wasn't cold, but the hair on the back of my neck stood on end. A quiver of foreboding ran up my spine—I felt like somebody had walked over my grave. It had been a long time since I'd had a feeling like that, and once again, I found myself wondering what was in store for me.

"You okay?" He lifted my chin. "You seem distracted to-night."

"I'm fine." I looked away from him, so he couldn't see the lie in my eyes. "It's just so beautiful out here. I keep losing myself. I'm sorry."

"Haven't seen you this way since … you know." He glanced at Dan.

Dan and Samantha were out of earshot, still dancing to-gether. "This took me by surprise, Cody. And, it's easy for me to space off out here with everything so perfect."

Cody dragged his hand along his jaw. "You're okay?"

It was obvious that he didn't believe me, but this wasn't the time or place to tell him that dragons had invaded my dreams. "I'm good." I held my hand out. "Do you want to dance some more?"

Cody bowed. "As you wish."

While we danced, I struggled to keep my mind from wandering. I didn't want Cody to think I didn't appreciate the evening he'd planned. I also didn't want him asking any more questions right now. I hated lying to him, but I couldn't talk to him about it here.

Besides, once I told them, everything would change. Once they knew, it would be real.

After a few more songs, Cody and I sat on a bench. I leaned against his chest and looked up. Stars twinkled in the darkened sky. Without thinking, I asked, "Do you think any more of my life is written up there, in the stars?"

"I don't know." He looked up. "Maybe they say, 'And they lived happily ever after.'"

"That'd be nice."

The waiter returned to the deck. "Does anyone have room for dessert?"

"Sure do," Dan said.

Cody nodded. "Always."

We went to the table. Cody pulled my chair out for me. He sat, then threw his arm over my chair.

I leaned into him. "Thanks for this wonderful evening."

"You're welcome."

"I'm trying to figure out how they'll ever top it," Samantha said.

Dan nipped her ear. "You'll have to wait and see."

The dessert was as amazing as everything else had been. I savored every bite, keeping my attention focused on my friends.

When they finished, Samantha and Dan wandered off. It wasn't long until *The River Otter* docked.

Once Matt tied up the boat, he joined us on the open deck. "I hope you had a great time."

"We did," Samantha said, and I nodded in agreement.

"Enjoy the rest of your night." He shook each of our hands as we walked past.

Cody drove with one hand on the steering wheel and one holding mine. I watched out the window, absentmindedly rubbing the back of his hand with my thumb.

"What's wrong?" Cody asked.

"Nothing." I smiled, trying to convince him I meant it.

By the time we got back to campus, it was after midnight. We got out of the car, and Cody and Dan walked with us toward the women's dormitory.

"You can't come in," Samantha said. "Marcy will flip out." Marcy, our hall monitor, for some unknown reason, hated guys being in the dorm after hours.

"She'll deal." Cody held the door open.

"What kind of guy doesn't walk his date to the door?" Dan asked.

I smiled at him over my shoulder. "One who doesn't want to get into trouble."

"We're not afraid of Marcy." Cody laughed.

We snuck through the hall, somehow managing to make it past Marcy's room without her realizing there were guys in the building.

Samantha kicked off her heels as soon as she crossed the threshold. "Does anybody want something to drink?"

"Water," Dan answered.

"Me, too," Cody and I said at the same time.

"You guys picked a great evening for this." Samantha twisted the cap off her bottle and held it in front of her mouth. "You couldn't have asked for better weather."

We sat and talked, not wanting the night to end, until around two when Dan stood and yawned. "I'm going to call it an evening. Do you want to walk out with me, Sam?" He held his hand out to her.

"Yeah."

When the door closed, Cody looked at me. "I'm not ready for this to be over. We live close, but it'll be different."

"Yeah, I'm sure our parents will have plans for us, and I was thinking about getting a part-time job for the summer. But, it won't be too long before we're back here again."

He pulled me onto his lap. "Leave some time for me."

"You know I will." I snuggled into him.

Samantha came back into the room. "Marcy just turned the corner. If you left now, you could probably sneak out."

"Guess I'll have to be quiet." He rubbed his hand down my leg. "I'm not leaving yet."

"If you're not leaving"—Samantha sat down and turned toward us—"we should talk about Dacia's nightmares."

Chapter 3
Unearthing Incubus

Samantha and Cody focused on me. I slumped down, and the excitement from the evening disappeared.

Cody slid his hand off my shoulders and folded his arms over his chest. "Nightmares?" His voice had a hard edge.

Samantha leaned forward, resting her elbows on her knees. "She's been keeping them to herself, but in the past week, I've seen two pairs of burnt pajamas buried in the trash."

"I'm sorry." I scrubbed my hands down my face. "I didn't want to worry you two." I wrapped my arms around my stomach. "I was going to tell you, but I wasn't ready yet. I guess that's why you were so concerned when I was spacing off, huh?"

"Yeah." Samantha nodded. "I've seen that look before. Something was troubling you. Wasn't it?"

I stared at the floor. "We were having a good time, and I wondered what Dan would think if he knew the truth about me. With these dreams"—I pulled my hand through my hair—"he's gonna find out."

"Dacia—" Cody grabbed my chin and turned my face toward him "—don't shut us out. We want to help."

"I know, but …" I pulled on the hem of my dress. "I wanted them to just be dreams, but after waking up from one last night, I think they're more."

"Is it …" Samantha's voice caught. She cleared her throat. "Is it Nefarious again?"

"No—" a humorless laugh escaped my lips "—I almost wish it was. I know that I can beat him." Cody stroked my arm from my shoulder to my elbow and back again. "They started after Nefarious. In the first one, I was flying on a pegasus. A fireball shot past us. A black dragon chased me. I've had several dreams since. They all have different dragons, and … I think I'm going to have to face them."

"Wow." Samantha sat back and shook her head. "I don't know how you handle it."

"Denial." I shrugged. "But, now I'm trying to figure out what I'm going to do when I'm home. My parents won't understand me waking up from nightmares burned or covered in blood."

Cody's hand stopped midway through its course. "Nope."

"It's not just that either. When you had dreams about Nefarious, you woke up screaming all of the time," Samantha said. "What if that starts happening again?"

"I don't know." I stood and paced in front of the chairs. "I wonder if it's too late to sign up for summer classes."

"This why you asked about the stars?" Cody asked.

"Yeah. I don't …"

Our conversation was interrupted by pounding on our door. "Cody Hawks, I know you're in there. Come out now." Marcy's voice reverberated through the wood.

Cody climbed the ladder to my loft. He piled my pillows around him to hide. "Not here," he whispered.

"Cody." Anger emphasized his name.

I opened the door a crack. "Marcy," I tried to sound aggrieved, "Cody isn't here. We went out. He dropped me off at the door. Samantha and I are sitting here talking, so please quit pounding on my door."

"Oh, I—I thought I heard him in there." She peeked past me. "I'm sorry."

"It's okay. Goodnight." I closed the door and walked back to the chairs. "That was way too easy. You'll have to be really quiet."

Cody descended the ladder, sat in Cookie Monster, and pulled me onto his lap. "Can't believe she left so easily."

"Me either." Samantha bit her lip. "Back to earlier, though. You know Cody's right, don't you? You need to let us know what's going on."

"I know." I twisted my bracelet around my wrist. "I just … I want a normal life. Sarah never said there'd be more. I thought once Nefarious was gone, I'd be free. I don't …" I took a deep breath. "I don't want to go through that again."

"Have you talked to Sarah?" Samantha leaned forward.

"No, I haven't." I dropped my chin to my chest. "I suppose I need to."

Samantha pulled her earrings out and hooked them together while she said, "It would be a good idea. Maybe she knows something about what's going on. Maybe she can help." She twisted her hands together, and I knew she had more to add. "You can tell Dan, too."

"Dan's a good guy." Cody squeezed my arm affectionately. "He'll deal."

I threw my hands up. "Oh, yeah? Then why were you so worried Matt was going to say too much?"

"Guys." Samantha glared at us. "Don't start this. I'm sure Dan would be …" She looked up, like the words were written on the ceiling. "Shocked, but I don't think it'd change anything."

I stared at the carpet, knowing Samantha wouldn't like what I had to say. "Maybe, but you'd be surprised to find out how many people have run from me because of them."

Samantha crossed her arms, her fingers squeezing her biceps. "Dan's a better person than that."

"Don't be mad, please." I rubbed my neck. "I've been through this before, and you and Cody are pretty much the only ones who have accepted me for who … no, for what I am. I hope Dan will, but I can't count on it."

"Fair enough. Just don't count him out yet." Samantha released her arms. The white marks from her fingers stood out. "Now that we've gotten all this out in the open, I'm going to get my jammies on and go to bed." She grabbed her stuff and walked to the door. With her hand on the knob, she turned back.

"Oh, Cody … thank you for such a wonderful evening. I'm sorry I brought this all up tonight, but it needed saying."

After Samantha left, Cody and I sat in silence, looking anywhere but at each other. "Pride," Cody muttered. "That's why I don't want Dan to know."

I reached for his hand, but he jerked it back.

"You have to trust us." A muscle in his jaw jumped. "No more hiding. No lying."

I stood and strode to the window, keeping my back to him. "I'm scared."

The chair rocked back. Cody's footsteps barely made any sound as he walked over to me. He slid his arms around my waist, resting his chin on my head. "We're here for you."

I turned, holding him, finding comfort in his warmth. "I can't do this again. I *needed* them to just be dreams. I thought I was done."

"I wish." He pulled me closer. "I'll help you. No matter how many monsters you face."

The slow rise and fall of his chest helped relax me. "You should go."

"No." His tone warned me not to argue. "I'm staying."

Chapter 4
Sleeping Is Bad For Your Health

While Cody slept in Cookie Monster and Samantha was snuggled up in her bed, I clutched Glacier and stared at the ceiling, too afraid to sleep. Besides not wanting to face my nightmares, if I woke up screaming or injured, Cody would never let me be alone. We went through this with Nefarious, and as much as I loved being around him, there were times I needed to go off on my own.

The urge to get up and go for a walk nearly pulled me to my feet several times, but if Cody or Samantha woke and found me gone, they would panic. *Why couldn't I have been smart enough to hide my stupid pajamas somewhere Samantha wouldn't find them?*

A little voice in my head answered, *Maybe you wanted her to see them.*

The sun rises above the skyline. Clouds explode in a wide array of colors, a sunrise to rival the beauty of the sunset we saw last night. A peaceful sensation sweeps over me, and I'm glad I snuck out of bed.

Birds race to the air, as if they each want to be the first in flight. One off in the distance soars closer, dipping and diving as it glides across the sky. The silhouette grows larger. My heart races. My breath comes out in short, harsh gasps. It's not a bird. I sprint from the bench, hiding in the shadows beneath the trees.

The enormous beast lands, and the ground trembles beneath its feet. I lean my head back to stare up at the dragon. Its emerald green scales shimmer in the sunlight temporarily blinding me. I blink back the spots, clearing my vision.

The dragon lowers its head, sniffing at the air, and a spiked fin flares up, extending from its nose to the tip of its tail. It strides toward the bench where I'd been sitting moments earlier, and talons the length of my arm scar the earth.

It scans the area, stopping when its bright green eyes stare into mine.

The monster springs. Lightning bolts explode from my fingertips. While the beast is distracted, I turn to flee, but I'm not fast enough.

The dragon's claws tear through the air, carving my back. Pain slices through my body, toppling me. I lie on the ground, unable to move. Panicked breaths rip at my throat. Spots dance in my vision. Just as I hear the whoosh of fire shooting through the air, everything goes black.

Darkness surrounded me. Distant voices pled with me to wake up. Try as I may, I couldn't answer them. I couldn't move. My consciousness hovered above my body.

"Dacia," said an unfamiliar voice that sounded closer than the others. "Dacia," he said even clearer this time. "I want Nefarious."

What? How can he know about Nefarious?

"If you give him to me, I won't send my pets after you," the man said. "If you refuse, my dragons can be very convincing." He laughed, and cold shivers crawled up my spine. "One way or another I will have Nefarious. There's no need to endure this pain. Give him to me. End your suffering."

Finding my voice, I screamed, "No! I'll never give him to you." As if emerging from a dark tunnel, light seeped in through my eyelids. Unsure where I would find myself, I blinked back the brightness. I lay in bed. Cody stood on my ladder, leaning over me. His blue eyes stood out against his pale face. When my gaze met his, he closed his eyes and sighed.

"Is she awake?" Sarah stood at the base of my ladder with Samantha.

"Yeah." He brushed my hair back with a trembling hand. "Scared me." His voice was ragged. "What happened?"

I pressed my hands against the bed to sit up, but pain pinned me in place. I whimpered. "Dragon attacked," I said through gritted teeth. "Passed out."

"How bad?" Cody asked. "Can you move?"

"No." I forced the word out. "Clawed my back."

"Cody, can you roll Dacia over, so I can look at her back?" Sarah asked.

"I'll try not to hurt you." The look on his face told me that if he did, it would hurt him just as much. His movements were delicate like he was afraid I might break. Waves of pain crashed over me, but I tried to hide it. "Dacia." Cody gasped. "This is awful!"

"Not … helping." The words came out strained. I chewed on my cheek to try to keep from crying.

"Sorry. This looks bad, really bad." Emotion left his voice raspy and his words forced.

"Let me see, Cody." Sarah stepped onto the ladder and gasped. "Oh, my. You lost a lot of blood. I think we're going to have to get you a new mattress."

"Still not helping." My hands shook. Trembling overtook my muscles. I clutched my pillow, and a sob escaped with the sudden movement.

"I'm sorry," Sarah said. "After what Nefarious did, I never imagined anything could be worse, but this is."

"But … Nefarious actually hurt Dacia," Samantha said. "This was a dream, and she usually heals faster from dreams."

"That's true," Sarah agreed. "Let's hope that's the case."

Sarah cleaned my wound, and the room spun. Pain was all I knew, all I felt, all that existed. It stole the breath from my lungs, took control of my muscles, forced a scream from my lips. The room darkened, and sound faded.

Then blessed numbness sought to destroy the agony, holding it at bay. I released my pillow, and blood returned to my fingers. My energy spent.

Exhaustion pulled at my eyelids, but there was something important, something I needed to tell them.

Cody climbed the ladder and brushed his hand over my cheek. "Want turned over?"

"No."

"Take some of my strength." He set his hand palm up beside mine.

I slid mine over the top of his, and he laced our fingers together. "I'll try." Nothing happened. I spread my fingers so he could pull away, but he squeezed tighter.

"Don't give up." He rubbed his thumb over mine. "This is all I can do for you. Let me help."

Nodding, I concentrated on healing. Warmth spread up my arm and across my back. Cody's eyelids drooped, and I pulled my hand away. "That's enough."

He climbed down the ladder and slumped in Cookie Monster.

Sarah patted his shoulder. "We should all try to get some rest."

"Wait." My voice sounded weak. "After I was attacked, someone talked to me."

"Who?" Sarah asked. "What did he say?"

"I don't know." I squeezed my eyes shut, not wanting this to be happening, not wanting to admit another fight rose before me. "He wants Nefarious."

"How …" Samantha's voice faltered. "How does he know about that?"

"Don't know." My body seized as I tried to roll onto my side. I sucked in a deep breath and held it until the spasm eased. "He'll use his dragons to get Nefarious."

Cody sat up. "*His* dragons?"

"Yeah." Emerald scales danced in front of my eyes. "I can't beat them."

Chapter 5
Change Of Plans

$\mathcal{A}$ deep, dreamless sleep enshrouded me. I woke to the sun streaming in through the windows and stretched like a cat before sitting up. When I looked down at my bed, the events of last night hit me. My sheets were covered in dried blood. Panic washed over me, and my hand shot up to feel my back. Blood crusted my torn shirt. My pulse quickened. My fingers pressed against unmarred skin—healed. I let out a relieved breath before I descended the ladder and gathered my clothes. I was about to sneak out to take a shower when Cody woke up.

"Hey—" he stifled a yawn "—you're up. Better?"

"Yeah." I turned my back to show him, then took a step toward the door. "I need to hit the showers before everyone else."

"Good idea." He stood and pulled me into his arms. "Glad you're okay." He brushed my hair back and hooked it over my ear, then rested his forehead against mine.

A warm blaze spread through my stomach. "Yeah, and here we go again." I nodded at the door. "I really gotta go."

Sunday mornings in the dorm were pretty lazy, so there was a good chance I would make it to the showers without being seen, but I put my robe on before I headed out the door—just in case.

I peeked out into the hallway and let out a relieved breath when I found it empty. Jogging toward the bathroom, I stayed on the balls of my feet to make as little noise as possible.

I reached for the doorknob but stopped short when I heard talking. I hadn't looked in the mirror. I didn't know if I had dried blood all over me or just on my back. Pressing my ear to the door, I listened.

My stomach dropped when I realized one of the voices belonged to Cassandra Nightshade. Even though she hadn't bothered me since I defeated Nefarious, I dreaded seeing her. She wasn't possessed anymore, and when questioned by Sarah, she swore she didn't remember anything about what had happened, but I didn't trust her. She had dragged me off to meet my death, and right then, feeling vulnerable, she was the last person I wanted to see.

A door closed down the hallway, and I had to decide whether to take my chances with Cassandra or hide in the stairwell. Pinching my eyes shut, I sucked in a deep breath, squared my shoulders, and pushed the door open, strolling in, pretending to be confident and in control.

Cassandra stood in front of the mirror putting her make-up on. She held a mascara brush in front of her face, and her hand trembled. *I wonder if she remembers me freezing her hands together.* A blonde girl straightened her hair a couple of sinks down from Cassandra. She smiled at me in the mirror as I walked past. She didn't seem to be terrified, so I assumed I didn't look too bad. I strolled into the first stall, set my bag down, and let out a deep sigh.

After showering, I shoved my pajama shirt into my bag, hiding it from any prying eyes, and went back to my room. Sarah and Cody sat in the chairs, talking in hushed tones. I grabbed a bottle of milk and stood beside Cody. "Hello."

"Good morning, Dacia." Sarah studied me like a sample under a microscope. "You look much better."

"Yeah, but"—I waved my arm at my bed—"I don't know what I'm going to do about that."

Sarah pursed her lips. "I'll see if I can scrounge up a different mattress for you." She returned her focus to me. "I came here to see if you'd be interested in enrolling in summer classes."

I nodded and closed my eyes, grateful for an excuse to stay away from home. "That'd be great." I pulled my hand through wet curls. "Hopefully, Mom and Dad will be okay with it."

Cody's chin jutted out. "If Dacia stays, so do I."

"I wouldn't expect anything else." Sarah chuckled. "There are nine days between semesters. You'll have to decide what you want to do then. You can stay here or go home."

My gaze settled on my bloody mattress. "I can't go home now."

"I'll probably—" Samantha yawned "—see if I can, too, but I'd like to go home."

Cody looked up at her loft. "Didn't know you were up."

"I'm not." She rolled over to go back to sleep.

Sarah looked from me to Cody. "Without Samantha here as a chaperone, I can't let Cody stay in your room."

"Noth—"

Sarah cut Cody off. "I'm sorry." She stood. "We'll have to figure something else out. Dacia, don't keep us in the dark. We can't help if we don't know what's going on."

I looked down at my feet. "I'm sorry. I didn't want …" I squeezed my eyes shut and pinched the bridge of my nose. "I didn't want to admit it was happening again."

Sarah patted my shoulder. "Trust me. Trust your friends."

"I do." I bit my lower lip. "Having you know about my nightmares makes them real."

"I've got to get going." Sarah strode to the door. "I'll stop by later to see what classes you want to take and if your parents will let you. It looks like it's going to be a beautiful day. You should get out and enjoy it, as long as you're ready for your tests." She shut the door with a soft click.

"Life's too short to spend it studying." I sat on Cody's lap and wrapped my arm around his shoulder. "I never know when a dragon might swoop down and eat me, so I might as well get out and enjoy it while I can. Right?"

Cody's grip on my waist tightened. "Don't say that. You beat Nefarious. You got this."

"There was one Nefarious." I cupped his cheek in my hand. His eyes locked with mine. "There are a ton of dragons and someone controlling them."

"Don't give up."

"In my nightmares, I've only had to face one at a time." My voice lowered. "What if they gang up on me? There's no way, Cody. Besides, you said that was the worst injury you'd seen so far. What if it really happens? *I can't do this!*"

"Thought that with Nefarious, but you did." Cody set his jaw, and determination flared in his eyes. "You're strong and smart. You can do it. Wish you'd see that."

There was no point in arguing with him. He hadn't seen the dragons, and if this was anything like it had been with Nefarious, they would be worse in real life. "I suppose I should call my parents." Butterflies fluttered in my stomach. I stood by the desk and took the phone out of its cradle. My hands trembled. I dialed their number three times before I got it right. "Hello, Mom." I fought to keep my voice from shaking. "How are you and Dad?"

"Pretty good." Mom's voice had a nervous edge to it. "I'm glad you called. I wanted to talk to you about this summer."

"Okay." I rocked back and forth, heel to toe.

"Your dad and I decided to take a vacation. We're going to the coast—" she cleared her throat "—for almost a month."

I jerked my head back. "Oh." *Since when do my parents take vacations?*

Her next words came out in a rush. "We thought about taking you along, but we decided since we never had a honeymoon or vacation with just the two of us that this would be the year." She paused, and I wondered if I should fill the silence somehow. "You're not too upset, are you?"

I shook my head. Other teenagers had acne. I had dragons. *So much for getting closer to my parents.* I plastered a phony smile on my face, hoping she would hear it in my voice. "No, Mom, I'm not. I'm glad. I was calling to tell you that I decided to stay here. If I take some classes this summer, I can graduate sooner."

"Oh, that's wonderful, dear." She chuckled, and her voice sounded more relaxed. For the rest of the conversation, we discussed the weather, Cody, Samantha, and my parents' upcoming trip.

When I got off the phone, I turned to Cody. "All set. They're going on vacation for a month, so they don't care."

"Great, Dacia," Cody said. "Call mine later. They'll be okay."

Samantha woke up at 10:30 and climbed out of her loft. Her brown hair was a tangled mess. "I'm going to shower." A silly grin lit her face. "Then I'm going to talk Dan into staying. I'll get to spend most of the summer with him." She squealed and practically skipped out the door.

I slumped forward, holding my head in my hands. "He'll want to know why. I don't want anyone else to know about me. I don't want to lose his friendship."

Cody rubbed my back. "She won't tell him."

My stomach was tied in a thousand knots. I wanted Dan to stay, to be here for Samantha. But, I wanted Dan to leave, so he wouldn't know about me. I didn't want to have to worry about another friend getting hurt.

"Let's go to Falcon Lake," Cody said.

"Sure." I sat up and stared out the window. The sky was bright blue. "After lunch." I pointed at my book. "I need to study more."

Cody scrubbed his hand over his hair, making it stand on end. "I gotta get cleaned up. You'll be okay?"

"Yeah, go ahead."

Samantha returned before Cody. She clapped her hands. "Dan said he'll stay."

I kept looking at my book, afraid of what my expression would show. "That's great."

"He wanted to know why the sudden change. I told him there were some openings, and it would be nice to spend more time with him. So, I guess, as long as our parents are okay with it, we're staying." She shrugged. "I didn't lie, just sort of bent the truth a little and left out the part about you."

"I appreciate it, Sam." I stuck my finger between the pages, closing the book around it. I wasn't sure what I'd done to deserve her as a friend. "I'm sure you're right about Dan, but I'm not ready for him to find out yet."

Her lips turned up in a sympathetic smile. "I understand, but he'll find out … eventually. It would be best if he heard it from you."

A dark feeling swept over me. I knew what Samantha was getting at, but I hoped she was wrong. Memories flashed through my mind. Nefarious' claws tore through my burned flesh.

Phantom pain tore through my leg, and I clutched the arms of the chair, waiting for it to subside.

If something like that happened again, there was no way I could hide it from Dan.

There was a knock on our door, and Samantha let Cody in. "Dan staying?" he asked.

"Yes." She wiggled her butt and swung her arms in a happy dance.

I clutched the hair above my ears. "I'll have to tell him, but I don't know how … or when."

Cody walked up behind me and massaged my shoulders. "Freeze fire. He'll be so amazed he'll forget to be scared."

"That might work," Samantha agreed.

"I don't know, maybe. I don't really think the day before finals is a good day to drop a bomb like that on anybody, though. We should wait until they're over."

"Yeah, you're right." Samantha sat in the desk chair and pulled books out of her backpack. "But, you should tell him soon … before he stumbles on it by accident."

"Cody and I are going to Falcon Lake. Do you and Dan want to come along?" I asked.

"I would love to, but no," she answered. "I'm shutting myself in here and studying all day. I should have started as soon as I woke up this morning."

"Well"—I flipped my hands up—"you could have if you hadn't gone to see Dan. He's a bad influence on you. You should call it off."

"Shut up, Dacia!" Samantha picked up her pencil and threw it at me.

Chapter 6

The trail to Falcon Lake wound through the forest behind the dorms. Trees stretched toward the sun, standing tall and proud. Their roots jutted from the ground. Ferns, mushrooms, and pinecones littered the forest floor. Squirrels yelled at us from high up in the branches, and chipmunks skittered for cover. Sunlight dappled the ground.

Cody and I stepped from the woods into a clearing. The mountains behind Falcon Lake reflected in its clear, deep water.

The lake was all but deserted. Most students were holed up in their rooms or in the library, cramming for finals.

"I'm glad they didn't come." Cody squeezed my hand. "It's nice to be alone."

"I shouldn't've invited them without asking you." I tugged on Cody's hand, leading him to the lake. "I just don't want Samantha to think I don't want to be around Dan."

"She won't."

We walked along the beach. "So much has changed in the last day." Staring out at the water, I dropped Cody's hand and wrapped my arm around his waist. "I was looking forward to going home."

Cody draped his arm over my shoulders, pulling me closer.

"I thought my parents would be proud when they saw my control. I was nervous about my nightmares, but I thought I might be able to hide them." I laid my head against his chest. His heart drummed in my ear. "After last night's ..." I let my voice trail off, not knowing how to finish my thought.

"I was, too." He pulled away, picked up several rocks, and skipped them across the lake one at a time. "My brothers've been pestering me. They had plans."

My hands fell limply to my sides. *How can I be so selfish? Why didn't I realize that Josh, Dawson, Brandon, and Britny missed their big brother and were excited he was coming home?* I didn't have any siblings to think about, and guilt ate at me for not thinking about his. "Cody, you can't stay here with me. You need to go home. You need to be with them. I can handle things. Sarah and Samantha will be here. I won't be on my own."

He turned to face me. "They'll be fine. I'll see them after. You need me."

"If you stay here …" I bit my lower lip pulling it into my mouth. "Sarah was killed because of me. You ended up in the hospital for helping me."

"You saved Sarah and healed me." Another rock bounced across the surface of the lake.

I hugged my arms around myself, holding in my fear and guilt. "What if I hadn't gotten there in time? What if something happened and I couldn't save you? I wouldn't be able to live with myself. You should go home, Cody. Your family needs you. You keep telling me how tough I am and how I'll be fine, so you should go spend the summer with your family. You can come see me on the weekends." I turned away from him so he wouldn't see me cry.

He grabbed my shoulders and spun me around. "I'm staying. You can't talk me out of it." He ran his fingers up my neck, tilting my head back. "You're tough. You'll get through this, but you'll need a shoulder to cry on, a friend to talk to. You'll need me to help you through those times." His thumbs swept over my cheeks, soft and tender. "I want to be a part of your life forever. I won't abandon you when you need me the most."

It was the most I'd heard him say at one time, but it did nothing to ease my mind. "I can't—"

He pressed his fingers over my lips. "Not your choice. Mine. I'm staying."

"Whatever." I shook my head.

He took my hand, leading me to the playground. I sat on a swing, twisting the chain, wrapping it tightly, then spun in circles. *How can I get him to go?* When the swing came to a stop, I asked, "Do you want to go sit on the beach?"

"Sure." He put his arm around my shoulders as we walked away. "Can't figure out how to get me outta here?"

"No." Heat rose in my cheeks, and I looked down at my feet. "You can't blame me for not wanting you to get hurt, can you?"

"You'll rescue me."

"I'll do my best."

We sat on the beach watching waves wash over the rocky shore. A girl sashayed out of the trees. She glided over to us, her movements so graceful she appeared to float on air. "Hi. Sorry to interrupt you. My name is Aurelia." Her long, golden hair bounced against her shoulders, glistening in the sun. "I will be taking classes at Phlox University this summer. Do you two go there?"

"Yeah, we do," I answered while Cody stared at the tall, slender supermodel with his mouth hanging open.

Aurelia's cat-like yellow eyes seemed to take in everything. Her gold skin shimmered in the sunlight. I wondered if she was human or if it was a disguise. Could she be an elf, nymph, dryad, or some other magical creature?

"I'm Dacia, and this is Cody." I nudged him hard in the arm when I introduced him.

"H-hi, nice to, uh, meet you." Cody stood, holding his hand out.

She shook it, then pointed at the ground beside me. "May I?"

"Sure."

Cody sat back down. I pulled his arm around my shoulder and leaned into him. I wanted both of them to know he was mine.

All my life I'd heard tales of a monster with green eyes. Never before had I realized that monster lived inside me. With the way Cody looked at Aurelia, the beast stirred. Its lips pulled back revealing bloodthirsty fangs. A low, menacing snarl filled me, daring me to let it escape.

"This place is beautiful." Aurelia stared at the lake. "As soon as I saw it, I knew I had to go to school here, but I know none of the students. I am sorry if I seem forward. I just wanted to meet some people, so I feel a little more like I belong here when I start classes." She turned her head toward us, and the motion looked predatory. "Are you taking summer classes?"

Cody cleared his throat. "Yeah."

"Great! I am glad I will know a couple of people here." She smiled, and I had never seen teeth so white before. "I doubt we will be in the same classes, but maybe I will see you around campus."

I lifted my lips in what I hoped might pass for a polite grin. "Yeah, maybe."

"I will see you later." She stood, smoothing out her white slacks, and walked away.

I threw Cody's arm off my shoulder and stood with my hands on my hips. "I can't believe you stared at her like that."

"Dacia …"

"You might wanna wipe the drool off your chin." I turned to make sure Aurelia was out of earshot. "Where'd she go anyway?"

He climbed to his feet and shrugged. "She just sort of …disappeared."

"Are you disappointed?" The beast bared its fangs again. I fought to keep the monster caged, but it was on the verge of escaping.

"Sorry, Dacia." He stepped toward me, and I backed up. "She's …"

I could tell he was sorry. I could hear it in his voice and see it on his face, but I couldn't think rationally. "She's what?" I got more perturbed by the moment. "Beautiful? Wonderful? Perfect?"

"She was … unusual." He rubbed the back of his neck. "I can't put my finger on it."

I poked his chest. "Make sure you don't put your finger on any part of her."

His eyes narrowed. "Something's off with her."

"Yeah, but you didn't see me stuttering and staring. Did you?"

"Said sorry." He squeezed his eyes shut and rubbed his hand down his face. "Enough of the jealousy."

"Then go home because if she's in any of your classes, you're going to act like an idiot every time you see her. And, you'll see the jealous side of me more often."

Why am I so upset? He acted like an idiot, but I noticed there was something different about Aurelia, too. Why didn't I just admit it? Was it because I was jealous or because I was worried about him staying here?

"Dacia." His voice was different. The regret was gone. It hardened and left no room for argument. "I'm not going home. Drop it! I'll never look at another girl."

There was no reason for me to be jealous, but I couldn't help it. "You can look at other girls." I laughed before adding, "But … only ugly ones."

Samantha sat at the desk surrounded by books. Her hair was pulled up in a messy bun, and a pen was tucked behind her ear. "How was Falcon Lake?"

"We met a new student." I rolled my eyes. "Aurelia. Make sure you have Dan on a short leash when she's around." I plopped down in Cookie Monster. "Cody couldn't keep his eyes off her."

She cocked her head. "Is that why he's not here?"

"No, he wanted to stop by his room. I guess he's planning on sleeping here"—I swept my hand over the chair—"again tonight."

"So, what's so special about … Aurelia, was it?"

"Honestly, I don't think she's human." I spun the chair, trying to gather my thoughts. "I know how stupid that sounds, but I think she's some sort of magical being. She sparkled."

She leaned back in her chair and looked at me instead of her book. "What do you mean *sparkled*?"

"I mean sparkled. Her hair and her skin shimmered. It was like they had flecks of gold in them, and the way she moved was so graceful. It wasn't natural. She came from nowhere, and then"—I closed my hands, then flicked my fingers out—"she disappeared."

"Well—" she tapped her finger against her bottom lip "—we know other creatures exist. Maybe she is something else, but what?"

"I wondered if she was an elf or nymph … maybe even a fairy. I don't know. She seemed nice enough, but I didn't like the way Cody looked at her. It was almost like he was infatuated with her, like she had some sort of spell over him. The way he was acting reminded me of the stories about sirens luring men to their deaths. I suppose it probably didn't help that we had been arguing … sort of." Talking about Aurelia brought the monster within me back to the surface. *Cody loves you,* I thought, *not her. Feed the love, not the jealousy.*

Fiddling with her bracelet, she asked, "What were you fighting about? Is everything okay now?"

"I guess his brothers were looking forward to him being home." I spun Cookie Monster around again. "They had all sorts of things planned for this summer, and I want him to go. At least there, he'll be safe. Here … who knows?"

Samantha stared at me with her mouth slightly open, then shook her head. "How do you expect him to go home when he knows every night you might wake up injured? When he knows, beyond the shadow of a doubt, something will eventually happen to you? You may or may not get hurt, but he would be so worried about you. The only way for him to go home is if you do. You have to know that."

I let out a hefty gust of air. "I could go home. Mom and Dad will be on vacation, so it's not like they'd know about my dreams. Maybe I'd be better off there."

"Yeah." Her voice was thick with sarcasm. "Do you really think you'd be better off in a house all by yourself? Give me a break, Dacia. Be sensible."

"I'm sorry." I swept my arm in front of me. "Why do you and Cody think it's wrong for me to want to protect you? If you're around, you're targets. I can't bear for anything to happen to you."

"We know." She pulled the pen from behind her ear and tapped it on the desk. "We really do, but even though we aren't much good to you, we can still help if you get hurt or if you need someone to talk to."

"That's what he said." I closed my eyes and tried to calm myself. As I released my breath, I felt Cody's aura slide over me. My lips tugged up in a smile. "Speaking of Cody, he's here now."

Cody let himself in and asked Samantha, "How's the studying going?"

She threw her arms up in the air as she said, "I'm going to fail all of my finals."

"Yeah." Cody shot her a lopsided grin. "You'll ace 'em."

"I don't think so." She shook her head. "I'm not the least bit ready for any of my tests."

Before demons and dragons had entered my life, I had felt that way about my grades and studying, but they were no longer a priority. Keeping my friends alive was far more important. "So, you don't want pizza tonight?"

"Did I say that? Pizza sounds good."

"See if Dan wants to join us." Cody patted her shoulder as he walked by.

Looking at the phone, she lifted from her chair. Then she turned back to her book and plopped down. "I'll give him a call as soon as I get done reading this section."

"Okay." I pulled my hair into a ponytail. "We're going to watch a movie while we eat. Will that bother you?"

"Nah." She thumped the pen against her notepad. "We'll probably join you. You were right."

"My three favorite words—" I smiled "—but about what this time?"

"Dan is a bad influence on me. I'd much rather spend the evening with him than studying."

"I'd much rather spend the evening with a dead fish than study," I told her. "Luckily, I only have one final to study for."

Samantha threw her hands up. "Why's that?"

"For painting, I just had to finish my last project. I had to write a short story for fiction writing. I'm about done with it. And, I have never figured out how to study for math. You either know it or you don't."

"That is so unfair." Samantha shook her head. "I've been studying for math all day."

"If it'll make you feel better, I'll try to study for geometry tomorrow while I should be studying American Lit." I laughed.

"Dacia, you are such a procrastinator! I wish I could do that even once, but I'd feel so guilty. Now, leave me alone so I can finish this!"

"Okay, okay," I said, still giggling.

Chapter 7

Draconian

After finishing my American Literature final, I sat outside to enjoy the fresh air, going back over every question in my head, hoping my answers were thorough enough. The sun shone over the mountains, and the sweet smell of wildflowers hung on the breeze.

Students meandered about with their heads in open books, trying to cram in last-minute knowledge. Strolling amongst them was a man dressed in a navy wizard's hat and robe. Though out of place, nobody paid attention to him. His long, white beard waved in the wind. What I could see of his skin appeared aged, almost leathery.

He prowled toward me. His gray gaze bored into mine, imprisoning me on the bench.

The sky darkened. Goosebumps lifted the hairs on my arms, and shivers danced along my spine.

I wanted to flee, but my legs wouldn't respond to my brain's command.

Students veered out of the man's path as he strode closer. The wind picked up blowing hair in front of my face. Strands stuck to my lips.

The man stopped in front of me, looking down at me like I was the winning lottery ticket. He brushed the hair off my face and tucked it behind my ear. His touch felt like a thousand spiders crawling over my skin. My stomach heaved.

"Hello, young lady." His voice was harsh, scratchy, and vaguely familiar.

"Hello," I responded. "Can I help you?" The words escaped before I could stop them. My mind felt cloudy—almost like I wasn't in control.

"Actually, you can. You're just the person I was looking for." He pointed at the bench. "May I?"

Against my better judgment, I said, "Sure," and scooted over to give him room.

"Let me introduce myself; I am Draconian, the Dragon Lord. I have a proposition for you, Dacia."

My head flinched back. *Dragon Lord? No, no, no. I'm not ready for this.* "How … how do you know who I am?"

"Well, Dacia Wolf is the only person on this entire campus who can see me, and since you were watching me, I immediately knew who you were." He paused, and for the first time in my life, I understood the expression, he looked like the cat that swallowed the canary. "I find you very interesting. For such a young lady, you have lived an exciting life, to this point, and if you do as I say, you will have many more adventures ahead of you. Now … for my proposition." He rubbed his hands together. "If you give me that beautiful little vase with Nefarious in it, I will keep my pets from ripping you limb from limb." His steely eyes drilled into me.

High above the clouds, two shadows circled. My instincts told me they were dragons. "What—" a lump stuck in my throat "—what are you talking about?"

"Don't play dumb with me!" His voice was low and hard.

"W-why?" I stammered. "Why do you want him?"

He waved his hand in the air like he was shooing a fly away. "That does not concern you."

With that comment, the fog cleared from my brain. Feeling confident for the first time since I laid eyes on him, I said, "*Actually, it does concern me.* You see if you release Nefarious, I have to battle him all over again. Since it nearly killed me last time, I really don't want to do that. I'm sure you can understand my dilemma."

"Do I look like I would set a demon loose on the world?" He feigned being offended. "Just what makes you think I would do something as irresponsible as that?"

"Oh, uh, I don't know. Maybe the fact that you send dragons out to attack teenagers?" I lifted my hands palms up. "Just a theory."

"You don't seem to understand." He wrapped his long, slender fingers around my wrist. As soon as he touched me, I felt like my body was being squeezed in and stretched out at the same time. When the feeling subsided, I was no longer on the bench. Draconian still held my wrist, but we stood in complete darkness. "You don't have a choice."

My muscles tensed, and I took a step back. "What did you do to me?"

"Transported you to my dungeon," he answered like I should have known what was going on. "I'll give you a few days to change your mind. Then I'll hand you over to my dragons. Your friends will be easy to persuade with you out of the way."

My heart pounded with a new intensity until it reached its crescendo. My fingernails dug into my hands, leaving crescent-shaped marks across my palms.

"Give me Nefarious, and no harm will befall them." His grip on my arm tightened. "Deny me, and they will die."

"Leave them out of this!" The words tore from my throat, leaving me raw.

I closed my eyes, pictured my room, and tried to teleport myself out of his dungeon. I managed to free myself from his grasp, but I wasn't any closer to getting out.

His laughter echoed through the dungeon. Bouncing off the walls, it intensified as it sought freedom. "I am a powerful wizard, and you think you can free yourself? My dungeon is guarded by magic more powerful than any you have ever imagined using. You are here until I release you."

I backed up against the wall. If magic couldn't save me, I'd find the door and free myself. The rough stones scraped my fingertips as I moved along them, searching for a way out.

Panic clawed through my stomach and chest, fighting to overcome me. I needed to escape. Without me to protect them,

Cody and Samantha wouldn't survive a dragon attack. I kept picturing their lifeless bodies. There had to be a way out.

"Dacia." Draconian's tone was soft, cajoling.

I turned toward his voice but couldn't see him.

"Be reasonable. I don't want to hurt you." Footsteps moved toward me. His fingers brushed against my arm, and I jerked back, scraping my arm on the wall. "Just give me Nefarious, and we can end all of this."

I didn't answer, afraid my voice would make it easier for him to track me. I kept moving along, searching with every step.

"I'll get him one way or another." His voice rose in frustration. "He will be part of my collection."

I stopped. My hands fell against my sides. "Your collection …" I pulled a trembling hand through my hair. "What do you collect? What makes you think you can control him?"

"Fifteen dragons at my beck and call and you don't think I can control a demon." His tone made me picture his lip turning up in disgust. "I could control the sun if I wanted to!"

"If you're so powerful, why don't you make me give Nefarious to you?" I slapped my hand over my mouth. I couldn't believe I'd said that. What if it hadn't occurred to him?

Silence filled the room. *Had I struck a nerve? Why would he be able to control dragons but not me?* The room filled with a blinding light. A loud boom like a clap of thunder shook the dungeon. The light was gone and, so it seemed, was the wizard.

Continuing my search of the room, I found a corner. Ten steps along that wall took me to the next. Thirteen steps to the next. I wanted to light a fire, but I was afraid someone or something would see me; I couldn't shake the feeling that I wasn't alone. I pictured myself sitting in my room and called upon all the energy around me to help me get there, but when I opened my eyes, I still stood in darkness.

Waving my arms in front of me, I walked through the center of the room. After making several passes without coming into contact with anything, I held my hand out in front of me. Flames ignited in my palm. Warmth radiated through my arm, driving off the chill fear had left behind.

The fire cast a blue glow over the cell. The walls, ceiling, and floor were all stone. There were no windows or doors.

Despair draped itself over my shoulders, weighing me down. I slid down the wall. The fire died out. Slumped on the floor, I clutched my knees to my chest.

What if Draconian goes after Cody and Samantha now? I can't protect them from here.

I rocked back and forth. Images of my friends being carried off by dragons filled my head. Hearing their terrified screams, I clutched my hands over my ears.

I have to do something. Think. I clenched my head. A heavy weight settled in my chest. *They'll die because of me.*

I sat up. "No." The word echoed through the room.

"Think, Dacia, think," I whispered under my breath. "There has to be a way out." I leaned my head against the wall and thought about all the extraordinary things I had done over the past year. I could conjure lightning, create fire, shoot ice from my fingertips, create a force-field around myself, teleport, fly, transport objects through the air without touching them, read some people's minds, heal myself and others, and walk through walls.

"That's it!" I rested the palm of my hand against the wall, hesitating before trying to push my fingers through it. I filled my lungs with oxygen and pressed my hand into the wall. The air on the other side was cool, and I felt a slight breeze. *Please don't let there be a dragon waiting for me.*

It took a moment for my eyes to adjust to the light, but when they did, I couldn't believe what I saw. I stood in a room the size of a football stadium. In the center was an enormous mound of gold, gems, and treasures of all shapes and sizes. The beauty and wealth of it took my breath away. I stood frozen for too long before coming to my senses. "Dacia," I said, waking myself up from my stupor, "get out of here while you can."

I closed my eyes and pictured myself sitting in my dorm room. Before I opened them again, I heard, "Hey, where did you come from?"

I couldn't remember Samantha's voice ever sounding so welcome. My voice, on the other hand, was lifeless. "A dungeon."

"What do you mean?"

I dragged my trembling hands through my hair. "Well, I met the guy who wants Nefarious, and he locked me in his dungeon."

"Pretty much just what you said then." We sat in silence for a few minutes before Samantha asked, "Well … are you going to call Cody and Sarah, or am I?"

"I suppose I will." Collapsing in the chair, I pulled my shoes off and threw them at the wall. They hit with less than satisfying thuds. "I was kind of getting used to my life being somewhat normal. As soon as I call them, that's gone."

"Dacia"—Samantha patted my shoulder—"that was gone as soon as you started having nightmares again. We just weren't aware that it was."

Cody arrived last. I waited by the door, opening it as soon as the strength and love of his aura blanketed me.

"Thought you'd wait." He brushed his finger along my cheek.

I pulled him into the room and closed the door.

Samantha waved at Cody from the desk chair. He nodded at her.

When he noticed Sarah sitting in Big Bird, his hand tightened on mine. "Why didn't you?"

I moved him toward Cookie Monster, then sat on the floor in front of him. "I did, but …"

"Dacia just spent the better part of the afternoon in a dungeon," Samantha said.

I nodded before plunging into the events of the day. I did my best not to leave out any details and finished by saying, "So, there goes the normalcy from my life."

Samantha waved her hand. "That was tossed out the window a long time ago."

Sarah looked at me for a moment. "How did he get into your head when you were unconscious?"

"I've been wondering that myself." I tugged on the lavender carpet threads. "With Nefarious, once I was comatose, I didn't have to worry about him anymore. I don't know if I'll ever be safe from Draconian."

"That's really scary." Samantha sat by the desk. Her books were still spread across it, but she hadn't even glanced at them since I came back.

I stared at my feet. "Don't I know it."

"I wish there was something we could do to help you." Sarah's expression was one I had dreamt of seeing on Mom's face. It told me that she sympathized with me and that she would take this from me if she could.

My mouth fell open. "Oh."

"*What?*" Cody asked.

"It just dawned on me why Draconian got so angry when I asked why he didn't try to control me."

Samantha's eyebrows pinched together. "Why?"

"He was trying." I stood and paced across the room. "That's why my brain seemed so cloudy. Why else would I have let him sit down by me? I even moved over for him. Somehow, he was making me passive … agreeable, but as soon as he told me that what he wanted to do with Nefarious didn't concern me, the spell was broken."

"How, though?" Sarah brushed lint off her heather slacks. "I imagine he'll try again. It would be beneficial to know how you broke the spell this time."

"Yeah, then maybe I can keep myself from being put under it again." I sat on Cody's knee. He gripped my waist. "I wish you could help train me, but unless you've suddenly learned how to use magic, I don't think you can control my mind."

"No, I haven't, but I will help you in any way I can." Sarah drummed her fingers on the arm of the chair. "Please don't hesitate to call me … day or night."

"Us either," Samantha offered. "What are friends for if not to help each other?"

We sat in silence for a moment. "This is a little off the subject, but have you met Aurelia, Sarah?"

"Yes, I have." She tipped her head to the side, and her eyebrows pinched together. "I signed her up for her classes a few days ago. Why do you ask?"

I glanced at Cody, who stared at the floor. "Well, Cody and I met her at Falcon Lake. She seemed unnatural. She was nice enough, but I've never seen anyone else who looks like her."

"Dacia thinks maybe she's an elf or something," Samantha said.

"That's definitely a possibility." Sarah drummed her fingers on the arm of the chair. "It would explain why she … sparkles. If that's true, I wonder what it means."

I dragged my hand through my hair. "Hopefully, nothing bad."

"She may just be another girl." The look on Sarah's face made it clear she didn't really feel this way. "Until we're sure, that's what we should assume," Sarah said. "Don't treat her any differently than you would anyone else."

"Yeah. Time will tell." *Could she be here to help me? Or is she Draconian's pawn?*

"Now"—Sarah smacked her hands, rubbing them together—"who is staying for the summer session?"

"Us and Dan." Cody waved his arm, indicating the three of us.

"Good. The more support Dacia has, the better." She held my gaze with hers, leaning forward. "Does Dan know about your powers?"

"Not yet." I lowered my head, rolling my neck. "But I doubt I'll be able to hide them from him for much longer."

"It would be best to tell him before something happens," Sarah said.

"Yeah, we've talked about that." My insides twisted. The thought of losing another friend because I was a freak was too much. "I'm just not sure how to let him know without scaring him off."

"You'll think of something." She nodded her head. "He seems like a good guy. It may take more to frighten him than you think."

"That's what Samantha says." Dragging my fingers along my forehead, I said, "I don't know how to go about telling him. 'Hey, Dan, I just wanted to let you know I'm a freak. Hope you don't mind.' For some reason, it just doesn't come across the way I want it to."

Samantha's hands tightened into fists. "Cody told you what to do." Her voice was stern.

"I'm sorry, Samantha." I clenched my jaw. The air in the room felt thick and hot. It stuck in my throat, not wanting to enter my lungs. I needed to get out of here, but I couldn't leave. Not now. "I don't want to upset you, but I'm scared."

"I know, but you're going to have to say something eventually. Try freezing fire like Cody suggested." The hint of a smile curved her lips. "Dan will be awestruck."

"I have to admit"—Sarah tapped her finger against her chin—"it sounds like a good idea to me. That is one of the more impressive things I've seen you do."

"I'll tell him. Just stop pushing." I rubbed my hands over my face. *How can I make them understand?* "You have to give me some time. I'm not about to spring this on him during finals. If I end up mortally wounded before then, I guess you guys can let him know I'm an abomination."

"It's okay." Cody gently kneaded my shoulders. "I agree. Finals are stressful enough."

"If you guys don't mind—" I stood up and tugged a hand through my curls "—this has been a long, hard day. I'd like to go to bed."

"Sure, Dacia." Samantha shot me a sympathetic smile.

Cody grabbed my hand and kissed the back of it. "Sleep good."

"Let me know if anything happens," Sarah said as she headed out.

I climbed into bed, aware Cody would be sleeping in Cookie Monster again tonight and knowing he would be doing it with Sarah's blessing.

Chapter 8

Torture Is Hell

storm looms on the horizon, the scent of rain fills the air, and lightning silhouettes enormous thunderheads. An ominous feeling crawls up my spine and perches on my shoulder. I hurry to class, worrying about what the day might bring.

Draconian hasn't bothered me since I was imprisoned, but I know that if he chooses today to come after me, this storm will shield him.

Apprehension tickles the nape of my neck. I fidget with my backpack and look over my shoulder. I tell myself I'm nervous about reading in front of the class, but I know there's more to it than that. I want to go back to my room and snuggle under a blanket. At least there, I'll feel safe.

Only one other student is in the classroom when I arrive. His dark head is bent over his desk. He furiously scribbles on his paper. I glance at the clock. I'm a few minutes earlier than normal. Shrugging, I sit down. As soon as I do, the other student stands, turning toward me. He doesn't look familiar, but I don't know everyone. For the most part, I keep to myself.

I pull my notebook out of my backpack and focus on my story. Parts of it grate on me, but I can't figure out how to re-word it. Deciding it's going to have to be good enough, I set my pen down and look around the room. When I catch a glance of the other student, I can't believe my eyes. I do a double-take and stare in horror.

His face isn't like anything I've ever seen. It looks like he's melting—like blobs of wax are running down his cheeks. His brown hair whitens and grows a couple of inches per second, and a long beard sprouts from his newly aged face. Before my eyes, the college-aged kid transforms into an old man.

It takes me too long to get over my shock and realize what's happening. Draconian had disguised himself. He'd waited here to ambush me. And, like an idiot, I'd sat and watched him. I spring to my feet, bumping my thigh on the desk, and run toward the door. Desks fly through the air, crashing down, blocking the aisles, bouncing against each other. I push one out of the way, and another slams in front of me.

Fury ignites inside me, sending heat pulsing through my veins. The desks around me quiver. I need to get a grip or risk losing control of my powers.

"Why won't you leave me alone?" I shout.

"Dacia, Dacia, Dacia." He shakes his head as he paces closer to me. "Don't play dumb with me; it doesn't become you. You have something I want. Give him to me, and this will end."

"Never! He will never be yours!" I shove desks out of my way, clearing a path to the door.

"So much defiance and at such a young age." He sounds like he's impressed. "Give me Nefarious, and come with me. Be my apprentice. Learn all I have to offer. My knowledge could be yours in time. We would make a great and powerful team."

Stopping, I stare at him, stunned. *Where did that come from? He didn't think I'd accept, did he?* "What is wrong with you?"

"Your anger could become your greatest strength. With time and instruction, you could be more powerful than me."

My mouth falls open. "Why …" I shake my head and try again. "Why would I let you teach me? I stand against evil. Don't you get it?"

"Evil? That's what bothers you?" He strokes his beard and steps toward me. "You and I were given these powers to use them. Controlling those who are weaker is our destiny. Good and evil aren't part of the equation."

"No." I narrow my eyes. "My destiny is helping those who are weaker, not controlling them, not making things more difficult for them."

He curls his lip and shakes his head. "You'll see it my way, Dacia. It may take torture and pain, but you'll come around."

Disgusted by the thought, I shout, "I'll never see it your way! I'll never be like you!" At the same time, lightning bolts shoot from my fingertips. Draconian dodges. Taking advantage of the distraction, I dart through the emergency exit.

A gust snatches the door from my hand, slamming it against the building. Raindrops pelt me, and thunder crashes in sync with the lightning. I lower my head and sprint into the storm. Flashes brighten the sky, and for a split second, a dragon looms in the distance.

The little girl inside me cowers, but somehow on the outside, I remain composed. The anger that overcame me earlier is gone now. "Dacia, you defeated Nefarious. You can do this," I say out loud.

A ball of fire races through the air toward me. I stop running and build a wall of ice between us. While hidden from the dragon's sight, I will myself to disappear. Watching myself become invisible is eerie, like being erased. I hold my hand in front of my face. Raindrops outline it. In these conditions, I'm still noticeable.

I sprint toward the dorm. Not being able to see where my feet will fall is disorienting. I stumble a few times before I quit looking at the ground. By the time the dragon's flames break through the ice, I'm far enough away I don't feel the heat.

The dragon roars, and for a moment, I feel sorry for it, knowing Draconian will punish it for failing.

The dorms rise up ahead of me. *Almost there, you can make it.* An extra burst of energy propels me forward. Draconian is still chasing me, but I don't waste time turning my head to see how close he is.

My breath comes out in heavy pants. Sweat mixes with the rain dripping down my face. My legs throb, but I'm almost there. The lights along the sidewalk beckon me on. I'm going to make it.

My body stiffens, and I can't feel anything. I plummet face-first on the ground unable to break my fall. My nose crunches against the pavement. Air rushes from my lungs, and I become visible once again.

Draconian's toes press against my side. "Didn't I tell you that you are no match for me? What will it take for you to learn this lesson?"

I try to scream for help, but like the rest of my body, I'm unable to move my mouth. He flips me over so I stare up at him. Rain pelts my eyes and runs into my nose and mouth. I can't blink, can't wipe the water away. If he doesn't kill me first, I'll drown.

"How are you going to get out of this one, Dacia?" He folds his hands behind his back and rocks onto his heels. "You will not flee from me so easily this time!"

Calm down. Use your powers to weaken his hold on you. Think of something.

"What torture will it take to make your anger consume you? What can I do to make you realize helping the weak is not your destiny?" He laughs, and intense pain courses through my body.

I scream, but no sound escapes my lips.

"How does that feel, Dacia?" he asks as the pain subsides. "Should we try again?"

A conflagration spreads through my muscles and bones, incinerating every part of me. My scorched lungs refuse to take in the air my body needs. On the inside, I writhe and scream as the wildfire burns through to my soul. On the outside, I lie perfectly, soundlessly still.

The pain diminishes, leaving smoldering embers where infernos had been. My brain feels fuzzy.

Draconian kneels beside me. He grasps my chin, turning my head so I stare directly into his face. Through the water pooled in my eyes, he's distorted. His nose looks enormous compared to the rest of his features.

"Let me in, Dacia, and this can all end." His voice is soft, comforting.

Part of me wants to give up, to hand him Nefarious, and walk away from the trauma. The more my thoughts lean in this direction, the more eager Draconian's features become.

"That's it," he coaxes. A smile spreads across his face, lifting his beard.

No. You can't give in. I fight to control my thoughts, to push him out of my head. I can't hand over Nefarious. The fuzziness retreats, like a cool breeze blowing the fog from my brain.

Draconian's nostrils flare, his chest heaves, and rage ignites in his eyes. "Your spirit is stronger than I imagined." He stands, turning his back on me. "But, I will break you."

Pain floods through my body. Waves of agony crash over me, threatening to drag me under. Darkness clouds my vision. I fight to control my thoughts, to keep them my own.

The torture is too much. My mind checks out, and I slip into unconsciousness.

I opened my eyes to my darkened room and sighed. Pain tore through my body with the slight movement. Every cell ached. Pinching my eyes shut, I whimpered.

Cody slept in Cookie Monster, and Samantha was curled up in her loft. They had no idea I had a nightmare.

I lay back against my pillows and clutched Glacier, flinching as pain shot up my arms. I bit my lip to keep from making any noise.

Staring up at the ceiling, I fought sleep. My eyelids grew heavy, and I fell into a tortured sleep where Draconian haunted my dreams.

Chapter 9
Dreams Do Come True, So Do Nightmares

The forecast called for a severe storm. Every time I closed my eyes, I pictured Draconian transforming from the college-aged student into the wizened wizard. *You don't know it'll happen. It could just be a dream.* But the fear bubbling up in my stomach led me to believe it was more.

I turned off the TV, threw my backpack over my shoulder, grabbed my umbrella, and kissed Cody goodbye. As I plodded off to class, my heart beat loud enough to drown out the booming thunder.

Lightning flashed across the sky, and fat raindrops pelted the ground. Most students dashed to their classes, but my steps were slow, held back by fear.

I stood outside Quartz Building gathering my wits, terrified of what waited inside. I took a deep breath and eased the door open. Stepping into the hallway, I closed my umbrella and trudged toward the classroom.

I peered in through the window, ready to flee. My class-mates sat at their desks or stood in groups, chatting. With a relieved sigh, I reprimanded myself for being so stupid. *How would Draconian've kept so many students from showing up for finals?*

I took my seat and pulled my story up on the computer to go over it one last time. A couple areas still needed tweaking. I stopped for a moment, trying to figure out the best way to say something.

The hair on the nape of my neck stood on end, and a shiver ran across my skin. I looked around the room and found the kid from my dream staring at me. There was no doubt in my mind. He was Draconian.

Fear clawed my chest. My thoughts jumbled. *I need to get out of here.* I pushed against my desk to stand. *I can't leave. I'll fail.* I sat back down and looked at my paper, devising a plan.

When Professor Mantis asked for volunteers to read part of their story, my hand was the first to shoot up. If I could get mine over with, maybe I could sneak out and get a head start on Draconian.

"Dacia," Professor Mantis called to my relief.

I walked to the front of the class and stood at the podium. The steady clacking of keyboards filled the room. Most of the students stared at their laptops or the inside of their eyelids, but Draconian never tore his gaze from me.

I concentrated on reading my story to the class and not on Draconian. As soon as I finished, I walked over to Professor Mantis. "May I be excused? I'm not feeling right."

Her hazel eyes appraised me. "You are quite pale. Go ahead." She waved me off, calling on the next student as I grabbed my stuff and strode to the door.

As soon as I stepped outside, I turned invisible and sprinted, knowing Draconian would be after me soon, and a dragon or two would probably be with him.

Rain fell, and like in my dream, I became more visible than I was comfortable with. I kept running … hoping to go unnoticed. Something roared, like a train bearing down on me. I turned to look. A fireball shot straight at me. The flames sizzled as rain splashed against them. I stopped and erected a force field around myself. Heat engulfed the barrier, slowing the flames. My hands blistered.

A colossal, blood-red dragon swooped down, landing in front of me. It folded its bat-like wings against its body and lowered its horned head.

The dragon roared. Razor-sharp teeth lined its mouth. The beast raced forward, spouting flames as it barreled toward me. I concentrated on my dorm room, but before I could teleport my body became rigid, and I fell to the ground, unable to move. Draconian stepped past the dragon, patting it like it was a cute little puppy.

"You recognized me? How? Don't bother answering that." He waved an arm in the air. "You'll find you can't talk." He knelt down, studying me. His beard draped over my arm. "Obviously, there is more to you than meets the eye. One day, when we're friends, you can tell me all about it, but for now, I want Nefarious."

He stood, raising his hands. I braced my mind for what came next, hoping to ward off some of the pain, but nothing could have prepared me for the agony. I screamed, but no sound escaped.

"Well, I don't think you're ready to tell me yet. Are you?" Excitement flashed through his gray eyes, brightening them until they looked like molten silver.

A thousand knives stabbed me at once, piercing my skin, slicing through muscles, bones, and organs, ripping the breath from my lungs.

My vision darkened.

He lowered his hands. "Now … maybe. Where is Nefarious?"

I couldn't answer him, couldn't move my mouth. Draconian stared into my eyes, and my mind went fuzzy.

Don't let him in. You're strong enough to defeat a demon. You can keep this buffoon from controlling you. My mind cleared, and pain flowed through my body with my blood.

"I will break you," he said through clenched teeth. "Nefarious will be mine. Why make this so hard on yourself?"

"Because you will not control me." His eyes widened at the sound of my voice, and I realized I'd broken his spell.

With the last of my strength, I imagined Sarah's office. My chest constricted. Darkness surrounded me. Carpet replaced concrete.

"Dacia?" Sarah sucked in a breath and pressed her hand to her chest. "Where did you come from?"

"Draconian attacked me," I managed to say before collapsing.

Sarah rushed over and knelt by my side, resting her hand on my shoulder. "Are you okay?"

Nurse Heron sprung from the couch. She lifted my hand, feeling for my pulse.

I sucked in a harsh breath, gasping.

"What happened?" Nancy looked from my blistered hand to my face.

"Just … give me a minute … please." I closed my eyes. I had no idea how I broke Draconian's control and got away. However I did it, I hoped I would be able to do it again. This wouldn't be the last time he'd try to control me, and next time, he wouldn't go so easy on me.

I slitted my eyes. Sarah and Nancy stepped away and were whispering to each other.

Exhaustion weighed on me. I fought its pull, I needed to know what Sarah was telling Nancy. I needed to figure out how to fix this. I never should have teleported here, but all I'd wanted was to escape. I hadn't thought about the consequences.

I tried to sit up, but my muscles protested. "Sarah?"

She and Nancy walked over and sat on the couch nearest me. Nancy leaned forward, cupping her elbow with one hand and tapping her lips with the other.

"Nancy knows the gist of it." Sarah waved her hand. "Why don't you tell me what happened?"

I squeezed my eyes shut and shook my head. *This isn't good. Too many people are finding out.*

"Draconian tortured me." My voice sounded hoarse, like the screams had ripped through it even though no sound was made. "Somehow I teleported here."

"He tortured you?" She bent down, staring at me. "You don't look hurt."

"Yeah." I laughed humorlessly. "Somehow, he made every part of my body scream in pain." I sucked in a breath, fighting the memory. "He does it in small doses. Otherwise, I think it would kill me."

Nancy glanced at Sarah, tilting her head to the side. Sarah nodded, and Nancy said, "Is that how you burnt your hands?"

I bit my bottom lip. "Can you help me onto the couch?"

Nancy and Sarah grabbed under my arms and hefted me to a standing position. My legs shook but held my weight. With measured steps, I moved to the couch. I sat, leaning my head against the back, staring at the ceiling, not wanting to see Nancy's face. "No, a dragon did that."

"A … a dragon?"

I heard movement on the other couch but didn't look. "Yep." The word came out with a popping sound at the end of it.

"A dragon. Wow."

"Dacia," Sarah said, "why don't you rest?" She quietly explained my powers and my current situation to Nancy. Then she told her about my nightmares.

Tears trickled out of my eyes, dripping into my ears. I didn't wipe them away. I didn't want to draw Nancy's attention.

Drowning out their voices, I fought the exhaustion, pain, and hopelessness that threatened to overcome me.

"Dacia."

I jumped when Sarah's hand came down on my shoulder, cringing as pain enveloped me.

"Sorry," she said. "Nancy was talking to you."

I wiped my tears with the back of my hand and looked at Nancy.

"When you came to my office—" she drew her finger along her cheek "—how'd that happen?"

I shook my head, looking down at my lap. "That was the first time I woke up injured. I didn't know I'd heal."

"And, that's why Cody came back from the hospital so quickly?" she asked with a little more enthusiasm.

I looked up at Sarah, and she nodded. "It's good that Nancy knows."

I reached my hand up to pull it through my hair, then dropped it, remembering the burns. "I had no idea I could do that. I was as surprised as anyone when his wounds healed."

She tipped her head back and laughed. "That is quite a power that you have." She rubbed her palms together. "Have you considered going into medicine?"

"Really … I just want to survive freshman year." I stared at my shoes.

"Think of all the good you could do, all the people you could help." Her hands were in constant motion, emphasizing every word she said.

I shifted on the couch. "How would any of it be explained? No one would understand."

Her shoulders slumped. "But, you could do so much—"

"I know, but I also know what it's like to have these powers—" I swallowed "—and how people treat me because of them."

She sat on the end of the couch and rested her hand on my shoulder. "People fear what they don't understand, but some people would accept it. And, that's a gift."

I snorted. "It's a rare gift."

Sarah cleared her throat. "Dacia needs to rest. She'll heal faster."

Nancy pursed her lips, but I wanted to jump up and hug Sarah.

After Nancy left, Sarah sat across from me. "I know you're concerned, but I think this is a good thing."

"Probably." I shrugged. "It's just too much right now."

"Are you okay?" She leaned toward me.

"I'm scared." I stared down at my hands. White blisters stood out against bright red skin. "I think Draconian will be worse than Nefarious." I looked into her eyes. "Maybe we should let Nancy know that if something happens to you, Samantha, or Cody, she should call me to help before she calls 9-1-1."

Her mouth opened, closed, then opened again. "Why do you think Draconian will be worse?"

"I have faced so many dragons in my dreams, not just one, and Draconian said he controls fifteen of them." My lips trembled, and I sucked in a deep breath, hoping to steady myself. "He attacked me on campus during the middle of the day. He can get into my head whether I'm conscious or unconscious. He's trying to figure out how to control me. If he does, you'll all be in danger—from me." I tapped my fist against my chest, emphasizing the point I was making. "If he's controlling me, you won't be able to stop me from handing Nefarious over to him."

She got up and paced, and I realized that like me, she seemed to think better on her feet. "I never considered that. Maybe I should move the vase."

"Somewhere I don't know about."

"I'll move it today." She looked at the clock. "I need to get going."

"If it's okay with you, I'd like to stay for a little bit while I regain some strength." I leaned my head against the couch again. "Then I might try to teleport to my room. I don't want to face Draconian or his dragons anytime soon."

She nodded, then patted my shoulder as she stood. "Be sure to let Cody and Samantha know what happened. You need to keep them informed."

"Yeah, and sometime after finals—" I yawned "—I'm going to tell Dan about me. He deserves to know what he's getting into."

"I think that's a good idea." She walked into her office and came out with her purse, fishing through it until she found her keys. "Be careful."

I stayed in Sarah's office listening to the rumbling thunder and pelting rain. After some of my strength returned, I called my room. When nobody answered, I hung up the phone and closed my eyes. My body squeezed in and stretched out. Darkness enveloped me for just an instant before I stood alone next to Cookie Monster.

Chapter 10

Coming Clean

*B*utterflies dive-bombed my stomach, and my feet tapped relentlessly, keeping time with my heart. Finals were over, and I was as free as a bird.

I should've spent the day enjoying myself. Instead, I paced from the door to the wall, ten steps, from the wall back to the door, eleven steps that time. I was more stressed about telling Dan than Samantha was about failing all of her finals. She'd gotten out of bed this morning mumbling about being a failure, but she'd gone to class. Deep down, she knew she'd get an A on her test. But, all I could think about was Dan's reaction. No matter how I pictured myself telling him, I saw fear dull his eyes and hatred harden his heart. Too many people had reacted that way for me to believe Dan would be any different. As

I crossed the floor for the thousandth time, ten steps again, I sensed Cody at the door and realized it was time.

He walked in and held my face in his hands, rubbing his thumbs along my temples. "You ready? Be here any minute."

Without meaning to, I siphoned some of his energy. It flowed into me, strong, reassuring. "I'm really nervous, but I can't let him stay here without knowing what he's getting into. It wouldn't be fair." I leaned into Cody for a hug, and some of my tension disappeared.

He held my head against his chest. "Sam and I are here for you."

When Dan and Samantha showed up, we made small talk for a while. Samantha swore she failed all her finals, but the rest of us agreed she aced them.

When we hit a lull in the conversation, I hid my trembling hands behind my back. "Dan, I have something I need to show you." My voice belied the butterflies fluttering in my stomach.

"It's really cool." Samantha squeezed his arm.

He looked from me to her. "What is it?"

"Remember to keep an open mind." She grinned at him, then nodded at me.

I took a deep breath. "This is going to shock you. Ready?"

"And waiting." He sounded like the only one left out of an inside joke.

I willed a ball of fire to life in the palm of my hand. Dan's eyes widened, and his mouth hung open. Blue flames grew to the size of a softball.

"Wha—what's going on?" Dan turned from me to Samantha to Cody. "This … this can't be happening. It's impossible!"

"It's okay, Dan." Samantha's voice was low and soothing.

"No, it isn't!" He threw the chair backward almost tipping it over in his rush to get out. "How can you do that?" He backed away from me, staring at me like I'd grown a second head. He gripped the back of the desk chair, his knuckles white from the force. "How can you just stand there and watch her?"

The fireball shrank in my hand as my concentration diminished. "Dan—" I swallowed the lump in my throat "—I didn't mean to scare you. I—"

"You didn't mean to scare me?" The color had drained from his face. "Maybe this is normal for you, but it's not for most people."

"Calm down, Dan." Cody thrust his finger forward, pointing at Dan, then at me. "Dacia, finish."

Cody moved in front of the door. His feet spread wide apart, his arms crossed over his chest. "Dacia," he said in a calmer tone, "please finish."

Samantha sat on the arm of the chair, her eyes full of tears. The ball of flames in my hand was only the size of a quarter. I concentrated on it, watching it grow, trying not to think about the fear on Dan's face. As ice flowed from my fingertips, I heard Dan gasp. When the last flame was extinguished, I sent the ice sphere flying through the air to Cody.

"You gotta admit that was cool." Cody sounded like my own personal cheerleader. He grabbed the globe and tossed it to Dan.

Dan jumped back from it. As the orb crashed to the ground, shattering, I jerked like I'd been slapped. Tiny shards of ice slid across the floor in all directions.

Dan's hands clenched at his sides. Veins popped out along his arm muscles. "Let me out, Cody."

"Calm down first." Cody reminded me of a bouncer with his face closed off and emotionless.

Dan shoved Cody. "I'm not going to calm down as long as I'm trapped in here with her." He stabbed his finger through the air at me, and I felt it like a physical blow.

Walking up behind him, Samantha raised her hand and held it out, hesitating before placing it on Dan's arm. He jerked away. Her forehead crumpled, and her eyes glistened. "Dan, please …"

"I'm sorry, Samantha. I really am." He ran his hand through his hair. "This is too much."

Samantha's voice stayed steady. "Dacia was afraid you'd react like this, but I told her she could trust you." She turned toward me. "Can you guys give us ten or fifteen minutes?"

"Sure." I forced the word out.

"We'll be in the hall." Cody reached his hand out to me. I walked to his side, avoiding looking at Samantha and Dan.

"Thanks." Samantha dragged Dan by the hand to Big Bird.

Cody and I stepped out, and he pulled me into his arms. "Give him time. He'll come around."

"What if he doesn't?" I stared down at the tile. The purple and black flecks blurred together over the white background.

"He will." He brushed my hair back. "He's in shock."

I wrapped my arms around Cody's waist and leaned into him, needing his strength and support. Time slowed. I wondered if Samantha would ever let us back in. A few people walked down the hall, casting curious glances in our direction.

Finally, Samantha opened the door. "Come back in."

Dan glanced up at me then looked back at his hands. He cleared his throat. "Sammi explained some things."

"So, are you okay with me?" My eyes were hot with unshed tears. I willed them not to fall no matter what he answered.

He kept his eyes lowered and shrugged. "What else can you do?"

"I—"

Cody interrupted, "Remember when I went to the hospital?"

"Yeah, kidney stones." Dan looked up at Cody. His eyebrows were furrowed in confusion.

"That's what we said, but I was in bad shape." Cody's face was stony. The anger, hurt, and sorrow he must've felt every time he thought about that day didn't show. "Four students beat me. I needed surgery."

"No." Dan shook his head. "I saw you the next day. We played basketball."

"Dacia healed me." Cody drew me closer. "She has powers. Before coming here, she couldn't control them, but with Sa—Dean Aspen's help, she's mastered them."

Dan's eyebrows shot up, disappearing under his hair. "Dean Aspen knows about this?"

"Sarah knew before I was born that she might train me someday." I couldn't meet his eyes. I couldn't handle finding fear or hatred in their hazel depths. "She called me into her office and informed me that we were part of a prophecy. I thought she was nuts, but she wasn't."

Dan looked at Samantha for help. His eyebrows were raised, and his mouth curled into a confused frown.

"It's all true, Dan." Samantha lifted her shoulders. "I wanted to tell you, but it wasn't my place."

"Why are you telling me now?" Dan rubbed his chin. The tiny hairs scraped against his palm, filling the silence.

Cody's fingers trailed up and down my arm. I didn't know if it was to keep me calm or him. I looked at Dan and said, "Since you're staying, you should know."

"Why?" Dan glanced at each of us, rubbing his neck. "You've kept it from me this long."

Cody and Samantha looked at me. I shook my head. Somebody else could tell him.

Samantha pinched her nose. "We wanted you to find out before something happens."

"Like what?"

"Let me explain more." I walked to the window and stared out at the trees. Aspen leaves rustled in the breeze. "The prophecy was that I would have to face a demon who wanted to conquer the world. Believe it or not, I did."

Dan wiped his hand over his face and laughed without humor. "Sure."

Samantha shrugged and nodded. "It happened."

Dan's smile faded, and his expression turned into a look of utter disbelief. "No offense, but how did you defeat a demon?"

"None taken. And, it was sheer, unadulterated luck. Do you remember me missing a lot of classes?"

He nodded.

"Nefarious, the demon, attacked me." I shuddered at the memory. "If I wouldn't have been able to heal myself, I don't think I'd be able to use my leg today. But, I don't even have a scar. Nefarious actually killed Sarah to keep her from training me, but I brought her back."

"You're kidding me. Right?" He sank down onto the chair, propping his elbows on his knees.

I shook my head. "No."

"So, how else would I find out about you?" Dan asked again.

"Bear with me for a minute." I held my hand up. "I've been having nightmares lately. When I dream that something or someone attacks me, I wake up with whatever injuries I dreamed about."

He scrubbed his hand down his face. "That's not possible."

"I wish." My voice trailed off. "And if that isn't enough, earlier this week a man named Draconian imprisoned me. He keeps dragons as pets."

"Dragons?" Dan snorted. "There's no such thing as dragons."

"Yeah." I sat on Cody's knee, and he rubbed my back. "I saw one up close and personal after my Fiction Writing final on Wednesday." I pictured the red dragon and saw flames shooting toward me. Shaking my head, I focused on my friends. Samantha stood beside Dan, her hand on his shoulder. He sat in Big Bird, one hand around her waist. The other pulled fuzz off the chair.

Cody's hand kept running along my spine.

"He wants me to give him Nefarious, and since I won't, he's started sending his dragons after me. We decided you should know before you come over here one day and find me covered in blood, burnt to a crisp, or whatever else they may do to me."

"You're serious?"

"She's serious." Samantha walked over to her closet. "I hope you don't mind, Dacia, but I saved these for when you talked to Dan." She pulled out a charred, bloodstained pair of pajamas. "Dacia had a dream about dragons the other night, and this is what she woke up in." Samantha tossed them to Dan who stared at them in horror.

"How would you give Nefarious to Dracon … what was it?" Dan asked, stumbling with the name.

"Draconian," Samantha answered.

"How would you give Nefarious to Draconian anyway?" He looked around the room as if searching for an explanation. "I thought you defeated him."

"I think I kind of turned him into a jinni. I encased him in a vase that is safely hidden away."

Dan set my pajamas down and wiped his hands on his legs. "This is going to take a while for me to wrap my brain around. I mean, how can you go through life knowing you might be attacked by demons or dragons?"

"Having Cody and Samantha helps more than you can imagine." I smiled at my friends. "But, it's not easy, and there are days when I … when I just don't know if I'm gonna make it." I stared down at my hands until my vision blurred. "I haven't dealt with it for months. Until earlier this week, I was in denial. Sarah told me about Nefarious … nothing else. I had no idea there would be other monsters. I thought I could have a normal life when I was done with him.”

Dan leaned back in the chair, and I could see he was trying to process all the information we'd given him. “So, this is real?” He looked me in the eye for the first time since seeing what I'm capable of.

“Unfortunately.” I lifted one shoulder toward my ear and tried to smile.

“Well, then, uh …” He stopped and cleared his throat. “Can you show me again?”

Slumping back against Cody, I let out a long breath. I looked over at Samantha and knew she felt the same way. Smiling, I lit a fire in my palm.

He held the ice globe, examining it as the last of the flames disappeared. “So, are there more things you can do? Fire, ice, heal, transport objects through mid-air, what else?”

“Well, uh, I can walk through walls, fly, read minds, tell when Cody's near, teleport.” I cocked my head. “I think that's all.”

Samantha tapped her chin. “You can crush things.”

“Yeah.” My stomach sank when I remembered Bryce's screams when I crushed his hand without knowing what I was doing. “Oh, I can also shoot lightning from my fingers and create like a force field thingy around me.”

He tilted his head, making his hair fall across his eyes. “Can you turn invisible or manipulate time and space?”

Tingles ran from my fingertips to my wrist as my hand disappeared.

"Wicked." He reached out, touching my fingers. "Can you make pizza appear?"

I waved my hands through the air. "It'll be here any minute."

Dan's mouth hung open. "Really?"

"Yeah." Cody laughed. "Ordered it earlier."

A few minutes later the pizza delivery guy knocked on the door. Cody took the pizzas from him and had a slice half-eaten before he set the boxes down.

"So, Superman has Kryptonite." Dan held a slice in front of his mouth. "Batman's just a regular guy with too much money and a sense of righteousness."

"Yeah." Cody put two slices on a plate and sat down.

"So, if you can do all that." Dan waved his arm, looking at me. "Do you have a weakness?"

"Well—" my eyebrows squeezed together "—probably."

Cody laughed, just about choking on his pizza. When he swallowed, he said, "Do warm chocolate chip cookies count?"

Chapter 11

Not So Bad

*N*ightmares pummeled me. I'd wake up from one and fall into another. Finally, deciding I couldn't take another beating, I grabbed my book and sat in bed reading. When morning's light crept through the window, I got up and headed for the showers, hoping one would invigorate me.

By the time I got back, Cody was awake. "Nightmare?" he asked as I set my bathroom bag down.

"Yeah," I grabbed my brush and pulled it through my curls. "I wish Sarah knew something that could help me against Draconian … or even his dragons. Maybe if I only had to worry about one, things'd be better."

Cody flipped the TV on. I looked up into Samantha's loft, expecting her to yell at him. Her bed was empty. "Where's Sam?"

"With Dan." Cody flipped through the channels. "They'll meet us for lunch."

He must've gone through the stations twelve times before deciding there was nothing to watch. I set my hand on his, pushing the remote down. "Is something wrong?"

"I, uh—" he flipped the TV off "—I should shower."

Shaking my head, I said, "So shower."

He ran his hands back and forth over the arms of the chair. The blue fuzz stood on end, then was smoothed down again. "All that's happened lately, don't wanna leave you."

"Alone." I sat in Big Bird with my chin in my hands. "You left off alone."

"Yeah." He stared at the black screen. "Took you twice this week. Don't want you alone."

Kneeling on the floor, I wrapped my arms around him and laid my head on his chest. "I'll be fine, Cody. I can stay here or sit in your room."

He tilted my chin up. "Promise you won't leave?"

"I'll stay in the building."

I walked with Cody to the door. When he opened it, Aurelia was stepping into the hall from the room across from mine.

"Hi." A grin spread across her face, and she tilted her head, reminding me of a bird for a second. I shook my head to clear the image. "I guess we are neighbors," she said.

"Looks like." I tried to return her smile, but the monster inside roared at me to get Cody away from her. I grabbed Cody's hand, tugging him along.

He lifted his eyebrow at me and nodded at Aurelia.

The three of us walked outside together. I tried to come up with something to say to break the tension, but I couldn't think rationally with the beast snarling inside me, fighting to claw its way out.

Aurelia's golden hair bounced as she walked. The silken strands glistened, not a hair out of place. I looked at my shadow. Its curls were tangled and unruly. Her legs were perfectly toned, her skin flawless. Next to her, I felt unkempt, insignificant, and washed out.

"Getting settled?" Cody asked.

She smiled at him, and a fire burned in the pit of my stomach.

"Yes. I just finished unpacking. I am looking forward to classes starting Monday so I can meet people." She looked at the mountains, and her eyes softened. "It gets lonely not having friends here."

Her loneliness spoke to me, quieting the monster. In that, I could relate to her. "I know what you mean." Without thinking about it, I asked, "Why don't you meet us for lunch? My roommate, Samantha, and her boyfriend, Dan, will be there, too."

"Really?" She looked from me to Cody. "That would be great. Thank you."

I shrugged, feeling guilty about how I'd been acting. She didn't deserve my attitude. "No problem."

I stayed in Cody's room while he showered and shaved. His roommate, Drew, had already gone home for the summer. Only Cody's things remained behind.

A picture of his family hung on the wall. Breathing deeply, I closed my eyes. Cody's siblings worshipped him. How long would that last? If he kept ditching them for me, the end was in sight.

I felt his presence in the hallway and turned my back on the photo. I'd made it clear that he should go home, and he'd made it clear that he wouldn't. I didn't want to argue about it again.

He grabbed some clothes, his toothbrush, and his pillow and shoved them into a bag. When he finished, we walked outside. His pace was hurried. His hand pressed against my back, pushing me forward. I couldn't blame him. His fear for me guided his steps.

Once we were inside my hallway, I pointed at the restroom. "I won't go anywhere else." I used my finger to draw a cross over my heart.

He nodded and walked toward my room.

Not wanting Cody to worry more than he needed to, I hurried to my room.

Raised voices stopped me outside the door. "She can't be alone," Cody shouted.

"And you can't sleep in her room unchaperoned," Sarah yelled.

I lowered my head. A problem. That was what I was. Just one big problem after another.

Opening the door, I stepped inside. Sarah and Cody stood inches from each other. Cody's hands were clenched at his sides. He glared down at Sarah. Her fists were on her hips, her feet spread apart.

They both turned, shooting me sheepish looks.

Cody dragged his hand through his hair. "I swear to you. I'll sleep in this chair. Nothing'll happen." He looked into her eyes, pleading with her to believe him. "She needs someone here."

Sarah looked from Cody to me and back again. Her hands dropped, and she let out a breath. "I am trusting you both but only because I won't be here to help her." She focused on Cody, her hazel eyes hardening. "Don't let me down."

The cafeteria was all but deserted when Cody and I showed up. We debated getting our food or waiting for the others, finally taking a seat at a table by the windows.

Aurelia showed up right after Samantha and Dan.

"Hi, Dacia, Cody." She nodded at us somehow making the movement look graceful. "Thanks for inviting me to join you."

"No problem," I said surprised to find the beast sleeping soundly. "This is my roommate and good friend, Samantha, and this is her boyfriend, Dan. This is Aurelia."

Dan stared. His mouth floundered but no words came out of it. Samantha smacked his shoulder, and his face turned bright red.

"Nice to meet you." Aurelia stretched her hand toward them.

Samantha pushed Dan's out of the way and clasped Aurelia's. "You too," she said. "Let's eat." She steered Aurelia away from Dan.

Dan sat at the table watching Samantha and Aurelia walk away. Cody patted him on the shoulder when we walked by. "Gets easier."

Dan got up from the table after he collected himself. He stood next to Samantha, keeping his eyes on his tray.

When we returned with our food, I asked Aurelia, "So, where are you from?"

"I have lived all over." Aurelia had a couple of hamburgers with no bun. She cut into one, and blood seeped out. "No one place. I do like the mountains best, though. They give me a sense of freedom."

I looked away from her nearly raw meat, focusing on my tacos and rice. "The mountains are beautiful. You can't beat the view."

Samantha pushed her salad around, occasionally taking a bite. Dan looked anywhere but at Aurelia.

"Where are you from?" Aurelia looked at each of us as we answered.

"Dan and Samantha are going home tomorrow morning," I said, pointing my fork at them, "but they'll be back for the summer semester."

"Have a major?" Cody asked.

Aurelia dabbed the corner of her mouth with her napkin. "I am undecided for now."

Cody and I asked several questions, and after Aurelia answered, she turned them back on us. Her actions were stiff and her words formal, but she didn't have the comfort of friends like the rest of us did.

Every student that stepped into the cafeteria seemed drawn to our table. Several came over and introduced themselves to Aurelia, but most gazed at her from across the room. I wondered if she realized the effect she had on them.

About halfway through lunch, Samantha and Dan loosened up. When Dan finished eating, he threw his arm over the back of Samantha's chair and rubbed her shoulder. Her smile told me he was forgiven.

While walking out of the student center, Aurelia said, "I want to thank you again for inviting me to join you."

I smiled at her. "No problem."

Aurelia turned away from the dorm. For a moment as she walked away, she looked like she was glowing.

When we were out of earshot, Samantha said, "Okay, I see what you mean. She sparkles."

"She did. Didn't she?" Dan held the building door open for us. "I've never seen anything like it."

"Yeah"—Samantha swatted his arm—"we noticed."

"Least I wasn't the only one," Cody said. "Feel better now, Dacia?"

"Actually, I forgot to be jealous." I laughed. "She's nice."

"She was," Samantha said, "but she didn't really talk about herself."

I unlocked our door and flipped on the lights. "She was probably just nervous."

"Or your first impression was right." Samantha pointed at Big Bird, and Dan plopped down. She sat on the floor in front of him, leaning back against his legs. "Maybe she can't say where she's from."

Dan's eyebrows rose. "Why not? What was your first impression?"

"The first time Cody and I met her"—I curled up on Cody's lap—"she sort of appeared out of nowhere, then disappeared again. Everything about her makes me wonder if she's really human."

Chapter 12
Death First

"Dacia, where are you, Dacia?" Draconian says in a singsong voice.

I squeeze my body into the corner and turn invisible, but I still feel exposed. Draconian knows I'm here. It's just a matter of time before he finds me.

"Give up, Dacia. You can't teleport out of here. You're trapped." His voice echoes off the walls. "I'll go easier on you if I don't have to track you down like a wild animal." He paces back and forth, waiting for me to show myself.

He steps so close I think my heartbeat will give me away. When he turns his back, my knees buckle. I grab the wall, holding myself up.

"Have it your way." He stands back and flames shoot from his fingertips.

There's nowhere for me to run. I can't get away, and I can't let myself be burned. When the inferno nears me, I place a shield around myself.

Draconian laughs wickedly. "There you are. I told you I'd find you." He turns his flames on me.

My shield magnifies the heat, scalding my skin. "Stop!" I scream as I sink to the ground, becoming visible.

"Dacia, will you never learn?" He saunters over to me, clasping his hands behind his back, reminiscent of lecturing teachers. "You're forcing me to punish you. I don't want to do this. I want you to become my protégée. I want to teach you all I know, but you insist on being tortured."

Without even glancing in my direction, he makes my muscles seize. I fall forward, and acid flows through my veins, burning me from the inside out. This time he doesn't steal my voice, and screams fill the room.

Mercifully, the pain stops. He kneels beside me, rolling me onto my back. His gray eyes light up with excitement. "Relax your mind, Dacia. You needn't say a word." He brushes my hair off my face. "This can all be over."

For a moment, I consider giving in.

"I leave the room for five minutes, Dacia, and you disappear." He stands, turning his back on me. "Did you really think you could get away from me this time? Do I need to surround you with my pets to keep you from misbehaving?"

I try to keep my voice from trembling as I whisper, "No." I want to be strong and face him, but I am defeated. For the past few days, I've been locked in a dark room with my only human contact coming from Draconian's long, drawn-out torture sessions. My strength is diminishing, and I don't know how much longer I can keep him out of my mind. As soon as he can control me or read my thoughts, my friends will be in danger.

Tears roll down my cheeks. "Just kill me. Please."

A tremor overtakes my body. Excruciating pain travels through my limbs, exploding in my chest, and for a brief moment, I think Draconian is going to grant my request. Relief floods my body, a blessed release from the agony.

"I'm not about to kill you, Dacia. I'll make you suffer greatly. I will break you, but you won't die. Once your spirit is broken, you'll give me what I want."

"Please," I whisper. "Please."

"No. I will bring you within the very grasp of Death himself, but he will not take you until Nefarious is mine." Draconian paces in front of me, changing his tone to one of sympathy. "That's all you have to do. Then you can end your suffering. I'll grant your wish, and your friends will live completely unscathed."

"I don't even know where he is!"

His face reddens, and his eyes darken. "Do. Not. Lie. To. Me."

"I'm not."

Draconian releases his hold on me. My muscles twitch involuntarily. A malicious grin lifts his beard, and fire flies through the air at me.

Death. I stare into the flames, wondering if I should keep fighting. I'm about to give in. Then I imagine Draconian torturing my friends. I lift my hands. Ice streams from my fingertips, deflecting the fire.

"You're slowing down, Dacia. You're not strong enough to continue fighting me. I will win. Why not submit now?" He waves his arms through the air. "Why put yourself through all this?"

He's right. My reflexes are slowing, and I don't have the strength to move. I can't fight him much longer.

"Just tell me who knows where Nefarious is, and this can end."

"No! I'll die first!"

"So be it!"

Flames race toward me. I try to throw up a shield to protect myself, but the blaze engulfs my body. I scream.

Cody stood on my ladder, leaning over me. "She's awake." His voice was jagged.

"Thank God," Samantha said at the same time Sarah said, "How is she?"

Haze clouded my vision. My skin felt like it was on fire, and my body ached. "Alive."

Cody wiped his eyes. "Been trying to wake you forever."

I squeezed my eyes shut. "I told him"—the words scraped against my throat—"I don't know where Nefarious is."

"It was just a dream," Samantha said.

"I hope so."

Chapter 13

Ally Or Enemy

*S*unday morning, I woke up to a hushed argument. Samantha, Dan, and Cody stood in front of the chairs, quietly yelling at each other and pointing fingers toward my loft.

I lifted myself onto an arm. Pain radiated through my body, sucking the air from my lungs. "What?"

The three of them looked up at me. They reminded me of puppies who'd been caught peeing on the carpet, glancing at each other, then staring at the floor. Finally, Cody said, "They're not sure about leaving."

"Why?"

Samantha wrapped her foot around her leg and rubbed her hand down her arm. "Last night's dream was pretty bad. I should stay to help you and Cody out."

"No." I shook my head. Pain surged through me with the movement, but I fought to keep it from showing on my face. "You need to go. I feel guilty enough that Cody's staying."

Cody lifted his shoulder in a half-hearted shrug. "Told ya."

Dan and Samantha finally decided to go home. They both wanted to see their families, and neither could come up with an excuse that would've satisfied their parents.

As soon as Samantha and Dan left, Cody slumped in the chair.

"What?" I asked.

Holding his head in his hands, he said, "Need a shower and my stuff."

"So …"

He shook his head. "And leave you alone?"

"I'm not going anywhere." I sat forward and winced. "I hurt too bad."

After Cody left, I sat in Cookie Monster, trying to read a book. I couldn't concentrate. Too many thoughts galloped through my head.

A knock on the door caught me off guard. "Just a second." I set my book on the floor and stood. The distance between the chair and door seemed insurmountable. My nightmare had happened too close to morning for me to heal completely. First and second-degree burns marred my skin, and my muscles ached from the torture I'd been subjected to.

I staggered across the room and looked through the peephole. Aurelia stood on the other side, not a strand of her gold-flecked hair out of place.

I plastered a smile on my face and opened the door.

"Good morning, Dacia." She stood perfectly still. "Are you alone?"

"Yeah." I ran my fingers through my hair in an attempt to tame it.

"I have something to share with you in private." She stepped closer, making me want to move back. "May I come in?"

"Sure." I shifted to the side to let her in. "Have a seat." She didn't so neither did I.

"I am not sure how to say this, so bear with me." A warm smile spread across her face. "I knew the moment I saw you on the beach with Cody that you were kind-hearted and would be easy to befriend. I wanted to get close to you before telling you how I came to be here, but it seems time may be running out." She stared into my eyes, and I fought the urge to look away. "I know what you are facing, and I am here to help you."

"What?" *How could she know?* I tilted my head and did my best to look confused. "Finals are over. I'm not facing anything right now. I'm not sure what you mean."

Her voice lost its friendly tone. "Dragons, Dacia, I know about the dragons. I am here to help you. Just as Sarah helped you with Nefarious, I am here to help you with Draconian and his dragons."

I teetered back. "I don't know what you're talking about."

"Do not play dumb with me." She bared her teeth. Her amber eyes hardened, burning into me. For the space of a heartbeat, the beautiful woman disappeared, and a ferocious beast stood in front of me.

"Fine." I pulled my hand through my hair, trying not to show any fear. "How do you know about all of this? Who told you? Who are you? What are you?"

"What do you mean by that? What am I?" She stood with her hands on her hips, and her chin jutted forward. "Does it matter how I know about all of this?"

I waved my hand up and down. "You sparkle. I've met a lot of people in my life, but you're the only one who sparkles without glitter."

Aurelia opened her mouth, but I kept talking. "And, it matters. I don't know you. I don't know if you're on my side or his. I can't trust everybody who walks into my life. Too much has happened."

"I offered my help." Frustration laced her words. "It is apparent you would rather not have it."

I paced the room. Each step sent a pulsating ache through my legs. "I appreciate your offer, but very few people know what I can do. How do you?"

"That is not important right now." Aurelia's voice and stance softened. "Just let me help you."

"It is important." I plopped down in Cookie Monster. "You can't expect me to trust you if you won't trust me."

"What do you mean?" She cocked her head to the side. Once again, the movement was reminiscent of a bird.

What is she? A phoenix? A fairy? An elf?

"You don't trust me enough to tell me how you know about me, but you expect me to take you at your word."

She sat down, folding her hands in her lap. "I am able to sense magic. I felt your prowess growing, and now I am here to help you learn to fight the dragons and their master … unless, of course, you would prefer to do it on your own."

"No. I need help." I looked down at my hands. "But how can I be sure what your intentions are?"

"I will prove my worth to you." She pointed at the burns on my hands. "It appears you had a rough night. I can help you with those."

"I'm okay." I shrugged. "They're healing."

"Please, let me help you." She reached toward me, stopping short of touching me.

I tugged my sleeves up and placed my hands in hers. Her touch was cool and soft. She ran her fingers along my arm in a circular motion. The blistered flesh disappeared, leaving behind creamy, unblemished skin.

"Thanks." She let go, and I pulled my feet up into my chair, wrapping my arms around my knees. "My dream wounds usually heal by morning, but these didn't."

"You are welcome." She stood. "Think about what I told you. I cannot interfere without your permission."

I cocked my head, not understanding. "What do you mean?"

"If you are injured and are unconscious, I cannot help you."

"Why?"

"You must decide, Dacia, if you want my help or not." She strode to the door.

I watched her, wondering if I should trust her, wondering if this was too good to be true. "Do you really think you can help me defeat Draconian?"

"Yes, I do," she said as she stepped into the hall.

I grabbed my book and read the same paragraph several times before picking up the phone. "Hey, Sarah," I said to her answering machine. "This is Dacia. I've got something important to talk to you about. Give me a call when you get back, please." Shortly after hanging up, I remembered her telling me that she wouldn't be around this week.

The conversation with Aurelia replayed over and over again in my mind, always leaving me with the same unanswered questions: How did she know? If she could sense magic, could she tell if Draconian used it on me last night? How did she find me? How did she heal my burns? Was she magic, or did she just have some abilities?

The walls closed in around me. Heat spread through my body. I walked to the window, hoping to fight off the claustrophobic feeling. My pulse pounded in my temples, quicker than it should have been. I closed my eyes and breathed deeply.

I wanted to go outside, to get some fresh air. But, I'd made a promise to Cody, and I intended to keep it. I pressed my face against the glass. When that didn't help, I opened the window. The fresh air did little to combat the dread welling up inside me, twisting my stomach. *Come on Cody. Hurry up.* I paced the room. Ten steps to the door. Ten steps back to the window.

Twenty minutes later, I felt Cody's presence and let out a heavy sigh. I looked at the floor half expecting a path to be worn through the lilac carpet.

I opened the door, and Cody's smile faded. He lifted his hand to my face. "You're upset."

His touch comforted me. The room seemed more spacious even though there was another body in it. I held my hand over his for a moment. "We need to talk." I walked to the chair and plopped into it, making it rock back.

"What's up?" He sat in the other chair and rubbed his chin. His eyes narrowed. "You're healed. How?"

"Yeah." I dragged my hand through my hair and looked into Samantha's loft, wishing she hadn't left already.

"What?"

"Aurelia healed me."

Cody's head snapped back. "Really?"

I replayed my conversation with Aurelia, trying not to leave anything out.

"Wow." Cody leaned forward. His elbows rested on his knees. "Someone to help."

"Maybe." I rolled my neck from side to side, trying to release some tension. "But how does she know?"

He shrugged. "How'd Draconian?"

Chapter 14

True to his word, Cody slept in the chair all week. His kisses were chaste, and his touch was scarce. When I mentioned it, he shrugged it off, quickly changing the subject. I couldn't help but wonder what Sarah had said to him or what was going through his mind. I fought the urge to read his thoughts, knowing I wouldn't like it if somebody read mine.

By the end of the week, dark circles ringed his eyes. Even when they didn't wake me, my nightmares woke him.

Every morning, Aurelia showed up at my door, asking if I needed to be healed. She never asked about my dreams. She didn't ask if I'd made a decision about her yet. She just treated my injuries, then left without trying to persuade me. Cody watched her, constantly on guard, no longer mesmerized by her beauty.

The third day, I asked her if she could help Cody.

She looked at him, taking in his rough appearance. "Cody needs sleep. I could help him rest. However, I do not think he would appreciate it."

"Why?"

Cody's head rested against the back of the chair. His eyes were only half-open. "You need me."

I knew the argument would lead to nowhere, so I dropped it. After Samantha returned, maybe he'd get some rest.

Saturday morning when Aurelia came over, Cody was finally sleeping. I held my finger over my lips and pointed to him.

Aurelia knelt in front of me, healing my dream injuries. "This is the seventh day I have treated your wounds," she whispered.

The pain in my muscles eased, soothed by whatever power flowed through her. "Thank you."

"Have I earned your trust yet?" She stood, keeping her eyes focused on mine.

I rolled my shoulders and looked out the window. It was unnerving to hold her gaze for too long. I imagined it was like having a staring contest with a top predator. "My undying appreciation."

"But not your trust."

Turning toward her, I shook my head. "Not yet. I'm sorry." Cody stirred. I closed my eyes and breathed for a moment, not wanting to wake him. When I continued, my voice was so soft I could barely hear it, but I doubted she had any trouble.

"My heart says I should, but my head says there are too many unanswered questions."

"Like what?" Her cornflower silk shirt and white shorts made her gold skin even more striking.

Looking down at my singed pajamas, I couldn't help but compare myself to her. She was elegant and always had it together while I always seemed to be falling apart. "How do I know you're not working with Draconian?"

She brushed imaginary lint off her shorts. "What can I do to persuade you?"

"I don't know." I tugged my hand through sleep-tangled curls. "Give me some time."

"I can do that. What else?"

"How did you find me? How did Draconian?" I walked toward the door to put more space between us and Cody. "It's hard to believe you both showed up at basically the same time."

She cocked her head like she was listening to something. I looked toward Cody, but he was still sleeping.

"Your magic called to me," she finally answered. "I imagine that is also how Draconian found you. It is purely coincidental that we arrived in the same time frame."

This was more information than she'd given me before. I thought about letting her go but decided I needed one more answer. "Are you like me?"

"No. I am not."

Throughout the day, more students returned to campus. There were far fewer than during the spring and fall semesters but more than had been around for the last several days. Laughter and conversations filled the hallway.

"Do you want to get out of here for a while?" I asked Cody.

He looked down at his hands, and I knew his answer before he gave it. "He's left you alone all week. Think it's a good idea?"

I shook my head. "I'll go crazy sitting here, though."

I read. I paced. Cody and I watched TV. I stared out the window. I thought about Aurelia. She'd given me no reason not to trust her. She'd healed my wounds all week. She'd answered some questions this morning, but I still didn't know much about her.

"Cody, I'm sorry, but I need some air." I stood, and he grabbed my hand.

"I'll come."

We stepped outside, and thoughts stopped whirring through my mind. I took a deep breath, and tension released from my muscles.

"Where to?" Cody asked. Being outside had the opposite effect on him. His shoulders were bunched. His voice was strained.

I pointed to a bench by the door. "I just needed to get out for a bit." Sitting next to him, I pulled his arm over my shoulders and laid my head against his chest.

The breeze rustled through the aspen trees, blowing my hair across my face. Birds chirped, and students made trips to their cars, hauling in their possessions.

Even though I was at ease, I kept an eye out for anything abnormal. Cody's grasp on my shoulder never relaxed. Finally, I stood and reached my hand down to him. "Let's go in." We walked toward the door.

"Hey!" someone shouted.

Cody's grip on my hand tightened. We continued walking. The door was only ten feet in front of us.

"Cody."

He looked over his shoulder and loosened his fingers. Blood returned to my fingertips.

"Hey, Justin," Cody said as the two of them did a complicated handshake. "Didn't know you were here for the summer."

Justin brushed his ebony hair off his face revealing dark brown eyes. "Yeah, I dropped a coupla classes. I'm gonna try 'em again."

While they talked, I saw Samantha pull into the parking lot. Dropping Cody's hand, I jogged over to her car and grabbed her duffel bag, carrying it up to our room for her.

I felt a little lighter knowing I would be able to talk to her and Dan about Aurelia tonight.

Samantha and Dan sat entwined together in Big Bird. Cody sat in Cookie Monster, and I paced while explaining what had been going on while they'd been gone.

Dan combed his fingers through Samantha's hair, never taking his gaze off hers. I wondered if they'd heard a word, but I kept talking.

When I finished, Dan said, "It sounds like she's on your side."

"If she can help you," Samantha said without looking away from Dan, "you should let her. It sounds like she's had plenty of opportunities to hurt you if she'd wanted to."

I sat on the arm of Cody's chair and pulled my hand through my hair. "That's what I've been thinking."

Cody slipped his hand under the back of my shirt. His fingers brushed over my waist, making my skin tingle. "Keep your friends close."

"And hope she's not an enemy?" I asked.

Chapter 15

I swatted at my phone, snoozing the alarm. Since we didn't get cell service here, that was all it was good for these days. Classes started this morning, and I wasn't looking forward to going. The next time my alarm went off, I flipped the blanket to the side and descended my loft's ladder.

"Morning, Dacia." Cody stood and stretched his back. "How'd you sleep?"

"Like I died."

"Strange—" Samantha yawned "—answer."

"Well, since I died twice in my dream, it seemed fitting."

Cody squeezed his eyes shut and pinched the bridge of his nose. "You don't sound upset … why?"

"Because"—I lifted my hands palms up—"last night I realized death isn't the worst thing in the world. Death is peaceful."

He strode toward me and gripped my shoulders. "You can't die." His voice was husky, his eyes wide with fear.

"I don't want to." I stepped closer to him and wrapped my arms around his waist. "But torture is a whole lot worse than death. And, we don't have time to discuss my dream right now. We can talk about it on our way to class."

Samantha looked at Cody and shrugged. "Sure."

A few minutes after I returned to our room, there was a knock on the door.

"That's got to be Dan," Samantha said. "Can you get it, Cody?"

"Sure," he answered, already on his way to the door. "Hey, Dan."

He looked around the room. "So, do you just stay here?"

"Can't say." Cody shrugged. "Sarah wouldn't like it." He patted Big Bird. "Not great for sleeping."

Dan's eyebrows pulled together. He looked up at Samantha's loft. "So, uh, how long has this been going on?"

"Sarah wouldn't want me to answer."

"So, you're here all the time? With Sarah's blessing?" Dan cocked his head. "Even while we were gone?"

Samantha stopped mid-swipe of her mascara brush and looked over her shoulder. "Dacia has some rough nights. It's good to have him here to help."

He shoved his hands in his pockets and rocked back on his heels, still looking at Samantha's loft.

She finished her makeup and clasped a clunky bracelet around her wrist. "The only problem is keeping it from Marcy."

"Well, that and the fact that Cody doesn't sleep worth a damn in these chairs." I leaned on Cookie Monster, making it rock. "They're not bad for a nap, but they're terrible for pulling all-nighters."

Dan finally pulled his gaze off Samantha's loft. "The two of us were going to room together this fall." He pointed to himself, then Cody. "I have a couch. We could bring it over and take the chairs to our room."

"That'd be great." Cody massaged his neck. "Appreciate it."

"You have to promise to take care of Big Bird and Cookie Monster, though." I looked at the chairs that had been part of my life for longer than I'd known Cody and felt more than a little sentimental. "But I think it would be a good thing. Who knows how long these dreams will last."

"Did you have another one last night?" Dan asked.

"I dreamed I died twice." Seeing their somber faces, I couldn't resist saying, "Seems like overkill, doesn't it?"

Samantha groaned. Dan chuckled. Cody pressed his lips together and shook his head.

I threw my hands up. "Okay, not the time for jokes."

When we stepped into the hall, Aurelia joined us. "Good morning!" Her sapphire shirt and pale gray slacks appeared to be designer quality.

"Oh, hello," I said.

Samantha raised her eyebrows and shook her head. "You're way too cheery for this time of day."

"I love mornings." Aurelia smiled. "They are full of promise."

"You and I"—Samantha pointed at Aurelia, then herself—"don't see eye to eye on that. Mornings are for sleeping."

"What classes are you taking?" I tugged on my faded green t-shirt, feeling a little shabby.

"Astronomy," she answered. "Then after lunch, I have calculus. On Tuesdays and Thursdays, I have photography."

"You have my schedule." Since she was here to keep an eye on me, it didn't surprise me.

The long walk to Kestrel Observatory would've been the perfect opportunity to talk to Cody, Samantha, and Dan about my dream. To get there, we had to walk past the majority of the buildings, through a forested area, and along the Rose River. However, I didn't know if I should discuss it with Aurelia there. I wanted to talk to Sarah about her first.

The further we moved from the buildings, the fewer students we passed. When we stepped into the trees, it was like being transported. The campus disappeared behind the thick foliage. The only sounds were the woodland creatures and the roar of the river.

Light filtered down through the leaves. Moss dotted with tiny white flowers covered downed trees. My fingers itched for a pencil and sketchpad.

When we arrived at the observatory, Sarah stood by the door. "Hello." She smiled at my companions, then focused on me. "Dacia, may I have a word with you?"

"Sure." I squeezed Cody's hand. "Save me a seat."

Sarah and I walked out of earshot of the passing students. "I'm sorry I didn't call you. I didn't get back until late last night."

"That's okay. I forgot you were gone when I called." I kicked a rock into a flowerbed. "I've got a lot to talk to you about, though. The others know most of it, but not all."

"Why don't the three of you stop by after class?"

"Well, can we make it the four of us?" I looked up at her. "I don't want Dan to feel left out. I told him everything before he went home."

She clasped her hands in front of her chest. "Good, I am glad to hear that. After class then."

The classroom was set up like most science labs. Tables and chairs ran through the center. Small telescopes were set against the walls. A projector screen was at the front of the room.

I sat between Cody and Aurelia a few rows from the front. "Dean Aspen would like to see us after class." I pointed down the row from me to Samantha. Then leaning toward Aurelia, I said, "I'm going to tell her about our conversation. I'll talk to you about it later."

"Thank you, Dacia." She inclined her head. "I appreciate it."

Vivian Caiman walked into the room with an air of author-ity about her. She was of average height and build with short black hair and a dark complexion. I had a difficult time paying attention to her. I wanted to talk to Sarah and was anxious to get out.

Because of that, class dragged on. I must have looked at the clock a thousand times. Finally, we were dismissed. Cody pulled me close to his side and hurried us to Sarah's office. When we arrived, she was waiting for us. Cody and I sat on one couch. Samantha and Dan sat on the other. Sarah's desk chair was in the room, but she stood.

Rubbing her hands together, she said, "I am now the only person who knows where Nefarious is being kept." She held onto the back of the chair and looked at me sheepishly. "I know I told you I would move the vase the other day, but I wasn't able to until this morning. Then I stuck a sealed envelope somewhere, so that if something happens to me, one of you will know where to find it."

"Why?" Cody asked.

"If Draconian got into Dacia's head the other night, I don't want any of you to be in danger. First and foremost, I am the Dean of this college, and I cannot stand back and watch my students get hurt." She paced with her hands behind her back. "Now, Dacia, what did you want to talk about?"

I told her about my conversation with Aurelia and about our concerns. Then I rehashed my latest dream. They all placed too much emphasis on the fact that I died, but what I couldn't make them understand was that there were worse things than death.

"So … what should I do about Aurelia?" I asked.

Sarah rubbed her chin. "Maybe I should have a talk with her and see if that helps me make a decision."

"That's a great idea." Samantha leaned forward with her elbows on her knees. "You're a good judge of character. Aurelia seems to be nice, but what are her intentions, and how does she know?"

Dan nodded. "I've been hanging around with them for quite some time, and they did a good job of hiding it from me." He lifted his hand, and his next words came out rushed. "Not that I'm upset."

"I'll talk to her." Sarah spun her ring around her finger and stared out the window. Finally, turning back to us, she said, "Why don't you get lunch before your next classes? Be careful."

We walked outside, and I lifted my face to the sky. A gentle breeze rustled the trees. Sunlight flickered through the leaves, dancing across the ground. The earthy scent of the forest mixed with pine lingered on the wind.

We were halfway to Wisteria Hall when Draconian's voice rumbled in my head. *Do you want to see your friends get hurt? It could be arranged.*

My blood ran cold. Dread crept up my spine, then clenched my heart. I bent forward, spitting the oxygen from my lungs.

"You okay?" Cody looked back at me.

"Run!" The word came out on a raspy breath.

They just stood there, looking at me.

"He's here!" I spun around, searching for Draconian and his dragons, searching for a way out.

Cody stepped toward me, his hand outstretched.

"Go!" I pointed toward the dorm.

I grabbed my backpack straps and started jogging. The others quickly caught up. Whether to humor me or because they realized I was serious, I could only guess.

A shadow darkened the ground. The beat of giant wings chased us. A crimson dragon swooped down, grabbed Cody by the shoulders, and flew off with him hanging from its talons. A moss-colored dragon plunged from the sky. I pushed Samantha to the ground.

The dragon flew into me, knocking me down. I skidded across the pavement, scraping my hands and knees, and landed on the grass. Looking up at the sky, spots swam in front of my eyes.

"Samantha!" Anguish filled Dan's voice.

My lungs struggled to fill. By the time I staggered to my feet, Samantha was gone.

Chapter 16

Daring Rescue

"What am I supposed to do now?" My heart plummeted, dropping me to my knees. I stared through the broken branches at the empty sky. Losing Cody was like the day losing the sun or the night losing the stars. One could not exist without the other. The realization that I would not ... *could not* live without him filled me with determination. I had to do something. I had to find some way to get him back, to have him safe. It didn't matter what happened to me. Without him, I was nothing.

Dan's mouth hung open, and his wide eyes stared into the distance.

I shoved my finger into Dan's chest. "Get out! Now! Do you want to be next?"

He grabbed my arms and shook me. "This is your fault!" He clutched his head. "Why didn't you stop them?"

"Not now, Dan." I made sure he was looking at me. "Get back to Sarah's. This isn't over."

Draconian's laughter reverberated through my skull. "My pets do love their new toys." He walked toward us, his navy robe billowed behind him.

"Bring them back," I said through clenched teeth.

Dan's gaze darted through the trees. "Who are you talking to?"

I thrusted my hands forward, but Dan looked straight through Draconian, staring into the trees beyond him. I grabbed Dan's shirt and pulled him behind me. "Don't move." Then I focused on Draconian. "Why can't he see you or hear you?"

A malicious smile twisted his lips. "It's so much more fun if your friends believe you're unhinged." He stepped closer. "Don't you agree?"

I tightened my grip on Dan's shirt, afraid Draconian might still try to take him, too.

Draconian tapped his lips. "Maybe they're not so much toys as dinner."

My chest tightened.

"Give me what I want, and you can have them back." He advanced, his mouth twisted in a cruel imitation of a grin. "I don't think they can handle torture as well as you. What do you think? Should we find out?" In a puff of smoke, he was gone.

"Come on." I turned around and grabbed Dan's shoulder. "I've got to save them."

"How?" His hands tightened into fists.

I tugged my fingers through my hair. "I don't know." My voice sounded hollow. "But I have to try."

We ran back to Sarah's, passing her receptionist without a word, and barged in. I breathed a sigh of relief when I realized she was alone in her office.

She rushed out of the backroom and looked from me to Dan. "What's going on?"

Dan plopped down on the couch and stared at his hands. "I couldn't hold onto her. The dragon ripped her right out of my grasp." When he looked up, his eyes were wide open and wet with tears. "We need to get them back."

"What?" Sarah's head snapped back, and she turned to me. Her eyebrows pinched together. "Hold onto who?"

I crumpled onto the couch and explained what happened. Sarah's face remained calm, but fear danced behind her eyes.

"I can't understand why he didn't take me." I walked to the window. "I was right there. He could've taken me with him or his dragons could've taken me."

"Maybe now would be a good time to talk to Aurelia." She placed her hand on my shoulder. "If you think she might have been sent here to help you, it might be a good time to find out."

I rolled my neck from side to side. "Okay."

"Teleport to your room." She squeezed my shoulder. "Dan can stay here."

Without another word, I closed my eyes and pictured myself standing next to Cookie Monster. I threw my backpack down and ran across the hall to Aurelia's room. I pounded on the door until she opened it. "They're gone." I stumbled forward. "He took them."

She pulled me inside. Plants filled the room, hiding the walls, growing all the way to the ceiling. A green couch blended in with the foliage. "I know."

A huge weight dropped into my stomach, nearly knocking me to the ground. *I shouldn't have trusted her. She knew where we'd be.* "How?"

She waved her hand. "I came here to protect you."

"So why didn't you save them?" I narrowed my eyes. Anger bubbled up inside me.

"You were being watched when it happened." Her voice was annoyingly calm and even. "I was unable to get there in time. I hoped you would come to me for help." She faced me and held her hands out. "And here you are."

I looked at her outstretched hands, then at her face. Seeing no malice in her eyes, I realized I needed her whether I trusted her or not. "Can you help me get them back? He's going to torture them. I can't let that happen."

She wiggled her fingers, and I placed my hands in hers. As soon as I did, I felt like I was caught in a whirlwind. Everything around me spun out of control. When it stopped, we stood in the treasure room of Draconian's castle.

I bent over, bracing one hand against the wall to keep from falling. When the urge to throw up subsided, I stood. "I've been here before. Draconian's dungeon is behind that wall. I can't …" I shook my head. "I hoped I would never see this place again."

Aurelia walked up to the wall and put her hands against it. "It is dark on the other side of this wall, but there are most assuredly two life forms in there."

"Life forms?" *Who talks like that?*

"I cannot tell for sure what they are," she explained. "I can sense the heat of two … beings. They might be dogs or people or dragons."

I closed my eyes and concentrated. Cody's aura flitted against my skin. It was weak, but definitely his. "One of them is Cody." I leaned my head against the cool stone.

I stepped through the wall, feeling the rock press against me, into absolute darkness. A hand grabbed hold of my arm. I gasped before hearing Aurelia whisper, "Shh."

I trailed my hand along the wall, slowly making my way to Cody. His aura was a beacon, pulsing stronger the closer I got to him. Knowing he was right in front of me, I stretched my hand out but stopped short of touching him. I didn't want to scare him. "Cody." His name was barely louder than a breath, but I figured he would hear it.

My fingers brushed his skin. Lights flared. I blinked, and when I opened my eyes, Draconian stood facing me. His laughter filled the dungeon. "So predictable." He shook his head. "It's not much of a challenge when you do exactly what I expect."

He flicked his hand, and my muscles seized. I fell on top of Cody, but he didn't move. Blood dripped from his shoulder. His face matched the pale granite wall he was propped against.

I prayed Draconian would keep his attention focused on me while Aurelia crept to Samantha's aid.

Draconian prowled toward me. His gray eyes narrowed. "You come to my home and try to steal my dragons' playthings." He kicked Cody's leg, and Cody groaned, a beautiful sound that let me know he was still alive.

Aurelia grasped Samantha's arm and disappeared. *One down, one to go.*

"Did you even consider bringing the vase?" He leaned down. His beard skimmed the floor. He grabbed my arms and pulled me to the center of the room. Then he stood, twisting around.

"Where. Is. She?"

In one quick move, he spun around and knelt beside me. Electricity sparked on his fingertips. He touched his hands to my temples.

My muscles flexed. Tremors shook me. A thousand fires ignited under my skin.

Draconian pulled his hands away. "Where is she?" He loosened his hold on me, freeing my voice.

My body relaxed slightly. Tears rolled out of the corners of my eyes. "I don't know." The words were barely a whisper.

He lifted his hands.

"No, please." I tried to jerk away from him, but I couldn't move.

He pushed his fingers into my temples, never taking his gaze off mine. "One more time. Where is she?"

"I … don't know."

Electricity flowed like lava through my veins, burning, searing. My screams bounced off the walls until it sounded like ten people were being tortured.

"Stop," Cody whispered.

Draconian moved to Cody's side. "Would you rather it was you?"

"No—" Draconian stopped my words with a wave of his hand.

Electricity arched from one of Draconian's hands to the other. He bent forward, and Cody's eyes bulged.

All I could think about was saving Cody.

Draconian inched closer. "She can heal. This will most likely kill you." The sparks jumped, lighting up Cody's face.

"Just do it," Cody said.

I clenched my fists. *I clenched my fists.* Electricity sizzled in my veins, lifting the hair on my arms. Lightning shot from my fingertips, slamming into Draconian. He fell to the floor, staring up at the ceiling.

Springing to my feet, I grabbed Cody under his arms and dragged him through the wall. My muscles screamed in agony, but adrenaline made me stronger than Superman. I screamed when someone clutched my shoulder.

Chapter 17

Healing Hands

"Sorry," Aurelia said.

I stumbled back ready to attack. Aurelia grasped one of my arms and one of Cody's. The world spun, and darkness swallowed me.

Before the room stopped spinning, I realized Aurelia had teleported us to Sarah's office.

Exhaustion and dizziness weighed on me, and I dropped onto the tan couch. Aurelia set Cody next to me. He reached his hand for mine as his head slumped against the back of the couch.

Aurelia sat across from us with Dan and Samantha.

"Thank God, you're back." Sarah rushed toward us. "Are you okay?"

I nodded, and Sarah placed her hand over her heart, letting out a relieved sigh. She looked at her watch. "I've got a conference call. Stay here please." She walked into her office, glancing back at us before shutting the door.

"Dacia, do you have the strength to heal Cody?" Aurelia held Samantha's hand.

"No," Cody mumbled. "I'm okay."

The adrenaline ebbed, and pain flowed over my muscles and bones. It saturated my cells, flooding my body. I entwined our fingers and sent what little strength I had into him. "No, you're not."

"He tortured you."

Aurelia's gaze fell on me. I closed my eyes and nodded slowly, trying not to cringe with the movement.

We sat in silence. As soon as Samantha's skin regained a healthy color and her breath evened out, Aurelia moved to the coffee table. She rested her hands on mine. "Let me help you." A surge of energy poured through me, strengthening me before siphoning into Cody.

He opened his eyes and smiled before closing them again.

"They will need sleep." Aurelia continued holding my hand, sending strength into me. "Since the healing power is not their own, they will need more rest to heal than you do. We need to give them a little time."

I looked over at Samantha. Dan sat next to her, holding her hand. Her shirt was covered in blood. I wondered if Draconian had done anything to stop the bleeding or if he just let them suffer.

Dan caught my eye. "Thanks." He nodded at Aurelia. "Both of you."

"Don't thank me, Dan." I looked down at the floor. "It's my fault she was taken to begin with."

"No." Dan's voice was soft. "It wasn't your fault. I was wrong to blame you." He held Samantha's hand, rubbing his thumb along hers. "You tried to protect her from that dragon. I did nothing, nothing at all."

"Don't be so hard on yourself, Dan." I looked him in the eyes. They were red-rimmed and greener than normal. "You've never seen a dragon before. Until just a few days ago, you didn't know any of this stuff was real. I've fought demons, dragons, and magicians before. You're new to this."

"I'll make you a deal." He tilted his head and looked at me like I was a moron. "When you stop being hard on yourself, I'll stop being hard on myself."

"It's not the same thing." I tightened my grip on Cody's hand, and he moaned in his sleep. "I could have protected them. You could've died."

"Like I said, I'll stop being hard on myself when you stop being hard on yourself."

Sarah came out of the office and stood between Dan and me. "There are more important things to discuss."

"Yeah." I sighed dramatically. "Like how am I going to get these guys to go home for the summer?"

"You're not." Sarah stood with her hands on her hips. "Draconian knows they're important to you. They'll be in danger no matter where they are. You need to figure out how you're going to protect them." She put her hand on Aurelia's shoulder. "We also need to learn a little more about Miss Aurelia here."

Dan and I turned our attention to Aurelia. Without a doubt, there was more to her than met the eye. "I was sent here to help Dacia." She let go of my hand. Without her energy flowing into me, my body ached, and exhaustion returned. "I know you would like more of an explanation, but that is all I can give you right now."

"She has powers like mine—" I lifted my arm and flexed my muscles "—only on steroids."

Dan looked between Aurelia and me. "How are your powers so much more advanced? You can't be too much older than her."

Aurelia laughed, a deep rumbling sound. "If it makes it easier for you, I can tell you I am not young, by any means. I may look like it, but I am more than two thousand years old. That is why my powers are stronger than yours, Dacia. They have had much longer to mature."

Dan's mouth floundered for a moment before he finally said, "You've got to be kidding."

"This is how I look now." She waved her hand from her head to her toes. "This is not who I am. Now, I have told you more about myself than I intended. We should be more concerned about the safety of all of you. I am in all the same classes as Dacia so I can protect her, but somehow, we have to figure out a way for all of you to be safe. I will do whatever I can to help, but you will all have to learn to trust me." She looked at Cody and Samantha. "I think they will be waking soon."

"Will I, uh …" I cleared my throat and tried again. "Will I live to … to be as old as you?" All eyes turned to me. I don't know if they hadn't thought about it or if they were surprised by me asking. "It's one of the things that keeps me up at night. I don't know if I will come back to life after dying or if I will actually be dead. It's … it's a scary thought."

Her golden gaze pierced me. I felt like she was looking into my soul. "I wish I knew the answer, Dacia, but I do not."

"Oh … well, thanks anyway." I tried to hide my disappointment. Sarah put her hand on my shoulder and squeezed gently.

Silence filled the room. I focused on Cody and Samantha, willing them to wake up, praying they would be okay.

"So … uh …" Dan fidgeted.

Aurelia looked over her shoulder at him. "What is it?"

"How can a dragon go unseen?" Dan's grip on Samantha's hand tightened, and his legs twitched like he was ready to flee. I couldn't blame him. He'd barely found out about any of this and already had been thrown into the middle of it.

She looked each of us in the eye before saying, "All of the mythological creatures have disguises and ways of hiding themselves from people. They are all real, hiding in plain sight. Most of the time, they try not to draw attention to themselves."

Sarah sat next to Samantha. "I've seen other creatures, but I haven't seen dragons yet."

"You don't want to see them." Dan shuddered. "But what have you seen?"

"Fairies, unicorns, pixies, gnomes." Sarah had a faraway look in her eyes.

Dan shook his head. "Why couldn't I have seen one of them?"

"Fairies helped heal me when I fought Nefarious." I stared across the room, remembering the silver-haired fairies. "I would've died without their help."

Samantha's eyes opened slowly. "Wh … what happened?"

Dan's face lit up like a Christmas tree. "Sammi, are you okay?" He didn't pause long enough for her to answer. "Dacia and Aurelia went after you and Cody and brought you back to Sarah's office."

"I'm all right but really tired." She rolled her shoulders forward and backward. "At least my shoulders don't hurt any-more." She looked first at me then Aurelia. "Thank you. Draconian was going to torture us, and I don't think either of us would've survived."

"I'm glad it didn't come to that." I rubbed my hand over my face. "He wanted me to go after you, so he might have just used you as bait."

"I'm still grateful." She yawned, one of those yawns that you can feel clear to your toes. "I'm sorry if I don't look like it. I'm just so tired."

"Aurelia healed you," I said, "but you still need to rest." I held my hand flat on Cody's chest. His heart thumped steadi-ly against my palm. "Why isn't Cody waking up?" I clutched Cody's hand in both of mine. *Please let Cody pull through this. Please let him be okay, Lord.*

Aurelia sat beside him and gripped his arm.

The room was quiet except for the steady ticking of the clock. I chewed on my lower lip and willed Cody to get better. I lifted one hand off his and caressed his face.

"Wake up, Cody." My words were soft but carried an edge of desperation. I put my hand back on his and looked at the clock. It had been almost an hour since we rescued them from Draconian. My grasp on Cody's hand tightened. I closed my eyes and tried to slow my breathing, needing to relax.

"You're … crushing … my … fingers," Cody said in a froggy voice.

I threw my arms around him.

His hand slowly trailed down my back. "How'd I get here?"

"Aurelia and Dacia rescued us," Samantha said.

He nodded at Aurelia. "So, she's a good guy?"

"Yeah." I pulled away from him and said a silent thank you to God.

Cody ran a trembling hand through his hair and looked down. "You okay, Dacia?"

"Yes." I smacked his arm. "Don't ever do something like that again. He'd've killed you." Tears pooled in my eyes.

Sarah hunched forward. "What happened?"

I tried to answer, but I couldn't talk over the lump in my throat. Shaking my head, I covered my mouth.

Cody stared out the window. "He was killing her." He clutched my hand. "So, I offered to take her place."

"If …" I cleared my throat and wiped my eyes. "If I hadn't gotten free, Cody'd be dead."

"Cody." Sarah shook her head.

Aurelia's face showed no emotion when she said, "She can heal on her own. You cannot."

He whipped his head around and glared at her. "What if her energy's gone?"

"Even then, she has a better chance than you." She sat perfectly still, not fidgeting, not blinking.

A muscle jumped in Cody's jaw.

I thought about all the books I'd read while trying to figure out how to defeat Nefarious. Had I read about her species? Would those books help me figure out what she was?

Dan looked from Cody to Aurelia. "You missed hearing that Aurelia is over two thousand years old."

"Huh." Cody shrugged half-heartedly.

Sarah clapped her hands together. "When Draconian captured you, did he say or do anything we need to know about?"

"The dragon carried me to Draconian." Cody rubbed his face. "Don't remember much. Kept blacking out. Draconian came in and asked me questions."

"Like what?" I brushed Cody's hair back.

"Basic stuff. Name, age, stuff like that. My head got fuzzier with each question. Don't remember him leaving." His eyebrows scrunched together in concentration. "Maybe it was blood loss."

"I don't think so." I shook my head.

Before I could delve into my opinions, Samantha said, "That's basically what happened to me."

I leaned my head against the couch. "When Draconian tried to control me, my mind went fuzzy, but I fought off what he was doing. I think he was trying to control you guys or at least get into your heads to figure out where Nefarious is."

Aurelia's posture was perfect, her face placid. "It sounds to me like it was a good thing we rescued them when we did."

"Definitely." Sarah paced behind the couch. "I can't help but wonder what Draconian may have found out. He may know I'm the only one who knows where Nefarious is hidden."

"I hope we didn't tell him." Samantha's voice filled with guilt. "But we could've. I don't know how you resist him, Dacia."

"He doesn't either." My pain and fatigue had diminished significantly while we sat there. "He can control all those dragons, but for some reason, he can't control me. It's the only strength I seem to have against him."

"I would like to help with that," Aurelia offered. "I think if you would let me, I could teach you a few tricks and strengthen some things you already know."

I looked at her, trying to figure out what kinds of creatures showed so little emotion. Mine always seemed to be on display for the world to see. "That'd be great. I would like to learn how you healed Samantha and Cody. Maybe we could borrow Sarah's office so other people couldn't hear us."

"Of course," Sarah agreed. "I've given Dacia all the instruction I can. I was afraid she was going to be on her own this time."

"You've no idea how glad I am to know I'm not completely alone." I rubbed my hand down Cody's arm. "Now, all I have to worry about is how to keep everybody in this room safe."

"Hopefully"—Aurelia nodded at me—"I can help you with that, too."

Cody sat up straighter and pointed at Dan and Samantha. "We have government together, so at least we're not spread out."

"Since it's not at the same time as my photography class, I can walk you to your class." I tugged my hand through my hair and dropped loose strands on the floor. "Maybe I can learn how to make you guys invisible or something."

"Can't risk yourself." Cody crossed his arms over his chest and shook his head. "Draconian could've killed you today."

I crossed my arms over my chest, bumping my elbow into Cody. "In case you didn't know, I'm your only shot at staying safe. And, if you get captured again, I'll risk my neck to go after you."

"Mmm-mmm." Aurelia cleared her throat. "You are not their only hope. But, you are right. One or both of us will have to walk to their class with them."

"I can't watch Samantha get carried off by another drag-on." Dan pulled her closer to his side. "We need protection."

Chapter 18
Fire And Ice

"I don't like this." Cody backed me up against the door, his hands on either side of me. "What if Draconian sends dragons after you?"

"What if he does and you're with me?" I pulled my hand through my hair and shook my head. "What if he sends them after you once we're safely inside our classroom? What if he sends them after you when you sneak over to your room to get your stuff?"

"I know." He took a long, slow breath, and when he spoke again, his voice was softer, tortured. "But, I keep hearing you scream."

I put my palms on his chest, pushing him back a step. "Aurelia will be with me. I'll be fine."

He bent down and crushed his lips against mine, teasing them apart. I hooked my fingers in his belt loops and pulled him closer to me, deepening the kiss. His body pressed against mine. His hand tangled in my hair. It was frantic and told me more about his fear than his words could have. He drew back and brushed the hair off my face. "Be careful." His voice was husky.

I stared at his mouth, wondering if I could skip class. Draconian could've killed Cody yesterday. How much more time would we have together?

Closing my eyes, I centered myself. I needed to spend time with Aurelia if I wanted to keep my friends safe. "We will. We'll be back for lunch." I slung my backpack over my shoulder. "Then we'll walk you to your class. Don't leave without us."

Aurelia waited for me in the hallway. "Be on your guard," she said after I closed my door. "Draconian will not be happy about your escape."

"Yeah." I tugged my hand through my hair. "That's what I'm afraid of."

Mandarin Center sat clear across campus from Wisteria Hall. Once we passed the main buildings, the trees grew thicker until we walked through a forest. A wooden bridge over the Rose River made the perfect place for an ambush. If a dragon stood on each side, we'd have nowhere to go.

I looked over my shoulder. Fighting the urge to run back to the dorm, I forced myself to continue.

Aurelia and I strode across the bridge, alert for danger. The rapid thumping of my heart grew louder with each step we took.

"If he is here"—Aurelia's voice was soft but authoritative—"teleport to your room. Do not concern yourself with me."

I nodded and kept searching the trees for any sign of danger. Birdsongs filled the sky, and squirrels ran amok. *If a dragon's hiding here, would they be so carefree?*

When my foot touched the ground on the far side of the bridge, I expected dragons to surround us, but nothing happened. My legs shook, and I struggled to keep walking.

Mandarin Center rose in front of us. The building was mostly glass to let in natural light. From inside, there was a fantastic view of the forest with the Snowfire Mountains rising in the background.

Aurelia held the door open for me, and I stepped into the entryway. The tension in my shoulders eased.

Artwork from years past lined the hallways. Aurelia pointed at a painting, the one piece I tried not to look at. A red and black-skinned beast rose from Falcon Lake. His clawed hand tore through the air. Even now, his yellow eyes sent fear shooting through my body. "Is that Nefarious?"

"Yeah." I fiddled with the straps on my backpack. "One of my dreams. Mr. Quercus liked it. I would've burned it."

Throughout class, Mr. Quercus emphasized the importance of taking unique photographs. I found myself wondering what he would think about a picture of Draconian's dragons.

Something told me that he might believe the print was real and not manipulated.

When class ended, Aurelia and I mixed in with the other students leaving Mandarin Center, hoping we'd find safety in numbers. Every noise had me looking over my shoulder, ready to run. Students broke off as we passed other buildings, but I felt safer in the open than I had in the forest.

"This is going to be rough." I rubbed my shoulder, trying to ease the knot rising there.

Aurelia's steps were hurried, but it didn't seem to wear on her at all. "Yes. Not knowing when or where he will appear is taxing."

Once we passed the classroom buildings, the trees thick-ened again. Only a handful of students were scattered around. I nodded toward a group of three girls. "Are we endangering them?"

"We may be." She quickened her pace so much that I had to trot to keep up with her.

When we got to Wisteria Hall, Aurelia held the door open and ushered me in. "You are safe now."

"Why?" I looked down the hall into the commons area. "Couldn't he be here?"

"I warded this building to keep him out." She tilted her head as if listening to someone. "You or I must be present for the wards to work."

"So, he could've snuck in." The words tumbled over each other in their rush to leave my mouth.

She pulled me toward the stairs. "Arion has seen no sign of him or his dr—" Aurelia's voice broke off when students stepped into the hallway.

"Who's Arion?"

"A friend." She waved to several ladies as we made our way to my room. "You will meet him eventually."

I grabbed the handle, and she turned toward her door. "Is he here to help, too?"

"Not in the same capacity."

As soon as we finished lunch, Aurelia and I escorted the others to class. When we stood outside of Dr. Cedar's classroom, Cody pulled me into his arms. "Be careful."

I leaned into him, resting my head against his chest. "We will."

"We will return as soon as class is over," Aurelia said. "Wait for us."

I stood on my tiptoes and pressed my lips against Cody's. He pulled me closer, deepening the kiss.

"Get a room," someone said.

Heat crept up my cheeks as I pulled away from him. "See you guys."

Aurelia and I walked through, exiting Primrose Hall through the backdoor. From there, it was a straight shot across the parking lot to Sarah's office.

The two of us were on high alert as we wove through parked cars. When we were almost to the door, Aurelia said, "Sarah and I believe it would be best for you and her not to have too much contact."

My steps faltered. "Wait. Why?"

"If Draconian is watching"—Aurelia waved her arm in front of her—"he will notice you spend more time with her than most students. If there is an emergency, do not hesitate to talk to her."

I kicked mulch off the sidewalk back into the flowerbed. Sarah treated me more like a daughter than my own parents did. She was proud of my powers, not embarrassed by them or ashamed of them. I'd enjoyed having an adult to look up to, and now that was being taken away from me, too.

"We will have our lessons in her office for now." She held the door open, ushering me inside. "There are other rooms in the building, so Draconian will have no way of knowing which one we are in. Most of the time Sarah will make a point to be gone during your lessons to keep suspicion down."

I waved at Alicia as we strolled past her to the staircase. Her spiky blonde hair had bright blue tips. She lifted her hand in response.

Once we were on the steps, I said, "It makes sense, but it's going to be hard to get used to. I was in constant contact with her during the whole Nefarious ordeal."

"It is the best way to keep Sarah safe and Nefarious out of Draconian's hands." Her voice was matter-of-fact. There were no inflections, nothing to clue me in on how she felt or even if she did.

"I understand." I ran my hand through my hair, catching in the tangled ends. "It seems like she's leaving Samantha and Cody hanging out to dry, though. Draconian will come after them, and she'll be safe."

"Sarah had a tough time with that." Aurelia strode off, prompting me to follow. "I talked her into it. Either you or I will be with Cody, Samantha, and Dan most of the time. Together we can keep them safe. It is impractical for either of us to be with Sarah constantly."

"Well, you better teach me what you know, so I can keep them safe."

We stepped into Sarah's office, but she didn't come out to greet us. Aurelia sat on one of the couches, and I sat on the other, facing her. She folded her hands in her lap. "I need you to tell me what powers you have. I have seen you use some of them, but I need to know all of your abilities and how strong they are."

"Okay, well there's invisibility, fire, ice, flying, walking through walls." I ticked them off on my fingers as I listed them. "I can sense when Cody's near, read minds, teleport, heal, create a force field thingy around me, and somehow I crushed Bryce's hand last fall." Tilting my head, I looked at the ceiling. "I think that's all."

"You are more advanced than I presumed." She sounded impressed, and hearing emotion in her voice caught me off guard.

Not wanting to stare at her, I gazed out the window, looking at the crisp, blue sky. Poufy clouds floated by. "They all kind of came when I needed them. Although, I'm not sure why I can tell when Cody's around and not anyone else."

"You have a special bond with him." She crossed her legs and clasped her hands around her knee. "You have known him most of your life and have shared many experiences with him."

"Yeah." A smile snuck onto my face. "We've been friends almost as long as I can remember."

"If you want to learn to recognize other people, all you have to do is be more aware of their essence."

My eyebrows pulled together. "How do I do that?"

"Concentrate on each person you meet. Let yourself into their minds. Once you have been in their heads, you will be able to sense them. You will know who each person is by their aura. Everyone's is different."

"I don't want to invade everyone's thoughts." I was uncomfortable with the prospect of it. "When I read Cody's mind, it was purely an accident."

"There is no need to read their minds." She stared over my shoulder. Her pupils contracted, looking like slits for an instant. "I am not quite sure how to explain it. You … just be."

Sitting across from Aurelia, watching her speak, she reminded me of a predator watching its prey, waiting for a moment of weakness. She sat almost perfectly still, taking in everything.

"Try it on me. Even if you wanted to, you could not read my thoughts. My mind is well guarded."

"Are you sure?" I bent forward with my elbows on my knees. "I know there are a lot of things you haven't told us yet." In my head, I finished by saying, *Like who or what you really are.*

"A mind as ancient as mine is not easy to comprehend." A smile touched her lips. "Go ahead, whenever you are ready."

I stared into her golden eyes, finding it difficult at first not to look away. After several seconds, I let myself relax. Images flashed through my mind—fairies, unicorns, fire, gold, and beautiful trees. Then serenity washed over me, peacefulness like I felt when I died in my dream. When I looked away from her, I knew for sure she was good and was here to help me in any way she could. I sighed and leaned back. "Why did I see those things?"

"I chose to let you." The edges of her mouth lifted slightly, almost forming a smile. "I saw no reason to conceal them. They give nothing away."

Fairies and unicorns. Were they plentiful where she came from? Was she an elf? "Are they clues?"

"They are memories."

"Will I be able to sense you now?" I twisted my earring around.

"You will only sense my presence if I want you to. I am not like the others, as you know. I can keep myself closed off to you. Though, if there is danger, I will not."

"If you're not like the others, are you like me?" I looked down at my pink shoes. "How did you come to be so old?"

Her voice softened. "I am not like you either. I am immortal. Please do not ask me anymore. When the time comes, you will know everything."

"Sorry." I closed my eyes and shook my head. "I'm curious. I want to know how I ended up like this. I'd also like to know what's going to happen to me. I just want answers."

"Youth is full of questions no matter the species." She turned her head toward Sarah's office. "Shall we see if Sarah will come out here? If you do the same to her, you will be able to tell when she is around. It may come in helpful if Draconian takes her."

"I'll get her." Walking to her door, my stomach clenched. *What if she doesn't want to see me?* I knocked softly on the door.

"Yes."

Peeking in, I said, "Can you come out here for a minute?"

"Sure." She pushed her chair back and followed me out. "What do you need?"

"You know how I can sense Cody." I plopped down on the couch. "I'm going to make it so I know when you're around."

She sat across from me, and I gazed into her hazel eyes. Images flashed through my mind. Nefarious attacked her. I lay on her couch, broken, bleeding, and burned. Cody sat on the floor next to me. His face was pale. Grief and torment distorted his features. When the images stopped, I felt warm and comfortable.

"That should do." I tucked my trembling hands into my armpits.

"I imagine I saw the same things you did." Sarah reached toward me, then pulled her hand back. "I've been dwelling on all of the bad stuff that happened with Nefarious. I'm worried about you and what's to come."

"Me too." I tried to summon a laugh, but it sounded more like a whimper. "Your aura is warm and comforting. Aurelia's is tranquil." My eyebrows pinched together. "I don't know what Cody's is. I'll have to pay attention next time I'm with him; I just know it's him."

"More importantly," Aurelia said, "next time you are around Draconian, you will have to see if you can read his aura. It would be beneficial if you knew when he was near."

"Yeah"—a chill prickled down my neck—"but, I'm scared to see what flashes through his mind."

Sarah stood and smoothed her cream slacks. "If you're done with me, I need to finish some things."

"Go ahead." Aurelia nodded. "I want Dacia to get some practice using each of her abilities."

Sarah went back to her office, closing the door behind her.

"Okay." I rubbed my hands together. "What's next?"

"Which of your powers do you use most often?" she asked.

"Fire, lightning, ice, or healing I suppose."

She thought for a while before saying, "Sarah's office is a bit small for lightning. Maybe we could go down to Falcon Lake some evening and you could show me then. There are not a lot of students here for the summer, so I think we would be able to go there without making a scene, especially if we went out on a stormy night." She pointed at my hands. "Show me what you can do with ice."

"Well, the easiest way to do that is to start with fire." I showed her how I could freeze fire, thinking I'd never get tired of watching ice devour the flames.

Her eyes widened a fraction. "Your control is impressive." She pointed at the floor next to the couch I was sitting on. "Now, hover and concentrate on ice. Instead of releasing it, hold it in."

Hovering a couple of inches off the ground, goosebumps raised the hairs on my arms. Shivers trembled through my body. I struggled not to shoot ice from my fingertips. Clenching my hands into fists, I fought to hold it inside me. My teeth chattered and my breath clouded the air.

"Keep it up," Aurelia said.

Looking at her was like peering through a frost-covered window. Prisms danced in the air. My fingers and toes went numb. A tingling sensation spread up my arms and legs. "I can't h-h-hold it anymore."

Aurelia held her hand up. "You are doing great, Dacia, a few more seconds."

"C-can't …" My vision cleared, and the chills subsided.

"You did it." Aurelia pointed at me. "Look at your hands."

I held them out, twisting and turning them, astonished by the transformation. My body was a solid block of ice. Staring at my hand, I studied it. The lines on my palms were etched into the ice. I opened and closed my fist. "Cool." I giggled at my pun.

Aurelia shook her head.

"It's almost as strange as looking down and finding I'm invisible, but … what can I gain from this?" I couldn't stop staring at my fingers. The flexibility I had was astounding. It didn't make any sense that ice could bend like this.

"If Draconian had hold of you and you did this, it would be like he was touching dry ice. He would be forced to let go, if only for a moment." She stood and walked around me. "You can grab onto something and freeze it instantaneously … just like you are now. If you held onto another living being that did not have your healing powers, you would do severe damage to it. Also, this comes in handy when you are fighting against ice. It is an excellent skill to have."

I flipped my hand over again, marveling at the detail, the veins, the creases. "So, uh, can I do something like this only with fire?"

"Yes, you should be able to. Do you want to try it?" She sat again. Her back was perfectly straight.

I stared at the hunter carpet. "Will I burn through Sarah's floor?"

"You would burn anything you came into contact with. Keep hovering, and think about fire. But, Dacia, do not stay ablaze for too long. You may start to singe things in here if the heat becomes too intense."

The thought of staying this way forever suddenly terrified me. "How do I go back to normal?" My voice trembled slightly but not from the cold.

"Just let it go," she said as if I should have realized that all along.

"You mean I have to freeze something?" My hand slid across the top of my head, and I couldn't help but smile. "I guess I can't pull my hand through my hair when it's frozen."

"No, you cannot." She smiled. "Let the moisture dissipate into the air."

I held my palm up and imagined releasing the cold, almost like evaporation. My fingertips pinkened. The thaw spread up my arms and over my body. My skin tingled as warmth returned. Then I was back to normal.

"That was weird. I never would have thought to try that on my own." I wiggled my fingers and toes and rubbed my arms and legs. Everything seemed intact and normal. "Do you want me to try with fire?"

"Yes. I believe that would be wise." She crossed her legs and waited.

I lifted myself about a foot off the ground and concentrated on burning. This time I had a better idea of what to expect. When the urge to shoot flames across the room threatened, I drew that power into me. Sweat dripped off my forehead. Warmth radiated up my arms. Then, within seconds, I became a blazing, blue inferno. Panic clawed at my chest. I slipped toward the ground but remembered to hover just in time.

"You are a quick study." Aurelia leaned forward. Her eyes lit up, reflecting the flames back at me. "How does it feel?"

My heart raced. I could feel it pounding, but was it there? Did have one right now? "Scary. Weird. Uncomfortable. I don't like it." I was afraid I was going to hyperventilate.

"You should extinguish yourself. Then we can talk about things."

By the time I did what she said, exhaustion had spread throughout my body. I slumped on the couch, closing my eyes. "What happens if somebody throws a bucket of water on me when I'm engulfed in flames or throws something at me and shatters me when I'm frozen?"

"If enough water is thrown on you, your flames may extinguish. You cannot be shattered or melted," Aurelia said. "You can still get hurt but not in those ways."

"How do you know—" I yawned "—something worse won't happen?"

"I have been alive in excess of two thousand years. I have seen more than you could ever imagine. You are still Dacia. You do not become the flames or the ice. Next time a dragon tries to capture you, try turning yourself into flames. Its claws will not be able to grasp you. They will slip through the fire, and you will be free. I know this is a lot to take in, but I need you to trust me. There is a great deal I can teach you if you do."

"I do trust you, but this is all so new." I shook my head, trying to ward off the sleep that threatened. "It'd be nice not to worry about being carried off by dragons. Their claws are sharp and painful."

"I can only imagine." A smirk touched her lips so quickly I wasn't certain I'd seen it. "It could also help you escape from Draconian's chains if he does manage to capture you. However, use these skills only as a last resort. Once Draconian knows what you can do, he may be able to counteract them." After a brief pause, she went on, "When you do face Draconian, he will have all of his dragons with him, but you will only have to stop him. Once he is out of the picture, the dragons will be free from his control and will no longer be concerned with you."

She always sounded so stiff. I wondered if it was a product of her age, her species, or her education.

"Draconian told me he has fifteen dragons. Do you think that's true?" I leaned my head back and closed my eyes. "And, how will I be able to get to him with them around?"

"Are you okay, Dacia?"

"Using my powers drains my energy." I peeked at her through half-closed lids. "I guess I did too much."

"Magic must be practiced, like exercising your muscles. You would not run a marathon without first training for it." I jumped when she sat next to me. My eyes shot open, and my heart raced. I hadn't heard her move.

"Sorry." She smiled and placed her hand on my arm. "My energy may help you."

Vitality surged through my veins, drowning the fatigue. "Thank you. I feel like I could run that marathon now."

"You need to build up your stamina. Do lots of little exercises every day."

"So, every day create fireballs or something?"

"Yes." She moved back to the other couch. "Do as much as you can and make sure you do a little more each day."

My leg bounced up and down. I stood and paced, needing to use some of the energy. "Back to his dragons."

"He has at least ten that I know of," she answered, "so fifteen is a likely number."

I stopped, tilting my head up, counting the dragons I'd come across so far. I had encountered eight or more either in dreams or in reality. Ten would be better than fifteen, but I didn't know if I could even handle one. I resumed pacing.

"We will have to figure out how to get to him." Her gaze followed me across the room. "I will be there to help you, though. You will not go through this alone."

"Unless he captures me and drags me off." Help would be nice, but I wanted to be prepared to fight on my own if it came down to it.

I looked at Sarah's clock. "We should go get the others."

Aurelia stood. "Where their safety is concerned, we must be diligent."

When we stepped across the threshold into my dorm room, I drew in a deep breath and slumped against the door.

Cody rubbed his thumb along my cheek. "What's up?"

"We're safe."

Fear darkened Cody's blue eyes. "Did you sense him?"

"No." I slipped my arm around his waist. Dan and Samantha were snuggled together in Big Bird. Samantha had a textbook in her hand, but she wasn't paying attention to it.

Aurelia stood by the desk, missing nothing. "As long as Dacia or I are here, this room is warded. Neither Draconian nor his dragons can enter."

"Good to know." Samantha put her book on the floor.

"Should … uh …" Dan scrubbed his hand over his face. "Should I be sleeping over here, too?" He looked from me to Aurelia. "Or, do you think I'm safe on my own?"

Cody sat in Cookie Monster, and I perched on the arm. "You should either stay here or have me or Aurelia teleport you to your room," I said. "When Draconian took Cody and Samantha, he saw you with me."

"For now, I'll sleep in my own bed." Dan nodded at Cody "We'll bring the couch over after class tomorrow."

Aurelia straightened. "The longer we are able to keep the three of you safe, the longer Dacia will have to hone her abilities."

"So …" Heat crept up my neck onto my face and ears when they turned their attention toward me. "I need to read your auras. Somewhere along the way, I read Cody's. That's why I can sense when he's near. I need to read yours in case something happens and I need to find you."

"Okay." Samantha's brow puckered. "What do we need to do?"

"Sit there and let me look in your eyes for a minute. I'll see images from your life flash in my head, and I guess you'll know what I see. Then I'll … sort of feel your essence. Once I do that, I'll be able to sense when you're around."

"Weird." Dan's lips pressed together. "Go ahead whenever you're ready."

I walked over to the desk and pulled out the chair. "Whoever's first." I pointed at the seat.

Dan came over. A nervous smile spread over his face like butter on a hot roll. I had a hard time focusing on anything but his dimples. Squeezing my eyes shut, I took a deep breath and centered myself.

Scenes from Dan's life flashed through my mind. Images of a couple I could only assume were his parents, a close-up view of Samantha's lips, our boat ride on Cougar Lake, a dragon carrying Samantha away. Blood dripped from her shoulders.

A reassuring strength flowed into me. I leaned closer and whispered in his ear, "Sorry to bring up that memory."

"It's okay. It's always in the front of my mind. I can't shake it, and it scares me to death."

I clutched his hand. "I worry about it all the time, too."

"Just stay strong, Dacia." He squeezed my fingers. Then louder, he said, "It's your turn, Sammi."

"What was it like?"

"Just like Dacia said it would be. Be prepared for what you might see, though." He held the chair while she sat. "Some memories are painful."

She cocked her head and looked at him with a question in her eyes. "Ready?"

"If you are." I stared into her soft brown eyes. The first images I saw were of Dan. Then I saw myself. First, my leg was torn to shreds and then I lay on Sarah's couch unconscious. The dragon flew toward Samantha. It seemed we were all full of fear. When the flashes stopped, I felt passion and determination intermixed with each other.

"All done." I pushed my hair off my face. "Sorry about the dragon."

"It's not your fault." She waved her hand between us. "Why'd it take longer with Dan?"

I looked at him. "Well, it's hard to focus when he's smiling."

"Don't I know it." She gazed at him with a love-struck gleam in her eyes. "What else?"

"What I saw."

"Oh."

"He's worried, the same as you. So, I saw the only horrific thing he's seen so far—you being carried off by a dragon."

"Yeah"—she glanced at Dan—"that was pretty hard on him."

I nodded. "Hopefully, it's the worst thing he sees."

"It is imperative for Dacia to use her powers more often." Aurelia sat in the desk chair. "Right now, she weakens too quickly. She must build her stamina before facing Draconian and his dragons."

Cody rubbed his jaw. "What can we do?"

"Remind her to exercise. Lend her some of your strength if she exhausts herself."

"I might as well start now." I stood in front of the chairs. "What I'm going to show you is really cool." Lifting off the ground, I took a deep breath and concentrated on ice. It didn't take as long for the cold sensation to work its way through my body this time. When I finished, I looked at the shock on their faces. "What do you think?"

"Really cool? No pun intended?" Cody reached up to touch my hand.

"Cody, stop!" Aurelia pounced between us and batted his hand away. "Do not touch her when she is like this."

"Why not?" Samantha asked. "What'll happen?"

"Your skin will burn." I backed up a step. "It doesn't hurt me, but it'd hurt you." Without releasing the ice, I concentrated on fire. It was awesome seeing myself turn from a giant ice sculpture into a flaming inferno. "Aurelia says that if I do this, I can make it impossible for the dragons to carry me off."

"Doesn't it burn? Don't you feel any pain?" Samantha sounded as panicky as I had when I first transformed into fire.

"No, I feel a little warmth, but that's it." I held my hand up and watched the flames dance. They didn't flare out but acted like they were in a container, under the surface of my invisible skin. "When I did this earlier, I panicked, but it's nothing to worry about."

"Wow." Dan leaned closer. "That's awesome. It must be amazing to do those things!"

I extinguished myself and curled up on Cody's lap. "Sometimes, but there are times I'd like to be normal. It would've saved me a lot of heartaches when I was growing up, and my parents would've liked to have had a normal child." For a moment, Jonathan's chubby-cheeked face flashed before my eyes. My parents would probably do just about anything for him to still be alive.

"Yeah," Dan said. "That'd suck."

I closed my eyes and rested my head on Cody's shoulder. "I didn't learn any control until I came here. Sarah helped with that." I looked at Aurelia. "Now hopefully from you, I'll learn a few more practical uses for my abilities. Either way, it's good to have the support of everyone."

Chapter 19

Hooves And Wings

$\mathcal{A}$urelia stood in front of me with a knife in her hand. In a quick, smooth motion, she sliced it down her arm. Gold blood spurted out from the wound.

I stumbled back. My hand shot up to my throat as I sucked in a quick, sharp breath. My mouth floundered open and closed. "What'd you do that for?" Panic filled my voice.

She hadn't flinched. Her expression never even changed. "I want to boost your healing power. Think about life while you try to heal me."

I took a deep breath in through my nose and slowly released it through my mouth. "Okay." I wanted to ask her why her blood was gold, but I knew she wouldn't answer anyway. So instead I fought to keep my attention focused on what she was saying. Anything that could boost my healing abilities was important for me to learn.

"Think about spring: plants budding, flowers blooming, baby animals of all kinds being born, butterflies emerging from their cocoons, those types of thoughts."

My mind filled with images of new life. I put my hands over Aurelia's wound and felt a stream of energy rush through them. Aurelia's skin wove together. Her wound healed before my eyes without a scar left to show for it. I turned her arm over, examining it. "Can I use this on myself when I'm wounded or only on others? I've always let my wounds heal on their own, but it would be great if I could help speed the process along."

"As long as you are not panicking, it should work on you, too. You are a quick learner, Dacia. The magic is very powerful in you."

I wish I knew why.

"So far we have worked on fire, ice, and healing." Aurelia sat on the couch. The silk of her pants swished when she crossed her legs. "We also made it so you can sense others. How is that going?"

"Good." I sat across from her. "I've been able to sense Samantha and Dan coming and going. I've even been able to sense you a couple of times."

"There are times when I will not let you, but most of the time, I will," she said. "There are times when I need my privacy. Next time Draconian shows up in your dreams, I want you to try to read his aura."

"In a dream?" I shook my head. That couldn't be what she meant. Could it? "How can I read someone's aura in my sleep? That seems a little far-fetched."

"I am not sure if it can be done, but I would like you to try. There are things you can do that I have no understanding of at all, so maybe you can do this."

"Sure." I nodded my head in disbelief. "Like what?"

She folded her hands together. "I have no idea how you can resist Draconian when he's trying to control you. Dragons have very powerful, old magic, and it seems they cannot fight him. You are more gifted than you realize. Just try. Maybe you will surprise us all. I am sure Draconian would not expect it."

On our way back from supper, Cody and I lagged behind the others. "Aurelia and I are going to Falcon Lake."

"When?"

I pulled on my lip with my teeth. Cody wasn't going to like this, but if I was training, I couldn't keep an eye on him, too. "As soon as we get you back to the room. She wants to see what I can do with lightning, and I guess it's supposed to storm tonight."

"I'm coming."

I shook my head. "Not this time."

"You sure?"

I shrugged, lifting my hands palm up, then dropping them back down to my sides. "I don't know, but I need to figure out something to stop Draconian. Aurelia thinks it will be safer for the two of us to go on our own."

"Going to the lake at night isn't a good idea." He ran his fingers through his hair and let out a deep breath. "You're inviting danger."

I stopped outside the door and took his hand in mine. "I'll be okay."

He reached up and traced his fingers from my ear to my chin. Holding my face in his hands, he said, "Anything happens, teleport back here. Don't be a hero. Be careful."

"I will." I slipped my fingers through his belt loops. "You do the same. Don't go anywhere. Aurelia has a plan to keep you safe."

"Hurry back." He brushed his fingers along my forehead. "Won't relax 'til you're with me."

"I'll be okay."

I felt his breath on my lips. It tasted like fear and desire. His mouth pressed against mine. A flash of heat coursed through my body. Cody pulled away, tucking my hair behind my ear.

"Go in." My voice trembled. "The sooner I leave, the sooner I can return."

"Come back. Okay?"

"Always."

Aurelia and I walked out of sight, then turned invisible. "Shall we fly?" she asked.

"If you think we won't lose each other."

"We'll communicate telepathically as we go. You could probably use some help with that skill."

"Honestly, I've never done it before. It's been done to me … a lot, but I've never tried it myself. I never even considered that I might be able to."

Without warning, she started using it. *Just think what you want to say. Then project only those thoughts to me. If you are not careful when you do it, I will be able to see everything you are thinking.*

I'll try, I thought to her.

I got that, she responded, *but I am also aware you have a headache right now and you feel guilty about leaving Cody behind.*

"Yeah, I should've taken something for my headache before we left, and I'm used to Cody being around." I was a little embarrassed she had been able to pick up on that, but at least we were invisible so she couldn't see the red glow on my face.

You also need to be careful when you project your thoughts. Make sure you only send them to your intended recipient. If you do not, anyone can hear what you are thinking.

So, why would I want to use this? I asked.

That was better. I only picked up on the headache that time. If you remember, Draconian was able to use it against you when he took Cody and Samantha. He only projected his thoughts to you, so they did not realize what was happening. Also, it comes in handy when you do not want your enemy to know what you are thinking but you need to communicate with your friends. You can send your thoughts to several people at once as long as you are thinking about all of them.

Oh, that makes sense. I don't know how often I will use it, but I imagine there will be times that it'll come in handy. Should we land now?

No, I want some shelter around us while we are here. Head for the trees on the left.

Hopefully, nobody decides to come down here tonight. So far it looks pretty deserted.

You are getting better. I have not heard any extra thoughts the last couple of times. We will have to try when others are around so we can be sure you are only projecting your thoughts to those you want to hear them. We can stop here. She stood under the trees. Her gold skin glittered in the fading light. *This should be good enough. You can show yourself now.*

I stood under the cover of the forest before becoming visible. *I hope nobody was watching that.*

Aurelia smiled. Then she turned serious. "Alas, it is not as foreboding as I had anticipated. I had hoped yours would not be the only lightning shooting through the sky." She looked from the dark clouds to me. "Show me what you can do."

I raised my hand and shot a bolt of lightning straight up into the clouds.

"How effective is that when you use it as a weapon?" Aurelia asked.

"Not very." I rubbed the back of my neck. "You'd think it would be. It's lightning after all. It usually buys me some time, but that's about it. I always thought it should do more."

"Point both hands and produce a lightning storm … a rapid succession of bolts. Make it rival Mother Nature's."

"Okay. Here goes." Bolt after bolt of lightning escaped from my fingertips in an awesome electrical storm. "That should be more effective."

"Now I want you to hold the lightning in, just like you did with fire and ice." She must have noticed the look of apprehension on my face because she added, "You will not turn into a bolt of lightning."

I closed my eyes, fighting the wave of nausea. A tingling sensation ran through my body, and my hair stood on end. I stretched my arms up to the sky but resisted the urge to let electricity shoot out of me. Dropping my hands, I watched as small charges arced across my fingertips. However, I wasn't transformed at all. "What happened?"

"You are electrically charged," she answered. "If anybody were to touch you right now, they would be electrocuted."

"So, uh, how do I make it safe for, uh, someone to touch me again?"

"The same way you released the ice and fire"—she held her hand up—"or you can release it as a bolt of lightning."

I pointed my finger at the dark clouds overhead. The largest bolt of lightning I had ever seen blasted into the heavens. "Wow!" I ran my hands over my hair, trying to smooth it down. "That was shocking."

Aurelia didn't even crack a smile. "For a human, your capacity for magic and your control are impressive."

"But not my puns?"

She shook her head. "They are not en-lightning."

I tried not to laugh, but I couldn't hold it in. Her response was totally unexpected. When I got myself under control again,

I looked at her and debated whether or not I should ask the question that was on the tip of my tongue. A silent war waged in my head. In the end, my curiosity won out. "Are you ever going to tell me what you are?"

"When the time is right, you will know. Now is not that time."

"I have a feeling that time will never come." The corners of my mouth turned down. "What could be so bad that you can't trust me? You're not some horrible monster. I would have been able to tell that from your aura. Whatever you are, you're good and honest."

"Yes, Dacia, you need to hold onto that." She turned away from me, watching the approaching storm. "When you read someone's aura, you know more about that person than they sometimes know about themselves. The aura does not lie. However, you will still have to wait until the time is right." She looked over her shoulder at me. Her gold eyes looked animalistic in this light.

I stumbled back as fear twisted my gut.

Aurelia blinked, and her eyes returned to normal. "I would like to get back to lightning. After all, that is why we are here tonight. I want you to try to release more than one bolt at a time. It is a bit of a challenge, but I think you can do it."

I shot one bolt of lightning into the sky followed by another. I shook my hands and tried again. Lightning bolts flashed through the night sky, illuminating the mountains and lake. Thunder crashed, rumbling over the peaks and through the valleys.

"You can do this, Dacia."

The next round went the same way. I sat down on the ground, pulling my knees up to my chest. "I need a minute." My arms and legs shook.

"Do you need some of my strength?" She walked over, standing above me.

"Yes." My fingers trembled when I lifted my hand to hers.

Strength flowed from her into me. Revitalized I stood and fired electricity into the sky.

"What am I doing wrong?" I tugged my hand through my curls.

"Patience. You will get this. Try one more time."

I squeezed my eyes shut and pictured the results I wanted. Then I opened them and repeated the process. Two bolts lit up the night, quickly followed by two more.

Then a lightning bolt tore through the sky, and the clouds rumbled violently, warning me not to compete with Mother Nature. "That one wasn't mine," I said as raindrops pelted us.

She smiled. "I know. We should head back now. We will have to stick to the ground. It is not safe to fly in a storm."

I let out a heavy breath. "I don't think I could fly now anyway. Even with borrowing energy from you, the lightning took too much out of me."

"This will give you a chance to rest." She smiled and stalked off. "There is someone I want you to meet on the way back."

"Really?" Who else would be out with a storm moving in? "Who is it?"

"A friend. He was going to try to meet us here tonight, but I believe he is waiting on the path"—she pointed into the forest—"over there."

A wave of panic threatened to pull me under. I stopped unsure if I should turn invisible and fly off or follow her into the trees where Alvin and Bryce jumped Cody and me last fall. My heart raced as I remembered her aura. *She's a good person ... or creature or whatever she is*, I reminded myself. *She would never lead me into an ambush especially after teaching me all these new ways to use my powers. That would be stupid.*

Aurelia turned and looked at me, "Are you coming, Dacia? It is only going to get worse out."

"Yeah ... uh, I'll catch up." I formed a force field around me to keep the rain off and also to help protect me from any unexpected attacks. I didn't know how long I could hold it with my failing strength.

We walked through the trees in silence. Aurelia stopped in front of me and said, "Dacia, I want you to meet my friend."

"Yeah. Where is he?"

"Right through those trees." Once again, she pointed into the shadows. I wondered if her night vision was that good. "Come on out, Arion."

A beautiful white stallion stepped out of the trees. Like Aurelia, he shimmered. It was like looking up into the night sky and watching the stars twinkle. I was mesmerized, unable to tear my eyes away from him. Then he turned to the side, and I was reminded of an angel. His wings were both delicate and powerful at the same time. They sparkled like the first snow of winter. He was the most magnificent thing I had ever seen.

"Arion, this is Dacia," Aurelia introduced me to him. "She is the one who stopped Nefarious."

The awe in my expression was mirrored in his eyes. I was embarrassed and flattered.

"It is an honor to meet you," he said in the most charming voice I had ever heard. "You saved this world from a fate worse than death. We are indebted to you, and for that, I am at your service. If there is any way I can help you, let me know."

It took a moment for me to find my voice. When I did, all I could say was, "Thank you."

"If you need Arion for any reason just project your thoughts to him. Wherever he is or whatever he is doing, he will come to you or let you know why he cannot," Aurelia said.

"I appreciate the help." I turned back to Arion. "I hope I don't offend you, but you are the most beautiful thing I've ever seen."

His ears twitched. "Why would that offend me?"

"Sometimes people get upset when, uh, others see them for what is on the outside." I dropped my force field.

"Humans are difficult to understand … conceit and arrogance do not make sense to immortal creatures. A compliment is always welcomed and those who give them are blessings." I felt myself begin to blush. "Do not be embarrassed, Dacia. You are a good person through and through. You have a beautiful aura. It shows that you are a powerful force to be reckoned with. Even though you could use those traits to harm others, you fight for people who are weaker. Your strongest attribute is compassion."

"Thank you," I said, humbled.

He lifted his head, staring at the sky. "The storm is ending. Would you like to go for a ride?"

"I would love to!" I clasped my hands in front of my chest. "Is it okay, Aurelia?"

"Yes, Dacia, but not too long," she said. "Cody will be waiting anxiously for your return."

As the clouds dissipated, light struck Arion. He shimmered in the moonlight like a diamond sparkles in the sun. It was captivating, and I was fortunate to witness such a vision.

Arion knelt in front of me and motioned for me to climb onto his back. "You can hold onto my mane, but not too tightly. Ready?"

"Yes." I trembled with excitement.

In a single graceful move, he ascended into the night sky. A sense of freedom overcame me. I laughed out loud.

His body shifted beneath me, like a horse galloping. The wind blew my hair back. Stars twinkled overhead, but in the distance, the storm seemed to have become fiercer. Lightning flashed through the clouds, illuminating the towering thunderheads. Thunder rumbled through the sky.

I spread my arms out, feeling joyful.

"I've had dreams about flying on a pegasus," I told Arion. "It was never this amazing, though."

"Reality is often better."

I glanced over my shoulder, suddenly uncertain. "Although every time I flew with you in my dreams, we were attacked by dragons."

"Have you had premonitions before?"

"Yes, with Nefarious, I was never able to tell if they were dreams or premonitions until they came true."

"Perhaps we should cut our flight short." As he flew back to Aurelia, he asked, "Have you told Aurelia about these dreams?"

"I honestly can't remember if I've mentioned any of them. I never thought it would happen. Every girl dreams about flying through the air on a pegasus or galloping through the forest on a unicorn, but how many actually get to?"

"Not many, but unicorns are overrated. All they have are horns. How can that compare with wings as amazing as these?" He laughed, and the sound warmed my soul.

I ran my fingers through his silky mane. "I can't imagine it does. Your wings are truly magnificent."

"Yes, you have a beautiful aura."

Arion landed down the beach from Aurelia and trotted toward her. She tilted her head ever so slightly. "That did not take long."

"Dacia told me she has had dreams of flying on a pegasus and being attacked by dragons while doing so."

I climbed off his back, and he folded his wings against his body.

"Do you believe they were premonitions?" she asked.

"I hope not." I patted Arion's neck. "My dreams tend to be fairly painful, and I'm not sure if the pegasus ended up getting injured or not. I'll understand if you don't want to help me."

"There is danger ahead." He shook his head. "The fact that you have had dreams which may or may not become reality changes nothing. Anytime evil is involved there is a chance somebody will get hurt. I pledged to help you, and so I will."

My stomach clenched. I knew I should fight my own battles to keep everyone safe, but I needed them. "Thank you." I swallowed hard. "I don't think I could do this by myself."

"It is our pleasure, Dacia." Aurelia walked toward the path. "We are always happy to help someone who is willing to stand up against malevolence. There are far too few who will."

I dragged my hand through damp curls. Flying with Aurelia and then on Arion had left my hair a tangled mess. "I should get back. I'm sure Cody is probably getting worried. He's used to being my protector."

"Everybody needs somebody to watch over them." Arion dashed off through the trees. I couldn't take my eyes off him. Seeing him disappear reminded me of watching a shooting star flash across the sky. He was beauty in motion.

"We should turn invisible and fly the rest of the way back," Aurelia said. "Do you need to siphon my energy first?"

"When I do, how does it affect you?"

"I have reserves of power. You merely take a sip."

"Yes, then." I placed my hand on her arm and drew strength from her. "Draconian's been too quiet lately. I'm worried about when and where he's going to appear again."

When Aurelia and I got back to my room, Samantha and Dan were snuggled together on the red couch, now named Elmo. I still wasn't used to seeing it here. We'd decided to keep the chairs here, too, since it was where most of our time was spent. Cookie Monster was at one end of Elmo, and Big Bird was under the bed, next to the TV.

Our room reminded me of a preschool with all the bright, primary colors. Sometimes it was a bit much.

Cody paced the floor. His muscles were tense, but when he pulled me into his arms, he relaxed. "How'd it go?"

"I learned some pretty cool tricks with lightning and how to communicate without talking." My voice rose with excitement. "I flew on a pegasus."

Samantha's eyes bulged. "You did what?"

"I met Aurelia's friend, Arion." I bounced up and down on my toes. "He's the pegasus who gave me a ride. It was awesome!"

"Wow." Dan shook his head. "Really?"

"What did he look like? Was it how we picture pegasus? Or are they different?" Samantha sounded like a kid at Christmas.

"At first, he looked like a white stallion, bigger than most but not as big as a draft horse … except he sparkled."

"Like Aurelia?" Samantha asked.

"Yes. Then he turned, and his wings were … magnificent. He was the most beautiful thing I've ever seen."

"Weren't you scared?" Cody's voice was cold and hard. I turned to look at him and couldn't believe the rage I saw burning in his eyes. "Even a little?"

"Why would I be?" I fidgeted with my earring. "I've flown before, and I've never been afraid of animals."

"Premonitions." His fists clenched and unclenched. "Didn't you worry? Or did you think about it?"

This wasn't like Cody at all. Anger radiated from him. He must've been even more worried about me when I was gone than I'd realized. I should've used my new ability to tell him I was okay, but until now, it hadn't occurred to me.

"I thought about it, but Aurelia was right there." I smacked the back of one hand against the palm of my other. "Every day of my life is spent worrying about everything. I know I will never live a normal life. Of course, I thought about it! I told Arion about my dreams, and he still offered to help me anytime I need him … and I can use all the allies I can get."

"Arion is a powerful ally to have." Aurelia placed her hand on my shoulder. "Dacia will need all the help she can get in this battle. Arion is both brave and caring. He will not let any harm befall Dacia if he can prevent it. He knows she is our only hope. Without her, we will be defeated."

I stood with my mouth hanging open, dumbfounded. "I'm a teenager. You're ancient. How can I be your only hope? There are others like you with more powerful magic than I'll ever have. Aren't there?"

"Yes, there are others like Arion and me. None of us— *none of us*—are able to do what you can. We cannot stop Draconian from controlling us. You are the only one, Dacia, and even without that ability, you are more powerful than you realize."

Suddenly, I felt how Atlas must. With the weight of the world bearing down on me, I wondered how I could keep from disappointing them. "Why me?"

"Each of us is given a path we must follow. Your path may be harder than some, but the more difficult the path, the greater the reward. It is amazing how much you have already achieved in your life. Do you not see that?"

"Yes—" I leaned against Cody "—I thought things would get easier once Nefarious was gone. I thought I would have a real life."

"If the path is worth taking, it is probably not an easy one." She strode across the room. "I am going to leave you and your friends to talk. If you need me, just project that thought to me." With her hand on the doorknob, she turned and said, "Oh, and if Draconian visits your dreams, remember what I told you. Good job tonight. You are progressing at an astounding pace."

"Goodnight, Aurelia," Cody said.

As soon as the door closed, Samantha turned toward me. "I am so jealous. Ever since I was a little girl, I have loved unicorns and pegasuses … or pegasi. How do you say it?"

"Pegasi." Cody rolled his eyes.

I plopped down on Cookie Monster, and the chair rocked back. "Arion says unicorns are overrated."

"Oh, really. Sounds like he's got some jealousy issues." Dan laughed.

"I hope you guys get to meet him. He's spectacular."

Chapter 20

Madness And Cruelty

The tension in the dorm room is palpable. I've apologized too many times for flying on Arion, but Cody still won't talk to me or even look at me.

"If you're going to be this way, I'm going for a walk. I can't take it!" Anger tears at my insides, trying to claw its way out. My fists clench at my sides. I close my eyes and try to steady my breathing.

"You can't. Not by yourself." Cody's voice is cold and angry.

"I'll get Aurelia or Arion to join me." On my way out, I slam the door and storm down the hall. I step out into the bright sunlight and think, *Arion, I need you.*

Is everything all right? His soothing voice softens the edges of my anger.

The wind blows through the leaves, and the aspen trees quake. *Yeah, I need to step outside, and nobody wants me to be alone. So, can you come?*

I am almost there. I would never let you down when you need me. You will not be able to see me until we are alone.

I understand.

Arion lands beside me with a soft thud. *Should I read your aura so I know when you're approaching?*

That would be a good idea. I will open my mind to you.

I place my hand against his neck. His fur is silky and warm. Beautiful sunrises and sunsets flash through my mind. I feel his joy as he soars above the clouds, looking down at the earth. A gold dragon flies next to him. It's magnificent, beautiful, and graceful. Illuminating energy flows through me.

"You have a dragon for a friend?" I chew on my lip. "Doesn't it frighten you?" We followed the path behind Wisteria Hall toward Falcon Lake, splitting off on a less-traveled trail.

"Gold dragons are benevolent, but under Draconian's control, even they can be malevolent."

We walk in silence for a while, heading deeper into the forest. Finally, I say, "I don't know if I could ever trust a dragon."

"Have you wondered if a dragon would ever trust you?"

His question surprises me. "I … I never really thought about it."

"We are out of sight now. Would you like to soar through the clouds?"

"Cody wouldn't like it. And I'm not sure if I should. What if dragons attack us?" My stomach vibrates with the wings of butterflies. "There are so many reasons not to, but I would love to."

Arion glimmers next to me like a mirage. If not for my hand on his neck, I might think my eyes are playing tricks on me.

He kneels, and I climb onto his back. His muscles bunch beneath me as he leaps into the air. Once we are above the clouds, he shows himself. Sunlight reflects off him, blinding me until my eyes adjust. Even then spots dance through the air in front of me.

Tension eases from my muscles, and for the first time since my dragon dreams started, I feel pure joy. I throw my head back and howl with delight.

Dragons burst through the clouds. Arion rears, and I clutch his mane. "No. No. No."

Arion pulls his wings back and dives. The dragons pursue. Their wings beat against the sky.

Flames shoot through the air. Arion rolls to the side, and I slip off his back.

As I fall through the clouds, I hear Draconian. "Just give me Nefarious."

He's here. I stop my fall, hovering in the air. I turn invisible and scan the skies for him. Before I teleport away, I need to read his aura.

"Give up already," I shout, then fly off so he doesn't know where I am.

I reach out for Draconian's mind. When I don't find it, I say to Arion, "Are you all right?"

Dragons circle through the skies, their wings beating the air, changing the air currents, making it hard to hover.

Yes, I am a skilled enough flier to avoid these silly creatures.

I need to find Draconian so I can read his aura. Can you help me?

As you wish.

"Dacia, come out, come out wherever you are," Draconian says in a singsong voice. "My dragons are ready for a game of cat and mouse."

"Show yourself, and she will come out." Arion's voice carries across the sky.

"Who is this? Somebody who wants to play with dragons," Draconian says.

What are you doing? I think to Arion.

I have a plan. When he shows himself, I will draw his attention while you read his aura.

Be careful.

"I will not let Dacia go until you show yourself," Arion shouts.

"How can I believe you have her?"

His voice comes from farther away. "You will have to trust me."

"Trust is for fools … and the weak."

"Well, if you are strong, you should be able to handle yourself against me. Show yourself! Only the weak hide behind dragons and invisibility."

"I am not weak!" Apparently, Arion has struck a nerve. "You are hiding behind invisibility."

"Yes," Arion's voice is taunting, "but not behind dragons, too."

"I am not hiding!" Draconian yells.

"Then show yourself."

Draconian appears astride a red dragon. His eyes dart across the sky, searching for Arion and me. His beard flaps over his shoulder. "Here I am. Now, where are you?"

This is your chance, Dacia, Arion thinks to me. Then to Draconian, he says, "You are still hiding behind a dragon so I will keep my invisibility for a little longer."

Smoke rolls out of the dragon's nostrils. Its cream-colored belly is alight with the fire burning inside. Flames burst from its jaws, incinerating the sky where Arion's voice came from. Muscles ripple as its tattered wings beat the sky.

I tear my attention away from the dragon and focus on Draconian, reaching for his mind.

Women burn to death, tied to stakes. Others are bound and thrown into lakes and rivers. Dragons are beaten, their eggs stolen from their nests. Torture and violence darken his memories. Finally, madness and cruelty wash over me.

I pull my mind away and fight against the nausea rising in me.

"What was that?" Draconian grasps his skull.

Let's get out of here, I say to Arion, but he doesn't respond.

"Your friend is under my control. Just to prove it, he's going to show himself now."

Draconian waves his hand, and Arion appears in the air in front of me.

"A pegasus … interesting. He won't do me any good, but I'm sure my dragons will like to play with him."

"Let him go!" My invisibility fades. "Take me instead."

Dragons swoop in, surrounding me. Terror rips the breath from my lungs. I want to escape, but I can't allow Arion to suffer.

"What did you do to me, Dacia?" Draconian flies closer.

"I didn't do anything." My teeth clamp together, and my chin juts out.

"You're lying. Shall I send one of my pets after your friend, or will you tell me the truth?"

Before I answer, a blue dragon lunges at Arion, and a ball of fire shoots through the air. I throw myself in front of it. The flames hit me in the chest, and I plummet to the ground.

"Don't let her die!" Draconian screams.

Arion flies toward me, diving with his wings pulled back.

I try to release him from Draconian's control. My vision swims, darkening at the edges … then nothing.

Dacia? Dacia, what did you want? You called for me, Arion said.

My mind was bleary. *I didn't want you to be under Draconian's spell. Did you save me?*

I have no idea what you are talking about, Dacia. You are not making sense. You are sending me too many thoughts. Concentrate!

Draconian had you, I tried to explain, but the pain was overbearing. *I can't do this now. I need to heal.*

I will send Aurelia.

Everything was quiet and calm for a while. Then hands covered my burns. A cool feeling washed over me. When I opened my eyes, Aurelia stood over me. I lay in bed, burned and bleeding. Aurelia covered my wounds and helped me put on a new pajama shirt.

"Samantha, you can get Cody." She placed her hand on my head, and strength seeped into me. "You are going to be okay. Arion sent me. He said you called for him, but you were incoherent."

"He must've been worried because he's outside right now."

"He is," she said, "but how did you know?"

"I can sense him."

She looked out the window. "When? How?"

"He let me." My eyes widened. "He probably doesn't know. I read it in my dream. Then dragons came. Arion made Draconian show himself so I could read his aura, too. I guess I got them both. Tell him I'm sorry."

"Rest now, Dacia." She patted my hand. "I will talk to Samantha and Cody. Then I will stay here and watch over you for the rest of the night. You need deep healing sleep."

My eyelids drooped. "Thanks," I mumbled. I was asleep before Aurelia descended the ladder.

Chapter 21
Close Call

$\mathcal{D}$an and Samantha walked in front of us. Her hand was tucked into the pocket of his shorts. Her flip-flops slapped against her feet with every step she took.

A smile tugged at my lips when I thought of how she'd react if she knew Arion was with us.

Sunlight danced through the leaves and onto the trail. The patchy light made it harder to tell if anyone hid in the trees.

"Do you learn anything?" Cody asked Aurelia.

Something rustled through the undergrowth. A squirrel scolded us from a branch overhead.

"I have forgotten more about the stars than your culture knew to begin with. I am able to keep an eye on Dacia, and that is why I am here." She added in a softer almost wistful voice, "Now from her, I could learn a thing or two."

I bit my bottom lip, pulling it into my mouth. "If I knew how to teach them to you, I would."

"That time may come, but for now, I need to continue teaching you all that I can so we can keep you alive."

I breathed easier once we were inside Kestrel Observatory. Throughout class, I wondered what Aurelia knew about the stars that we didn't. I knew her knowledge must be vast. *What is it like to live forever? Does she miss the way things were or welcome change? Will I live forever? Will I have to watch my family and friends die? Or will I age with them?*

I imagined Cody growing old and feeble and me staying the same. *How can I watch him wither away and die? Will it make me as warped as Draconian is if I do? Is that what made him this way?*

"Dacia, wake up." Cody snapped his fingers in front of my face. "Time to go."

"Sorry." I blinked and jerked my head back. "I was spacing off."

"Yeah, we noticed." Samantha nodded, and her lips pressed together. "Hopefully, whatever you were thinking about was worth it because we're having a test next week, and you didn't learn a thing."

"I'll study." I rolled my eyes. "And, no, what I was thinking about wasn't worth it. It was just a lot of unanswerable questions."

I stuffed my books in my bag and followed the others. As soon as I stepped outside, I sensed Arion. Even though I couldn't see him, knowing he was there helped me feel at ease.

Cody hung back with me. "You okay?"

"I'm just dwelling." I rearranged my backpack on my shoulders. "Nothing important."

"You sure?"

"Yeah." I wrapped my arm around his waist, and he threw his over my shoulder.

As we passed through a grove of trees about halfway back to the dorm, I felt Draconian's aura. My steps faltered.

Cody stopped. "Dacia?"

"Draconian is here," I warned in a fierce whisper. "I can feel him, but I can't tell where he is."

"Continue cautiously." Aurelia cocked her head in a bird-like movement. "Keep talking. Act like everything is fine."

"So, uh, what are you guys doing tonight?" I asked, trying to sound casual. "I was thinking pizza and a movie. What do you think?"

My question was followed by a long uncomfortable silence that was broken when Cody volunteered, "*Pirates of the Caribbean.*"

"Yeah, that sounds good." Dan's voice was tense.

"I've always wanted to see that movie." Draconian stepped out of the trees in front of us. His charcoal robe swirled around his feet. "Mind if I join you?"

"Don't you have something better to do with your time than chase teenage girls?" The harshness of my voice surprised me.

He narrowed his gray eyes and stroked his beard, stepping closer. "You don't seem surprised to see me."

"I'm not. I knew you …" My voice trailed off before I could finish.

Arion projected his thoughts to me, *Dacia, do not rush to show your cards. Keep things from him as long as you can.*

I cleared my throat and started over, "I knew you'd show up sooner or later. You don't seem to be able to stay away from me."

"Yes." He sauntered closer to me. "You are such a charming young lady. I am drawn to you."

"Oh, I thought you were just attracted to my power." I concentrated on lightning. Electrical charges leaped from my fingertips.

"No need to be aggressive—I came alone." He held his hands out in front of him. "I just want to talk."

"Please forgive me if I don't trust you." I surreptitiously glanced at the trees, not wanting to take my eyes off Draconian for too long. "I'm sure your dragons are around here somewhere."

Aurelia walked over and stood beside me. She looked over her shoulder at the others. "Stay behind us."

Draconian stopped moving and stared open-mouthed at Aurelia. "I know you. *I know you.*" He pointed at me. "Does she?" With a puff of smoke, he disappeared.

I narrowed my eyes at Aurelia. "What did he mean by that?" The urge to grab my friends and run off tugged at me.

"Apparently, he knows what you figured out the first time we met … I am not human." Her face was unreadable.

"Is that all he meant?" I stood between her and the others, shielding them.

"He might think he knows what I am, but it would be nothing more than a guess."

Widening my stance, I crossed my arms over my chest. "I suppose this still isn't the time to tell me."

"No, Dacia. Now is the time to get you and your friends to safety." When I didn't move, she added, "Before he returns with reinforcements."

"Is he afraid of you?" Cody asked.

"Yeah, why did he disappear so quickly?" Samantha asked before Aurelia could answer Cody.

"Arion, show yourself, please." Aurelia ignored the questions. He appeared right beside me. I realized for the first time how serious he was about protecting me. Draconian didn't know about him, and I needed to make sure it stayed that way. The element of surprise was on my side for now.

Samantha's mouth dropped open. "You are beautiful."

Aurelia didn't give him the chance to respond. "Take Samantha and Dan to the dorm. Keep them safe."

"When I turn invisible, you will too." Arion knelt in front of them. "It is a very strange thing to watch yourself disappear."

Excitement flushed Samantha's cheeks and lit up her eyes.

"What now?" I asked Aurelia.

"Now we do the same," she answered as if it was as obvious as night following day.

"What about me?" Cody pointed at himself.

"I will take you with me," Aurelia said.

I looked from Cody to Aurelia and tried to imagine her carrying him. He had four inches on her and at least fifty pounds. "Do you need help?"

"No, Dacia. I am very strong." A smile lifted her lips but went no farther. "Looks can be deceiving."

With that, we turned invisible and flew off. *Draconian really must have been alone,* I thought to Aurelia. *Why?*

I do not know the answer. Maybe he really wanted to talk to you.

Maybe. You were right to leave quickly. If he comes back with his dragons, the farther we are from there the better.

Aurelia and I landed in the trees outside Wisteria Hall. We became visible and hustled to the dorm room.

As soon as the door clicked shut, Samantha bounced up out of the chair and clapped her hands. "That was amazing! I thought it would be awesome just to see a pegasus, but I got to ride one."

"She almost fell off because she was so excited." Dan laughed. "But it was pretty cool."

Cody crossed the room and sat down. He leaned forward with his elbows on his knees. "Aurelia carried me like—" he held his palm out, staring at it "—like I was a fly. Weightless."

Even though I was safe here, the room felt too stuffy, too closed in. Too many colors overloaded my senses.

I walked to the window and opened it. The breeze blew across my face, helping to fight the claustrophobia. I closed my eyes and breathed in the fresh air. "So, why did Draconian run away when he saw you?" I asked. "Don't say now is not the time."

"I imagine he was afraid to take on one of us while the other was there." Aurelia pulled out the desk chair and sat down. "You asked me what I was shortly after you met me. You admit you thought I was different the first time we met. You should understand what he saw in me. Just because we are friends now does not mean I am human. It does not mean other people who know see me as a person. Remember that."

"You're right." Cody walked to me. His fingers brushed the back of my hand for just an instant.

"No matter what else you are"—Samantha sat next to Dan on the couch—"you're our friend. That's all that matters."

"Then trust me." Aurelia's voice held an emotion that I couldn't decipher. "I will tell you more, but you have to give me time. There are things I have to do first. I know you are curious. Humans, especially the young ones, often are."

"We'll do our best." I turned away from the window. I owed her so much. The least I could do was give her my trust. Cody, Samantha, and Dan all nodded in agreement. "You have to remember, though, we are human … curious humans who can't always trust, even when we want to. Human nature isn't what it should be."

"Well said." Aurelia inclined her head. "I, too, will have to try to be more understanding."

"What is Draconian up to? Why would he just want to talk?" I turned my back to her, hoping she'd see it for what it was—a sign of trust. "Do you suppose he knows I read his aura?"

"We can only speculate," Aurelia said.

"I don't know what to think of this."

"None of us do." Cody slid his fingers through mine.

"I hate to change the subject, but we need to decide," Dan said. "Do we take our chances and go to calculus, or do we skip?"

The thought of spending the day trapped in this room made my gut clench. Panic gripped me, threatening to suffocate me.

I took a deep breath, inhaling the pine scent, letting it soothe me. "Well, I'm not spending my life hiding." I faced the others. "However, I can't blame any of you if you want to skip. You can't heal yourselves or fight back. You have to decide for yourselves."

"I'm going," Cody said in his don't-even-think-about-arguing-with-me voice.

"Me too." Samantha stood. "I can't let Draconian take my grades down."

"Well, let's get going then." Dan walked to the door. "We don't want to be late."

Aurelia frowned at me. "Though I disagree with your decision, I will not hold you back."

Cody and I led the way to class with Aurelia following Samantha and Dan. We didn't dilly-dally.

As Cody took his seat, he let out a sigh of relief. "Made it."

"Yeah," I agreed.

"You don't sound too happy about it." Dan leaned over his desk, looking around Cody and Samantha to see me.

I tapped my pen against my paper, trying to figure out how to put my feelings into words. "I don't know what he's waiting for, and that scares me more than I'd like to admit."

"Every day he waits is another day for you to learn to perfect your skills." Aurelia's optimism wasn't contagious.

"I know, but it also gives him a chance to come up with a plan." I pulled my book out and sat it on the desk.

"Maybe we should come up with a plan of our own." Samantha rubbed her finger over her lip. "Maybe there's a way to get Draconian out on his own."

"I'm open to suggestions." I didn't see how we could lure him out without his dragons, but I was willing to give almost anything a try.

"That is a good idea." Aurelia stood out like a rose in a patch of dandelions. She didn't belong here, slumming it with mere mortals. "We should try to come up with something. If we can fight Draconian alone or even with just one or two dragons around, that would be much better than dealing with all of them."

"Yeah." A fake laugh followed the word. "But how am I going to defeat even one dragon, let alone Draconian?" A shiver ran down my spine as I pictured myself surrounded by fifteen dragons. They crept toward me, bloodthirsty fangs yearning to sink into my skin. I would be lucky to survive five minutes in a fight with them. Draconian wouldn't show himself until it was over. He would hide behind his dragons while they tore the flesh from my bones.

"Remember, Dacia, you will not have to beat all of his dragons. You only have to stop him." Aurelia kept her voice quiet.

Without meaning to, I rolled my eyes at her. "Sure, but the dragons won't stand by and watch me battle Draconian. They'll protect him."

"Guys, too many people." Cody waved his arm at the classroom.

Aurelia wasn't ready to be done, though. She projected her thoughts to me, *Do not give up, Dacia. There is always hope.*

I'm sorry, I thought to her, *but I'm terrified of dragons. They're evil, vicious, cruel monsters with only death and destruction on their minds.*

Aurelia's face hardened, and her eyes flashed dangerously. *It is not their fault. Those dragons are under Draconian's control. They are not evil, vicious, or cruel. You know they are being tortured.*

Sorry, but all of them that I've had the pleasure of meeting have been just that ... evil, vicious, cruel, horrible monsters! I slammed my fist down on the desk. Pain shot through my hand, but I kept my face hard.

If your only experience with a dog was a bad one, would you assume all dogs were monsters? Dragons are the same. Some are evil, but not all. She stared at Professor Granite, watching him write calculations on the whiteboard. *I could say people are evil, vicious, and cruel because Draconian is, but I would be wrong. Not all people are bad ... you are not.*

You're right. I looked down at my hands fisted on my desk, feeling guilty for assuming the worst. I lifted my head, meeting her golden eyes, hoping she would understand. *I've encountered several dragons, and they've all been under Draconian's control. I guess I just thought it was their nature to be evil.*

Her face softened. *You are forgiven. It seems a reasonable assumption. I have actually met a dragon or two, and they were benevolent.*

Maybe someday I can meet them. It would be nice to be proven wrong about this.

I doubt the dragons that remain free will come out of hiding until Draconian is stopped. Throughout history, dragons have been hunted and feared but never controlled ... until now.

Samantha reached over Cody and poked me in the leg with her pencil. I looked into her narrowed eyes. "Are you two listening at all?"

"No," I answered, "we're having a conversation."

"Do that later," she whispered fiercely. "You're going to fail all your classes!"

"Maybe astronomy," I agreed, "but I can do most math in my sleep."

"Ladies," Professor Granite snapped, "if you think you can do a better job teaching this class than I can, please, by all means, come up and teach it. Otherwise, zip it!" I had never seen him angry before. His salt and pepper mustache lay unmoving over his pinched lips, and he stared at us through very angry gray eyes.

"Sorry, sir," I said.

"Sorry," Samantha mumbled.

Well, Aurelia projected to me, *it seems your telepathy is pretty good. Obviously, Samantha was not able to hear us.*

Yeah, but I need to pay attention now. If I don't, Samantha will get in even more trouble.

"We're going to your room," I said to Cody and Dan. Kalmia Hall was twice as far from the women's dorm as the men's.

Aurelia nodded, and the five of us left together. We strode to Dracaena Hall, glancing over our shoulders, fearing what might be hiding behind every tree, jumping at every sound.

We strode through the hallways to Dan and Cody's room. The blinds were down and the curtains drawn.

"You need to let some air in here," Samantha said.

Dan shrugged. "I never know if I'll be coming back, so I leave the window closed."

"I'm sorry, Dan." I sucked in a deep breath. "I never meant to put you in danger."

He shook his head. "That's not what I meant." He brushed his auburn hair back. His hair was longer than I'd seen it since meeting him. "One of these nights, I'll be too scared to be on my own."

Aurelia took Dan's and Samantha's hands in hers. "This room is also warded as long as you or I are in it." She nodded at me before teleporting away.

"Guess she thinks we need some time alone," Cody said.

I pulled my hand through my hair. "I think she realizes I feel like a caged animal." With Elmo in our room, the furnishings here were pretty sparse. I sat on the floor under the window, pulling my knees up to my chest. "We had a pretty intense argument in class."

Cody sat down beside me. His arm and leg brushed against mine. Warmth seeped into me.

"I don't know if I'll live through this, Cody. How am I gonna fight them all?"

He tucked one arm under my knees and wrapped the other around my shoulders, then lifted me onto his lap.

"Felt the same with Nefarious. Still here." He rubbed his hand along my arm. "Have faith."

I laid my head on his shoulder. "I'm trying."

He pressed his lips to my forehead. "You'll get through this."

I tilted my face up, brushing my lips along his neck. A low moan escaped from him. His hand slid under my shirt, clasping my waist.

My fingers wove through his hair, pulling his mouth to mine. I turned, wrapping my legs around his body.

His hands explored my back, drawing me closer. His fingers slid into my sleeves, and he looked at me, asking permission.

I shook my head. "Not yet."

He slid his hands down, kneading my tense muscles, trailing kisses from my mouth to my ear. "When you're ready." His teeth scraped against my earlobe. "I love you."

Cupping his face in my hands, I said, "I love you, too." My voice was throaty.

I knew Cody wanted more, but besides not being ready, there were other things holding me back. I might not survive, and if I did, I might not ever die. Cody deserved better.

"Dacia?" Cody clenched my waist. His eyes were tender. "I'll wait forever if you want."

I brushed my thumbs over his cheeks. "Not forever … just not yet." Standing, I reached my hand down to him. He took it, letting me pull him to his feet.

Grasping my shoulders, he said, "Don't shut me out."

I stepped closer, wrapping my arms around his waist. He clutched me against him. I didn't know what to say, so I just nodded. "Ready?"

"Sure."

Closing my eyes, I pictured my room. My body felt like it was being sucked into one tiny spot in my chest before being stretched back out again. Darkness surrounded me. Then Cody and I reappeared near the sink, still holding each other.

He staggered back, stumbling out of my embrace, slightly off balance. Out of the corner of my eye, I saw Dan and Samantha separating from each other, sitting up on the couch, and finger-combing their hair.

I gave them a minute before turning to face them. "Where's Aurelia?"

"Her room." Dan nodded toward the door.

Samantha furtively untwisted her shirt. "It seems she just needs to be in the building to keep the wards up."

We're back, I thought to Aurelia.

Thank you for letting me know.

I tossed my backpack against the wall. "If anybody is up for that pizza and movie, I'll buy."

"Yeah, that'd be good," Dan said.

"We'll all chip in." Samantha shrugged. "We need it as much as you do."

"Dan, catch." Cody tossed him a ruler. Without skipping a beat, Dan was on his feet in a frantic sword fight with Cody. They danced through the room banging ruler against ruler. Then Dan struck Cody.

Cody slipped away with Dan's ruler stuck between his arm and ribcage. He stumbled backward and fell to the ground. "Dacia." Cody gasped as he clutched his chest. "I'm fading fast. Grant a dying man his last wish?"

"What is it, Cody?" I joined in, acting like I was about to lose him forever.

"A kiss … from your beautiful lips … is all … I need … please." He wheezed as if taking his last breath.

I leaned over and kissed him. With that, his head fell to the side, and he died with a smile on his face.

Dan and Samantha stood up and clapped. "A death scene like that deserves a standing ovation," Samantha said.

Cody jumped to his feet and took a bow. "Thank you … thank you. Where'd I be without my fans?"

"So, are you going to start taking acting classes?" I asked.

"You never know," he said with a twinkle in his eye. "If it'd get you to kiss me, I might."

"Cody." I rolled my eyes.

After the movie, Samantha and Dan stretched out on the couch. The red fabric clashed with the lavender carpet, but Cody appreciated being able to lie down to sleep.

It didn't take Samantha long to fall asleep wrapped in Dan's arms.

I grabbed my pajamas and started for the door.

"Can I stay here tonight?" Dan asked. "Seeing Draconian today has me a little freaked out."

"Yeah, no problem." I stepped into the hall and slumped against the door. Hopefully, I could make it through the night without a nightmare.

Chapter 22

A Witness To Madness

Without the moon to interfere, stars brighten the night sky. Cody and I walk hand in hand from the student center. The cool breeze blows the scent of grilling hamburgers across campus.

I point to a bench. "Let's sit over there."

"Sure." He sits, spreading his arm across the back.

I lie down with my head on his lap, looking up at the stars. "They're so much brighter here than at home. I love looking at them and watching the moonrise."

Cody's fingers trail through my hair. "Uh, don't think that's the moon."

"Over there." I jab my finger toward the sky.

"That's not east."

I sit up and stare in disbelief. Flames stretch toward the heavens. "You're right. We need to get outta here."

I stand, reaching for Cody's hand, but he doesn't take it. His gaze is glued to the sky behind me. Dread clutches my heart as I turn to see what Cody's looking at.

An amethyst dragon soars toward us on bat-like wings. Flames spew from its beak-like jaws, illuminating the two twisted horns protruding from its angular head.

The ground ignites below the beast. It narrows its eyes and darts toward us.

"Cody, we need to leave now!"

I grab his hand and tug. We sprint for the dorm. Lights line the winding sidewalk, but we cut through the trees, jumping over roots and ducking beneath low branches.

The creatures of the night go silent, and my heart plummets.

A rumbling growl sends a chill down my spine. An ebony dragon stalks forward. Its body clings to the ground. Its demon-like wings are tucked into its muscled sides.

Cody and I inch backward. The dragon strikes, grabbing Cody around the waist, lifting him into the air.

I clutch Cody's hand. My feet lift off the ground.

The purple dragon pierces my shoulders and yanks me away. Pain clouds my thoughts. The dragons beat their wings, rising above the rooftops.

Let us go, I think to the dragons. *In return, I might be able to help you.*

Help? The dragon carrying me snorts and smoke puffs out of its nostrils.

The black dragon's bronze eyes narrow, and its talons clench.

Cody screams. Blood runs from his side, dripping off the dragon's knuckles. It roars back to me in an earsplitting baritone voice. *Why would I need the help of a puny human? Look at me. I am the top of the food chain.*

But Draconian controls you.

Nobody controls me! I have no master!

Then why are you taking us to him?

He knows I am powerful. He fears and respects me. He asked me to do it for him because he cannot.

"Dacia, if you can't save us both …" Cody's voice is laced with pain. "Promise you'll escape."

"I can't do that, Cody." My heart drums in my ears. "I know what Draconian's capable of. His torture is ruthless. You won't survive."

"Promise or I'll make this dragon kill me."

"Fine! I promise."

Cody's head sags. His blood still drips from the dragon's talons.

"Hang in there, Cody." I turn my thoughts to the black dragon. *Let me help him. He'll die.*

The beast whips his head toward me. His ebony horns slice through the air.

He is insignificant. You are the one Draconian wants.

Fire consumes my thoughts. I hold it in until I'm engulfed in flames. Slipping out of the dragon's claws, I hover between them. *If you want to take me to Draconian, you'll let me heal Cody now!*

The black one roars, and the stench of rotten flesh hits me with the force of a gale. *You are testing my patience, little one.* The dragons descend.

I asked you nicely. You could have cooperated.

As he alights, he relaxes his grip on Cody. "You have one minute."

Just before landing between the dragons, I extinguish my flames. My stomach rolls. I want to dart away, but I kneel and place my hands over Cody's wounds. "If you let go of him, this would be so much easier."

"You will not leave without the boy, and I will not give you the chance to leave with him." The dragon's voice rumbles low and deep.

If I teleport while the dragon holds Cody will it come along? It's too great of a risk.

I close my eyes and think about life. Cody's injuries slowly begin to mend. His skin draws together, and he gasps.

"Thanks." He squeezes my hand. "Wondered if I'd see you again."

"I need you to stay with me."

He tries to sit, but the dragon forces him down. "Shall we continue?" the beast asks. "Or must I listen to you drone on?"

I stand and stare into the dragon's bronze eyes. "Carry him carefully. I'll fly alongside you until we're almost there. Then I'll let that one"—I jerk my thumb over my shoulder at the other dragon—"carry me in. If you hurt him, I'll disappear."

The purple dragon growls and steps closer to me. I stiffen but don't turn. Sweat beads along my hair and upper lip.

The black dragon lifts Cody, not allowing its claws to dig in, and they both launch into the air. I fly along beside them, watching Cody, hoping for a chance to free him.

"It's time," the dragon snarls.

"Are you sure about this, uh … what is your name?" I ask.

The dragon hisses. "You are an insolent pest."

"I'm sorry." I'm not sure why he's angry. "I just wanted to ask if we could come to some other arrangement. I don't want to go to Draconian, but I can't let you take Cody without me."

"It is too late." The amethyst dragon reaches up as quick as lightning and grabs me out of the sky. I scream as its talons pierce my body.

"Dacia, you okay?"

"I've been better." I bite back the pain.

The dragon takes me to Draconian and drops me at his feet.

"Let the boy go," Draconian says.

There's a long pause, and I know the dragons are communicating with Draconian. "So, you can free yourself, yet you stayed for him." Draconian strokes his beard, looking up at the ceiling. "Maybe he is not insignificant. Maybe I can use him. My friend here will hold onto him until you give me what I want."

"Dacia, save yourself," Cody says as he's dragged off.

"Shut up, boy." Draconian yells before turning his gaze on me.

My body goes limp. I fall to the ground at Draconian's feet. The first thing that comes to mind is that I need to have Aurelia teach me how to get out of this. I'm completely powerless. My thoughts are interrupted when fire sears through my body.

"Your boyfriend here can't hear how much pain you're in." Draconian shakes his head like it's a tragedy. "That will never do." Once again, pain envelopes me. This time when I scream, instead of silence, an agonized cry echoes through the cavernous room.

"Dacia!" Cody yells. "Don't do this for me."

"You have a choice, Dacia. You can either give me Nefarious, or we can continue. Which will it be?" Draconian's voice is fierce.

"I … I will n-nev … never give him … to you," I say through my sobs.

Electricity buzzes through my body, burning my muscles. The stone floor cools my skin, easing some of the pain.

"Anytime." Draconian growls.

I close my eyes and shake my head.

Draconian jabs his fingers against my temples. Electricity jolts into my brain.

My hands clench. My toes curl. My body convulses, then goes limp.

Serenity surrounds me. Pain is a memory.

I stand on the beach of Falcon Lake at sunset. A boat glides through the water, scarcely leaving ripples in the reflection. It drifts toward the shore, stopping in front of me. I feel compelled to climb aboard.

I step onto the gangway. Something grabs me and yanks me backward. The invisible force drags me against my will.

Air rushes into my lungs, sending me into a coughing fit.

Draconian stands above me, laughing. He rubs his palms together, and electricity dances across his fingers. He clasps my face in his hands, and the current surges through my body. A scream tears from me.

"Dacia!" Cody's voice is ragged, desperate.

"Dacia." Cody shook my arm.

I forced my eyes open and breathed deeply, trying to orient myself.

Cody stood on my ladder. His eyes were wild.

"I'm okay." I tried to smile, but every muscle in my body ached. My pajamas were bloody.

Dan stood on the floor, staring up into my loft. His hazel eyes looked huge against the backdrop of his pale face.

"Sorry," I whispered to Dan.

"Don't apologize." Cody brushed the hair off my forehead. "You okay?"

"I'll survive."

"Let me see your back." Samantha knelt in her loft. "It looks like a dragon carried you in its talons again." She rubbed her shoulders as if remembering the pain.

"Yeah, then Draconian tortured me"—I tried to shrug it off for Dan's benefit—"nothing new."

"I'm sorry, Dacia, but I can't handle this." Dan held his hand over his mouth, staring up at me. "Whether Aurelia comes to get me or not, I think I'll go back to my room from now on."

Cody helped sit me up. "Some people can't handle blood."

"Yeah, it's not that," Dan said. "It's the screams and the fact that she wakes up like this. If it was, uh … real, I think it would be different."

"What do you mean?" Anger flashed across Cody's face. "It is real!"

"I–I mean, if it happened in, uh, you know …"

"You know what he means," I said through clenched teeth.

Cody closed his eyes and pinched the bridge of his nose. "Sorry."

Dan looked like a rabbit that was about to bolt. "I didn't mean to upset anybody."

"The good news is her injuries will be gone by morning." Samantha grabbed ahold of Dan's elbow.

"That's amazing."

"I thank God for it every day," I said as Cody eased me back down.

The color slowly came back to Dan's face, but he still looked shaken up. "Yeah, I would, too."

I wrapped my arms around my body and thought healing thoughts. My muscles relaxed, and my pain receded. When I finished, I opened my eyes and looked at my wounds. They weren't completely healed, but they were much better.

"I wish you hadn't seen this." A weight settled on my chest. "I wish you hadn't heard me screaming. I know it's hard on all of you."

"It's not your fault." Dan plopped down on Elmo. "I thought I knew what I was getting into by staying here, but I was wrong. It's too much." He stared at the floor. "I don't know how you do it. I couldn't."

I thought about it for a moment and said, "If you had to, you could. We all do what we must."

Chapter 23

Taken

unlight filtered through the trees. Chipmunks darted along the path in front of us. Birds chirped. The forest was alive, but Aurelia and I walked to photography class on high alert.

"Draconian paralyzes me, and there's nothing I can do." I tugged my hand through my hair. "When he had Cody that time, I got free, but I don't know how. Anyway, can you help me with it?"

"I will have to try to figure out what he does." She cocked her head. "Can you sense Draconian's presence now?"

"No … why?" I was concerned that somehow she could, and I couldn't anymore.

"I need to skip class. There are things I need to discuss with Arion. We will both be gone for a while. We should be back before class is over, though."

"Oh … okay." I was surprised she was willing to leave me alone. "I'm sure I'll be fine. It's not too much farther. Go ahead."

"Be careful." She disappeared.

I couldn't remember the last time I'd been alone. The freedom was exhilarating, but I was afraid that if something happened I'd never be left on my own again.

"I could get used to this," I mumbled as I walked along enjoying the silence.

Dry leaves rustled across the ground behind me, but the air was still. My breath caught in my throat, and a chill vibrated in my chest. A twig snapped. I slowly turned, fearing the worst.

A green dragon stood still, trying to blend in with the trees. Icy fingers clutched my heart, holding me in a vice-like grip. This was the same dragon that had ripped my back open in my dream.

You have to get out of here.

I turned to run, but before I could, Draconian appeared in front of me.

"I came to you alone … without my pets, and you wanted to battle me." He lifted his hands, palms up. "I wanted to talk. So, tell me, Dacia, who is the evil one?"

I stared at him. Maybe I had been eager to fight him, but that didn't make me a bad person. Did it?

"Maybe," he answered his own question, "it's both of us … or neither. Maybe we're both a little self-serving. What do you think?"

Before I could answer, I fell to the ground in a heap, paralyzed. "This time, I have my dragons with me, and I am not prepared to be civilized. This time, you will give me what I want."

He bent down, grabbed my arm, and transported me to his castle.

My breath caught in my throat. I tried to swallow it, but it stuck there, aching. My eyes darted from side to side. The room was dank and dark. The air smelled stagnant. The stone walls, the massive doors, it all looked familiar. Draconian had killed me in this room.

Without releasing me from his spell, Draconian chained me to a table in the middle of the room. I tried to teleport, but as expected, I couldn't. I tried to turn to fire, to free myself from the restraints, nothing. Giving up on freeing myself, I fought to close my eyes so I wouldn't have to witness my torture, but I couldn't even manage that.

"Dacia, give up." Draconian stood over me, his gray eyes gleaming. "I brought you here because, as powerful as you are, you cannot teleport out. You are trapped."

Aurelia. Arion. Draconian has me. Help! There was no response to my plea. I could only hope Draconian hadn't stopped that power, too.

"Don't make this worse than it has to be." Draconian paced the length of the table, running his fingers along the edge. "Who knows where Nefarious is? If not you ... who?"

I couldn't answer him even if I wanted to. He hadn't released me. "Cat got your tongue?" His mouth curled up into an evil snarl. "Should we see if we can loosen your lips?"

Draconian placed his hand on mine. Bursts of colors popped behind my eyes as pain traveled along my nerves. I gasped for breath, but he didn't stop. The edges of my vision blurred, then darkened. My consciousness slipped.

Stepping back, Draconian said, "Tell me who knows."

My jaw and neck relaxed when he gave me back the ability to talk. I took advantage of the opportunity and thought, *Aurelia, Arion, help!* Then to Draconian, I said in a calm, controlled voice that belied my fear, "I don't know, and if I did, you'd be the last person I'd tell."

"I warned you not to make this difficult, but you couldn't resist. Could you?" He put his hands on my temples, and I braced myself.

The electrical current cleaved through my body, and violent spasms trailed in its wake. Everywhere metal touched my exposed skin, my flesh burned. The pain lasted for an eternity before I went limp.

Gentle waves lapped against the shore. Birds sang. It was peaceful. As I stared at the reflection on Falcon Lake, a boat glided across the water, stopping in front of me. I reached out to climb aboard, but as my hands touched the rail, I was dragged back to life. Immense pain returned to my body. Tears rolled down my cheeks. I didn't want Draconian to see them, but I couldn't turn them off or turn away.

"Did you see a white light?" Draconian taunted. "Was it like everybody describes it?"

"Why … why didn't you let him take me?"

"Death will not have you until you give me what I want!" He reached down and wiped a tear from my eye. His hand was rough. "Poor baby." Draconian's voice filled with contempt.

"Give him to me, and you won't have to go through this anymore."

"What do you want with him?" My voice was weak, and the words scraped on their way out.

"Power." Draconian stepped away, clasping his hands behind his back. His burgundy robe dragged along the stone floor.

His answer revolted me. "Power? You've got a teenage girl chained to a table, torturing her. You should feel pretty powerful."

He spun around, jabbing his finger at me. "You will give me Nefarious, or you will die."

I clenched my teeth to keep from biting my tongue.

Draconian jabbed his fingertips onto my temples and blasted electricity into my brain. My hands clenched, and my toes curled. My body convulsed.

I stood by Falcon Lake. The sun-warmed sand squished between my toes. I no longer felt blood trickling down my face. My pain was gone. Draconian tugged on me, but I swatted him away. This time I was climbing aboard the ship. I wanted to see where it would take me.

My foot hung in the air over the gangplank when Draconian tugged. I pressed my feet down, fighting Draconian's pull, but he became harder and harder to resist. I was losing ground. With a final jerk, Draconian yanked me back to my life. Chained to the table, I struggled for breath. Pain ransacked my body, cleaving my muscles, burning through my veins.

"I thought I lost you that time." Draconian's voice was soft, giving the impression that he cared whether or not he killed me. "You're losing the battle, Dacia. Tell me where he is, or I will have no choice but to kill you this time."

"Death." I croaked.

"Tell me, Dacia. Ease your suffering. You don't …"

A roar echoed down the hallway. I twisted my head to the side, craning my neck to see the door. A gold dragon slammed into a scarlet beast with a deafening crash. The ground shook.

The golden intruder shimmered with a radiance I hadn't seen in any of the others. Spikes framed its head, reminding me of the crest of a cockatoo. There was a regal elegance about this dragon that belied its power. Golden claws slashed through the air, and massive fangs tore into the red dragon's flesh. Blood gushed from open wounds. Flames erupted, blocking my view.

As I lay there watching them battle, it dawned on me I was free from Draconian's spell. This was my chance to escape. I thought about fire until I was engulfed in flames. My body slipped through the chains.

Run to the dragon, Dacia. Arion spoke into my thoughts. *Do not be afraid. I sent her to help you.*

I flew to the far side of the gold dragon before relinquishing my flames. The creature stood at least seven feet tall at the shoulders. It knelt down. I couldn't draw in a breath. Terror clutched my heart.

Dacia, she's a friend.

Arion's voice prompted me to move. I climbed on her back, and she tore through the hall.

As soon as she stepped outside, she unfurled her wings and launched into the air. Pine trees stretched to the heavens.

Dacia, Arion said, *teleport to Sarah's office. Aurelia and I will be there as soon as we can.*

I'm not sure if I'm strong enough. The thought left my mind before I remembered to focus on who I was sending it to.

You must try. Fear laced Arion's voice.

I clutched the dragon. Its scales felt like a thousand razors slicing through my sensitive skin. *What if I don't make it?*

Be careful, he warned. *You are sending extra thoughts.*

I didn't respond. My mind was still fuzzy from torture, and my body ached. I needed to get to safety, but I was scared I wouldn't be able to teleport where I wanted. A fireball hurtled through the air beside us. I looked over my shoulder. Three dragons barreled toward us.

"I'm going to teleport. Will you be okay?"

"Yes," the dragon answered in a beautiful voice. "Once you are gone, I will have no problems evading them."

"Thank you."

I closed my eyes, picturing Sarah's office in detail. The dragon rolled to the side, nearly throwing me from its back.

Taking a deep breath, I said a silent prayer and teleported.

My concentration held, and I found myself in Sarah's office. I heard voices behind the door. Whoever was in there got up. I dashed into the bathroom.

I turned the light on and stared at my reflection. Blood trailed down my face from my temples, and my eyes were ringed with dark circles. "You look like a corpse," I told the girl in the mirror before leaning over the sink and splashing water on my face. Opening the door, I peered out. The room was empty, so I knocked on Sarah's office door. When she didn't answer, I staggered to the couch.

I leaned forward and struggled to keep my eyes open. Mere moments later, my senses were assaulted. I felt serenity, encouragement, passion and determination, comfort, enlightenment, strength, and love. Aurelia, Dan, Samantha, Sarah, and Cody walked into the room together.

I am out here if you need me, Arion said.

"Dacia?" Cody sat beside me and wrapped his arm around my shoulders, pulling me into his side.

I cringed.

"Sorry." He jerked his arm away.

"Torture's hell." I closed my eyes and pictured Draconian standing over me. My pulse raced, my breaths were shallow and rapid.

"Dacia"—Sarah's voice was soothing—"you're going to hyperventilate. Breathe."

Pain echoed throughout my body. The memories were as harsh as the reality had been. I tucked myself into the corner of the couch, drawing my legs up and wrapping my arms around them.

Aurelia stepped toward me with her arm outstretched. "May I?"

Draconian's hands reached for my temples. "No!"

Cody's face was pale, his eyes haunted. "Please."

I nodded at Aurelia and squeezed my eyes shut. Healing energy flowed through me, cooling the fire in my veins.

I looked up at her and tried to curve my lips into a smile.

Thank you. I thought to Arion. S*ending the dragon saved me.*

I am sorry we did not arrive sooner.

Did the dragon get away?

"Dacia?" Samantha chewed on her lip.

I lifted my hand, halting her.

Yes, she is safe.

Please thank her for me.

I will.

"The dragon that saved me is okay." I loosened my grip on my legs.

"A dragon saved you?" Dan said thoroughly confused.

"You okay?" Cody reached toward me but stopped. I nodded, and his hand rubbed down my calf, but it was Draconian's touch that I felt.

Fighting the urge to pull away from him, I pressed my hand down on his, stopping its movements. "I'm better than I was."

"I explained to everyone why you were on your own, and I am sorry for leaving you." Aurelia stood behind me with her hands on my shoulders. Strength surged through me. "I thought you would be okay, but Draconian must have had one of his dragons keeping an eye on you. I will not leave you again."

Called it, I thought to myself. "Sometimes I'm going to be on my own." I scooted toward Cody and rested my head on his shoulder. "I need to figure out how to handle myself."

Cody tenderly slipped his arm around me, and I dove into my story. Panic stole my breath and took me back to Draconian several times. Aurelia's strength flowed into me, counteracting the terror. I paused when I got to the part where Draconian killed me. I wasn't sure if I wanted to tell them about that but decided the truth was the best option.

Cody's face fell. I watched him swallow over the lump in his throat. He opened his mouth, but no sound came out. When he managed to find his voice, it was weak. "You … died?"

"Yeah, it was like the dream I had." I rubbed my thumb over his. "Don't be afraid. Death is peaceful. Torture isn't."

Cody's grip on my arm tightened. "I can't lose you, Dacia."

I clutched his hand and stared into his red-rimmed eyes. "My only regret was that I wouldn't see you again, but even with my abilities, it's hard not to want to die when you're being tortured."

He leaned his forehead against mine and closed his eyes. "You can't think that. You have to come back to us."

"You are giving up too easily," Aurelia said. "We all depend on you."

I threw my hands up in the air. "Have you ever been tortured?"

"No, I have not," Aurelia answered.

"Then you have no idea." I narrowed my eyes. "There was nothing easy about it … except dying."

"I haven't been tortured, but I've been there," Sarah said. "I know what Dacia's going through. Death might be different for everyone, but it was very peaceful for me. When Dacia pulled me back, it was an awful feeling. I was dragged back to a safe life, though. Dacia was dragged back for another round of torture. It would seem quite unbearable compared to the serenity of death."

"Exactly." I didn't want to talk about death anymore. It wasn't like I had a death wish, but if my only choices were death or torture, death seemed the obvious one. To change the subject, I asked the first thing that popped into my head. "Why was the dragon in my dream so upset when I asked his name? Up until that point, I had the impression he respected me."

"I am sure he did." Aurelia's hands tightened on my shoulders for a split second.

"Really?" I asked.

"Yes, your magic is very powerful. Even if he had not seen what you were capable of, he would have sensed your strength." Aurelia sat beside me, resting her hand on my arm. "Immortal beings only give their names out to those we know, those we trust not to hurt us. You are fortunate if any are willing to trust you. That should tell you something about your character."

"But I knew Nefarious' name," I said.

"No. You knew what Sarah's ancestors called him. It is not his true name. His true name bound him here once. That is why he seeks to destroy Earth. The names of immortals can be dangerous."

"What do you mean by that … his name bound him here?" Samantha asked.

"A magician found out his name and kept him here to do his bidding." Her strength slowly seeped into me. "Not many can bind immortals here, but I think Dacia has the power to."

"Wow." Dan looked at me, then Aurelia. "Think of all you could do with that power."

"No, Dan," I said. "That's not something I want."

"Dacia would lose the help of all immortal beings if she tried to control one." Aurelia focused on Dan. Her eyes were hard, and there was no doubt she was the apex predator in the room. "We do not look kindly on it."

"I'm sorry. I didn't realize." Dan sounded ashamed.

I turned toward Aurelia. "Aurelia must not be your true name then."

"Why?" Samantha looked at everyone. "Oh … the whole school would know it."

"Keep Arion's name safe." Aurelia stood, walking toward the window where Arion waited. "He chose to trust all of you with it."

I dropped my head into my hands. "I hope Draconian didn't hear it from me earlier."

"Arion is not the sort of creature Draconian is interested in," Aurelia said, "but he will use him against you if he can."

"Do we go to class?" Samantha looked at her watch.

"Yes," I answered. "You go." Cody's grip on my arm tightened, and I knew he was getting ready to argue. "I need my lesson with Aurelia. I need to know how to prevent Draconian from paralyzing me. I need to know what to do if he does. I can't let this happen again."

"If that's what you want," Cody said.

"I will do my best to help you." Aurelia looked out the window. "Arion and I discussed that while we were away."

"Did you come up with anything?" I twisted my hair around my finger.

She returned her focus to me. "In the words of your kind, we are going to wing it."

"Well, let's get them to their class and get back here." I pressed my hands down on the cushion, hoping I would be able to stand but afraid my legs wouldn't hold me.

"I'll be here when you get back," Sarah told us. "I still want to see what Dacia has been learning."

Hopefully, it will be a quick trip with no problems. Draconian will be really mad that I escaped from him again, I thought to Aurelia.

"You should stay here and show her while I take them." Aurelia stood. "That will give us more time to work."

Cody pulled me to my feet. My muscles felt tender but no longer ached. Cupping my face in his hands, he kissed me gently. "Be careful. Stay safe."

Chapter 24

Worse Than Death

As soon as Aurelia returned, Sarah excused herself. Before her door closed, my body stiffened, and I collapsed to the floor. I couldn't move, couldn't even blink.

"Try to free yourself." Aurelia sounded detached. "Fight back. I know you cannot move, but you can still think. Envision a way out of this."

I got away from Draconian once by teleporting, so I decided that was my best option. I pictured myself across the room. Nothing happened. My chest tightened, and my stomach roiled.

Aurelia's face was pinched whether in determination or remorse I wasn't sure.

Heat built inside me, coursing through my veins. Steam puffed out of my nose, dispersing the air.

"Come on, Dacia. You can do this."

I turned my thoughts from heat to healing. Vitality surged into my body. I pictured myself across the room. Standing by Sarah's door, I closed my eyes and rolled my neck. "Yes."

"Good job." Aurelia paralyzed me again without warning or hesitation. I fell to the ground. "I am truly sorry, Dacia, but this is the only way."

Pain sizzled through my body, crackling through my veins, searing my muscles. A soundless scream tore from my throat. Tears ran over my cheeks.

Aurelia's voice was nearly devoured by the agony. "You need to block out the pain. Once you have done that, you should be able to teleport again."

Excruciating pain radiated through me, leaving me unable to think. I couldn't concentrate on anything else. I felt like I was going to pass out. The room spun. My mind was nearing its threshold. I focused on life, closed my eyes, and pictured Sarah's couch. Sitting there, my muscles ached, but no new pain was inflicted on me.

"I did it." I leaned back and let out a hefty breath.

"Yes, you did. Prepare yourself."

I held my hands up in front of me and shook my head. "I need a break. My body is about to give out on me."

"I am sorry, Dacia, but Draconian would not stop." Anguish flooded her voice. "If you want to be able to fight him off, this is the only way Arion or I could think of."

She paralyzed me again. Pain enveloped my body.

"Fight, Dacia."

I thought about kittens, lambs, butterflies, flowers, and all the wonderful things spring brings. The pain lessened, and my head cleared. Strength returned to my body. In about half the time, I teleported across the room and freed myself from her control.

"Much better." Her compliment helped put my mind at ease. She wasn't doing this for fun. She did it to help me. "I am truly sorry for doing that. I had no idea how to tell you to free yourself."

If there was a muscle in my body that wasn't screaming out in pain, I was unaware of it. What Aurelia did was worse than anything Draconian had done to me.

"You handled yourself well." She smiled at me, and I saw pride in her eyes. "I am impressed by how quickly you freed yourself. Your strength amazes me. The only thing we have not addressed is how to free yourself from Draconian's dungeon, and I think that will have to wait until our next lesson. We should go, or we will be late to pick up Samantha, Dan, and Cody."

My muscles shook when I stepped forward, but I didn't want to use more energy. "Hopefully, with everything you've shown me, Draconian won't be able to get me into his dungeon again anyway. If I can escape from him, like I could you, I don't know how he would capture me. You've shown me how to escape from his dragons and, now hopefully, from him."

Standing at the top of the stairs, my legs trembled. From up here, they looked insurmountable. I put one foot down, and my knee buckled. Clutching the railing, I took the next step. Closing my eyes for a moment, I thought about life, just enough to stop my legs from giving in, but not enough to drain me.

We walked down the steps, and my legs trembled. "I need to find a safe place to teleport to. If I'd've teleported here just a moment after I did, I would've teleported right in front of Sarah's guest."

"You should be able to teleport into your room now that Dan knows about you," Aurelia said. "If you told everybody you needed it to be your safe place, I am sure they would keep it that way for you."

"Most of the time I can count on that," I said. "Because of me, Samantha doesn't have a lot of other friends. She actually told some of them that if they can't get over their problems with me, she doesn't want anything to do with them, but that hasn't worked too well for her."

"For the life of me, I cannot understand why people do not accept you. What you are capable of is amazing." Her face was twisted into a mask of confusion.

"Well, I'm sure a lot of them think it's amazing, but fear controls them. As a general rule, people are scared of what they don't understand. And, let's face it … I don't even understand my differences. I'm just lucky to have the friends I have."

"Maybe so. There are so many differences between humans and …" Aurelia didn't finish that thought.

"And what?" I asked, knowing she wouldn't answer.

She looked at me, and for a second, I thought she would tell me. "Not yet."

"You can't blame me for trying."

"Immortals, that is the only answer I can give right now. I need to be sure you can handle the truth before I tell you anything more. If I rush into it, I could jeopardize everything."

Now I was even more confused. What could be so terrible she wouldn't tell me?

Aurelia and I stood outside Primrose Hall, waiting for the others.

Cody stepped through the doors and stopped. He looked me over from head to foot, and his face fell. "What happened?" He hurried forward. "Take my strength."

"I'm fine. Why?"

"You look like you did after Draconian tortured you," Samantha answered. "You look like you've been through the wringer."

"Oh … uh … yeah." I ran my hands along the side of my head, pulling my hair back. "Aurelia tortured me."

Anger radiated from Cody. His jaw clenched and un-clenched. His blue eyes were hard and icy. "What?" He glared at Aurelia and ran his hand through his hair. "First you leave her. Then you torture her. Care to explain?"

"It was the only way to train her," Aurelia said. "Dacia knows how to escape from Draconian now, and that is what is important."

"It's okay." I put my hand on Cody's chest, pushing him back. "Aurelia did what she had to, and I'll be fine. Let's just get back before Draconian tries to stop us."

"Once we get you back, I need to leave with Arion again," Aurelia said. "We were unable to finish what we were doing."

"Stick around 'til Dacia's safe." Cody's voice was venomous.

"Cody." I curled my fingers around his shirt and pulled him toward me. "Stop it. Aurelia thought I was safe when she left. I couldn't sense Draconian. I wasn't far from the classroom."

"Sorry."

"Dacia is essential to the welfare of this planet," Aurelia said. "What happened was unfortunate, and I will do my best to keep it from happening ever again. However, Dacia is going to have to face Draconian at some point in time, or she will always be looking over her shoulder."

"Not 'til she's ready." Cody stood rigid.

"I am trying to get her ready." Aurelia started walking toward the dorm. "She is almost there."

"Do you really think so?" I twisted my blue t-shirt around my finger.

"Of course you are." Samantha grabbed Dan's hand and followed Aurelia. "You defeated Nefarious. I'm sure you can handle Draconian. This time you have Aurelia and Arion to help you."

I trudged along, every step was agony. "With Aurelia's help today, I might stand a chance against Draconian, but …" I closed my eyes and shook my head. "He has so many dragons."

It was well past midnight when I sensed Aurelia returning to her room. *Is everything okay?* I thought to her.

Dacia, you should be sleeping. You need your rest.

Sleep isn't always peaceful and relaxing. What were you doing anyway? I asked, expecting a non-answer.

Arion and I are trying to recruit allies. Most immortals are afraid of Draconian. His ability to control dragons has sent many fleeing. Several of whom I would normally count on will not come out of hiding until he is stopped.

Help would be good.

Even without it, I believe you can defeat Draconian. You are powerful.

I hope you're right.

Chapter 25

The trail to Falcon Lake twisted through a heavily forested area. The air carried the scent of pine and dank, dark earth. Light flickered through the trees. Squirrels chattered and birds sang.

My friends and I walked in silence, listening for anything out of place. An uneasy feeling clung to my body, threatening to drag me into despair.

While I'd been in the shower, Samantha, Dan, and Cody had talked to Aurelia about going to Falcon Lake for a picnic. They thought a change of pace would be good for me. Surprisingly, Aurelia had agreed.

As soon as we stepped out of the trees, some of my tension dissolved. Samantha and Dan strolled along the lake. Faint traces of their conversation caught on the wind as they got farther away.

"I cannot give you the privacy you desire." Aurelia nodded toward the trees. "I will be over there keeping an eye on you. Stay where I can see you."

"Who's going to keep an eye on you?" I knew she could handle herself, but I also knew she worried about Draconian controlling her.

"Arion." She pointed at the sky. "He is flying above us."

I looked up. The sky was a deep cerulean blue, dotted here and there by puffy clouds. "He must be able to keep me from sensing him. I didn't realize he was there."

"Unless we tell you otherwise, Arion will be around you at all times, Dacia. Draconian thinks of him as a mere horse, not a threat. I believe his arrogance will be his downfall."

"It'd be nice if he had a downfall."

"Everybody does, Dacia." She flipped her golden hair over her shoulder. "Have some faith."

"That's part of the problem." I kicked at the ground, watching rocks tumble into each other. "I have a downfall, and Draconian knows what it is. He will exploit it."

"What's yours?" Cody asked.

"She thinks it is you." Aurelia stood perfectly still, her face expressionless, looking regal. "However, love is an asset, not a liability."

"Draconian *will* use Cody against me. I *won't* be able to let him hurt Cody, so I'll hand Nefarious to Draconian in exchange for Cody's life." I crossed my arms and stared into Aurelia's gold eyes, daring her to contradict me. "A dragon will capture

Cody and me, and even though I could escape, I will let it take me so I can free Cody. Things will go terribly wrong. I've seen it in my dreams so many times. I know you think I need to be optimistic, but I'm not. I'm a realist, and realistically, this can't end well."

"It can." Cody stepped in front of me and took my hands in his. "It will."

A deep sigh escaped my lips, and my shoulders hunched forward. "This isn't how I wanted to spend my day. Can we try to enjoy ourselves?"

"Be careful," Aurelia said. "I will be here if you need me—even if you cannot see me."

Cody and I walked to the water's edge. The gentle waves lapped over my feet. I took a deep breath and tried to relax. I knew what I said had been hard on Cody, but deep down, he had to know it already, even if he couldn't admit it. The ones I loved gave me strength. There was no doubt about that, but at the same time, they were my Achilles' heel.

I looked over my shoulder and saw a gold light shimmering where Aurelia had been, then nothing. I couldn't help but wonder why she disappeared. When Draconian saw us together, he had backed down. Now, I felt like she was setting a trap and using me as bait.

Cody cleared his throat. "I'm your downfall?"

"Do you want the truth?" My voice was as icy as the chill running up my spine. I didn't mean for it to come out like that, but maybe it would help him realize I was serious. "Sit down." We both sat. I dug my feet down into the rocks and rested my hand on Cody's knee. "You're the best thing that's happened to me. You've helped me through so much. Ever since we met, you've been my knight in faded denim, and that's part of the problem. I can't sacrifice you for me or even … or even for the world. You come first. I'd have no problem laying my life down for you. I can't let Draconian hurt you, and we know he won't let me die instead. To save you, I'd give up Nefarious. I'd hand him over and watch the world burn. Unfortunately, Draconian knows this, and he won't stop until he gets what he wants."

Cody stared out over the water, his shoulders hunched. "Keep me safe then. I can't leave and can't let you die for me." He ran a finger from my ear to my neck. My pulse soared, and I closed my eyes. "I'd die for you, too."

"Yeah, but Draconian won't care if you die." I lowered my head, forcing him to lean in to hear me. "That's the problem."

You're right about that, Draconian's voice reverberated in my head. *He's nothing to me, but you … you could be a force to reckon with if you would let me mold you.*

"Cody, run to Aurelia *now*." I pulled him to his feet, then shoved him toward the trees.

"What's wrong?"

"Draconian … I can't sense him, but he's in my head." *Aurelia, I need you.*

As we ran back to the place we'd left her, we saw her reappear. For a moment, I wasn't sure if my eyes were playing a trick on me or if I caught a glimpse of her true identity. I shook my head and brushed the thought away. Right then, Cody's safety was my only concern.

Don't run, Dacia. Stay and play with my friends. The sound of Draconian's laughter cut me up and left me bare.

Shadows raced over the ground, and I looked up to see two dragons, their wings pinned back in a dive. I grabbed Cody's hand and pictured my room.

The rocks, trees, and lake swirled together. My body seemed to suck into my core, pulling Cody along. I squeezed my eyes shut until I felt carpet beneath my feet. The room was empty, safe.

I dropped Cody's hand and stepped away. "I have to go back." Leaving him standing by Big Bird, I teleported back to Falcon Lake. I searched the area for them, finally spotting Samantha's pink shirt through the trees.

"Come on." I held my hands out. "I'll get you out of here." They ran to me, and I grabbed them both by the hand. In the blink of an eye, we stood in our room. "I have to go back to help Aurelia."

"Be careful." I heard Cody's worried voice as I disappeared.

Dragons circled in the sky. One was as white as the new-fallen snow. Muscles rippled as it darted through the air. The beast's head was slender with a bearded chin that flowed into a long neck. Its wings frayed at the edges as if they'd been torn. A long, spiked tail whipped through the air.

The other dragon was azure with scales that glistened in the sunlight. Large frilled ears and two long ivory horns adorned this beast's massive head. Enormous fangs jutted from its mouth.

Aurelia, where are you? Are you okay?

I am fine, Dacia. Get yourself back to safety.

"I can't just leave you here," I shouted.

Then we will both teleport back.

I reappeared in my room. Samantha and Dan huddled together on the couch, and Cody strode toward me, wrapping his arms around me. "You're okay." His breath brushed my cheek.

"Where's Aurelia?" Samantha asked.

"Here." She appeared beside Cody and put her hand on my shoulder. "You did well."

"Thanks."

"I don't think we should go to Falcon Lake again anytime soon." Dan gripped the arm of the couch with white knuckles.

"Probably not." I tried to move to one of the chairs, but Cody's grip tightened on me, holding me in place. I wrapped my arms around his waist and leaned into him, knowing that he needed this. His heart raced against my ear, and his body trembled. I didn't understand why he was acting this way. We'd gotten to safety with no difficulty.

When Cody loosened his grip, I looked up into his face. His eyes were red and his cheeks tear-stained. He smiled at me, but it wasn't convincing. A lump rose in my throat.

"Are you okay?" I asked.

He shook his head before leaning it back against mine.

"Aurelia, can Cody and I go to your room for a minute?"

"Take all the time you need."

Cody started to walk away, but this time, I didn't let go. We teleported into Aurelia's room, and he crumpled against me when we sat on the couch. I ran my fingers through his hair, waiting for him to let me in.

"Watched you disappear." His voice was quiet and broken. "Twice."

"I'm sorry, Cody." I brushed my thumbs over his cheeks, wiping away his tears. "I had to go back for them."

"I know, but I …" His voice cracked. "What if you didn't come back?"

My hand slipped down to his shoulder as I bent to kiss his forehead. He sat up, pressing me against the arm of the couch, and crushed his lips against mine. His kiss was desperate and fierce. His hands traveled up and down my spine, pulling me against him. Then he pushed me down, propping himself above me. My hands tangled in his hair, before moving to his shoulder blades and pulling him down on top of me.

He made a low sound in the back of his throat, arching his neck. He brought his lips back down on mine. Fire flowed through my veins. His mouth moved to my neck, and a wave of desire crashed over me.

I pulled his mouth back to mine, then slipped my hands under the hem of his shirt. My fingers explored his back: tracing over his ribs and up his spine, feeling the flexed muscles in his shoulders. I moaned softly against his lips.

The kiss deepened, and he wrapped his arms around me, pulling me against him. His lips veered off mine again, kissing my chin, my cheek, my ear, and my neck. He lifted his head and looked down at me. The sadness was gone from his face. His eyes were lit by desire, his cheeks flushed, and his lips swollen. "I love you." His voice was husky.

"I love you, too." I brushed my fingers over his lips. "Are you okay?"

He nodded. His hand drew a path from my arm to my shoulder and up my neck. Then gazing into my eyes, he brought his mouth down on mine again. This time the kiss was gentle, intensity and desperation gone.

I lay on my side with my head on Cody's chest. He squeezed my shoulders, and with his other hand, he traced circles on my arm. "They're worried about us, aren't they?" Cody asked.

"Probably."

"We should go back."

"Only if you're ready."

Chapter 26
Unlikely Allies

$\mathcal{D}$an, Samantha, Cody, and I walked to class. Aurelia and Arion were trying to recruit help, so I was on high alert.

Something rustled in the trees, and I stepped in front of the others. A deer ran across the trail in front of us, and a nervous laugh escaped from me.

Three more deer darted through the trees, separating me from my friends. The hair on the back of my neck lifted. Something was wrong.

Movement beneath the shadow of the trees stopped me. I stared into the woods, but the light flickered through the leaves, constantly shifting, making it impossible to see what was hidden behind them.

"What is it?" Cody stepped up beside me.

I positioned myself between him and the forest. Glancing into the foliage again, I shook my head. "Maybe nothing." I waved them ahead of me, wanting to keep them in my sights.

Following my friends, I watched the trees through my peripheral vision. Something was there, but all I could see were the greens, browns, and blacks of the timber. I couldn't make out its size or shape. I didn't know if it was a deer, a moose, a bear, or a dragon.

A twig snapped, and I stopped and stared into the woods. Nothing.

Was I letting my imagination get the better of me?

Realizing how far ahead of me everyone had gotten, I pulled my focus from the forest and jogged to catch up. I skidded to a halt when the smallest dragon I had ever seen stepped through the undergrowth. It was only a little taller than an average-size horse.

Even in the open, it was difficult to see the beast. Its scales were all the colors of the forest, camouflaging it, making it blend with the trees, and keeping it unnoticed until it was ready to be seen.

The dragon lowered its horned head and flames burned in the back of its throat. Its tail swung around, trapping Dan, Samantha, and Cody. A fin opened on the end of it, blocking them from my view.

I'm going to get you out of this. I sent the thought to each of my friends, hoping it worked and didn't go to the dragon, too.

"Let them go." Initially, I'd thought I could fight this beast, but I wasn't sure anymore. I didn't know how strong its tail was or how badly it could hurt my friends. The most menacing thing about it seemed to be the spikes on the backs of its elbows and knees and along its spine, but looks could be deceiving. "Take me to Draconian instead."

"He wants them, not you," it said in a sibilant voice.

"He only wants them so he can use them as bait to trap me"—I stepped toward the beast—"but I'm giving myself to you willingly. He will reward you greatly if you take me to him in their place."

The dragon moved toward me without relinquishing its hold on my friends. Its head cocked to the side like it was contemplating what I said. "What does he want with you?"

"I am a powerful magician."

The beast leaned its head back and let out a strange guttural sound that I assumed was laughter. "You must take me for a fool."

Aurelia told me that immortal creatures would be able to sense my powers, so I was thrown off by the dragon's response. "I also have something he wants," I told it. "Take me to him. If he really did want them and not me, you are clever and cunning enough to capture them again."

"Yes," the beast agreed. "Dragons are so much more intelligent than puny, insignificant, worthless humans."

In a fraction of a second, the dragon turned and grabbed me in its claws before leaping into the air with ease.

Get back to the room. I spoke into my friends' heads. *I can get away from him, but I need you safe first.*

I let the dragon carry me nearly all of the way to Draconian's castle before I engulfed myself in flames. Once I did, I slipped out of its talons.

A deafening roar filled the air, followed by a burst of flames. "You tricked me!"

"And, you fell for it. You should've listened when I told you I was a powerful magician." I teleported back to the place where the dragon had ambushed us. The others were gone. I breathed a sigh of relief before teleporting to my room. I expected them to be waiting for me, but when nobody else was there, I contacted Aurelia. *I need your help*, I said trying not to sound too desperate.

What is wrong?

We were ambushed. I tricked the dragon into taking me instead, but the others aren't back. We need to find them!

Dacia, Draconian's voice filled my head.

Aurelia, Draconian is in my head.

Wait for me, she said. *Do not do anything until I get there.*

What do you want? I focused on Draconian. Anger squeezed my chest and curled my hands into tight fists.

Bring Nefarious to me, and you can have your friends back.

What makes you think I won't walk in there, right under your nose, and take them back? I filled my voice with as much arrogance as I could muster.

I considered that scenario, so I decided to take it out of play. Your friends are in three separate places, each of them guarded by one of my most ferocious pets. If you even try to rescue one of them, that dragon will signal the others, and your friends will pay dearly for your insubordination. You can't save them all. Don't keep me waiting for too long. My dragons do get hungry.

Let them go!

No, I don't think I will. His voice crashed through my head. I pressed my hands to my ears, but it did nothing to block the noise. *Their insignificant lives are in your hands. Bring Nefarious to me!*

I sounded defeated when I relayed the news to Aurelia. *Draconian has them, and they're not all in one place. If I try to rescue one of them ...* my thought trailed off. *I'm scared, Aurelia.*

Wait for Arion and me. Do not do anything without us, Dacia. We will get them back. I promise.

Hurry! Please.

While I waited for Aurelia, I paced the room, chewing my fingernails. Then I plopped down on the couch, hugged Cody's pillow to my chest, and breathed in his scent. I fought the urge to go to Sarah's office and force her to tell me where she'd hidden Nefarious. Clutching Cody's pillow to my face, I screamed into it.

When I pulled the pillow down, Aurelia stood in front of me. "What took so long?" I shouted.

Aurelia stood in front of me with her hands behind her back. She was dressed all in black, and I wondered how she thought that would help conceal her. Sparkly skin tended to stand out.

"I am sorry, Dacia. I should have stayed with you today," she said, completely ignoring my question.

"It's not your fault." All of my anger drained away, leaving me weak. I tossed the pillow down and put my head in my hands. "I couldn't keep them safe." Tears pooled in my eyes, blurring my vision. "I had one job, and I couldn't do it."

"Dacia, we will get them back." She sat beside me.

"Why?" I tried to keep my voice from cracking. "Why did he take them?"

Wrapping her arm around my shoulders, she answered, "He is testing you—your determination, your strength, and most importantly your abilities. He is trying to see how far he can push you before you give up or decide to stand against him."

"So … Draconian won't leave them alone until I hand over Nefarious or die?" I bent forward over my knees, trying to make myself as small as possible.

She narrowed her eyes. "If you are this negative, it will be more difficult to win." She squeezed my shoulder, and I winced at her strength. "You were chosen for a reason."

"They weren't." I sat up, raised my hands, and dropped them again. "I can't let him hurt them."

"We can always hope he will grow tired of this game."

I sat there, feeling sorry for myself. Then my resolve hardened. I'd given into grief. Now it was time to act.

"We need to hurry." I sprang to my feet. "We can't leave them with Draconian any longer than we have to."

"We will get them back." Aurelia patted the couch, but I didn't sit. "I am sorry for making you wait. I spent the day trying to find help."

I tucked my hands into my pockets and paced. "And … did you have any luck?" *Why are we talking about this instead of freeing Cody?* I winced at the thought. *And Samantha and Dan.*

"Not as much as I would have liked. Hopefully, it will be enough."

The way she said it gave me a bad feeling. I stopped in front of her. "Who or what is helping us? Do you have a plan?"

"They are called grigs. They are small enough that we can send them into Draconian's castle without the risk of being seen. We will have the grigs search for Cody, Dan, and Samantha. Once we know where they are, we will teleport in, grab them and get out. If we synchronize it, we should be able to get in and out before they know what is happening. Because they are under Draconian's control, the dragon's reflexes are slower than they normally would be. That should give us a small advantage."

"Well, that's a scary thought." I shook my head and sighed. "Their reflexes are so much faster than mine. How fast would they normally be?"

"Of course, they seem fast to you. You must remember you are talking about creatures that are centuries or even millennia older than you. They have had hundreds of years to perfect their abilities."

"Who else is going in with us?"

"Arion."

"I didn't realize he was here. I can't feel his presence."

"He is bringing the grigs. He should arrive any minute."

I couldn't bear the sound of silence. I knew it would cause my mind to wander, and I would imagine my friends being tortured. "Tell me more about them while we're waiting. I've never heard of a grig before."

"Most people have not. They are mischievous little sprites who love playing tricks on people."

She couldn't be serious. Could she? My friends were in danger, and she was sending in tricksters. "And we're supposed to trust them?"

"Yes, Dacia, we have to trust them. They are all we have. They promised to be on their best behavior."

"I hope so."

"Grigs have a head, body, and arms like you would expect to see on any fey creature, but their legs and wings are cricket-like," she said. "Their hearing is exceptional, far superior to that of a human."

The creatures my imagination conjured were hideous. I shook my head, deciding I should just wait to see them. "That should help them find my friends."

"Yes, it should." She pulled a gold strand of hair off her shoulder and incinerated it. "Unicorns will fight to the death to protect the grigs that live in their forests."

"Have you seen unicorns?" I cocked my head, remembering them showing up when I read her aura. But had she actually seen them? "Are they overrated?"

"Yes, I have seen them, and though some tend to be excessively vain, they are extraordinary creatures. Arion was trying to get a reaction from you when he told you they were overrated. Most young girls dream about seeing unicorns, and he knows that." She smiled. "Shall I continue?"

"Yes, please."

"Grigs enjoy playing pranks on unsuspecting passersby. They do not ever intentionally harm anyone and always make up for their tomfoolery. They are mischievous, not cruel."

When Arion arrived with the grigs, Aurelia explained her plan. While she did, I couldn't help but stare at them. All three of them had wild, dark green hair. Their skin was pale blue, except for their legs which were brown and hairy. They were a lively bunch who didn't seem to have a care in the world. When they talked, their voices were shrill. I had to strain to understand what they said.

"Dacia, this is Persimmon, Okapi, and Tinamou. They have generously agreed to help us rescue your friends from Draconian," Aurelia said, sounding very formal.

"Thank you so much." Had they been bigger, I would have tried to shake their hands. I didn't know what to do or what proper etiquette was.

"The pleasure is ours, Big One," Persimmon said in a screechy voice. She was the only girl. She had on a bright purple shirt and skirt that clashed with her hair. A tiny knife hung on a belt at her side.

"It is an honor to be of service to you." Tinamou bowed. He was more subtle looking in a brown tunic with bright red buttons. He had a knife at his side, but he also carried what appeared to be a tiny instrument.

"Is that ... is that a violin?" I asked.

"Actually, it is a fiddle," he answered. "With it, I have the power to make creatures dance until I cease playing."

"Does it work on dragons?" I asked in a skeptical tone.

"Most likely, it will not." Okapi bowed slightly when he answered me. "We shall go now."

"Be careful," Aurelia told them, and with that, they disappeared. "Dacia, the grigs would prefer it if you keep them to yourself until this is all over. They do not want word spreading that they helped free your friends."

"Why not?" I sat on the edge of the chair, but restless energy pulled me back to my feet.

"They are afraid of the repercussions they could face if Draconian found out. They would rather you did not mention them to anyone, including Cody, Samantha, and Dan. They will not come back here after we free your friends."

"Okay." It seemed odd the grigs wouldn't want my friends to know they saved them, but if that was what they wanted, I would respect their wishes. As long as my friends were freed, I didn't care about the rest.

Flames sparked in my palm while I paced. I'd been slowly building my stamina since Aurelia told me magic was like any other muscle. I just hoped I'd have enough for tonight.

It felt like the grigs had been gone for hours. I pulled out my phone and looked at the clock on it. It had to have frozen. According to it, they'd only been gone for mere minutes.

With each step I took, fear clenched my heart tighter. I let go of the flames. Trying to distract myself, I made electricity dance over invisible fingertips.

Aurelia sat motionless on the couch. Her head was tilted as if listening for something.

Dacia, Draconian's voice hammered against my skull.

My magic dissolved, and I stopped pacing. I closed my eyes, trying to hold my terror back. *Draconian.*

Why are you delaying?

The condemnation in his voice twisted my stomach. I hated myself for not being strong enough to confront him, to end his control of the dragons, and to stop him from hurting anyone or anything else.

Why haven't you brought Nefarious to me? Do you want your friends to suffer needlessly?

My breath caught. He didn't know about the grigs. Everybody was still safe. Silently, I thanked God. Then I answered, keeping my words confident, *I don't keep Nefarious tucked under my pillow. I have to get him. I'll be there, but you have to give me time.*

Time is nearly out. Draconian sent me an image of a black dragon guarding Cody. Cody leaned against the wall. His blue t-shirt was covered in blood.

If you hurt them, you will never see Nefarious!

We'll see about that. Won't we?

"Dacia, is everything okay?" Aurelia asked.

"Draconian wants to know what is taking so long. He told me the clock is ticking." My voice sounded strained, fearful.

"We will have them out of there before he knows what is happening." She stood beside me. "Everything is going to be okay."

"I hope you're right," I mumbled. "He knows we'll come for them. He'll be waiting."

"Do not give up hope." Aurelia rested her hand on my shoulder. "We will get them back."

I dragged my fingers through my hair and focused on breathing. *Inhale ... exhale ... inhale ... exhale.* "How can you be so sure?"

She raised one shoulder to her ear. "Why not be optimistic?"

"You're right. It's just ... well, I knew this would happen, and I'm terrified." I looked into her golden eyes, hoping to find some answers, but there was nothing. "What if something happens to them?"

"We will save them."

I shook her arm off my shoulder and paced again. It seemed like an eternity passed before Aurelia turned to me and said, "The grigs found your friends. Are you ready?" She told Arion and me where to teleport to. "As soon as you have them, teleport back here."

She turned invisible, and I followed suit. "Wait! How do I teleport out of the dungeon if I have to?"

"You know how you can keep Draconian from controlling you, but I do not. With magic, some things are not as easy for one person as they are for another. My best advice is for you to want it with all of your being. Even then, you may not succeed."

My shoulders sagged forward, and my chin settled on my chest. Taking a deep breath, I slowly raised my head. "Let's hope it works today."

Arion, Aurelia, and I teleported into Draconian's castle simultaneously. I found myself in the room where Draconian had held me prisoner, where he had killed me. I saw myself lying on the table. Draconian stood over me, and electrical charges flowed through my body. Blood dripped from my charred temples. Then my body convulsed, and I was dead.

I shook my head, chasing away the image. I took one more look at the table where I had been welcomed into death's arms. As I turned away, my nostrils were assaulted by the smell of rotting flesh. I stumbled backward when I saw the dragon guarding Cody. He was black as midnight. I could sense its desire to tear Cody limb from limb. It was with a great deal of restraint that he held himself back.

Cody slumped against the granite wall. His skin was pale. Dark circles rimmed his eyes. He watched the dragon as if waiting for it to lunge.

My heart broke at the sight of him, and I imagined Samantha and Dan were no better off.

Cody, I'm here. I'll be standing by you in just a second. Don't be surprised when I grab hold of you.

Cody's expression didn't change. He didn't let on that he'd heard me, didn't give me away.

The dragon's head lowered. His nostrils flared, and he scanned the room. *He can smell me,* I thought to Aurelia.

I have Dan. Arion has Samantha. On the count of three, get out of there. One ... two... three.

The dragon lifted his snout and prowled toward me. I teleported right next to Cody and grabbed his arm. With every fiber of my being, I willed myself out of the room. Nothing happened.

Turning his head, the dragon stared right at me. I wondered if I'd lost my invisibility or if the beast's bronze eyes could see through it.

I ran, pulling Cody behind me. He hesitated at the wall, but I pulled him forward. Resting my hand against the cold stone, I pushed Cody through, following close behind him.

The dragon's claws tore through my back. I screamed. The pain was blinding, all-encompassing. I fell forward, pushing us through the wall, knocking Cody to the ground.

Blood ran down my back and pooled on the ground. I clutched Cody's hand and pictured us in my dorm room. Blackness crept in at the edges of my vision.

"Dacia." Cody's voice sounded far away. "Please wake up, Dacia. I don't know where we are. I need you. Please, Dacia, please wake up." Cody knelt above me, his hands grasping my shoulders.

"Was I dreaming?" I asked. My back throbbed, and everything was blurry. I blinked several times, trying to clear my eyes. Seeing the blood on Cody's clothes and the desperation in his eyes, everything came back to me.

We were on the edge of a rocky cliff. Stunted trees sprouted up sporadically. Far below us, moonlight reflected off lakes.

"Oh, God. I could've killed us."

The whites of Cody's eyes shone in the pale light. "Don't know where we are." Panic twisted his voice. "Don't know where to go."

Scenes from the day flashed before my eyes—the camouflaged dragon surprising us and carrying me off, my friends kidnapped, grigs, Draconian's castle, the dragon attacking me. "Aurelia and Arion … they were supposed to save Samantha and Dan." My voice was thick. "Did they make it out?"

"Don't know." He cupped my face in his hands. "Can you get us back?"

I tried to move, but my body seized. Pain sucked the air from my lungs and blackened my vision. "No." The word was a whimper.

"Take my strength, Dacia." Cody lay on the ground alongside me.

I siphoned off his energy, knowing I couldn't take enough to heal myself. "How long?"

"Feels like hours. Maybe fifteen or twenty minutes." An uncertain smile lifted his lips. "Time stopped when Draconian came to the room and took us to his castle. That dragon kept saying how satisfying a meal I would make. It was awful. Then you came, and everything was going to be okay. But, you're not okay. What happened?"

"The dragon …" My words caught in my throat. "Thank God he got me, not you." Focusing on life, I healed myself a little more. "Help me stand."

Cody pulled me to my feet. I wobbled like a newborn foal. He wrapped his arms around me, careful not to touch my back.

Once I thought I had control of myself, I closed my eyes and concentrated on every detail of my room. I didn't want to screw up again. When I opened them, we stood in front of the couch. Dan and Samantha huddled up against each other. Black circles rimmed their wide eyes, making their faces even paler.

"Dacia," Samantha said. "You guys are okay. We were so scared. We expected to find you waiting for us here, but when you weren't, Aurelia took off. We haven't seen her since. We were scared Draconian would show up and kidnap us again."

My legs wobbled, and I fought dizziness and nausea. I reached out to steady myself, but there was nothing there to hold onto. I fell to my hands and knees.

"Oh my, God, Dacia. I had no idea …" Cody's words faded. When he spoke again, the husky timbre of his voice surprised me. "You need to heal yourself."

"Can't." My arms and legs trembled. I fought to steady them, to find the strength to go after Aurelia. "Need to find Aurelia."

"No, Dacia," Dan said. "You have to heal yourself. I'm not sure how you're even alive."

Aurelia, I thought. *Arion.*

Dacia, where are you? Are you all right? Is Cody with you? Arion's voice sounded panicked.

In my room. Cody with me.

Aurelia left to find you. I will bring her back.

Thank you, Arion. The room spun. Then everything went black. When I woke up, I lay on my stomach on the couch. Aurelia stood over me with her hands on my back.

"Take it easy," she said. "Your wound was severe. I have no idea how you made it back here. You should have died."

"Glad … you're okay." My voice scratched my throat.

Aurelia's strength flowed into me. "Cody, can you lend Dacia some energy."

"Whatever she needs." He sat on the floor in front of the couch and grasped my hand.

Closing my eyes, I focused on healing, but my powers didn't respond. "Aurelia, I can't feel even a flicker of energy."

"I believe you depleted your magic, keeping yourself alive." I heard something in her voice I hadn't expected. Fear. "You will need to rest."

"I can't." I looked at my friends. It would be amazing if they didn't suffer from PTSD. "I need to confront Draconian so they don't have to worry about being carried off by dragons."

"You can't just go off and challenge him. You need to be ready." Samantha sounded stern.

"We're going to stand by your side," Dan agreed. "But you can't even move right now. Don't look for a battle until you can win it."

"I can't let this go on forever. Worrying … wondering if you guys are safe … I can't keep doing that."

"You won't, Dacia." Cody rubbed his thumb along my hand. "You'll know when it's time. You can't rush it. This is your destiny, and you're on its timeline. It's not on yours."

"Your friends have been blessed with intelligence," Aurelia said. "You should listen to them."

"Maybe … but that doesn't mean they're right. If I don't do something soon, it's going to be too late."

Dacia! Draconian's voice blasted through my head.

I squeezed my eyes shut, wincing.

How dare you! How dare you come into my castle uninvited and steal from me! You and your friends will pay for this!

Cody rubbed his thumb along my forehead. "You okay?"

"Draconian … is really angry."

"What did he say?" Aurelia asked.

"That we're going to pay."

My dragon enjoyed the taste of your blood. He longs for more.

Chapter 27
Nightmares For All

Dragons plunge at me from every angle, soaring back into the darkened sky before they strike. Their master's rage is mirrored on their faces. If he would allow them to, they would tear me apart.

My stomach twists. The knots trying to double me over, but I keep a brave face for Cody. Dragons circle where he stands near Falcon Lake. I can't figure out how to get to him without the beasts attacking.

Draconian strolls out of the forest, his green robe snagging on branches. Dark anger simmers in his eyes. "How will you save him this time, Dacia?"

"Let him go." My voice is strong and holds the threat of retribution. "This is between us."

Draconian focuses on Cody and strokes his beard as if in consideration. "I don't think so." He returns his attention to me. "If I keep him here, you'll be less likely to disappear."

I step toward him, but a cobalt dragon lands between us, baring foot-long fangs at me. "As long as my friends are in danger, you'll never get Nefarious."

A sinister smirk creeps across Draconian's lips. "I believe you've forgotten something."

"What's that?" I stare at my fingernails as if contemplating a manicure.

"I don't think you'll live through this confrontation. I don't have to bring you back from Death's doors."

My breath catches in my throat for an instant, and fear flashes across my face.

"You're right to be scared." He strides toward me. "For the last time, hand over Nefarious."

"I can't."

"Once you're gone and nobody is around to save your friends, they will hand him over." He is right. He knows it, and so do I.

Waves of rage surge inside me, and for the first time in months, I worry I'll lose control of my powers. I need to channel this energy—to use it to free Cody and me.

Draconian shrugs. "Have it your way." Paralyzed, I fall to the ground.

Knowing I can free myself, I bring to mind images of life, but my anger swells, washing them away. Pain drives my thoughts further back. I'm unable to move, unable to focus, unable to control my rage.

"What's wrong, Dacia?" Draconian taunts. "Not as strong as you thought? Cody can't hear you crying for help. We shouldn't deprive him of that, should we?"

The scream tears from my throat, ripping my vocal cords. Electrical charges flow through my body. The cry becomes distant, then nonexistent. The pain is gone. Peace settles over me. *Cody needs me. What will happen to him without me?* The boat drifts to shore. I think about life. Unlike when Draconian jerked me back from death, my spirit slowly returns to my body.

Draconian saunters toward Cody. My body trembles, and I don't know if my legs will hold me. Determined and unsteady, I climb to my feet. I feel disoriented, but I have to stop Draconian. Lightning bolts shoot from my fingers, but in my condition, none of them hit their mark.

"I gave you to him!" Draconian whips around. "Why did Death send you back?"

"He didn't." I fight to keep my voice steady. "I wasn't ready to cross over. Did you really think I'd leave Cody with you?"

Draconian stumbles backward. I can tell by the look on his face he hadn't realized I'm powerful enough to cheat death on my own. "So, you're going to make this more of a challenge."

"I'm not taking the easy way out so you can torture my friends." I step toward him. "You're not going to win."

"I always win! Always!"

"Not this time." I jab my finger at him, then turn it toward the ground. "This time I win."

Draconian raises his hand, and I fall to the ground, paralyzed. Images of life fill my mind. My body relaxes, and when

I'm able to move, I teleport to Cody. The black dragon clamps his jaws shut around my waist. His fangs pierce through my flesh and into my organs. Life drains from my body. When the dragon releases his grip, I crumple to the ground. Blood pools around me. Cody pulls me toward him. His fingers run through my hair while he sobs. Then while I lie there wondering if my life is over, I realize I can't feel any pain. A heavy silence fills the air. The background fades, and the last things I see are Cody's tear-filled eyes.

"Dacia." The whisper was barely audible. "Dacia." This time it was louder and had an edge of panic in it. "Dacia, please. Please wake up."

I forced my eyes open. At first, I had trouble making out shapes. Shadows moved against a darker background. As my vision cleared, I realized Aurelia stood over me. Cody was beside her. "Dacia," his voice was filled with relief. "Thank God. I ... I didn't think you'd wake up this time."

"If they had waited any longer to get me, we might have found out the answer to your question." Aurelia's voice was somber. "I am not sure you would have lived through this."

If my wounds are that bad, why can't I feel anything? Am I paralyzed? Oh, God, please no. My eyes fluttered shut.

"Dacia, stay with me," Cody said.

Am I going to be okay? I thought to Aurelia. *I can't feel anything. I can't move.*

I think you will be fine, Dacia. It might take until morning to heal completely. If I were you, I would not try to move. Let your body recover.

Okay. "Sorry I woke you."

"You didn't." Cody focused somewhere over my head. "Had a nightmare and woke up. You were covered in blood. You weren't breathing. Made Samantha get Aurelia." Tears choked his voice. "Thought I lost you. Without Aurelia … who knows?" He swiped his hand over his red-rimmed eyes. "We might've found out if you can die."

"We've all had nightmares tonight." Samantha's voice sounded small, like she wasn't sure if I was going to pull through either.

"Ours just aren't as bad as yours," Dan added.

"You seem to be handling this better," I said.

He shrugged. "I've seen a lot since the first time I stayed over here." He squeezed Samantha's shoulders. "Besides, somebody needed to be a rock."

"I have given you all the strength I can." Aurelia pulled her hands off mine. "Try to heal yourself a little more before you go back to sleep." She descended the ladder and left.

"You okay, Dacia?" Cody's words caressed my cheek.

"Aurelia thinks I will be."

"But, what do *you* think?" Samantha asked.

"I think I hope Aurelia's right." I tried to move to see her, but my body didn't respond. "I'm not sure. I can't feel any pain."

"That's good. Isn't it?" Dan asked.

"I'm afraid I'm paralyzed." My voice rose, and my heart raced. Breath entered and retreated from my lungs too quickly to do my body any good.

I watched Cody put his hand on top of mine to comfort me, but I couldn't feel it there. "You're gonna be okay." His fingers squeezed mine. "If you could feel your wounds, you wouldn't want to be alive right now." Fear and doubt clouded his eyes and were written in the lines of his face.

"Thanks, Cody." He was probably right, but what if he wasn't? "We should get some sleep," I said. "Morning comes early."

"Yeah, way too early." Samantha sighed.

"You didn't scream," Dan said quietly.

"It happened fast." *But I screamed before that.* I had seen the pained expression on Cody's face, seen him watch me die.

The room darkened, but I refused to close my eyes. If I fell asleep again, I didn't know if I'd survive another nightmare. I tried to focus on healing, but I kept seeing dragons, fangs, violence, and death. *Concentrate, Dacia.*

Eventually, my eyelids became so heavy I couldn't force them to reopen. I had no choice but to sleep.

Draconian waits with his dragons. I'm alone. I won't have to fight for anybody but myself. While Draconian saunters toward me, I check out my surroundings. We stand in a clearing in the middle of a forest.

Draconian stops a few feet from me, his hands lifted in front of him. "Can we talk, please?"

"Why?" I close my eyes and rub my face. "I already know what you have to say. You know my answer. Neither of us will give in."

"Violence doesn't seem to be working, so I thought we could try to solve this problem diplomatically." He waves his hand. "I would like to have Nefarious for my collection. I won't free him. I just want him. I would also like to train you, Dacia.

You could be the greatest sorceress of all time if you would let me help you hone your skills."

"Nefarious is safely hidden away from all of us … where he should be. Hopefully, he will stay there for eternity," I say. "And, as far as being the greatest sorceress of all time, I would rather be a normal college kid right now. I'd love to have a normal life with normal worries and struggles."

"But … you could be magnificent."

Stifling a humorless laugh, I say, "I don't wanna be."

"How can you not want to live up to your potential?" He slams the back of one hand against the palm of his other. "Why do you want to be average … when you could be extraordinary?"

"I don't want to control everything and everyone. I want to live and let live. I want a normal, wonderful life." It is like explaining something to a brick wall. He can't comprehend what I'm saying.

"I'll have to keep you captive until you see the light. You will be my protégée!"

Before he has a chance to paralyze me, I teleport away. *Is that really what he wants? Why?*

Chapter 28

"*D*acia."

"What?" My eyes jerked open. "Is something wrong?"

"No, it's morning." Cody's voice was soft, timid. "How're you?"

"Don't know." I tried to sit up but couldn't. My breath accelerated. I felt like a bug trapped in a spider web. *Why? Did Draconian do something to me, or were my powers diminishing?* I tried to keep my expression neutral, to hide my fear. "C-could you …" I cleared my throat. "Can you get Aurelia?" I could've tried speaking to her mind, but I was afraid my thoughts were too scattered.

"Guys … no talking." Samantha yawned. "It's too early."

"Sorry, Sam," I said, not wanting to worry her yet.

"Dacia can't move," Cody practically yelled at her. "Sorry I woke you."

"Cody, calm down." I stared at the ceiling, unable to do anything else. "Losing your temper doesn't help anyone."

"Is there something I can do?" Dan asked.

"No, Cody's going to get Aurelia." I could've sent Dan to get her, but Cody needed something to do.

"Be right back. Don't worry. You'll be okay." He ran out the door.

As much as I wanted to, I didn't share his opinion. If I was going to heal, it should've happened by now. Something was wrong. I couldn't help but wonder if I'd ever be able to move again.

"I'm sorry, Dacia," Samantha climbed out of her loft. "I assumed you'd be fine by morning. You're always fine by morning."

"Don't worry about it." I tried to sound confident, but I just wanted to cry. "I know you didn't mean anything."

Dacia, Draconian said. *Are you ready to face me?*

Not this morning. I have class. I couldn't let him find out I was paralyzed. If he knew, there'd be no end to the havoc he'd wreak on my friends.

Maybe later this week ... maybe you won't be scared stiff by then.

"That was weird." The urge to pull my hand through my hair was overwhelming. The action helped me center myself.

"What was weird?" Aurelia asked.

Her voice startled me. I hadn't heard her and Cody come back. "Draconian wanted to know if I was ready to face him."

"It seems a little odd that he contacted you." Her voice was closer, but I still couldn't see her. "Did he say anything out of the ordinary?"

"He asked if I was ready to face him." I shrugged my shoulders, but they didn't move. "He must be as anxious to get this over with as I am."

"Maybe." Aurelia didn't sound convinced. "Try to sit up."

I tried to force myself into a sitting position, but my body didn't respond. My heart pounded in my ears, drowning out everything else. Sweat beaded at my temples.

Aurelia placed her hands on my stomach and closed her eyes. When she opened them, she said, "Maybe something was still trying to heal. Now, try again."

As I tried to sit up, I realized what Draconian had said earlier. "He said something about being scared stiff. Do you think he has something to do with me not being able to move?" The words raced off my tongue.

"What do you do when he tries to control you?" Cody asked.

"Yeah, try that," Samantha said.

Aurelia pulled her hands back. "If that does not work, try to teleport."

"It's worth a shot," Dan added his two cents worth.

I closed my eyes and concentrated on clearing my thoughts. "It's not working." Tears welled up behind my eyelids, and a feeling of despair threatened to overwhelm me.

"I am going to hold your hand," Aurelia said. "Teleport somewhere safe."

"Where?" I asked.

"Try Dan and Cody's room." Samantha sounded wide awake now. "Nobody is staying there. It should be empty."

I concentrated on Cody's room. I moved through space and fell to the ground with a thud. The room was dark and smelled stuffy. I needed to remember to tell him to open his window and air it out.

"Are you okay?" Aurelia asked.

"Still can't move." I grew more disheartened.

"We are going to teleport further away to see what happens," Aurelia said. "I will lead the way."

We teleported to a cave heaped with treasure. I staggered back. "Where are we?" Gold, jewels, and art filled the enormous cavern.

"You can move again."

Spinning in a circle, I stared in amazement at the wealth contained in the room. "Yeah, but where are we?"

"Sometimes Arion is here." Her eyes twinkled, reflecting the treasure. "I figured it would be safe. Apparently, Draconian had you under a spell."

"Yeah, I guess." I pulled my hand through my hair, then held it in front of my face, watching my fingers wiggle. "Why couldn't I free myself?"

"If he combined his magic with one of the dragon's, it would be far superior to yours," she said. "I hoped that bit of information had eluded him, but judging from this, he may have figured it out."

"Great, so what can I expect now?"

She stood with her hands behind her back, ignoring the treasure like only someone who'd been there several times before could. "I do not know, Dacia. Maybe this is just his magic. Maybe it has nothing to do with dragons."

What kind of things can he do to me if he combines his magic with the dragons'? Will I be able to stand a chance against that kind of power? I shivered and hoped I would never find out. "We should get back. The others probably wonder what's going on."

When we got back to the room, Samantha and Dan sat huddled together. Cody paced, rubbing the back of his neck. His hand fell to his side. He strode across the room, pulling me into his arms, and rested his forehead against mine.

Samantha let out a relieved sigh. "You're okay."

"Yeah." I ran my fingers along Cody's jaw and stepped back. "We had to teleport farther away to break the spell, but it was Draconian."

"I don't know how you do this day after day," Dan said.

"I don't have a choice." I laughed humorlessly. "If I did, I think I'd choose a normal life."

"Would you?" Aurelia raised a golden eyebrow. "Could you really sit back and see evil happen around you and not try to stop it? Unlike most, you have the power to make things better."

"Probably not"—I shook my head—"but … ignorance is bliss. If I wasn't directly involved, I might not know any of this was going on."

"I imagine anyone who's ever been in a situation like this wished it wasn't them." Samantha fiddled with her bracelet. "But, you rose to the challenge, and that makes you a hero."

"I wouldn't say that."

"I would," Aurelia, Dan and Cody echoed the sentiment.

I looked down to keep them from noticing my blush. "Thanks."

"We're going to be late for class if we don't get moving." Dan stood, reaching his hand down to Samantha.

"I'm skipping." I held my shirt out in front of me. "I'm covered in blood, my pajamas are ripped to shreds, and I need a shower."

"I'll stay," Cody said.

"That sounds like a good idea to me." Dan patted Samantha's shoulder.

"Hmph … fine." Samantha sounded frustrated. "I don't want to be taken hostage any more than either of you, but I hate skipping class."

"It sounds like a wonderful idea to me," Aurelia said. "I think you will all be safer this way. Too much has happened over the last couple of days."

I took a long shower. It was meant to be relaxing, but my mind kept wandering. I wanted to know where Draconian's newfound power came from and how to stop him. *Was there a way? Could I put an end to this?*

I dressed in jean shorts and a black graphic tee and was lacing up my sneakers when Draconian's voice echoed in my head. *How's my future apprentice?*

I wanted to come up with a witty response, but the best that I could think of was, *I'll let you know if I meet her.*

You, Dacia. Anger inhabited his voice.

Unmoved by your desire to control me.

What a pity. Sarcasm dripped from his words. *I noticed you skipped class this morning. Is something wrong?*

Nothing I can't handle.

You have two weeks. If I don't have Nefarious in two weeks, I will kill your friends. Do you understand?

I will face you in two weeks if you swear to leave all of us alone until then. If these are to be my last two weeks, I want to live them peacefully.

Have you figured out what your friend is yet?

Which one? Aurelia's face danced behind my eyes, and I wondered why she wouldn't tell me. *Unlike you, I have many.*

It doesn't matter. I know what she is. He laughed, and it was laced with madness. *You'll find out soon enough. You have two weeks. After that, you will become my protégée, or you will die!*

I will never belong to you!

The choice is yours. For now, you are free to go.

Did he think he'd released me from his spell? Could I trust Draconian to leave us alone for the next two weeks? Was it a trick, or would he stay true to his word? No matter what, I had a lot to learn in the next two weeks.

Closing the door to my room, I leaned against it. Samantha and Dan were snuggled together on the couch. Aurelia perched on Big Bird, and Cody sat in Cookie Monster. Except for Aurelia, sleepless nights were evident on their faces. Dark circles crouched under their eyes.

Pushing away from the door, I stood beside Cody. "I have good news and bad news. Which do you want first?"

"How about you give us the good news and never tell us the bad?" Samantha said.

"Don't think so." Cody grabbed my hand. "Give 'em to us."

"In two weeks, I have to face Draconian, but until then, he will leave us alone."

"Two weeks." Dan leaned back, and a smile spread across his face. His dimples made him look younger than he had since Draconian became part of his life. "Two weeks without worrying about being kidnapped, without being attacked by dragons, but … then what will you do?"

"He said my choice is to be his protégée or die." I studied my fingernails, trying to look unconcerned. "I'm not fond of either choice, so I'll have to come up with a third option. Two weeks of freedom sounds good, though."

"Will he keep his word?" Cody asked. "Can we trust him?"

"I don't know." I sat down on Cody's lap.

Samantha leaned forward, resting her elbows on her knees. "We'll have to keep our guard up."

"He knows Dacia is strong." Aurelia nodded at me. "I think he will be true to his word. He wants to put an end to this. He wants to get his hands on Nefarious, and his way has only proven how resourceful Dacia can be. I imagine he believes that if he keeps his word, Dacia will keep hers."

Cody held me tighter. "Don't like having a deadline."

"I don't know how much I like it either"—I rubbed my hands along Cody's arms, trying to relieve some of his tension—"but the end is in sight. And, more importantly, as long as I face him, you guys will be safe."

"What do you mean by that?" Samantha sat back and tugged on her lip.

"There are always consequences." I stood up and walked to the window. "If I don't confront him within two weeks, he'll come after you guys."

"Oh." Dan's face fell.

"You don't have to worry." I squared my shoulders and held his gaze. "I'll face him. I won't let any of you be hurt because of me."

"We know that, Dacia," Samantha said. "It just sounds worse when you throw in his threat."

"What else did he say?" Aurelia didn't show any emotion, but her eyes took in everything.

Turning away from them, I stared out the window. Fat clouds floated lazily across the sky. Pine trees stretched, reaching for the sun. Students scurried about, hustling to classes. I turned back and looked Aurelia in the eyes. "He asked if I know what you are yet." I twirled a crimson strand of hair around my finger. "I told him he'd have to clarify because I have many friends. Then I told him I was unmoved by his concern, hoping he'd think I was still paralyzed."

Aurelia's smile was dazzling. "The less he knows about your skills, the better off you are."

"If he really is going to leave us alone for two weeks, do you guys want to spend the day in Althea?" I rubbed my hand down Cody's arm, hoping he wouldn't get upset at the suggestion.

"Lunch at The Avalanche." A grin spread across Samantha's face.

"Sounds good." Dan rubbed his hands together. "Oh, and maybe I can sleep in my own bed tonight?"

"Don't see why not." Cody laughed and wrapped his arms around me, holding me closer. "I'll be here. Draconian can promise the moon, but Dacia'll still have nightmares."

"You guys can do whatever you want." I waved my hand at the door. "Just be back here between ten-thirty and eleven, so we can leave."

"Do I have to go, too?" Cody asked in his best poor-me voice.

"None of you have to." I shook my head at him. "I just assumed you were all ready to."

"I am chomping at the bit to get out of here," Dan said. "I feel claustrophobic, and I've only been here awhile. I can't imagine how all of you feel."

"I felt the same way when I dealt with Nefarious. If I hadn't been so worried about the three of you this time, I'm sure I'd feel that way now." I laid my head against Cody's shoulder.

"She kept wandering off while we were sleeping." Samantha's lips pressed together, and she shook her head. "It was bad."

While they talked about me, I focused my attention on Aurelia and projected my thoughts to her, *I'm sure Dan and Samantha will stay together. Can you have Arion keep an eye on them?*

I am one step ahead of you. He said he would be honored to help you, and he will be discreet.

I smiled at her as a little weight lifted off my shoulders.

"Luckily, she's been well behaved this time." Cody laughed, and even though they were talking about me, I welcomed the sound.

"With Nefarious, I was hunted, and you were *smothering* me," I reminded them. "This time I'm more of a guardian … or a protector … or something. Draconian wants something from me. If he didn't, he would've killed me already. Right now, I'm fairly safe."

A relieved grin spread across Samantha's face. "Well, as it turns out, none of us have to worry right now. We're all off the hook for two weeks."

"Don't be so sure." Cody rubbed the back of his neck. "Be cautious. Can't trust Draconian."

"I know I'm being optimistic, but that doesn't mean I won't be careful. I was actually thinking about maybe having Arion keep an eye on us. What do you think, Dan?" Samantha asked.

"I would feel more comfortable with that." He nodded. "That way, if something happens, you'll know right away."

"It has already been arranged," Aurelia said.

"Thanks. Let's get out of here." Samantha grabbed Dan's hand. "We'll see you for lunch."

Aurelia followed them out the door. When she was in the hallway, she turned back. "Be careful."

"I need to go to my room. Do you wanna tag along?" Cody asked.

Without lifting my head from his shoulder, I said, "Yeah." We stayed like that for several more minutes, enjoying the peace, before leaving.

A thick fog rolled across the ground, making its way toward campus. Only the tops of the mountains were left exposed. The hair on the back of my neck stood on end as fear took hold of me. My initial response was to turn around and run back to safety, but I resisted the urge. Any other day, I would have been worried about Draconian attacking. However, today, I was free. Today, I didn't have to worry about what was hiding around the next corner. Today, I could be the college kid I longed to be. Today, I could relax.

"Today is a great day." I pulled Cody's arm around my shoulder. "If only they could all be like this." Fog swallowed the campus, but even its gloom couldn't dampen my spirits.

We were almost to his building when Sarah stepped through the fog and into our path. "Well, hello." Her hand went to her chest. "I'm surprised to see you two out here."

I squeezed Cody's hand and whispered, "Change the subject." There was always a possibility Draconian was listening, so while he talked to Sarah about the weather, I projected my thoughts to her. *Sarah, I'm sorry to talk to you this way, but we can't be too careful. Draconian promised us a two-week reprieve if I will face him at the end of it.*

She looked worried for a moment but quickly regained her composure. "Why don't you stop by my office later? I would like to find out what different students think about summer classes. We need to do whatever we can to improve," she said as she walked off.

Chapter 29
Stipulations

*T*he four of us piled into Cody's car. After he pulled out of the parking lot, I reached for his hand. I felt a lightness that had been missing since we went to Cougar Lake.

Patchy fog clung to the valleys, rising up through the lodgepole pines. Wildflowers of every color grew along the road. Snow-covered peaks stretched into the blue sky.

Samantha and Dan sat in the back, talking quietly. Cody rubbed his thumb over mine, his expression soft. My friends were at ease, and even though the little voice in my head warned me not to let my guard down, I relaxed.

Tourists filled the streets and sidewalks of Althea. They carried souvenir bags and cameras. Many of them wore Snow-fire Mountain sweatshirts or t-shirts and smiles. Several licked ice cream cones. Others chewed on freshly made taffy.

We parked three blocks from The Avalanche, then fought the crowds on the sidewalk to put our name in. There was a half-hour wait, so we sat outside on a bench, soaking up the sun.

"We should spend all day in town." Samantha clapped her hands together excitedly.

"We bumped into Sarah this morning." Cody's hand ran up and down my arm. "She expects to see us this afternoon."

"She wants to talk to us about summer classes." I winked while telling them. "I'm sure she has a lot of questions. But, I didn't feel like talking this morning. It was so foggy and yucky and who knows who would overhear us … not that it would have been anything important."

Our pager went off, and we were seated at a table near the front. I couldn't watch the entire restaurant, and I didn't feel inclined to. Cody scooted his chair closer to mine and threw his arm over my shoulders, loosely, not in guard dog mode.

Lunch away from campus was exactly what the four of us needed. The tension that had taken up permanent residence on all our shoulders was evicted.

"Maybe we should skip classes for the next two weeks," Dan said.

"Dan"—Samantha rolled her eyes—"school is important. Don't you feel guilty about skipping today?"

He grabbed his drink and downed about half of it before setting it on the table again. "No, I really don't. I know I should be there, but things have been so stressful lately, and it feels good to take it easy."

"Dacia Wolf, is that you?" A tall, handsome guy with dark eyes and even darker hair walked toward me. "You don't remember me, do you? It's Ben … Ben Vole. We went to high school together."

"You're right. I don't remember you," I said. Why would he remember me anyway? Cody would be a lot more memorable. He was a popular athlete. So, why would Ben recognize me and not him? "Are you going to college here?"

"No, just vacationing. I'll be around for two weeks. Then I'm heading home. It's good to see you having so much fun." He bent down like he was going to kiss my cheek. Instead, he whispered in my ear, "Don't go too far away or the deal's off."

My body stiffened as he walked away, and my napkin-wrapped silverware fell from my hand.

Cody tilted his head, watching Ben leave. "I don't remember him. Do you?"

"What's wrong, Dacia?" Samantha's food stopped halfway to her mouth.

It took a moment for me to regain my composure and answer her. "Th–that was, uh, Draconian."

"What?" Dan looked from me to Cody.

"Why didn't I sense him? Was I too relaxed, or did he figure out how to disguise his aura?" I pulled my hand through my hair. "I can't let my guard down again."

"How do you know it was him?" Samantha set her fork back on her plate. The uneaten bite clung to its tines.

"Well, he whispered in my ear that if we stray too far from campus, the deal's off." I looked down at my burger. Bacon, cheese, and lettuce hung over the toasted bun. I'd only taken a couple of bites of it before Draconian came over. I pushed my plate away, wishing he would've waited to say anything until we were done eating. "So, *nobody* goes home for the next two weeks."

Everybody sat in stunned silence until Cody broke it. "Maybe we should have Arion keep an eye on us, too."

"I'm willing to bet Aurelia is watching as we speak." I drummed my fingers on the table. "Somehow, she can make it impossible for me to sense her."

"I can see that." Samantha nodded. "After all, she had Arion appointed to us before I asked."

I fiddled with my napkin, not looking at my friends. "I suggested it to her, too, but by then, she'd already asked him."

"It seems logical then that she would be keeping an eye on you two." Dan ran his fry through ketchup. "We're just pawns in this game, but you"—he pointed at Cody and me—"you're the king and queen."

Aurelia.

Yes, Dacia.

You can show yourself. I know you're watching me.

No, I will not show myself, however, I am trying to keep you safe. Nothing can happen to you, or all hope will be lost.

You're putting way too much pressure on me. I chewed on my bottom lip. *That guy that just left our table was Draconian, and for some reason, I couldn't sense him. What's going on?*

I am not sure. Try to enjoy yourselves for now. Nothing is going to happen here, especially not with all of these people around. We will talk back on campus.

I hope you're right.

"Hello … Dacia. Is anybody home?" Cody waved his hand in front of my eyes. "Snap out of it."

"Sorry." I blinked several times. "I was having a conversation with Aurelia. She's watching over us, and she doesn't think Draconian will start anything with all these people around."

"She has a good point." Dan put his hand on Samantha's leg. "This really wouldn't be a good place to try to nab us."

I folded my arms on the table. "I would've liked two weeks of peace, two weeks to enjoy myself, but I'm going to have to be aware of my surroundings at all times. I can't afford for something to happen to any of you."

"Don't forget to keep yourself safe, too." Samantha stabbed her salad.

The return trip was solemn. Cody grasped the steering wheel with white knuckles. Samantha and Dan held hands in the backseat without saying a word. My mind raced. *Did Draconian find a way to keep me from sensing him? Did his dragons teach him how? Or, is he using their magic to intensify his own? Please, Lord, don't let that be the case.*

I heaved a dramatic sigh and chewed on my fingernails.

"Don't do that." Cody took my hand in his.

"Can't help it."

"Try … for me."

Cody held one hand, and I sat on the other the rest of the way to campus. Once we were back in our room, Aurelia showed herself. "You should not worry about not sensing Draconian. He was in disguise, and you were not expecting to run into him today."

"But I still should've known when he showed up." I held my head in my hands. "I should've known he was near."

She squeezed my shoulder. "Do you always know when Cody or Samantha are coming and going?"

"No, I don't." I remembered the day Cody was attacked. "I hadn't thought of that."

"In order to sense his approach every time, you need to be diligent … always expect him to be around. Then you might always be able to tell when he is near."

I let out a relieved breath. "That makes me feel so much better. I was really worried that he'd found a way to elude me."

"I do not believe that is the case this time." She focused her attention on Samantha and Dan. "Arion will watch over you wherever you two decide to go. I am going to walk with them to Sarah's. I will not go in with you, though. I do not want Draconian to suspect anything."

I stood, looking at them. "Be careful."

"You, too." Samantha pulled out her braid and combed through her hair with her fingers.

On the way to Sarah's office, Aurelia asked, "Is there anything you want to learn before you face Draconian?"

I shrugged, making Cody's arm bounce against my neck. "How to defeat him."

"I wish I knew the answer to that." Her voice sounded apologetic.

"Will I have to … kill him?" The last part came out as a whisper.

"I wish I knew the answer to that, too. I cannot foresee him giving up if you let him live, but there is always a chance you can scare him enough that he will."

"I was afraid you were going to say something like that." My heart plummeted. "I don't know if I can. He's a horrible, bad, evil man, but how can I kill him? How can I live with myself if I do?" Cody pulled me closer. Normally, it would have been comforting, but today it couldn't reach the chill that settled inside me.

"Those are questions only you can answer," Aurelia said. "We are almost there. I will be here when you come out, though you will not see me."

Sarah paced the floor in her office when we arrived. Papers were scattered across the coffee table. "Oh, thank God. You're okay. I was getting worried about you."

"We're fine," Cody said. "As it turns out, we weren't even alone. Aurelia watched over us the whole time."

"That's good to know." Sarah sounded relieved. "So, tell me what's going on."

"Let's sit down," I said. Cody and I sat beside each other on one of the couches. His arm was wrapped around my shoulders. Sarah sat across from us with her hands folded in her lap. Without preamble, I told her about my conversation with Draconian and about our trip to Althea.

"So, where are Samantha and Dan? Are they safe?" Sarah's forehead wrinkled with concern.

"Arion's watching over them." Sarah's hair had been infiltrated by more strands of gray since I first met her. It couldn't be easy for her to run the college and deal with my problems.

Trying to soften my voice, I said, "Aurelia doesn't think Draconian'll hurt any of us. She believes he'll keep his word."

"Can you defeat Draconian?" She lifted her hands as if realizing how discouraging she sounded. "I don't mean to sound like I don't think you can. After all, you defeated Nefarious. I guess what I'm asking is, are you ready?"

So much for trying to relieve some of her stress. "I'm ready for this to be over, but I don't know if I can defeat him. Aurelia isn't sure if he'll give up, and I don't have another vase to keep him in." Taking a deep breath, I paused to get the courage to say the next part. "She, uh, she thinks I might have to … kill him, and I don't know if I can."

"I understand why you would be concerned about that. It wouldn't be an easy thing to do." She picked her coffee cup up off the table and spun it in her hands. "Maybe there's another way. After all, you didn't know how you would defeat Nefarious until it happened."

"Good point." Cody squeezed my shoulder.

"Let's hope I'm victorious. The alternative is unthinkable." This was a battle I couldn't lose, but one I had no idea how to win.

"Keep me informed, Dacia." Sarah rested the cup on her knee and held my gaze. Her hazel eyes were filled with concern. "I don't like not talking to you every day. I worry about what's going on."

"Does Aurelia keep you informed?" Cody asked.

She smiled at me, and it was wistful. "Yes, but I feel better hearing it from you guys. Just do me a favor. Be careful. I know you are. Even though Aurelia thinks he'll leave you alone for the next two weeks, don't take it for granted."

"We don't plan to." I leaned forward and rested my hands on my knees. "I'm afraid he's trying to loosen us up so it'll be easier to catch us off guard."

"Stay safe." She looked at her watch. "You should go in case he's watching."

We walked over to the door together. "Thanks, Sarah. It's good to know people care."

"It's no problem, Dacia. I'll talk to a few other students today, so it doesn't look like I was singling you out." She gave me a hug and patted Cody's arm on our way out the door.

Dan and Samantha were snuggled on the couch when we got back. "How did it go with Sarah?" Samantha sat up.

"It was fine." I plopped down in Cookie Monster. "She just wanted to know what was going on and warned us to stay safe."

"Do you two want to go to Falcon Lake with us?" Dan asked. "We thought about taking stuff for a picnic and having a bonfire on the beach."

I tilted my head, and my eyebrows furrowed. I couldn't believe they were ready to go out again so soon after seeing Draconian in Althea. "What do you think, Cody?"

He rubbed his neck. "We have a bonfire, we'll be out late. Think it's safe?"

"What do you think, Aurelia?" I asked.

Suddenly, Aurelia stood in the room with us. "I think you will be fine. Arion and I will go with you and make sure you are safe."

Samantha's face lit up. "Do you think he'd give me another ride?"

"You'll have to ask him yourself."

"I think I might." Her grin spread from ear to ear.

Cody and I snuggled together on the beach. The fire danced in front of us, casting shadows over Dan's, Samantha's, and Aurelia's faces. The sun put on a spectacular show before retreating under the horizon. Stars filled the sky, twinkling against the black backdrop.

"This is perfect." I rested my head on Cody's shoulder.

"Yeah, couldn't've asked for a better night." He shoved the last of his S'more into his mouth.

"I haven't seen anybody else for quite a while," Samantha said. "Do you think Arion could show himself now?"

He appeared next to Aurelia. His fur glimmered as brightly as the stars. He bowed his head in greeting.

"Oh, hi." Samantha clapped her hands. "Um, may I … may I have a ride?"

Arion knelt, allowing Samantha to climb onto his back. In one graceful movement, Arion ascended to the heavens with Samantha squealing in delight. I would've enjoyed flying with him, but since I knew the idea terrified Cody, it'd have to wait until Draconian was defeated.

When Samantha and Arion returned, Cody asked, "Wanna walk?"

"Yeah, that'd be nice."

As we strolled away from the fire, I realized how chilly the evening had become. Cody and I walked hand in hand in silence. I leaned close to him, and his arm wrapped around my shoulders. "This is living." My voice was soft and relaxed. "No fears, no concerns, just happiness, and peace. I can handle this."

"Wish. With all my heart, wish you had this, but if it was offered, Don't think you'd take it." He kissed the top of my head. "You'd choose the noble route. Wouldn't let pain and suffering go on, not knowing you could stop it."

"No, but I can dream. Can't I?"

We stopped and looked out over Falcon Lake. The moon reflected on the water giving it a surreal appearance. Cody gently grabbed my shoulders and turned me to face him. Placing his hands on the sides of my head and caressing my cheeks with his thumbs, he said, "Dream whatever you like. Just make sure I'm part of it."

"You always are, Cody." I rested my hands on his. "You're what makes this life worth living."

He leaned down and brushed his lips over mine. He started to pull away, but an inferno ignited in my chest. I wrapped my arms around his neck and pulled his mouth down. He smiled before crushing his lips against mine. My fingers twisted in his hair.

His hands traveled up and down my spine, pulling me against him. Then they dropped to my hips, lifting me. I wrapped my legs around his waist, clinging to him. My heart pounded against his chest.

Cody pulled his mouth away from mine. His voice was low and ragged. "Best thing to happen to me was you. I love you."

"I love you, too." I kissed his cheek, then the tip of his nose. When my mouth touched his, everything else disappeared. Nothing but the two of us existed. My heart soared, filled with the love Cody felt for me. I pulled back, and he sat me down, not letting go until he was sure I wouldn't lose my balance. Then he took my hand in his and walked toward our picnic table.

Seeing my friends around the fire, my heart sunk. I couldn't keep them safe forever. "I'm sorry I got you involved in this," I said to Cody. "The three of you must've been terrified yesterday."

"Scared to death. Knew you'd save us." He dropped my hand and draped his arm over my shoulders, pulling me close to him. "How did you, though? How'd you get us all out at once?"

"We had help, but it's not something I can talk about," I answered. "I made a promise."

"Won't ask again, but whoever they are, I'm grateful."

"You and me both. I couldn't have done it myself."

Chapter 30

$\mathcal{T}$he days passed quicker than I would've liked. With a little over a week to go, Aurelia and I hadn't come up with a way to stop Draconian without killing him.

And, with each passing day, it became more apparent to me that I couldn't. Life was valuable, and I couldn't end somebody's, not even his.

I left my training sessions with Aurelia feeling more despondent by the day. I stood in the hall outside my room until I could screw a smile on and pretend that things would be okay.

Every day, Samantha had something planned to get us out of the building. I imagined she did it in part to keep my thoughts away from Draconian, but it had the opposite effect.

She decided to spend another afternoon at Falcon Lake. When we got to the trail, Cody and I took off on our own. "What's going on, Dacia?" he asked.

"What do you mean?" The path was worn into the forest floor by all of the students who'd needed a break through the years. Boulders and roots thrusted through the dirt, striving to catch a glimpse of the sun. Orange mushrooms crouched at the bases of trees. Chipmunks, squirrels, and birds watched from the branches, careful not to draw too much attention.

"Everybody is relaxed and enjoying this, but you're tense. Even when we're all together, you seem to be alone. It's like you're …" He spread his fingers out wide, then fisted them. "You're waiting for something to happen. I don't know."

"I'm scared." I tugged my hand through my hair. Individual strands broke free, clinging to my fingers. I wiggled them and watched the hairs flutter to the ground. "I don't trust Draconian to stay away. He didn't even manage it for one day."

"Since then?"

I couldn't lie to Cody as much as I would've liked to at that moment. When asked a point-blank question, it was my nature to give a point-blank answer. "Yes, he has. I didn't want to tell you guys because he hasn't been threatening." Kicking at the dirt, I said, "I didn't want you to worry."

"You don't have to deal on your own."

"Maybe not, but you shouldn't have to at all."

"I chose to." He reached for my hand and laced his fingers through mine. "Don't think you should go through this alone."

"I know, and I appreciate it."

"Don't let me in, and I worry more." His words were spoken so softly that if there had been a breeze, they would've drifted away on it. "Even if you don't tell them, tell me."

"I can do that." I turned toward him and ran my finger down his chest. "By the way, you read my mind earlier. I wanted to spend some time alone with you. I know Samantha and Dan feel safer with me around or maybe, with me and Aurelia around. But, it's nice to be alone with you." I leaned my head against him, and we walked along in silence for a while.

"Enjoy yourself tonight."

"I can't let my guard down." The thought of going to Althea later didn't sit well with me, but I felt a responsibility to keep my friends safe. "If I do, I can't sense him, and I don't want to be surprised again. Maybe I can figure out how to keep an eye out for him without being so distracted."

When we got back to our room, Samantha asked, "Bowling or movie?"

Neither the continuous noise of the bowling alley nor the dark secluded nature of a movie theater sounded appealing. Really, I just wanted to stay in and take it easy. I knew Samantha would go along with it if I suggested it, but I would spend the whole night feeling guilty. "We could go to the park and play on the swings."

"Really?" Cody tilted his head, and one eyebrow arched upward.

"That sounds like fun." Samantha's brown eyes sparkled. "I haven't done that in ages."

Dan flipped his hands palms up. "The park it is."

Cody turned to me and as quiet as a church mouse whispered, "Nobody'll be around."

"Let's get going." Samantha practically bounced to the door.

"Go ahead. We'll be right behind you." When they left the room, I turned to Cody. "I didn't think about that. We'll be okay, though. It'll be fun."

Dinner was at The Avalanche again. We were on a first-name basis with our waitress, Abigail. "Hey, my favorite customers." She flipped her blonde ponytail over her shoulder as she strolled to our table. "You're back again."

"Campus food gets old after a while." Dan flashed her his charming smile.

She blushed in response, and I couldn't blame her. It was a great smile. "I won't know about that for another year. I'll be a senior this fall."

"You going to Phlox?" Cody asked.

She tapped her pen against her ruby lips. "I haven't decided. I grew up in Althea, and I've never been away."

"Where would you go that is this beautiful?" I waved my hand toward the window.

"I don't know. It's great here." She had a faraway look in her brown eyes. "I'm lucky to have lived here my whole life, but part of me wants to get out … to see what else is out there."

"I get that"—Dan picked up his menu—"but this would be hard to leave behind."

"Yeah, that's my dilemma." Abigail lowered her pen to her pad. "I should take your order."

Right after she walked away, my stomach dropped. Madness clung to the air. *Draconian.* I unwrapped my silverware, scanning the room. No one seemed out of place.

I grabbed my purse. "Be right back." Walking toward the restroom, I peered into booths and studied people's faces. *Where is he?*

I stood at the sink, trying to gather myself before returning to my seat. Draconian's presence saturated the air, but I saw no sign of him.

Cody lifted his eyebrows in question. I gave him a small shake of my head, hoping he'd let it go. He squeezed my knee when I sat but didn't say anything.

Finally, Draconian's aura disappeared. I leaned back and let out a breath. Cody rested his hand on the back of my chair. His fingertips trailed along my neck.

By the time our food arrived, a little of my appetite had returned, but not enough to finish my supper.

Abigail refilled drinks and cleared plates. When everyone else was finished, she asked me, "Do you need a box?"

"Yes, please."

She returned with our bill and my box. "Thanks for coming."

When we got up to leave, Cody reached for my food. Making sure Samantha and Dan weren't looking, I shook my head. He narrowed his eyebrows but didn't say anything.

We were almost to the door when I said, "Crap. I forgot my leftovers."

Dan and Samantha turned to follow me back to the table, but Cody said, "We'll be out in a sec."

My hand shook when I reached for the box. "He was here."

"Figured." Cody picked up my food and slung his other arm over my shoulder.

"Hey, you're back," Abigail said.

Cody held up the Styrofoam container. "Yeah."

She tugged on the end of her braid. "So, uh, are your friends together?"

"Yeah." Cody smiled at her.

"Too bad." She sighed. "He's got the best smile I've ever seen. It kinda makes you melt."

"You can say that again." I agreed with her.

Cody raised his arm above his head and pointed down. "Hey, uh, boyfriend here."

I looked up at him. A mischievous grin pulled my lips upward. "He's got the smile, but you're the whole package."

"I gotta get back to work," Abigail said. "Come back soon."

As we walked out, Cody asked, "Really? His smile?"

"It's pretty cute, but I love you." I bumped into his hip. "Draconian, remember."

"Thanks for telling me. We'll have to be careful."

"What took so long?" Samantha asked when we got back to them.

"Ran into Abigail." Cody looked at Dan, shaking his head. "Seems you have a great smile."

Samantha slipped her hand into Dan's back pocket. "He does."

"Geesh." Cody shook his head. "What am I … chopped liver?"

"You've got blond hair and blue eyes," Dan said. "You don't need a great smile to get girls."

We squeezed through the crowd on the sidewalk, stopping at Cody's car to grab our jackets and drop off my food.

Music rumbled through the air. The bass and drums thumped inside me. Samantha's hips moved in time to the beat. She grabbed Dan's hand and squealed, dragging him toward the park.

The scent of popcorn and funnel cakes filled the air. Dancers crowded together on the tennis court, bouncing and writhing to the beat. The song changed from pop to country.

"Well, how about that?" Samantha looked over her shoulder at us. "It looks like we're dancing." She spun toward the music.

"Man." Dan stopped, and his head fell forward into his hands. "Slow songs are good. I get to hold her close, but how do you dance to this?"

"Don't look at me." I laughed. "I've never been able to figure it out."

"Me either," Cody told him. "You're on your own."

"Maybe with my winning smile, I can charm her into only making me dance to slow songs."

"Good luck." Cody pointed at himself and grinned like a madman. "I'm not dancing. Maybe the smile is overrated."

"Maybe." Dan walked away, dragging his hands through his auburn hair.

The playground equipment nearby was overrun with giggling children. "Higher. Higher." One girl laughed in delight when someone pushed her swing into the sky.

Beyond the glow of the lights, a few swings sat empty. Cody and I meandered toward them. The swing hugged my hips. The chains creaked as I gained momentum. I pumped my legs, soaring higher. Cody stretched his legs out, pointing his toes at the stars. Then he let go. He flew through the air, landing on the balls of his feet.

Jogging back, with laughter lighting up his face, he said, "Haven't done that in ages."

I slowed my swing to a gentle sway. My fingers threaded loosely through Cody's.

The music switched between country and rock. The tempo stayed upbeat.

"This is nice." Cody squeezed my hand. "Alone, but people nearby … hopefully, keeping Draconian at bay."

"Yeah. This makes it easier to relax."

"Dan's smile must not've worked because he's dancing." Cody laughed and pointed toward the tennis court. "Or trying to."

"Dan can't say no to Samantha. I doubt he even tried his smile on her."

A gentle breeze lifted my hair. I closed my eyes and rolled my neck. When I opened them, I caught Cody staring at me. He turned away, but not before I saw stress etched in the lines of his face.

"What?" I tightened my grip on the chain.

"Know what to do—" he dug his toe into the dirt "—about Draconian?"

I pulled my hand away from Cody's and held the chains at shoulder height, gazing at nothing. "No, I can't kill him."

He rubbed his chin. "Didn't think you would."

"If he hurt one of you, I could do it out of anger or grief." I spun in the swing, twisting the chains together. "I think maybe he knows that. Maybe that's why … never mind."

"Why he hasn't killed one of us," he finished.

"Yeah."

"Wants you for his apprentice. Must respect you." Cody barely swayed in his swing. "Maybe he's afraid of you."

"Maybe." The chains groaned, not twisting any higher. I let go, spinning around until the chains twisted in the other direction. "I have no idea what to do and only a week to figure it out."

Cody sighed. "Wish I could help."

"I know."

The music slowed. A ballad drifted over to us. Cody stood and reached for my hand. I let him pull me to my feet. His arms circled my waist and drew me to him. I rested my head on his shoulder, and together we swayed to the music.

This. This is why I need to survive. This is why I'll have to kill Draconian if there is no other way.

"Well, don't you two just dance beautifully together?"

I jerked away from Cody and stared at the owner of the voice. He was a rugged man in his forties. A cowboy hat sat low, hiding his eyes.

"Thanks." Cody's voice was cautious.

My stomach rolled. I'd let my guard down while Cody and I danced, and I didn't know if this was Draconian or just somebody who happened upon us.

"Don't let me stop you." He pointed at the row of houses across the street. "I'm just passing through on my way home." He tilted his hat back a little. I half expected to see Draconian's gray eyes looking back at me, but I felt no malice from this stranger. "I've had enough music for one night."

"Have a good evening," Cody said as he walked away. When he was out of earshot, Cody turned to me and asked, "Was that him?"

"It didn't seem to be." I put my hands on my knees and leaned forward. "I think I'm going to be sick."

Chapter 31
Phoenixes, Tigers, And Dragons

Aurelia and I stood on the fifty-yard line. I hadn't been to Phoenix Stadium since football season ended, but Sarah promised the dome would be empty.

"Did you have something in mind?" Aurelia asked.

I paced toward the end zone, knowing she'd hear me no matter how far away from her I wandered. "I wish I knew Draconian's weakness. Maybe I could use it to my advantage." Pivoting, I walked back toward her.

Aurelia stood with her hands in her pockets, watching me. "He wants to be the most powerful magician in the world. That, in itself, is a weakness." She met me at the forty-five and squeezed my shoulder. "I would love to tell you that you can find something to use against him, but I think the only way to deal with him is to kill him."

I scrubbed my hand down my face and laughed without humor. "I can't."

"I know. It would not be easy for me either," she said. "You will not have to stand against Draconian and his dragons alone. I will be there with you when you fight him. I will help you any way I can."

"Maybe I could hold him down for you." My hand flew to my mouth. *I just asked her to kill for me.*

"It is not in my nature to kill any more than it is in yours."

"I didn't mean it. I just said it. I wouldn't wish this on anybody, let alone a friend." I turned away from her, feeling her hand slip down my back as I strode away. "Draconian doesn't seem to be afraid of anything. How am I supposed to beat somebody who fears nothing?"

"I imagine his greatest fear is death." She crossed her arms, tapping her fingers against her elbows. "That is probably why he wants you for his protégée. He wants his legacy to continue after he dies."

"So, we're back to death, a punishment I can't give him." I fisted my hand in the hair at the back of my head and spun toward Aurelia. She stood so still, always watching, sizing everything up. "Am I ever going to find out what you are?"

"Back to that again?"

"I just wondered if I would find out before I die."

"You will. I promise."

"Since I'm going to die next week, you're running out of time."

"You are not about to die, Dacia. I will be there with you." She cocked her head to the side, and I couldn't help but picture her as a bird. Maybe she was a phoenix or a griffon or something like that. "However, if for some reason, it looks like you are not going to make it, I will transform into my true shape. Now can we move on?"

"Sure." I continued pacing. Every time I stopped, my thoughts threatened to devour me. "Is there a way to ward the room without us there?"

She tracked my movements without turning her head. "The magic exists, but it is easily broken."

I tugged my hand through my hair. "I need to find a way to keep Draconian away from them."

"What are you planning?" She turned to face me.

I stopped moving and looked at her. If I told her, would she try to stop me? Or would she stand by me?

"I'm going to call Draconian out, but somehow, I have to make sure they're safe when I do." I started pacing again. "In my nightmares, he uses them against me. Every. Time."

She placed a comforting hand on my shoulder on my next pass. "When do you plan to confront him?"

"Next weekend. I don't want to wait for him to show up. I'm gonna meet him head-on." I lit a fire in my palm and watched it grow. "On my terms."

"What do you need from me?"

The fire died, and I ticked off a list on my fingers. "A way to keep my friends safe mand away. Anything you can teach me that might help. A miracle."

She tilted her head but said nothing.

Turning away from her again, I said, "Draconian can change his appearance. How?"

"I am not sure it will help you, but I can teach you."

"It probably won't help now, but it might in the future."

She stepped back. "Close your eyes and picture what you want to look like. Do you have the image in your mind?"

"Yes."

"Now I want you to visualize yourself that way." She paused. "Concentration is crucial. Make sure you focus on all the little details."

I nodded while continuing to picture myself as I wanted to be seen. I imagined my body lengthening, my hair straightening, and growing longer. Opening my eyes, I looked down to see nothing had changed.

Once again, I closed my eyes. I pictured the lake that I'd used to calm myself when I first started learning to control my powers. Peace settled in my body, pushing the turmoil and fear to my extremities. My shoulders loosened, and I tried to change my appearance.

This time when I opened my eyes, I stared down at golden hands. "It seems to have worked."

"Yes." Aurelia's eyes widened. "I feel like I am staring in a mirror. It is odd."

A thrill of excitement ran through me. "Can I change into anything or just other human forms?"

"There is only one way to find out." Her voice sounded off, but I couldn't place the emotion. "Obviously, I can change into other forms. I am unaware of the limitations transfiguration has on humans or if there are any for that matter. Picture something in your head that you would like to transform into, and see what happens."

I closed my eyes and pictured an Amur tiger. The majestic creature with its orange and black stripes and rippling muscles filled my mind. Releasing the magic, my body grew. My arms and legs stretched out, and my muscles bulked up. I fell forward, standing on all fours. A long tail twitched from side to side. My neck elongated. Razor-sharp fangs filled my massive jaws. I turned my head to catch a glimpse of myself and found I'd become what I feared most, an enormous black dragon.

I lowered my head to look at Aurelia. Her mouth hung open in astonishment, but her eyes were fierce, a mixture of contempt and awe. Through gritted teeth and with a strained voice, she said, "That is not what I expected. I doubt any other human has ever transformed into a dragon before."

"It's …" I cocked my head. My voice was deep and booming. "It's not what I intended." I tried to hide my excitement but didn't succeed. "I wanted to change into a tiger, but dragons have been first and foremost on my mind for days. I guess it makes sense that I transformed into one."

"Can you breathe fire?" she asked still sounding strained.

I had no idea how to see if I could. I tilted my head. The movement made the field spin. I tottered but righted myself. Deciding magic would be my best option, a fireball escaped my massive paw, but I didn't breathe it. "Maybe with some practice, but I don't think so."

Focusing on my body, I transformed back into myself. My muscles burned. My body shrank, and I fell onto my hands and knees. The breath squeezed from my lungs. "That …" I gasped. "That could help me defeat Draconian."

"It could." She spun around so her back was toward me. Her voice sounded forced. "However, his dragons will tear you apart if you take that form in front of them."

"Why?" I raised my eyebrows and rolled onto my back.

"Dragons are exceptionally arrogant creatures. They believe they are superior to all other living things, especially humans." Tension made her normally graceful movements rough. "Dragons can change into human form, and when they do, they respect humans. They actually like the lifestyle humans lead, but in dragon form, they will not appreciate your ability. Even if you free them, they may attack you."

Hope faded, like the stars lost to the morning sky. It was almost as if it had never been there. I thought being a dragon would help me defeat Draconian, that maybe it was my way out. Now she was telling me if I used it, I would be lucky to survive the dragons' wrath. I closed my eyes. "How do you know so much about dragons?"

"I have been around for thousands of years. I have met creatures of all types." She turned toward me again, meeting my gaze for a moment before looking into the empty stands. "Dragons, as a species, are by far the most egotistical of them."

"Okay, I won't try to change out of human form again until dragons are off my mind—" I sighed "—but it was pretty cool. Wasn't it?"

"Yes." She smiled, but it was strained. "I was shocked you chose to emulate me."

I was thrown off by her comment. I was more impressed by turning into a dragon than by turning into her. "You were the first person I pictured. After all, I saw you right before I closed my eyes."

"That makes sense." She nodded and turned away. "It was weird looking into my own face. You had it perfectly, down to the eyes, and nobody else has eyes like mine."

"That's for sure. You have awesome eyes." I struggled to sit up. Aurelia clasped my hand, sending a burst of energy through me.

"We should return." She helped me to my feet. "Transformation seems to have taken a toll on you."

If transforming into Aurelia and into a dragon expended that much energy, how did Aurelia stay in human form all the time? How much stronger was her magic than mine?

Outside the stadium, puffy, white clouds dotted the sky. A soft breeze blew down from the mountains, bringing crisp, cool air with it. We walked in companionable silence until we were nearly at Wisteria Hall.

"I'm no closer to stopping him." I opened the door and held it for her.

"We will think of something."

I grimaced. "I hope so."

By the time we stepped into the dormitory, my legs were shaking. A few girls wandered the halls. All of them shouted hellos to Aurelia. A few even included me.

She waited until we were past them before saying, "There is always hope, Dacia. Do not give up so easily. I believe in you. You will find a way to defeat him."

Cody turned off the TV when Aurelia and I stepped into the room. "How'd it go?"

"I have no idea how to beat Draconian, but I transformed into a dragon!" I knew Aurelia didn't like it, but I couldn't keep the excitement out of my voice, even to placate her.

"You what?" His voice rose, and his eyes widened.

"First, I turned into Aurelia. Then, I transformed into a black dragon, the one that was guarding you." I pointed at him. "It was awesome."

"So, can you turn into a dragon and eat Draconian or something?"

I glanced at Aurelia. Her face was covered by an unreadable mask. "No. Aurelia says the dragons would kill me if they knew I could turn into one."

He focused on Aurelia. "Why?"

She sounded like she was forcing herself to remain calm when she gave him the same answer she'd given me.

Cody seized the arms of the chair. "But, she's helping them!"

"Most dragons do not believe humans can help them." She sat on the edge of the couch and looked at the floor. "The majority feel they are superior, and therefore, they are not willing to admit needing help. Arrogance is the biggest flaw dragons have. That is the main reason why they have been given such a bad rap throughout history. It is not because of their violent tendencies. It is because of their superiority complex." Her voice had a hard edge to it, and her gold eyes narrowed.

"Their loss." Cody reached his hand out to me. I sat on the arm of the chair.

"Think of them like wolves," Aurelia said in a more peaceful tone. "Wolves would not be thought of as monsters if fairy tales had made them seem less vicious. Stories about their cunning and cruelty made them out to be bad guys. They are an important part of the ecosystem." She looked up, and sorrow filled her eyes. "Dragons have been made into villains throughout history. Those who have seen them tremble at the mere mention of their name. They have been made into horrible, menacing, awe-inspiring beasts, and unlike wolves, because of their arrogance, they have embraced this role. Thousands of years of conditioning are not going to be undone because Dacia is helping them. Some may hold humans in higher regard after she frees them. Others may become infuriated that a human saved them."

Cody rubbed his hand along my back. "Dragons sound like people."

"They are. Some are friendly and outgoing. Some are mean." She leaned back and stretched her legs out in front of me. "Almost all of them are arrogant and would not appreciate seeing Dacia as a dragon. Also, unlike people, dragons are not fooled by appearances. If Dacia transformed into a dragon and freed them, they would see a dragon standing before them, but they would be aware it was Dacia. She would not be able to hide that fact from them."

"Well, it doesn't matter. I'm not going to change back into a dragon again." I walked to the window and looked outside. "I didn't mean to do it in the first place, but dragons are constantly on my mind. I can't think about anything without wondering what the dragons are going to do … or when I'm going to have to face dragons. If I change again at all, it will be into somebody else … just a disguise."

"That sounds like a wise decision." Aurelia's stance relaxed slightly. "Now, unless you want me to stick around, I have some things I need to do."

"No, that's okay." I folded my arms around my waist. "Thanks for your help today."

After she left, I turned to Cody and asked, "Where are Samantha and Dan?"

"Don't know." His gaze shifted, looking anywhere but at me. "I shouldn't ask, but would you?"

"Cody, I shouldn't." I pulled my hand through my hair, gathering it as I went, then held it at the back of my head. "If Aurelia is watching us, she'll be really mad. When all of this is over, I think I'll be able to change shape without turning into a dragon. Can it wait until then?"

"Sure." His shoulders dropped, and he rubbed his neck. "I shouldn't've asked."

I hated to let him down, so I closed my eyes and concentrated. Focusing on every minute detail, I thought of a tiger: the exact color of orange, the amber eyes, the stripes, the curve of the ears. When that was all that was on my mind, I began changing. My arms and legs became muscular. I fell forward, landing silently on padded paws. A long tail swished behind me. When I opened my eyes again, I looked into Cody's awestruck face.

"You're … you're a tiger," he stammered.

He stood and reached out, scratching under my chin. I chuffed. The noise startled me. I bumped my head against his waist, nearly knocking him over. Lying down, I rested my head on my paws, then returned to my body.

My muscles quivered. I tried to push myself up off the floor, but I fell back down.

"Dacia." Cody lifted me, cradling me in his arms. "Why didn't you tell me?"

My lips moved, but the words wouldn't form.

He sat down, lifted his shirt, and placed my hand on his chest. "Take as much as you need."

Draconian stares down at me from the back of a blue dragon. "Your friends will pay for your defiance. They will suffer unless you hand Nefarious over." Spittle flies from his mouth while he shouts at me.

The beast stands on me. Its razor-sharp talons pierce my chest. Spots dance in front of my eyes, making it impossible to focus. Blood soaks the rocky ground beneath me. My breaths are ragged and shallow. *How does he expect me to tell him where Nefarious is? I can't talk.*

"Time's up." His cruel laugh echoes through the still, evening air. "Bring them out," he orders his dragons. "She can watch them die!" He climbs down and kneels beside me. "You should've given him to me." His beard brushes my face. He smells like sulfur. "Now, I get the satisfaction of watching you lose all that you love."

Three dragons fly into the clearing. Each one carries one of my friends in its talons. Blood runs down their chests and backs. My heartbeat edges up a notch, as fear twists my stomach. I try to lift myself off the ground, but my muscles shake, then give out. I've lost too much blood. Fuzziness creeps into my vision, softening the edges, blurring images together. Consciousness slips from my grasp. As their faces go in and out of focus, I see desperation in their eyes. There has to be some way to help them.

Where are Arion and Aurelia? I close my eyes, fighting off the wave of nausea that threatens.

"Kill them!" Draconian shouts. The dragons tighten their grips on my friends. Talons pierce their flesh, and their cries fill the air. One by one, I feel their auras fade to nothingness.

"No!" I scream. The jagged pieces of my heart pierce my soul. Tears flood my eyes. "This … this can't be … happening." I sob. *I could've given him Nefarious. I could've defeated him again if Draconian freed him.*

Anger like a caged beast rises inside me, slamming against the bars, breaking free. Rage tears through my body, flowing through my veins until I can see only hatred and pain.

I push to my feet. Adrenaline gives me strength. Fireball after fireball flies from my fingertips, driving Draconian back.

Long, black claws tip my fingers. Ebony scales penetrate my skin as I transform into a dragon. Spikes run from the top of my head to the tip of my tail. Razor-sharp fangs fill my jaws, and my body burns from the fire within. Flames stream from my mouth, and for the first time, I detect fear in Draconian's eyes.

I advance on him without relenting. His defenses diminish. He falls to the ground, trembling.

"They will k-kill you for th-this." Draconian's voice quivers as he tries to back away from me.

I smell his terror, drinking it in, wanting it to last.

Draconian lifts his hands in surrender. "I can stop them."

Low growls rumble all around me. I tear my eyes from Draconian. Dragons surround me, stalking toward me, death in their eyes. "You unworthy, insignificant fool! How dare you!" the purple dragon shouts at me.

Draconian's fear turns to pleasure. "You chose the wrong form, Dacia! You have sealed your fate."

The dragons attack me with a ferocity I haven't seen before … tearing me limb from limb, and the last thing I see is a gruesome look of satisfaction cross Aurelia's face.

Chapter 32

Trust Issues

$\mathcal{M}$y eyes burst open. I'd fallen asleep drawing energy from Cody. *Oh, God. What did I do?* I sat up and looked around. I was on the couch, and he was sleeping in Cookie Monster.

"Cody," I whispered.

He forced his eyes open, blinking several times. "What?"

"Are you okay?" My words were rushed. "Did I take too much?"

He blinked again finally focusing on me. "Why …" His voice caught. "Why are you covered in blood?"

The light flicked on. Dan stood by the door, and Samantha looked over the rail of her loft. "What's going on?" she asked.

I closed my eyes to keep the room from spinning. Aurelia's face took shape, the anger, the hate, the satisfaction.

Does she want me dead? Why? I thought we were friends. Dream or premonition? Will I know before it's too late?

"Dacia." Cody's voice snapped me out of it. "You okay?"

I shook my head.

Cody sat down beside me, pulling me onto his lap. "Do you need more?"

"I can't. It's too much."

"What happened?" Samantha asked.

"Draconian ... dragons." I closed my eyes to think healing thoughts, but all I could concentrate on was the smugness in Aurelia's eyes. I slumped back.

Cody tightened his grip on me. "Dacia."

"I can't concentrate. I can't heal." Everything was far away and slipping further with each breath.

"Why?" Dan asked.

"I watched all of you die," I whispered. "Then I died. Aurelia seemed ... happy about it. What am I supposed to think?" Panic cracked my voice.

"Why would she want you dead?" Samantha asked.

"I don't know." I leaned my head against Cody, breathing in his scent. "Every time I close my eyes, I see her face."

"It was a dream," Dan said.

Cody's chest vibrated when he said, "Some come true."

"Yes, I'm aware of that," Dan's voice was calm and soothing. "But, what makes you think this one is a premonition? Aurelia has done nothing but help you."

"The look she gave me was so ... hateful."

"Concentrate on healing." Cody rubbed my arm. "Take my strength."

"I can't. I took too much earlier."

"Dan, Samantha," Cody said.

"I got it, Sam." Dan sat beside me on the couch and clutched my hand. "Go ahead."

While I pulled energy from Dan, Cody told Samantha and Dan about my lesson.

"She did what?" Samantha's voice was filled with excitement.

"Aurelia didn't like it," Cody said.

"Wow, I've gotta see that when you're better," Dan said.

"Not until this is over." Cody's voice was stern. "If she turns into a dragon and they find out, they'll kill her."

"We can wait," Samantha said. "Nobody wants Dacia to get hurt, including Aurelia."

"It's …" I gulped in air. "It's not … working."

"Do you want me to get Aurelia?" Samantha asked.

"Don't know … if I can trust …"

"You can, and you will." Samantha strode to the door.

My head fell back against Cody's shoulder. I shut my eyes, trying to block out the pain.

Aurelia's hands were hot, like she had been warming them by a campfire. Her eyes filled with concern, and I realized my friends were right; it was just a dream. She didn't mean me any harm.

I heard Aurelia's voice in my head, *Arion told me about your dream. He did not mean to eavesdrop. He is here to protect you. Please do not think I intend to harm you in any way.*

I know. I'm sorry, I answered so only she could hear. *The dream was so real. I wasn't thinking.*

"You are healing nicely now, Dacia," she said aloud. "You will be fine."

I pushed myself off Cody's lap and staggered across the room to my robe.

"What are you doing?" Samantha asked.

Pointing at myself, I said, "I've gotta get this blood off me."

Samantha tossed off her sheet and joined me. "You don't look very steady. I'll go with you."

"Thanks," I said.

Cody looked down at the blood on his clothes. "Aurelia"—Cody stood—"could you?"

"Of course." She rested her hand on his shoulder, and they disappeared.

Cody and Aurelia were waiting when we returned. I plopped down in Cookie Monster. "Cody, take my bed. I don't have the energy to climb the ladder."

Aurelia grasped my shoulder. "Rest."

My eyes fought to stay open. I leaned back and fell into a deep, dreamless sleep. When I woke up, everybody except Aurelia was gone. "Where is everyone?"

"I convinced them it would be good to go to class," she said. "Samantha thought it was a good idea, but Cody was hesitant."

I chuckled. "I imagine."

"How are you feeling?"

"Much better. I slept like I haven't slept in a long time." I thought about last night's events. "You put a spell on me."

She nodded. "Yes. You are very observant. You needed to heal, so I made you sleep. I hope you are not upset."

"Well, uh …" I raked my fingers through my hair. "It makes me a little uncomfortable knowing you can do that to me. I couldn't do anything to fight it."

"Had you not been injured, you could have. Your injuries were severe—worse than you realized, and your agitation caused them to worsen. I need you to understand I did it to help you, not to harm you."

"I do." Walking to the window, I tried to get my emotions under control and find the right words to explain myself. "It's just unnerving knowing somebody can do that to me, and there is nothing I can do about it."

"I have had thousands of years to perfect my abilities." Aurelia crossed her legs, tugging her skirt down. "Also, I am a magical creature—all of my kind are magical. Humans produce one child in a million who has the ability to use magic. If those capabilities are not nurtured and honed, the child may lose its power. You are a unique creature, Dacia. One day, if you continue training, you will be even more powerful than I am, but you will never be more powerful than me when you are standing on death's doorstep."

Turning away from the window, I focused on Aurelia. In all the time I'd known her, I couldn't remember her joking or being sarcastic, but she couldn't be serious. Could she? "Do you …" I bit my lip and cocked my head. "Do you really believe that?"

"Yes, your magic is limitless."

"So, uh, in your opinion, am I going to …" I pressed my fingers over my lips and turned away.

"Say what you want, Dacia. You will not upset me, and if it is bothering you, it is better asked."

"Am I going to become more powerful than you because I won't die either?" The words ran out of my mouth.

"In my experience, death is inevitable for all of us. Yes"— she nodded—"even me. You may live a very long time, or you may not. That is not something I can answer for you. I know you do not want to live forever, but most likely, you will live longer than the majority of people. However, there are no guarantees in life. If you are reckless, your life will end sooner rather than later."

I plopped down on the chair hard enough to make it rock back and forth. "That's more than you said before."

"Yes, I have learned you are a very persistent person, so I decided I might as well tell you. Otherwise, you would keep hounding me until I did. I have never met anyone else quite like you."

"Thanks, but what can I say?" I smiled and twisted my index fingers on my cheeks. "I've gotta be me."

"That you do, Dacia. The world needs you just the way you are."

"Maybe you don't know, but … uh, how long has Draconian been alive?"

"I am uncertain of his exact age." She spread her arms across the back of the couch. "However, he was around during the Salem witch-hunt. What I am unsure of is how long he was alive before then."

My eyebrows pinched together. I tried to remember when they happened, but remembering dates had never been one of my strengths. "When were they?"

"1692." Her eyes filled with visions of the past. "That was a trying time."

"Were you in Salem then?"

"No, I was not." She folded her hands in her lap and looked down at them. "If I had been, I would have disappeared, never to be seen again. If the judges and accusers understood magic, none of those poor, innocent people would have been forced to go through that. There have been many times throughout history when 'witches' were persecuted. I doubt any truly magical being was ever convicted. Draconian was there, and I imagine he influenced the young girls who claimed to be bewitched." She lifted her head. Her gold eyes hardened. "He is a monstrous man."

"Why didn't somebody stop him then? Why was it ever allowed to escalate to this?"

"Why is anything ever allowed to escalate?" She dropped her head to her chest. "Somebody should have stopped him, but we did not feel it was our place. It was a human problem, and as it turned out, humans had no idea what they were up against."

I leaned forward, resting my elbows on my knees. "Is he more powerful than you?"

"Draconian possesses powers I do not. He can do things I cannot. However, I can do things he cannot. Which of us is stronger, I do not know. He takes too much for granted, and that weakens his powers."

"Can I win?" The words surprised me. I hadn't planned on asking that, and I wasn't sure I wanted to know her answer.

She tilted her head, examining me like a bug under a microscope. "I believe you can."

"Let's hope." Knowing Draconian had been keeping an eye on me, I didn't want him to think now would be the opportune moment to strike. I needed more time before I faced him, more training, and a chance to say goodbye. Just in case. "I'm feeling better. I should get cleaned up so I can go to class this afternoon."

Aurelia stood and walked toward the door.

"Thanks for everything, Aurelia. I'm sorry I doubted you."

"I forgive you." She looked over her shoulder at me. "You are going through a trying time, and you will have doubts. Try to stay positive. The world needs you."

I shrugged and sighed. "No guarantees."

"Arion should return with your friends soon. You better be back before them, or they will be worried."

By the time I finished my shower and returned to the room, Cody, Dan, and Samantha were back. "How're you?" Cody asked before I closed the door.

"Better. My wounds are healed, and Aurelia and I had a good talk after I woke up."

"I'm glad you're better." Samantha pulled her hair up into a messy bun. "Tonight, we have to go to the observatory for our astronomy class. It's supposed to be a clear night, and this little outing counts for half our grade."

I rubbed the towel over my head. Tangled curls fell below my shoulders. I put some leave-in conditioner in my hands and pulled my fingers through my hair. "I guess I better show up then." I tipped my head back, staring at the ceiling. "Don't let me take a nap before then."

"We'll find something to do." Cody grabbed my hand and pulled me toward him.

"I'll tell Professor Caiman I had a migraine." I leaned into Cody. "I need you guys to help me stay focused … keep my mind off Draconian."

"Whatever you need." Dan stood behind Samantha with his head on her shoulder.

"It's not going to be easy."

"Yeah, we know." Cody wrapped his arms around my waist and kissed my forehead. "Nothing's easy anymore. A week from tomorrow things will get better."

"Hopefully." I turned away so Cody couldn't see my face. I didn't plan to wait that long to face Draconian, but I wasn't ready to tell my friends.

"I am confident you will defeat him," Aurelia said. "I will be there to help you."

"We'll see when it's over," I told them. "I don't know how it's going to turn out, but if I defeat him, I hope it's a while before I have to save the world again."

"The world is always in danger. However, you are not its only guardian. Others, who you will probably never meet, play a part in protecting it."

"I just want a break." I felt selfish for asking for it.

"Well, I don't know about you guys"—Dan stood back and folded his arms over his chest—"but I don't think we're doing a great job of keeping her mind off this."

"You're right," Cody said. "We suck."

After lunch, we went to calculus. I did my best to listen to Professor Granite, but my mind wandered back to Draconian and his dragons. The same question kept haunting me. *How can I win?* As far as I was concerned, I couldn't. *How can I face Draconian and fifteen dragons and walk away?* It was an impossible endeavor.

"Dacia, please answer the question." Professor Granite tapped his foot rapidly.

"I'm sorry. I, uh, had a migraine this morning, and it's coming back. I didn't hear your question," I hated lying, but it was better than telling him I was preoccupied with dragons.

"Cody, why don't you take her to Nurse Heron's office?" he suggested. "Feel better, Dacia. Now … Tanya, please answer."

Are you okay? Aurelia's voice echoed inside my head.

Yeah, I can't concentrate. All I can think about is Draconian and his dragons. I'm scared … really, really scared. I don't see how I can defeat him. I can't think.

The answer will come when you least expect it, just as it did when you defeated Nefarious, she told me with a confidence I didn't feel. *Go back to your room. Arion will watch over you.*

"What's going on?" As soon as we were out of the classroom, Cody turned me toward him, holding my arms at the elbows. "You don't have a headache."

"No, I don't, but it seemed better than telling him I was zoning out."

"What were you thinking about?"

"Nothing really … I was just spaced out." The lie tasted like a mouthful of vanilla extract.

Cody grimaced, but he didn't say a word. We continued in silence. I shouldn't have done it, but I wanted to know what he thought. *She's not telling the truth. How do I get her to let me in?* I heard his voice in my head.

We hurried back to my room. I didn't expect Draconian to attack me, but I couldn't take the chance. Cody sat on the couch and patted the seat next to him. I shook my head and leaned on Cookie Monster, my hands folded over the back, my chin resting on my arms.

"I'm scared." I didn't want him to think I didn't care about him. "All I can think about is Draconian. I can't win, Cody!"

"But, you can. Aurelia believes in you … I believe in you." He stood beside me and squeezed my shoulder.

"I know you all think I've got this"—I closed my eyes—"but I don't. I can't see a way out."

"You'll find it." He wrapped his arms around me in a protective embrace. "You have to. I can't live without you."

I turned in his arms and nuzzled my head into his chest. "You might have to. I don't want to die, but I don't know how to survive this."

"You will survive," Arion's voice filled the room. "You are stronger than Draconian, and you have more reasons to live."

"I hope you're right …"

Cody and I sat on the couch. He pulled me against his side and held me until the others got back from class. Cody told them what was going on. I ran my finger over his arm, tracing his veins. I didn't interrupt, didn't add anything to it.

Dan and Samantha sat in Big Bird and Cookie Monster. Dan leaned toward us. They listened to Cody without interrupting, then responded exactly how I expected them to: everything would be fine. I'd see.

"We really aren't doing a good job." Dan's apologetic smile didn't brighten his face as much as his usual one, but it still showed off his dimples.

"We have to be at the observatory by nine," Samantha said. "So, what do you guys want to do until then?"

"We need to get Dacia out of here for a while," Dan said. "We need to help keep her mind off things."

"Racquetball." Cody sat up straighter. "Wanna play racquetball? It's been a long time."

"Sure, why not?" I lifted my shoulders. "If I don't concentrate, my head'll get knocked off. That should help keep me focused."

"Are you sure you want to?" Samantha asked.

"Yeah, let's do it." I rubbed my hands together, trying to garner some enthusiasm.

The others were in a good mood as we walked to the racquetball court. However, I saw dragons everywhere—in the distant trees, in the clouds, hiding behind buildings, standing in every shadowed place. My heart raced, anticipating the worst. Fear welled up inside of me until it was all I could do not to scream.

Calm down, I thought to myself, but the irrational fear grew. "I need to sit for a minute." I plopped down in the middle of the sidewalk, closed my eyes, and tried to picture Falcon Lake. My breathing evened out, and the sound of waves lapping against the shore washed my terror away. As the last of my fear subsided, I thought I heard Draconian's laughter in the distance. Was all this because of him? Did he cast a spell to give me an anxiety attack?

When I opened my eyes, the concerned faces of my friends stared down at me. Cody knelt beside me and traced his fingers over the back of my hand. "You okay?"

"I'm fine," I said. "Panic attack, but I'm over it."

"Are you sure?" Samantha didn't sound convinced.

"Yeah. Shall we?" *Did Draconian do that to me, or am I losing my mind?*

They looked at me like they wanted me to say more, but none of them pressed me for information. Instead, they followed when I walked away.

"It'll be nice when this is over, won't it?" Dan asked quietly.

"Let's hope," Samantha whispered back to him.

Yes, let's, I thought.

Racquetball was a good distraction. I didn't know if we played by the rules, but for a couple hours, all I thought about was hitting the ball and not getting hit by it in return. By the time we left, the four of us were soaked in sweat.

"I think we have enough time for showers and dinner before we head for the observatory," Samantha said.

With that comment, a crushing weight crashed down on me. The idea of being out wandering around campus in the dark did not appeal to me in the least.

My stoic mask slipped and trepidation showed on my face. "What's wrong, Dacia?" Dan asked. "Do you need to sit for a minute?"

"No … no, I'm fine." I tried to muster up a smile but failed.

"No, you're not." Cody brushed my cheek. "You were, but now you're white as a sheet and obviously upset."

"We're going to the observatory at night … in the dark, and you don't think Draconian will try to take advantage of that situation? I'm sorry if I seem a little distraught or overwhelmed, but I'm scared to death. I don't want you guys to be around when he decides it's time. Maybe that won't be tonight. Maybe he'll wait like he promised, but what if he doesn't?"

"We probably will be," Cody said.

"I know, and he will kill you." I was surprised by how calm my voice sounded.

Chapter 33

Stargazing

*L*ong shadows stretched across the sidewalk and into the forest. I clutched Cody's hand. Every noise, every stray breeze had me grasping tighter.

"Dacia"—Cody's voice was strained—"you're crushing my hand."

I loosened my grip. Light danced through the trees, making it seem like something was moving in them. I clenched it again. He wiggled his fingers, spreading mine out.

I stepped into Kestrel Observatory and leaned against the wall. When my legs quit shaking, we took the stairs to the roof. A few other students were there already and had staked claims on their telescopes.

Professor Caiman walked over to us and handed us a list of stars, nebula, clusters, and planets that we needed to find.

Once we found them, she would sign off. "Split into groups of two or three. As soon as it's dark enough, we'll begin."

"I will go with Dan and Samantha," Aurelia said. *If either of us notices something out of the ordinary, we can contact each other and teleport back to the room,* she thought to me.

"That's fine," I told her. I figured that simple statement worked for both what she told me and what she thought to me.

"How are you?" Cody asked when we were alone.

"All right." I scanned the sky and the ground. "I just feel like something bad is going to happen. Who knows? Maybe I'm just paranoid."

"Maybe, you've been through a lot."

"So, what's on the list?" I rubbed my neck.

"M27, M13, M11, M57, Vega, Deneb, Polaris, Arcturus, Altair, Regulus, and Saturn." He waved the paper. "Gonna take a while to find all this."

"Hopefully, we have time," I mumbled. "You'll have to help me out with the M numbers. I wasn't in class this morning, and I don't remember what all of them are."

"We can look for the stars and Saturn first."

My hands wouldn't stop shaking, so I shoved them into my pockets. "I think that'd be best. The sooner we can get done, the better. Dan and Samantha should have quite an advantage with Aurelia helping them."

Before long, stars filled the night sky. Looking up at them comforted me. The sky was cloudless, and the moon wouldn't rise for another couple of hours. Cody and I took turns looking through the telescope.

We were searching for Regulus when I noticed a dark shadow moving across the sky. One of my classmates said, "There's a cloud in the way. I can't find Saturn." But, I knew better. It wasn't a cloud. The amethyst dragon swooped and dived in a rhythmic dance, twisting and turning gracefully through the night sky. For some reason, it didn't evoke a sense of fear.

Do you see it? I asked Aurelia.

Yes, she answered. *She is not going to harm us, though. She is not one of Draconian's dragons ... not yet anyway.*

I watched her weave across the heavens. *Why can I see her? Why can't anyone else?*

You know what you are looking at. You know dragons exist. Your classmates are deceived by a spell. All they can see is a cloud drifting across the sky.

Oh. I looked through the telescope at the dragon. *Do you think she would help us?*

She will not. I have already asked her. She sounded disappointed. *She would be a worthy ally. However, she has eggs in her lair and cannot risk being under Draconian's control. Baby dragons are very rare.*

Baby dragons. That would be neat to see.

Yes, it has been a long time since I have seen them. Longing floated through my mind along with Aurelia's words. *Keep your eyes open for anything else. If Draconian notices her flying around, he will try to make her his.*

My stomach twisted, fear and desperation clinging to my gut. *Can you warn her? Let her know that Draconian is probably keeping an eye on me, and she is vulnerable right now.* I didn't want her eggs to be jeopardized, and I also didn't want to have to face another dragon.

Yes.

I watched the graceful dragon through my telescope. One minute she was there, and the next she was gone.

She was grateful for the warning, Aurelia's voice sounded in my head. *She teleported back to her lair.*

That helped set my mind at ease. Even though I had no idea how to fight them, fifteen dragons were better than sixteen.

"Dacia, where've you been?" Cody sounded annoyed. "You're always off in your own world."

I looked around to make sure nobody was paying attention to us. "I'm sorry," I whispered. "There was a dragon." I pointed to the sky where she had been flying. "Aurelia and I were discussing it."

"Why're we still here?" Panic rose in his voice.

"She's not one of Draconian's."

"Let's get done," Cody said. "I gotta bad feeling, too."

"Too many things could happen … too much could go wrong." I turned back to the telescope. "We've only got one more. Let's find it. Hopefully, they're about done, too."

While we waited for Professor Caiman to come over and verify our results, I felt Draconian's presence. *I can feel him,* I thought to Aurelia. *I don't know where he is, though.*

Are you finished?

We're just waiting for Professor Caiman. What about you?

As soon as she gets here, we are also done. We can walk out of sight and teleport back to the room.

I don't want to tell them, I thought to her. *I don't want them to worry.*

When Professor Caiman came over to check our telescope, she said, "You're definitely in the right area, but until that cloud moves, I won't be able to tell if that's the Wild Duck Cluster for sure."

Aurelia, I thought, *is there a cloud blocking M11 right now?*

No, Dacia, she responded. *It is one of Draconian's dragons. He must have sent him to look for the dragon you saw earlier.*

We've got to get out of here.

"Well done," Professor Caiman said. "You two are done. You can stick around and keep using the telescope, or you can head back."

"I think we'll go back," I said. "I haven't been feeling very well today. As soon as Samantha, Dan, and Aurelia are done, we'll head back with them."

I breathed a sigh of relief when she checked their findings next and excused them. Grabbing Cody's hand, we hurried downstairs. I led them off the path, and when we were hidden out of sight, Aurelia and I teleported the others back to our room.

"What was that about?" Samantha asked.

"The cloud blocking M11 was one of Draconian's dragons," Aurelia answered. "He was not there for any of us, but we saw no reason to take a chance."

"Why was he there then?" Dan lifted his hands, then dropped them back to his sides.

"Another dragon had been flying there earlier. She was not under Draconian's control," Aurelia said.

"Aurelia believes Draconian sent the dragon to recruit her." I squeezed my forehead between my thumb and fingers and brought them together. "I felt Draconian's presence right before Professor Caiman came over."

"Hopefully, Draconian and the dragon don't find her." Samantha plopped down on the couch, pulling Dan with her. "You don't need any more enemies."

"No, I don't." I looked out the window, wondering how many others were patrolling the skies.

"Why didn't you tell me?" Cody asked.

"Professor Caiman was standing there." I turned toward him. "I couldn't."

"You could've, Dacia, and you know it." He tossed his hands up.

"If I would've sent my thoughts to you, you wouldn't have shown fear or said anything?" I couldn't keep the doubt out of my voice.

"Probably would've, but I'da known what was happening."

"I thought I was doing what was best." I grabbed my pajamas. "I'm going to bed." I stomped out the door.

When I got back, Cody walked over to me and put his arm around my shoulders. Part of me wanted to pull away from him, but the rest of me knew I needed him, knew I didn't want to be angry, and knew he was scared and meant well.

"Please don't be mad." His voice was soft, the anger gone. "You're doing what you feel is best, but we're here to help. Don't keep us in the dark."

"I'll try, but … don't expect me to tell you about Draconian or dragons in front of a bunch of people. Just trust me to keep you safe."

"I'm sorry to interrupt, but I think I'll stay over here tonight," Dan said. "I think I'd feel more comfortable not being alone."

I tried to smile at Dan, to reassure him, but I wasn't sure that was the expression that came across. "You're more than welcome to."

"Sleep on the couch tonight." Cody rested his chin on my shoulder. "After all, it's yours."

"I brought it over for you. Dacia needs you here more than she needs me," Dan said.

"Slept in Cookie Monster half the year. A few more nights won't kill me."

"You two can work it out." I pulled away. "I'm going to bed. Sleep good."

"You too, Dacia," Cody said.

Chapter 34

Hardening My Resolve

$\mathcal{A}$urelia and I stood in an auditorium in Kalmia Hall, facing each other. Fireballs erupted from my fingertips. She deflected each of them with ease.

"Your stamina is improving." She lifted her hand and froze four fireballs. They dropped to the ground with a thud.

I lowered my hands and yawned. "Isn't there anything new you could teach me?"

"I could show you how to close your mind to keep others from being able to sense your presence," she said. "However, I am not sure that would be the brightest thing to do right now … maybe after the fight."

"So, basically, I'm left with what I already know." I closed my eyes and tugged my hand through my hair. "That's great."

"When we first met, your powers were more formidable than I had anticipated." Aurelia stepped toward me. "Your skills are advanced for your age. If you continue progressing at this rate, you will be one of the most powerful magicians I have ever heard of in just a matter of years." She patted my shoulder. "I am sorry, but I have no more to offer."

I scrubbed my hand over my face. I'd hoped Aurelia would be able to teach me something that would help me defeat Draconian, but I'd have to figure it out on my own.

On our way to pick up the others from class, Aurelia walked tall with her head held high. I studied the cracks in the sidewalks, my shoulders slumped and my hands stuffed in my pockets.

"Dacia, you okay?" Cody asked when he stepped out of Primrose Hall.

I lifted my shoulders half-heartedly and headed toward the dorm without saying a word. Cody walked beside me. Samantha, Dan, and Aurelia fell in behind us, talking quietly. Their voices turned to fuzz inside my head. Cody's hand slid around my forearm, jerking me to a stop.

"Aurelia, take Samantha and Dan back?" His voice lifted into a question. He pointed at me, then at himself. "We need a minute."

She took a long, slow breath and made her decision. "I think Dacia could use some time alone with you, too. It will be good for her," she said as if I wasn't even there.

She was right—physically, I was walking along beside them, but mentally, I was light-years away.

Cody took my hand and led me to a bench. He sat and pulled me onto his lap. I curled up against him, and he held me, nuzzling his face in my hair. His arms shielded me from all of the dangers, real, and imagined like nothing could harm me as long as I stayed there.

"Hate seeing you so upset," he breathed in my ear.

I buried my head deeper into his chest. I didn't want him to see the tears streaming down my face or the hopelessness in my eyes. I knew this wasn't how I should be spending what little time I had left. I should be living … enjoying myself. *This will be the last time I let grief overwhelm me before I battle Draconian,* I vowed to myself. *This is the last time self-pity will control me.*

"I'm sorry, Cody," I said when I found my voice.

"Don't be. You hold it all in. Some point, has to come out. You can't always be brave and strong. Sometimes, you have to be vulnerable." He brushed my hair back and tucked it behind my ear. "Believe it or not, you're not Wonder Woman."

I cupped his jaw in my hand, rubbing my thumb along his cheek. "You're good at making excuses for me."

"Not an excuse. You're human. Only so much you can take." His hand lingered on my face. "Don't know how you do it."

I watched students walk by. One guy dribbled a basketball, between his legs and behind his back. He nodded at Cody as he went by. "Why don't you play basketball or hang out with your friends anymore?"

"You need me more." He held my eyes with his. "Mean more than anything, and not gonna let you go through this alone."

Guilt pooled in my stomach, weighing me down. "You still need your life."

"You're my life. All I need."

"But … I might not always be here." I brushed my fingers along his hairline and over his ear. Birds chirped, jumping from branch to branch in the pine trees. "You need to go on with your life if that happens."

"You're gone, mine won't be worth living." Cody covered my hand with his. "Draconian wins, want him to kill me, too. Can't live without you, Dacia. Don't—" he cleared his throat, and I noticed how shiny his eyes were "—don't even wanna try. Don't even wanna imagine life without you."

"Please … don't say that, Cody." My chest tightened. The thought of a world without him in it was more than I could bear. I bit my lip, pulling it into my mouth. The wind blew my hair back, and Cody brushed it off his face. "I don't think I can beat him. If I don't, I want you, Samantha, and Dan to get out of here and never turn back. You'll find somebody else … somebody better for you. Don't let him kill you."

"You think I'd find someone else?" His eyes narrowed, and he drew in a quick breath. "There's no one else. Something happens to you, lose half myself … the better half."

"I'm sorry, Cody." Tears threatened to flow. "I can't imagine the world without you. If something happens to me, you can't be lost, too."

"If something happens … if you don't make it, won't be anything lefta me worth saving." He wiped tears from my eyes. "Love you, and can't live without you. Don'tcha see that?"

I set my hand over the top of his and gazed into his sapphire eyes. "I wouldn't be able to live without you either. I guess I just don't know why you feel so strongly about me." A chipmunk ran across the sidewalk and sniffed my foot before zipping off again in search of food. My lips turned up in a wistful smile.

His hand was still on my face, lending me warmth and strength. He gently rubbed his thumb over my cheek. "Because you're beautiful and wonderful and perfect and unique," he answered as if it was obvious. "You're my heart and soul. Why can't you see that?"

"Nobody's ever cared about me like this before. I don't see how you can." I dragged my hand through my hair and stared off at the mountains. "Every girl here stares at you when you walk by. They all wonder what you're doing with me. I wonder what you're doing with me."

"Loving you. Hoping you love me half as much in return." He didn't lower his voice. He didn't try to hide his declaration from the people walking by, and my heart swelled in response.

"I have always loved you—I will always love you." I leaned my head back against his shoulder. It broke my heart knowing that if I failed, Draconian would probably kill him, too. That was the hardest thing about going into this battle. All of my friends might pay because my morals stood in the way of me killing Draconian. Just the fact that I knew that should've made it easier for me to decide what to do, but it went against the very essence of my being to take another life, no matter how evil that life was.

I was pulled out of my reverie when Cody's hands slid up my neck, tilting my head back. His lips crashed against mine, desperate, starving. I clutched his shirt, pulling him toward me. He pulled away, leaving me breathless. When I regained control of myself, I looked at him with raised eyebrows.

The light danced in his eyes, softening them. His fingers drew intricate designs on my arms and back. His breath was ragged, his voice husky. "Only have a week, should make the most of it." He kissed my forehead, my nose, my cheek, and my ear. I grabbed his head and pulled his lips to mine.

Heat spread through my body and settled in my chest, bringing with it a sense of determination. I slid my hand under Cody's shirt, trailing my fingers over his skin.

He moaned and tugged me toward him, leaving only a tiny strip of air between us. I scooted closer, eliminating it.

There was nothing in the world except the two of us. Nothing else mattered.

The kiss slowed, and I leaned my forehead against his. Both of us were breathing hard.

We sat in silence, my head resting against his shoulder. His heartbeat, a steady rhythm, helped me feel at ease. The warmth of his body chased the chill from me. I wanted him to hold me tighter, to pull me closer, but that would have been impossible. I was already as close to him as I could be.

Bees buzzed, zipping from flower to flower. Butterflies flitted through the air. Clouds drifted across the sky. For a moment, everything seemed perfect.

Cody broke the silence. His chest bounced against my ear. "Anything you want to do?"

"I'm pretty comfortable here." I lifted my head just enough to look at his face.

"Not alone much." He rubbed his hand over the top of my head and down my back. "Should take advantage."

I looked into his eyes and laughed without humor. "I doubt we're alone now. I'm sure Arion is keeping an eye on us."

"Yeah." He rubbed his chin. "Outta sight and all."

"If he wasn't able to, I imagine Aurelia took the others back to the dorm and then came to watch us herself." I stretched out on the bench with my head on Cody's lap. He brushed his fingers through my hair. Once again, I found myself wondering why life couldn't always be this easy. Why had fate dealt me such a difficult hand to play?

A small voice in the back of my head asked me, *If this hadn't been your hand, would you be here with Cody—like this—right now?*

"Probably not," I mumbled.

"What was that, Dacia?"

"Sorry." Heat flooded my cheeks. "I was just talking to myself."

"About what?"

"I was, uh … trying to make sense of my life."

He twined his fingers through mine. "Having any luck?"

I shrugged. "Not too much. But without Nefarious, there might not be an us."

"We'da figured it out."

A wave of emotions washed over me. I knew what I wanted out of life. I wanted to marry Cody, have his children and grow old with him. I wanted to watch our grandchildren grow up. None of this could happen if I didn't defeat Draconian. Maybe for this … maybe for Cody, I could find the strength to kill Draconian. If nothing else, I had to try. I couldn't give up my future before it had a chance to happen.

Cody and I spent most of the day alone. We wandered around campus, holding hands and enjoying each other's company. Every so often, we sat on a bench, and he held me. It was during each of these moments that I felt my resolve strengthen. I could do it—for Cody—I could defeat Draconian. I could face fifteen dragons and walk away. I had to.

Chapter 35
Death Is An Option

The mountain clearing is beautiful, the perfect place for a picnic. It shouldn't be the scene of a battle, but that's what it is today. Wildflowers are trampled beneath dragon feet. Draconian's laughter hushes the birds. The trees surrounding us have been singed by dragon flame.

"Your confidence is incredible," Draconian says. "Where did this come from?"

"I made my mind up," I answer like I don't have a care in the world. "I won't let you steal my future."

"Whatever it takes?" His eyebrows rise, and he nods. "You really think you can stop me?"

"Yep." I make a popping sound at the end of the word.

"I have a different future planned for you." He lifts his hands in front of him, and I fall to the ground. Draconian turns and walks away from me. "First I'll kill Cody. You'll be suicidal for a while, but I'm patient. You'll get over him … with my help. That anger will make you stronger." He spins around and smirks at me.

Channeling my strength, I push myself up. "Leave him out of this!"

"It's too late for me to do that." His laugh is vicious.

I follow his gaze and see three dragons heading my way. Cody dangles from the talons of the black dragon. Blood stains his shirt, dripping from the hem. I'm not sure how much longer he has to live. A blue dragon and a red one fly over the clearing. Samantha and Dan hang limply from their talons.

"Give me Nefarious, and I will let your friends go. I'll even let you heal them before I take you away."

"How about I kill you instead?"

I don't give him a chance to answer. I remember my lesson on the beach with Aurelia and discharge lightning bolt after lightning bolt in his direction.

Draconian disappears, re-emerging across the clearing. His black and silver robe is singed. Fear dances through his gray eyes.

I fling more bolts of lightning at him, not giving him a chance to retaliate. I need to keep him occupied while I figure out how to free my friends.

He teleports, again and again, looking more haggard each time he appears.

A roaring rushes toward me. I think about fire until I turn into flames. Just as I do, the fireball passes through my chest.

The menace radiating off Draconian is like a thousand pin-pricks on my bare skin. "Kill him," he orders the black dragon.

As soon as the words leave his mouth, the strength and love that I sense in Cody's aura sizzles, then fades into nothingness. The light vanishes from his eyes. The flames engulfing me extinguish themselves, and I fall to the ground in a heap. I clutch my chest. My heart shatters. The slivers tear through me, shredding me.

"Oh," Draconian's voice is heavy with sarcasm, "I thought you were going to fight me. I thought you were going to kill me."

A sob tears from my throat. "Just kill me—put me out of my misery." My voice sounds lifeless. All the fight flees from me. "I don't want to live in a world without Cody."

"I thought I already made it clear to you." His tone turns condescending. "I'm not about to kill my newest pet. You will be my apprentice. In time, you will get over the loss of this insignificant boy, and you will learn all I have to offer. You will come to see the allure of power and immortality."

My mind feels muddled. I know he's trying to control me, but I no longer have the desire to stop him. Maybe under his control, I won't feel this pain. Maybe under his control, I will be numb. Right now, I feel like my heart has exploded, and with it, my will to survive disappeared. How can I live without Cody?

I don't fight Draconian, but for some reason, he can't control me. He growls in frustration.

"Take them," I scream. "Take my memories. Take my pain. You promised." I curl into a ball, tucking my legs into my chest. I stare at Cody's body, willing it to move, willing him to breathe.

Draconian reaches for my mind again. When he can't get in, the pain that overtakes me is fierce and relentless. I'm not paralyzed—I could scream—instead, I lie there silently. Tears stream down my cheeks.

"Fight back." He kicks me in the stomach, rattling the shards left behind when my heart broke.

I don't respond, hoping if I make him mad enough, he'll kill me.

"Would you like your other friends to suffer the same fate as Cody?" His voice is soft, but menace boils under the surface.

What a friend I am—I'd forgotten all about Samantha and Dan. They have to be terrified. "Just let them go. You won. I won't fight anymore. You didn't kill me, but you took my life." I swallow over the lump in the back of my throat. "You took everything I was living for."

"No, I don't think I'll let them go. I would much rather have you fight for them." An evil smile lights up his face.

I want to give up—to lie there and die—but, how can I with my friends' lives in danger? Is there some way for them to escape death … for me to escape Draconian?

"Let them go!" I jump to my feet. "I'll go with you willingly once they are free."

"Do you really think you are in a position to negotiate?" Rage emanates from him.

"Actually, I do." My confidence makes him hesitate.

"I will let one of them go," he responds after a tension-filled pause. "Then, when you are in my dungeon, I'll release the other."

"That's the wrong answer." My legs shake, but I stand in front of him, holding my ground. "They will be healed by me before I go anywhere with you. Your time is running out. Decide!"

He glances at the dragons carrying my friends. "Release the girl."

Samantha falls to the ground without making a sound. Her body is limp. I start toward her but stop. I have to stand firm. "What about Dan?" Sparks flicker on my fingertips, lifting my hair. I rise off the ground, hovering above Draconian.

Sweat beads on his forehead, and his eyes dart around the clearing. "Drop him." He waves his hand toward the dragon. Dan's body crashes to the ground.

I fly toward them, knowing I'll only have one chance. If Draconian suspects anything, his dragons will kill my friends. They are far enough apart that I can't reach both of them at once. I kneel beside Samantha, grab her hand, and teleport to Dan's side. Before the dragons realize what's happening, I have hold of Dan and teleport back to my room.

Fighting to keep my thoughts from wandering, I heal Samantha and Dan. Then, without saying a word to them, I teleport back to the battlefield. Draconian and his dragons are still there.

Cody lies lifeless on the ground. Hoping to go unnoticed, I teleport to him. As soon as I reappear, pain tears through my body. I collapse.

Draconian laughs. "You're so predictable." He saunters closer, smirking as fire burns me from the inside. "I knew you couldn't leave the boy's body behind."

Lava burns through my veins, melting me. Sweat beads on my face. I force myself onto my hands and knees. The fire within surges as I crawl to Cody's side and drop onto the ground next to him.

I wrap my arms around him. His skin already carries the paleness of death. Laying my head on his chest, a sob tears through me, catching in my throat. I squeeze my eyes shut and teleport back to my room.

Samantha and Dan gasp when they see me with his corpse. "I couldn't leave him there," I explain. I sit on the floor cradling Cody in my arms, rocking back and forth as sobs cleave through my body.

Pain slashes my heart. Cody is dead. He'll never hold me in his arms again, never try to protect me, never open his beautiful blue eyes. Grief devastates me. Every fragment of my broken heart screams in agony. The force takes my breath away.

"Dacia … Dacia." Samantha wraps her arm around my shoulders, but I won't let go of Cody.

"Dacia." *How can I be hearing his voice?* "Dacia, wake up."

Cody wiped the tears from my eyes. "What is it, Dacia? Where are you hurt?"

"I … I'm not. I'm fine now." I threw my arms around his neck, pulling his mouth down on mine. I planned to never let him go.

Samantha knelt at the end of her bed and cleared her throat. "Uh, not to interrupt, but would you mind telling us what your dream was about?"

Cody tried to pull away, but I clung to him, not willing to be separated from him.

"Dacia, it's okay." He entwined his fingers with mine and lifted them to his mouth.

I squeezed my eyes shut. "Cody died. It was so real." Rubbing my hand along his jaw, a lump formed in my throat. "I thought I would never see you again."

"I'm sorry, Dacia." Samantha's gaze flicked to Dan. "That had to be terrible."

"I can't imagine losing Samantha," Dan said quietly.

"Yeah." I swallowed hard, trying to force my emotions down. "I really don't want to think about it. It hurts even though he's standing here in my arms."

"Sleep better." Samantha crawled back under her covers.

"It's okay." Cody brushed his fingers through my hair. "I'm here. I'm not going anywhere."

"I know you don't plan to, but I'm scared." My whole body trembled. "I'm not ready to face him, but I'm ready to get this over with. I'm tired of being scared."

"Next week … will all be over by this time next week." He kept running his hands through my hair and along my arms, trying to soothe me. "I'll be sleeping in my room. Then a coupla weeks later, we'll be home for the rest of the summer. It's almost over."

"I hope you're right." I sighed. "I wish I had your confidence."

Chapter 36

Wednesday … only days remained until I either died or killed someone—what a choice. No wonder my stomach was a ball of nerves.

I was tempted to skip classes for the rest of the week, but if I was fortunate enough to survive, I'd have way too much to make up. If Draconian killed me, the others would miss enough days of school because of my funeral—if they could find my body and prove I was dead and not a runaway or something. My friends would know the truth, but nobody else would believe them.

"Don't think about it," I said to myself, but how could I not? Impending doom … who wouldn't think about it?

Groaning, I threw my covers off. Astronomy started in a little over an hour. I climbed down from my loft and woke the others.

"How're you?" Cody stifled a yawn.

"I'm tired." I rummaged through my closet, looking for something to wear, settling on sage capris and a tan shirt. "I didn't sleep well. I was afraid I'd dream about you dying again." Even though I was done in the closet, I kept my back to him. "I couldn't bear that."

"Sure you wanna go?"

"She's already skipped too many classes." Samantha turned away from the sink, folded her arms over her chest, and tapped her foot.

He walked up behind me, his steps cushioned by the carpet, and lifted me to my feet. "I'll try to keep you awake then."

"Thanks." I turned and wrapped my arms around his waist. "It'd suck to have nightmares in front of the whole class."

I was glad Cody made me that promise. Every time he saw my eyelids droop, he kicked my foot.

I didn't take notes, didn't hear Professor Caiman, didn't even register the other students. I would've been better off skipping class. Cody probably would've learned more without me there, too.

When we stepped out into the fresh air, I woke up a little, but I was still dragging when I felt Draconian's presence. *He's watching us again,* I thought to Aurelia. *I can't fight him today.*

Pick up the pace a little ... but nothing too obvious, she responded. *I think he is just doing surveillance.*

Relief washed over me when we got back to the dorm and I could let my guard down. I sat down on the couch with Cody and put my head on his shoulder. He wrapped his arm around me and pulled me closer. "Go to sleep, Dacia," he whispered as he caressed my arm. He laid his head on mine, and I felt protected. Sleep was inevitable.

"Dacia." Cody sounded far away. "Dacia." His voice was closer now. "Dacia, wake up."

I dragged myself back into reality. My eyes were heavy with sleep. I was still curled up on the couch next to Cody.

"Sleep okay?" He smiled down at me.

"Mmm-hmm," I answered. "What time is it?"

"Almost two. We're skipping class. Hope that's all right with you."

"Yeah, that's fine." If we were skipping class, I wondered why he bothered waking me up.

"Didn't think you'd want to sleep all day." His heart steadily beat beneath my ear. "Afraid if you did, you wouldn't sleep again tonight."

Now, I wondered if he could read my mind. "I probably shouldn't. I didn't mean to sleep this long, anyway."

"Wasn't sure, but my stomach decided. I'm starving."

"Okay." I laughed. "Let's go feed you."

We walked to Sedum. After getting our food, we sat at a table looking out at the green space. Several students lay on the grass, soaking up the sun or napping. Some played catch, and others had their noses buried in books.

While we ate, I asked, "How did you talk Samantha into letting me sleep … letting me skip class?"

"Wasn't easy." He took a long drink of lemonade. "She thought you should go, but you were sleeping so peacefully—you don't do that very often—so she finally gave up."

"I'm glad. I feel better now."

"You need sleep before …" He pushed his food around on his plate, careful not to look at me. "You have to, uh … have to beat him."

I tapped his foot with mine, and he met my gaze. "I hope so, Cody, but I'm not sure if I can."

"Well, can't live without you." He shrugged. "Sure of that."

"And, I don't know if I can die. But … death would probably be better than being tortured, imprisoned, and ending up as his apprentice," I said in a detached voice.

"Don't say that, Dacia!" He slammed his fist down on the table for emphasis. "Don't even think it!" His tone was harsh. Cody never let his temper get out of control. When I looked at him, I realized he wasn't mad. His face was pale, and fear washed the vibrancy from his eyes.

"I … I …" Reaching across the table, I covered his hand with mine. "I wouldn't try to die. I would try to free myself—no matter how long it took."

"Sorry, Dacia." He turned his hand, twining our fingers.

"It's okay. I know you're scared. So am I."

"Wish I could take your place." He looked out the window, then back at me. "Can't stand to see you go through this. Hate not keeping you safe."

I lifted my lips in a pathetic imitation of a smile. "This is my life. We both need to learn to accept it."

"Sure."

Chapter 37

Hardening My Heart

The wind howls, bolstered by my grief. Lightning tears through the sky, and fat drops pelt the ground.

Draconian stands above me. His robe and long beard cling to his body, but his eyes sparkle with delight.

The lifeless bodies of my friends litter the hillside. Dragons perch beside them, bowing their heads against the storm.

"Why?" I ask through my sobs. "Why … why them? Why like this?"

"You know why." He waves his hand at the sky, and the rain slows. Looking at me, he crinkles his brow, then turns his face to the storm clouds above us. "You were warned. You have no one to blame but yourself."

Hatred fills my body … seeping from my pores. My heart hardens. *What's the point of love when everything ends in death? Why should I care about anybody but me?* As these thoughts occur to me, I feel myself growing stronger. The storm swirls around us, picking up in intensity until Draconian stumbles back against the wind. I'm not a fragile little girl any longer. Like the tempest, I'm a force to be reckoned with.

The world took everything from me—my future with Cody is gone. Suddenly, I understand killing. I understand evil. I'm empty inside. *Why shouldn't everybody feel the same way as me? Why should I have to go through this alone? Death is inevitable for most ... why put it off?*

"Teach me," I yell at him. "Teach me everything you know!"

A gold dragon lands beside me. "No!" Her beautiful voice sounds tortured.

I turn toward the beast. Hatred narrows my eyes as I stare into hers. "I control you now. You will do as I say."

The dragon's eyes glaze over, and her essence combines with mine. Her strength surges through my veins. My blood feels like liquid fire. I'm powerful and alive.

How Draconian must feel controlling fifteen dragons! I envy him. I want more ... I want to feel that power. I want to take them from him.

"Dacia, come to the castle with me." Draconian reaches his hand out. "I will teach you everything; you will be the most powerful magician ever."

As I turn to go with him, I see Cody's face. It's twisted in fear and pain ... the most horrible thing I've ever seen. My heart tears. He would've hated for me to end up like this.

"No!" I scream.

"Dacia, it's okay. It's just a dream," Cody said. He traced his fingers along my cheek, leaving a trail of electricity in their wake.

I sat up and hugged him. "You're alive."

Samantha looked at me from her loft. Her lips were pinched together in an imitation of a smile. "It was just a dream."

"He killed all of you this time." I stared at the ceiling, but all I saw was Cody's lifeless face. "I can't let it happen."

Cody didn't say anything. He just pulled me closer to him, running his fingers through my hair.

"You won't let that happen." Dan's voice came from somewhere below us and was filled with a confidence I didn't share. "You'll keep us safe."

"I'll try, but unless I figure something out soon, I have no idea how to defeat him." After the room had been quiet for a few minutes, I said, "We should get back to sleep."

"You sure?" Cody's hand stopped moving, and I immediately missed the soothing effect it had had on me.

"Yeah, I'll be fine." I wouldn't be going back to sleep. Too many unanswered questions ran through my brain.

Cody cupped my face in his hands and kissed my forehead. "Try to sleep," he whispered.

Once the others were asleep, I allowed myself to think about my dream. I had to think of it that way … as a dream. It couldn't have been a premonition—could it? I couldn't turn out like that no matter what happened. Ending up like Draconian would be a fate worse than death.

I'm going to have to kill him. My stomach reeled at the thought, but I couldn't see any other way out. As long as my friends lived, I would find a way to deal with the torment.

෫ 349 ෬

Chapter 38
Dreams Of The Future

*S*itting on the floor by the couch, I contemplated skipping classes. It could be my last day of classes ever, but I decided I wasn't going. I rested my head by Cody's, watching him sleep. He looked peaceful. The lines of tension that had marked his face lately smoothed out. His tousled hair made him look boyish.

My touch was gentle, to keep from scaring him, as I caressed his face and ran my fingers through his hair. I wanted to take him and run away from this, but I knew Draconian would find me no matter where I went. There was no escaping my destiny.

"Cody." My voice was soft so as not to wake the others.

"Mmm, morning, Dacia." He pulled me up onto the couch with him.

I stretched out beside him with my head against his bare chest. His body was warm from sleep. "Morning. I'm not going to class today."

"Why not?" He no longer sounded drowsy, but on edge. "Everything okay?"

"Yes." I ran my fingers along the lines that puckered above his eyes, wishing I could take his stress away. "I don't wanna go. I thought maybe we could spend some time alone today … maybe go to Falcon Lake or even Althea."

"Just the two of us?" He pulled me closer. His eyes reminded me of sparkling blue pools.

"Just the two of us." I threw my leg over his and snuggled in closer. Feeling content in Cody's arms, my eyes drifted closed. I forced them open and stood. "I better wake up Samantha and Dan so they can go to class. Then I need to tell Aurelia. She can have Arion keep an eye on us if she wants to."

Dan was sleeping in Big Bird. I walked over and gently rocked the chair back. "I'm awake," Dan said. "Have fun skipping."

I nodded and turned to Samantha's loft. "Hey, Sam, morning has arrived."

She grunted and plopped her pillow on top of her head.

"Samantha'll tell you, you're being irresponsible." Cody smiled. "But, I think it's a great idea."

"You shouldn't talk about me when I'm trying to sleep." Samantha yawned.

"We're skipping." Cody pointed at the two of us.

"You really shouldn't." She sat up and stretched her arms out to the sides. "It's kind of irresponsible."

I tried to hold in my laughter, but it erupted from me, followed by Cody's.

"What is so funny?" Samantha demanded.

"That's what Cody said you'd say." I tugged out shorts and a graphic t-shirt. "Anyway, you need to get ready for class."

"Well, are you sure you're not going?"

"Sam, I love you, but I'm skipping class today." I sat next to Cody on the couch. "I want to spend some time alone with Cody."

"That sounds nice." She climbed out of her loft. Dan stared at her the whole time. "I'm sure you'll have fun, but you missed class on Wednesday. Are you sure you want to skip again today?"

"I know you're looking out for my best interests, but I'm not going," I told her.

She looked a little disappointed, but she didn't say anything more. I was surprised she let it go at that. I figured she would try harder to convince us. Maybe she could see I wasn't going to give on this, or maybe she knew I needed some time off. Either way, I was glad I didn't have to argue.

When she left, I went over to brush my teeth. While doing that, I let Aurelia know we wouldn't be going.

Enjoy yourself, but be careful.

We will.

I will get Dan to his room, then get him and Samantha to class.

Thanks. I plopped down next to Cody and draped his arm over my shoulders.

"Liked it better how we were." He leaned back, pulling me down with him. My head lay on his chest, and his arms wrapped around me. I felt safe and loved. *Why can't things always be like this?*

"Mmm … me too." I traced my fingers over his chest. "Maybe we should just stay here all day."

"Whatever you want, Dacia."

We stayed that way for longer than I intended. I fell asleep to the steady beat of his heart.

Cody and I stand on The River Otter. Cougar Lake reflects the sunset, a flawless mirror image of pinks and purples.

While I appreciate the beauty surrounding me, Cody kneels beside me. I turn toward him, and he takes my hand in his. "Dacia, without you, my life isn't worth living. You are my heart and soul, the most beautiful thing I have ever seen. The stars, the moon, the sunset … they all pale in comparison to you. You would make me the happiest man in the world if you would be my wife. Will you marry me, Dacia KayLee Wolf?"

"Yes." My hand hovers over my heart. Words tumble out of my mouth, higher pitched than normal. "Oh, Cody, yes."

He slips a diamond ring on my finger, and I stare at it in amazement.

The smile on his face holds the promise of forever. His eyes dance with happiness. He climbs to his feet and wraps me in his arms, embracing me like he'll never let go.

He tips my chin up, and his lips crash down on mine. I moan in response and clutch him tighter. I can taste the excitement in his kiss. Our bodies press together, but I want him closer to me. The kiss softens, and he draws back slowly as if he can't bear to be separated from me.

"I forgot to tell you something," he says in a soft whisper.

"What?" My voice trembles.

"It's kind of embarrassing. I left out the most important part." He tucks a loose strand of hair behind my ear. "I forgot to tell you that I love you."

"I love you, too, Cody," I whisper.

"I love you, too," Cody breathed in my ear. With that, the sunset faded away, and I was lying on the couch in Cody's arms. "Look content. Good dream?"

"Yes," I murmured.

We sat in silence for a moment. Then Cody asked, "You going to tell me about it? Or do I only get to hear about the bad dreams?"

"If I tell you, you need to keep in mind that I'm not pressuring you into anything." I didn't know what he'd think of my dream, but I didn't want to scare him off.

He caressed my cheek and neck. The touch was intoxicating. "Wouldn't mind hearing ones where you're saying I love you. Gotta be better than the ones you're screaming in."

"Promise." My tone was adamant.

"Okay, no pressure." He crossed his heart. "I promise."

"I dreamed you proposed to me. It was beautiful and perfect. But, I'm not in a hurry for it." To be honest, I hadn't really thought about it. I knew Cody and I would be together forever. There was no sense rushing into anything, but now that I'd dreamt about it, I knew I wanted that future more than anything.

"We'll always be together," he told me. "Nobody else for me."

I walked my fingers over his chest before wrapping my arm around him. "I know. That's why I'm not in a hurry. Besides, if we got married, my parents would quit paying for my college, and I can't afford to pay for it myself."

"No sense starting further in debt than we have to, but they'd pay if we were engaged. Wouldn't they?"

"I'm sure they would." I closed my eyes and sighed. "I'm not pushing you, Cody. I love you. I know you love me. That's good enough for me."

He trailed his fingers along my jaw. "What would they think about a ring?"

"My dad would wonder why you didn't get his permission. Mom would be ecstatic. They both think the world of you," I answered. "But, you don't have to get me a ring—now or ever, unless it's your choice. It was just a dream. Besides, you don't even have a job."

"Not now, but did. Saved mosta my money." A fox's smile crept over his face, and he winked at me.

Falcon Lake was practically deserted when Cody and I arrived. We sat at one of the picnic tables. Cody's leg was pressed against mine. After the nightmares I'd been having lately, feeling it there was warm and reassuring. He watched me from the corner of his eye, making sure I ate my sandwich.

As soon as I finished chewing the last bite of it, he stood and held his hand out to me. We strolled along the edge of the lake, our fingers entwined.

Snow piles crouched in the shadows of the trees, hiding from the afternoon sun, but everywhere else, bright wildflowers sprung up. Yellows, reds, pinks, and purples.

I should have been worried about Draconian, but for once, I let myself relax.

"Wanna sit?" Cody nodded toward the spot where we'd snuggled on the rocky shore several times since we'd started dating.

"Sure."

We sat on the sun-warmed rocks, and Cody draped his arm over my shoulders. "Glad we skipped."

"Me, too." I laid my head against his chest, listening to his steady breathing, and we stayed that way, gazing at the lake, enjoying each other's company until his stomach growled.

Chuckling, I pulled back and looked into his eyes. "Avalanche?"

"Sounds good." He kissed the top of my head before standing up. "Inviting Samantha and Dan?"

"No." I brushed off my capris. "Just you and me this time."

We drove to Althea in a comfortable silence. I didn't want to ruin the day by talking about Draconian, and I knew if I opened my mouth, there was a chance he would come up.

When we finished eating, we still weren't ready to go back to campus, so we sauntered along the boardwalks, peeking in store windows.

Cody stopped at the display in the local jewelry shop's window. He looked at me, raising one eyebrow, and asked, "See anything you like? Wanna go in?"

My heart swelled. It was the future I wanted, but I hadn't intended to pressure him. "Are you asking because it's what you want or because you think it's what I want?"

"Both," he answered, grinning wider. "Never thought much about it, but uh … now, keep thinking how wonderful it'll be when the world knows you're mine, to hear you say 'yes.'" He squeezed my fingers. "Can't stop thinking about it."

I turned to face him and wrapped my arms around his waist, pulling him closer. "Everyone who sees us together knows I belong to you. They wonder what spell you're under to make you stay with me, but …" I let my voice trail off. "And, whenever you ask, I'll say yes. My life wouldn't be worth living without you."

"Mine either."

"Well, if we're just looking …" I pointed to an oval diamond solitaire. "That one is beautiful. You don't see too many oval-shaped diamonds."

"Beautiful and unique—just like you. Sounds perfect."

By the time we headed back to campus, it was late. While Cody navigated the winding road, I thought about Samantha and Dan, hoping they wouldn't be too worried. I felt guilty about staying out so long without warning her, but I hadn't planned on it. Shaking my head, I pushed those thoughts away. I didn't need to dwell on anything unpleasant right now; I needed to enjoy my time with Cody. There wasn't enough time in the day. The seconds ticked by too fast—reminding me there were only so many of them left.

Standing in the hallway, I stared at my doorknob. "Do you think she'll be mad?"

"No." His hand was on the small of my back, not guiding but comforting. "Knew you needed this."

I pushed the door open to find the lights off and the room empty. A relieved sigh escaped from me. I gathered my stuff and hurried down to the bathroom to change into my pajamas and get ready for bed. When I got back, Cody and I snuggled up on the couch together and watched some random movie that was on TV.

"Look tired." He brushed my hair back. His touch was soft and tender. "Should go to sleep?"

"Do you"—my cheeks heated as a blush crept over them—"care if I sleep here?" I looked down at my hands.

He tilted my chin up so I was looking at him. "If that's what you want."

"You kept the nightmares away."

He pulled his shirt over his head, threw it on the floor, and lay down.

I grabbed a blanket. Then I snuggled against his chest, pulling his arms around me. He held me close, rubbing my back, pressing kisses to the top of my head.

Guilt tightened my chest. In the morning, he'd understand why I didn't want to be separated from him tonight. He'd probably hate me for what I was doing, but it was comforting to know that if I didn't make it back, this would be his last memory of us together.

I threw my leg over Cody's and pressed my body against his. His breath hitched, and he tugged me closer.

Eventually, Cody's breathing evened out, and his grip on me loosed. After what seemed like an eternity, my eyes grew heavy, and sleep found me.

Cody stands at the end of a long aisle, more handsome than ever … debonair. I walk toward him, my steps drawn out. The scene widens, and I notice all the people sitting in pews. My arm is on my dad's. He pats my fingers, and I look up into his damp eyes.

Cody gazes at me, flashing a radiant smile. The extent of his love for me is obvious to everyone there. When we reach him, Dad places my hand into Cody's. At the touch of his skin, I woke up.

Cody was propped up on his elbow, peering down at me. "You okay?" He brushed my hair back. "Nightmare?"

Closing my eyes, I pictured Cody in his tuxedo. "No, it was wonderful," I whispered. When I looked up at him, tears pooled in my eyes.

Ever so gently, he traced his thumb along my jaw. His lips pulled down. "Then what's wrong?"

"I just …" I clung to Cody, pressing my face into his chest, breathing him in. "I don't know if it will ever come true."

"What was it?"

"Our wedding."

"Why wouldn't it?" His hold on me went rigid. "Told you we'll always be together."

I smiled at him, but it was full of sadness. "I don't think I can beat him."

He scooted back and looked down at me. His blue eyes were intense. "You've got this. I can feel it." He tapped his fingers over his heart. "It'll be okay."

"I hope you're right." I sighed.

His hands delicately trailed over my arm, leaving a tingling sensation behind them as they moved on. I kissed his neck, then his chin. He lowered his face, and in an instant, my lips were on his.

He drew back. "Something you're not telling me?"

I ran my hand along his side. "Why?"

"Don't know." He rubbed his jaw. "Feel like you're …"

"What?" I pushed him, even though I should have let him drop it.

He squeezed his eyes shut, pinching the bridge of his nose. "Feel like you're saying goodbye. Like you wanted as much time as you could get so you could get your fill of me."

"Oh, Cody, I could never get my fill of you. I want forever with you." I dragged my hand through my hair. "I really don't know how much time I have left, and I don't want to waste one minute … not even one second of it."

He blew out a long breath. "Just don't do anything stupid."

I was glad he worded it that way because I didn't want to lie to him, and I didn't think challenging Draconian to keep him from hurting my friends was stupid. "I won't."

"Sleep good, then." His lips brushed my forehead, and he stroked my arm.

I fell asleep feeling safe and loved.

Chapter 39

Saturday morning when I woke up, my legs were twisted with Cody's, and his arms were wrapped around me. Despite what awaited me, a smile stretched across my face.

I lay beside him, memorizing the way he looked, his warmth, his smell.

Slowly, to keep from waking him, I disentangled my legs from his. My foot was on the floor when his eyes popped open.

"How'd you sleep?" He brushed his finger from my temple to my chin.

"Good," I whispered, "well … great, actually." Heat flushed my cheeks.

"Yeah." His blue eyes sparkled. "Liked having you here."

I snuggled up against him, not quite ready to let go yet.

Dacia, Aurelia's voice chimed in my head. *It is time.*

Trying not to show any reaction, I thought, *I know.* I pulled away from Cody. "I'm going to take a shower before they get too busy. You better stay put until you're supposed to be here."

"Know the routine." He laughed.

I brushed my lips over his, intending to leave.

Holding his face in my hands, I stared into his eyes. There was so much I wanted to tell him in case I didn't make it back. Instead, I pressed my mouth to his, threw my leg over his, and clutched his waist, pressing our bodies together.

Cody's fingers twisted in my hair. With his other hand, he tugged me closer. Groaning, he deepened the kiss.

Heat blossomed in my core. I slowed the kiss and drew back. My breath came out in ragged gasps.

"Dacia?" Cody's voice was husky.

I grazed my fingers along his arm as I stood. "I love you."

He clenched my hand, and fear flashed through his eyes. "Love you, too."

Grabbing my bag, I walked to the door. I looked back at my friends. Samantha and Dan had returned sometime after I fell asleep last night. She was buried under covers and pillows. Dan smiled at me from Big Bird. I waved and pulled the door shut.

As I stepped into the hall, I wondered if Cody realized I was saying goodbye. If not, he'd figure it out soon enough. When I didn't come back from my shower, he wasn't going to be happy, but hopefully, he'd forgive me.

While I changed into black yoga pants and a blue shirt, Aurelia set the wards protecting my room. I braided my hair and sent a silent prayer to God. *Please keep my friends safe and help me survive. Help me figure out how to stop Draconian without killing him, but if it comes to that, please give me the strength to defeat him.*

Aurelia and I met outside, heading into the forest. We plodded along without saying anything. Neither of us was in a hurry to find out what fate had in store.

As soon as we were hidden beneath the shadows of the trees and out of view of prying eyes, we turned invisible and launched ourselves into the sky. My shirt rustled in the wind. Goosebumps spread across my arms. A few stray hairs unraveled from my braid, whipping around my face.

The ground rushed below us quicker than I would've liked. As I flew, I reached my mind out to Draconian, making sure Aurelia could also hear me. *I'm on my way here.* I sent him an image of a clearing in the mountains far away from any humans.

Why do I care? His voice entered my mind, and I cringed in response.

Now or never. My stomach twisted. I closed my eyes fighting off my fear, opening them before I flew off course or hurt myself.

"Aurelia"—my voice was quiet, broken—"I can't do this."

You have to, she spoke into my mind, *otherwise Draconian will come after you.*

We landed in the clearing. A field of purple and yellow wildflowers stretched all around us. A few pine trees dotted the area. Rocky peaks stretched to the sky, capped by snow. The air smelled crisp and clean.

Stretching my senses out, I searched for Draconian. When I didn't find him, I turned visible and sank to my knees. Trembling began deep inside me, my chest tightened, and I thought I might collapse. "I should have …" My voice caught in my throat. "I should have told them goodbye. I shouldn't have left like that."

"No, you did the right thing." Aurelia stood beside me with her hand on my shoulder. "They never would have let you go. You will be back with them before you know it."

"How can you be so sure? What if I don't make it back?" My pulse thrummed in my ears. The sound drove out all of the background noises. My heart attacked my ribs, trying to break free from its prison. I clutched the grass, struggling not to lose myself. My breath rushed in and out too fast to fill my lungs. Tears pricked my eyes, and spots darkened my vision.

Aurelia's energy flowed into me. Her strength vanquished the panic attack. "Everything will be okay."

"I'm terrified." A chill shuddered through my chest, and bile rose in my throat.

She nodded. "I would not expect any less. Without these emotions, you would not be who you are. Use them to your advantage."

"How … how am I supposed to do that when right now, I just want to run away?"

Silence filled the space between us. "Draconian shows no fear; that does not mean nothing scares him. He is arrogant. His overconfidence will be his downfall. You, on the other hand, know you are vulnerable. Because of that, your will to live is stronger than his. Use your fear to stay alive."

"I'll try." I tugged on the end of my braid. "I'm really not ready to die … or to become Draconian's apprentice."

"Stand." She reached her hand down to me. "You must not let him see you like this."

I grabbed her hand and let her help me to my feet. Then I wrapped my arms around her. "No matter what happens, you've been a good friend. Thanks for everything." I cocked my head. Madness and hatred buzzed inside my mind. "He's almost here."

Aurelia disappeared. "Let him believe you came on your own," she whispered.

Draconian landed about fifty yards from us. He folded his hands behind his back. His gray robe dragged over the ground. Walking toward me, he said, "You had two more days. Why meet now?"

I shrugged. "It's time to end this."

He scrutinized me. "Where is Nefarious?" His cold voice shot through me like daggers. His fury simmered just below the surface.

"I decided it wouldn't be in my best interests to bring him along." Defiance kept my voice from shaking.

He made a clicking noise before saying, "That wasn't the answer I was looking for."

"Why do you want him, anyway?"

"I've already answered that." He narrowed his eyes at me. "Power. That's it. Controlling a demon would bring me great power. Nobody would dare defy me. Nobody would doubt my strength."

Anger blossomed in my belly, taking my fear and hardening it into determination. "So, you're nothing but a bully?" I had dealt with bullies all my life, and he was the worst of them.

Draconian swung his arms toward me. Lightning shot from his fingertips.

I thought of fire, willing my body to turn to flames. Sparks danced over my hands and up my arms, but nothing more happened.

Aurelia threw a shield up in front of me just before the bolts pummeled it.

"So, I see your pet is going to help you." Draconian sneered. "I wonder … has she told you her secret yet? No matter. Maybe I should bring my pets out to play, too." He waved his hands.

Dragons flew at us from all angles: diving down from the sky, crawling out from the trees, appearing from thin air. Gusts of wind whipped around me as the beasts' wings beat the air. The ground shook when they landed. A rainbow of dragons surrounded us.

A chill rippled along my skin. I stood frozen in place, unable to move even as fire shot through the air at me from every direction. Aurelia's shield held the flames at bay, but I felt like I was about to be the main course at a barbecue.

"Dacia! Snap out of it!" Aurelia's gold skin glistened from the heat.

I fell to my knees, grasping my stomach. *I'm going to die throwing up*, I thought to myself.

Chapter 40

"acia!"

I lifted my face to Aurelia, still clutching my stomach. "I don't know what to do. I can't stop them."

"Concentrate on stopping Draconian." The strain of holding the dragon fire back showed on her face. "Ignore the dragons."

I laughed, and even to me, it sounded crazed. "How?"

Aurelia grabbed my hand and teleported us back to the cavern where she had freed me from Draconian's spell. Treasure glittered in the vast space. The air smelled earthy but not musty.

A golden haze surrounded Aurelia. The shimmering fog spun through the air, whirling like a tornado, growing larger by the second. The dim light of the cavern reflected off it, casting a multitude of small rainbows over the walls, ceiling, and floor.

The cloud continued to grow until it became so dense I couldn't see Aurelia at all. My breathing hitched.

I stepped back, unsure of what the shimmering mist was. Coins clanked under my feet, tumbling down the stack.

The haze dissipated, and in its place stood a gold dragon. It turned its head toward me, and a spiked crest flared up, framing its face. Fangs jutted out from its jaws.

Scrambling back, I sucked in a breath. My hand rose to my mouth. My feet slipped on the treasure, and I fell. My heart pummeled my chest.

The beast lowered its head, and I found myself looking into Aurelia's eye.

"You're—" my words caught in my throat. I took a deep breath and started over. "You're the dragon that saved me and … you're from Arion's memory."

"Yes." Aurelia's voice was richer, fuller. "I came to you in human form because I knew you would not trust a dragon." She shrunk. Her crest transformed into golden locks. Her features distorted, morphing into the person I knew as Aurelia. "I will help you, but you have to trust me."

My stomach plummeted, and Aurelia's words ran through my head. *However, if for some reason, it looks like you are not going to make it, I will transform into my true shape.* "Y-you th-think I-I'm gonna die."

She tilted her head to the side, shaking it slightly. "No, I think you defeat him."

"Then why did you show me?" I pointed at her. "You said you'd show me if I was going to die."

Her jaw dropped, and I was shocked that she had actually shown a reaction for once. "I thought it would give you strength knowing you had a dragon on your side." She looked down at the gold beneath her feet. "I did not mean for you to misconstrue my actions."

Hope settled inside of me, warming my heart, filling me. With her, there was a chance. I stood up, brushing myself off. "Turn into a dragon and fight with me."

"I cannot resist him in dragon form." She stepped toward me. "No other dragon has."

"All you have to do is fight it. Find the strength inside, and push him out of your head."

"I cannot take that risk. I will do what I can in this body." She pointed at herself. "I could not live with myself if I turned on you."

I stared down at my feet. "I don't know if I can kill him."

"Killing is not easy to do. It should only be done when there are no other options."

"I don't think there are any other options when it comes to Draconian." Forgetting my hair was braided, I tried to pull my hand through it. "He is evil. He will never give up."

"No, he will not." She took another step toward me, and I got the impression she was trying not to scare me. "I may be able to draw the dragons to me while you go after Draconian. However, if we do not kill him, you and your friends will always be in danger."

"Then help me kill him, Aurelia. I can't do it by myself," I begged her.

"We will go out there together and stand against him." She reached for my hand. "If the opportunity arises, I will take it. That is all I can promise."

Placing some distance between ourselves and Draconian's dragons, we teleported back. We hadn't been gone for more than a few minutes even though it felt like an eternity.

As I stood there, preparing myself to face death, I took in every sight, every sound, every smell. The sky was the beautiful cerulean blue that can only be found in the mountains. Big, puffy white clouds floated high above. Birdsongs rang out, the individual harmonies joining in a natural melody. The cool mountain air filled my nostrils with the scent of pine trees—a scent I had loved since the first time I had smelled it. People always noticed the worst things in life—evil, hatred, fear—but there was so much good to be had if you just took a look around yourself. Even here, standing on death's doorstep, there was beauty and wonder. If these were to be my last moments, I wanted to take in as many blessings as I could before I died.

"I knew your courage would falter." Draconian pressed his hands down, and the dragons sat, lowering their heads to the ground. "I'm surprised to see you back, but then again, I thought you'd last longer to begin with."

"I'm here now, so let's get this over with." False bravado filled my voice.

He paced like a teacher lecturing his class. "You do realize that if you would have held up your end of the bargain, this would be over by now; don't you?"

I clenched my hands into fists. "Maybe if you'd've held up your end, I would've, but you didn't leave me alone. I worried about my friends every day."

Draconian jerked back like I'd slapped him. "What makes you think that?" He pulled his fingers through his beard.

"I felt your presence everywhere we went. You were always watching us." I ground my teeth together. "I had no peace. I couldn't enjoy myself. I was constantly looking over my shoulder, wondering when you would try to ambush me or come whisper in my ear again."

"Impossible!" He staggered back, his mouth floundering. "How could you know that? I never let you into my head. How?"

"That's not what's important here!" I stabbed my finger toward him. "*You* are the reason I didn't bring Nefarious! When you can't be trusted to keep your word about something as simple as that, how am I supposed to believe you won't unleash a demon on the world?"

His face darkened, and his eyes narrowed. "You never intended to bring him. You always planned to attack."

I sucked in a deep breath, filling my lungs to capacity, and blasted lightning bolt after lightning bolt from my fingertips. Draconian dodged and weaved, managing to avoid any harm.

"Is that all you've got, Dacia?" He ducked under a thunderbolt. "I won't give up. If you want to end this, if you want your friends to be safe, you'll have to hand over Nefarious."

"No, there is always another way!" I willed a small icicle into my palm. Stretching it into a javelin, I launched it at Draconian.

"Not this time." He spun to the side. The shard tore through his robe, slicing his arm. Blood beaded on his pale skin. *"I always win!"*

A blast of fire shot toward me. With a wave of my hand, I deflected it.

"If I kill you, my friends will be safe."

Silence was the only response.

"You've shown me how easy it is." *How am I gonna do this? Kill or be killed. I'll just have to learn how to live with it later.* "You actually killed me. Didn't you think I would return the favor someday?"

"I thought you stood against evil." Electricity sparked between his fingers. "If you kill me, won't you succumb to that which you hate most?"

I thought about the fear I heard in his voice. For the first time, I realized how much power I had. Draconian wouldn't be afraid of me if I was insignificant.

Flames danced over my skin. Heat built up inside me until an inferno engulfed my body. Then I shot through the air at him.

Draconian's eyes widened. "Get her!" He shouted to his dragons. They leaped up, flying toward me.

I slammed into Draconian. He shot through the air. Smashing his head against a tree, he slumped forward.

I flew toward him, wondering if he was dead, if this was over. The black dragon stepped between us.

A low rumble sounded deep within his throat, sending a ripple along the spikes that ran the length of his spine. With a shake of his horned head, his jaws opened. The scent of rotten flesh hit me with the force of a gale. "I will end this even if he won't," the beast snarled.

My flames extinguished, and I crashed to the ground. *No. No. No.* I'd been so close to ending this, but if the dragon still defended him, Draconian lived.

Smoke curled over the dragon's nostrils. The beast stepped toward me, lowering his head and pulling his lips back in a snarl.

I lifted my hands palms out, showing him that I meant no harm. "Let me …" My words caught in my throat. I couldn't believe I was about to ask to murder someone. Shaking my head, I said, "Let me kill him. Let me finish this."

The dragon's head jerked back, readying to strike.

Oh, my God. I'm gonna die. My mind went blank. I didn't try to protect myself, didn't try to fight.

A gold dragon shot through the air like a torpedo. Her teeth were bared, and her talons tore through the black dragon's flesh, knocking him to the ground. A deafening roar filled the air as he turned to face Aurelia.

Climbing to my feet, I forged a sword from ice. It felt heavy in my hand, a weight that tugged on my heart and my conscience. Once I used it, I couldn't go back. I'd never be the same. Blood would stain my hands for eternity.

I stood over Draconian. Blood trickled from his nose, staining his mustache red. His gray eyes were open but unseeing.

Killing him was the only way to ensure my friends' safety, but killing him when he was unconscious seemed wrong.

A dragon roared. I looked up. The black dragon's talons tore through Aurelia's flesh. Gold blood dripped from several wounds.

For Aurelia. I lifted the sword and was rammed in the side. The force knocked me to the ground, flinging the sword from my hand. It shattered against the rocks.

Scrambling to my feet, I faced the intruder. The beast tossed its scarlet head in challenge.

I stared into its amber eyes. Fire and hatred flashed through my mind. A crimson hatchling rubbed its cheek against mine … not mine. The dragon's. Its thoughts flowed into my mind.

Delving deeper into its mind, I saw its … no his pride as he taught his hatchling to fly and to hunt. Another dragon called out his name.

"Pyrus"—I filled my voice with command—"you are free. Go home."

Pyrus shook his head, like he was waking up, and then launched into the air, flying away without a backward glance.

Warmth spread through me as hope dared to plant its seeds in my heart.

"What did you do to *my dragon*?" Draconian screamed from the base of the tree.

"I freed him. I'm freeing all of them." I stepped toward him, forging my ice sword. "Without your pets here to protect you, we'll see what you're really made of."

Fear flashed across Draconian's face. "Bring me her friends!"

Three dragons rose out of the pine trees down the mountain from us. The whoosh of dragons' wings grew louder as

Draconian's smallest dragons flew with my friends dangling from their talons.

"No." The word was a gasp. My heart plummeted. The room was warded. They were supposed to be safe.

"If you want to win, you can't show all your cards at the beginning of the hand." Draconian pushed himself to a sitting position, leaning against the tree.

Aurelia and the black dragon flew above us, striking at each other. Flames tore through the sky.

The three dragons landed, spreading out enough that I couldn't get to them all. They held onto their prisoners.

My friends' faces were pale and contorted with pain. Blood trickled from their shoulders, soaking their shirts.

Cody only wore one shoe. I wondered if it'd fallen off or if he'd been taken while trying to put it on.

"You are down to two choices." The smugness in Draconian's voice made me want to puke. "You can become my apprentice or they can die. What'll it be?"

"I can fight you." Without my concentration, water dripped off the tip of the sword. I let it fall to the ground, knowing I couldn't use it on Draconian while his dragons held my friends.

"Yes … if you want to watch your friends die, that is definitely an option." His voice sounded like it was getting stronger. "Make your choice, Dacia."

"If I surrender—" I dropped to my knees in front of him "—will you let my friends live?" Desperation clung to my voice.

"No, Dacia, don't," Cody's weak voice carried to me. "I can't live without you."

"Well, at least one of your friends doesn't want to live," Draconian said as he tried to stand. "I guess we should grant him his wish. Shouldn't we?"

Stretching my hand out in front of me, I said, "Don't move." My voice was steel, the threat in it clear.

Draconian gripped the tree, struggling to pull himself to his feet.

Lightning shot from my fingertips. "I said, don't move."

He threw up a shield in time to deflect the bolt, but it cost him.

He fell to the ground, exhausted. I couldn't understand why he wasn't healed yet. As powerful as he was, he should've been back to one hundred percent by now. Then the answer hit me. Somebody with his total disregard for life would never realize how much it could help him.

"You made your choice," he said in a feeble voice. "Capture her, and kill the boy," he ordered his dragons.

A dragon as white as the new-fallen snow swooped at me. I rolled across the ground, dodging its claws. It flew up into the sky, readying itself for another pass.

I teleported closer to Cody, sensing Arion's presence. *Can you free Samantha and Dan?*

Yes ... I failed to keep them safe. I will not fail in this.

Cody's dragon, the brown one from the forest, dropped him. The dragon stood on his hind legs. His body swayed as he readied himself to strike.

"Stop!" I shouted. "Here I am."

"The trickssster," the dragon hissed.

"I told you Draconian wanted me. Now's your chance."

As he deliberated over which command to follow, I searched his memories for his name. I had to find it before he decided to kill Cody. Finally … "Taipan, you are free! Draconian no longer controls you."

I ran to Cody, kneeling beside him. His breathing was shallow and erratic. My heart plummeted. Dragons raced toward us. I cradled Cody against me and teleported him under the cover of the trees. I held his face and focused my thoughts on healing.

His breathing evened out, and some color returned to his cheeks.

Brushing his hair back, I said, "I have to do this."

"I know." His voice was rough, pained. He grabbed my hand. "Come back to me."

I gazed into his sapphire eyes, seeing his love for me and his fear mingled together. "I'll try."

Dragons screeched above us. Aurelia and the black dragon were locked together. Their claws dug into each other's scales. Their jaws snapped.

Aurelia, I thought as I teleported away from Cody. *If you tell me his name, I can free him.*

It is Malus Tribulus. Along with her words, I felt her pain.

"Malus—" A blue dragon dove at me. Its talons tore across my back as I dropped to the ground.

Through the pain, I tried to focus on the dragon's thoughts. They were scattered, giving me the impression that it didn't have a very long attention span. I searched thought after thought until I deciphered his name.

Valerian, you are free, I thought to the dragon.

Looking up, I searched for Malus Tribulus and Aurelia. They burst through a puffy, white cloud. The black beast held Aurelia in his claws. She still fought, but it was obvious Malus Tribulus had gained the upper hand. Without wasting any more time, I yelled into the sky, "Malus Tribulus, you are free to go back to your home."

He released Aurelia and flew off. She spun through the air, spiraling toward the ground, tumbling through the sky. She flapped her wings, but the membrane had been slashed apart. Panic widened her eyes.

I watched in horror as she plunged, realizing seconds before she hit me, that I was about to be crushed. Waving my hands at the sky, I conjured a gust of air to hit her from below. It slowed her descent and helped cushion her fall.

I set a shield around me, kneeling to the ground and covering my head.

Aurelia's body battered the shield, bounced off it, and crashed to the ground with a sickening crunch. Gold blood gushed from several wounds. Her breaths were ragged and wet.

Dragons circled in the sky above us. I blasted lightning bolts at them as I rushed toward Aurelia's head.

Her eye fluttered open. "Thank ... you." Blood trickled between her fangs.

I held my hand next to her long, slender neck. "Can I heal you?"

"Please."

I erected a shield around us. It was a drain on my energy but necessary while my attention was focused on Aurelia.

A white dragon landed outside the shield, close enough that the ground shook. The beast lowered its head, and sorrow filled its lavender eyes.

"Get her!" Draconian shouted.

The dragon sank down, tucking its wings in, and making itself appear as small as possible. It crawled around the shield, checking for weaknesses in it.

Keeping an eye on the newcomer, I inched my hand closer to Aurelia. Smooth scales met my trembling fingers. Images of life floated across my eyelids. I poured all my strength into healing her.

Aurelia sighed, and I pulled my hand away.

"Shall we end this?" She lifted her head. Her gaze landed on the white dragon. "That is Arabis."

The dragon lifted its head at the sound of its name.

"Arabis, you are free," I said.

"Thank you, Little One." Her voice was musical. "You are very brave. If you ever need anything …"

"Will you get my friends to safety?" I asked before she could rescind her offer.

"As you wish." She bowed her head and launched into the sky.

Aurelia stood slowly as if unsure her legs could hold her weight.

Arion, I thought, *Arabis is going to help you get them out of here.*

Draconian still sat against the tree. His arms hung limply at his sides. A dragon stood on either side of him.

Aurelia nodded her head toward them. "The purple dragon is Acacia."

"The green one?" I asked.

She shook her head.

"Acacia!" I strode toward Draconian and his guards. Draconian's head snapped up at the sound of the beast's name. "You are free."

The dragon narrowed its eyes at me. "You insolent fool," his foul voice was hate-filled, "of course I am free."

He stepped toward me, tossing his horned head. Then he unfurled his wings and leaped into the air. The gust of wind knocked Draconian back. He pulled himself to his feet, staggering forward. "Enough!"

His dragons swooped in, landing all around us. The ground trembled, and I stumbled.

Draconian stepped through the beasts. His pale face was damp with sweat. "Aurea," his voice was soft.

Aurelia stopped. Her eyes dimmed.

"What a beautiful name." Draconian sneered at me. "You didn't think she'd give you her true name. Did you? You're just a pawn in her game."

"Aurea, fight him." I pressed my hand to her neck, sending her my strength. "You don't have to let him in. You're free, Aurea."

"Yes, Dacia, as long as you are here by my side, I am free." Her words vibrated against my hand. "I cannot stop him from controlling me, but I can count on you to keep me true."

I kept funneling my energy into her, hoping it would keep Draconian from gaining control. The world spun, and I wobbled. I clung to Aurelia.

Aurelia pulled away from me. *You must save your strength. You have to end this.*

I'm okay.

Draconian staggered toward us. "Aurea, if you will not join me, you will die"—he thrust his finger at me—"just like her."

Aurelia, I thought to her, *turn invisible ... now.* As she did, I transformed into her human form. My body shimmered, and long golden hair flowed to my waist.

"Dacia!" Rage distorted Draconian's face.

What are you doing? Aurelia's voice echoed in my head.

I didn't answer, afraid that in my exhaustion Draconian or his dragons would hear my thoughts.

"Aurea," Draconian purred, "join me."

"Never!" Aurelia's voice shouted from my lips.

"Then die." Shards of ice flew from his fingertips.

I flung my arms up, erecting a shield that only covered me from the waist up. My power was too diminished to cover all of me and hold Aurelia's form.

I pressed forward. Icicles burst against the shield, creating mini snowstorms each time one hit.

A shard pierced my thigh. I screamed in response. Gold blood trickled down my leg. *Weird.*

Fire ignited beneath my skin, melting the dart. I grew the flame in my palm and threw it at Draconian, quickly followed by several others.

He stumbled backward.

"Attack!" he screamed at his dragons.

Aurelia's gold scales glinted in the sunlight as she reappeared. Her head lowered toward the ground. She bared her teeth, and a low growl escaped her lips as she stalked toward me.

"Well, isn't this an interesting turn of events?" Draconian laughed out loud.

The magic drained from me, seeping away like a balloon deflating. *How had I not realized his magic would still affect her?*

Dragons rushed at me. I engulfed myself in flames. Spinning in circles, I shot lightning bolts off in all directions. The dragons held their ground but didn't venture any closer.

"Aurea," I shouted, "you are free. You do not have to obey Draconian."

Her eyes cleared, and she shook her head.

Draconian raised his weathered hands, and my body went limp. I crashed to the ground. The flames that had licked my skin sizzled then extinguished themselves. "She will obey me."

Pain blazed through my body, boiling the blood in my veins, searing my muscles. Through my screams, I heard Draconian try to gain control of Aurelia.

"Aurea," he crooned. "Dacia is a threat to your kind. You must stop her. If you do not, she will slaughter all the dragons."

Thinking about spring and all the life that it brings with it, healing power slowly trickled through my veins. My pain diminished, and strength returned to my limbs. When I was free from his paralyzing spell, I remained as still as possible and spoke to Aurelia telepathically, *Aurea, you are free. Draconian is not your master. Do not listen to him. Please help me, Aurea. I am your friend.*

Aurelia didn't acknowledge me. With a predatory gaze in her eye, she prowled closer like a hungry wolf. Fear held me in its grasp. Even though she was a terrifying dragon … she was Aurelia. She was my friend. I couldn't fight her. Hatred flashed in her eyes, and I knew it was over. I never imagined I'd die at the hand of a friend. I looked into her eyes and hoped she would give me a quick death.

Aurelia whipped her neck around, turning on Draconian. Relief chased my fear away, leaving me lightheaded. A low growl erupted from the depths of Aurelia's chest, and she swiped at Draconian with her razor-sharp claws.

Draconian screamed in agony as her talons tore through his flesh. Blood poured from his wounds. His eyes filled with terror. He stumbled backward and fell to the ground.

The green dragon sprung on Aurelia, knocking her back. Aurelia growled and attacked the other beast.

Dragon claws and teeth flashed through the air. Their necks snaked together. Their tails flicked.

I stood and formed a third sword in my hand. Closing my eyes, I took a deep breath and strode toward Draconian. He lay on the ground. Blood saturated his robe. The edges of his wounds had already begun stitching themselves together.

Pressing his arms down on the ground, he lifted himself up and pushed back, sitting against a boulder. His body shook. His face was ashen.

Looking at the ice sword, he smirked. "You're not fooling me. You won't use that."

I glanced down at the blade. My stomach clenched, and my shoulders slumped. When I looked back at him, tears were pooling in my eyes. "I don't think I have a choice."

"Join me." He coughed. Blood splattered his hand, staining his beard. "There is … so much I can teach you."

"Will you free the dragons?" I stepped forward. "Give up on Nefarious?" I took another step.

His eyes flicked to something behind me. I turned. A red dragon swooped toward me. I blasted the beast with a lightning bolt, knocking it from the sky.

I turned back to Draconian. Fire danced over his fingers. He raised his hand. "You'll all be mine." The flames merged together forming a ball. He lifted it.

The world slowed. I plunged the sword into his chest. Dropping the grip, I staggered back.

Draconian looked at the sword, then at me. His gray eyes bulged. Blood gurgled out of his mouth. The flames in his palm extinguished, and he grabbed the blade, pulling it out, slicing his palms open. Blood spurted from his chest, soaking his robe.

His breath hitched, then stopped. His features slackened. He slumped forward, and the dragons launched into the sky, flying off.

Aurelia landed next to me, changing into her human form. She lifted the sword. "Turn around."

I looked at her, hearing what she said but not comprehending. My hands shuddered. *I killed him. Oh, my God. I'm a murderer.* My knees buckled, but Aurelia clasped me under the arm, stopping my fall. When I regained my balance, she gently turned me around.

The sword slashed through the air. Something thumped against the ground. Then Aurelia grabbed my arm, sending her energy through me, and teleported us to my room.

Chapter 41

Ding Dong The Wizard Is Dead

Cody stood at the window. Samantha and Dan huddled together on the couch, and Sarah paced nervously.

I slumped into Cookie Monster. Turning my hands, I stared at them. I could still feel the blade sliding through Draconian's flesh, piercing his heart.

Voices drifted toward me, but the words may as well have been gibberish.

A hand slammed down on my shoulder, and I jumped up. Cody stood by the chair. His arms were lifted. His palms faced out by his shoulders.

"Dacia?" He slowly reached out to me.

Shaking my head, I stepped back. "I … I'm … a murderer. I killed him." My stomach heaved. I ran to the trashcan and knelt in front of it. I threw up until nothing was left in my stomach. Shivers wracked my body.

Leaning against the wall, I closed my eyes and pictured Draconian's dying expression, his pain, and his surprise. Tears slid down my cheeks, dripping off my chin.

Cody sat next to me, wrapping his arms around his knees, careful not to touch me, his eyes dampened by concern.

Aurelia narrated the day's events. Samantha, Dan, and Sarah asked questions every so often. I stared at nothing, occasionally wiping my eyes. Cody watched me, not touching me, not saying anything.

When Aurelia finished, Cody said, "You promised." His jaw clenched. "Weren't going to do anything stupid." He reached toward me but dropped his hand between us. "Then you confronted Draconian."

Unable to look him in the eyes, I dropped my chin to my chest. Blood splatters were all over my shirt. I jerked back, my feet scrabbling against the floor. My breath came in quick, harsh gasps. I tugged at my shirt, ripping the bottom of it.

"Dacia." Sarah grabbed my hands. "It's okay."

"There's blood." My voice was shrill.

"Samantha get Dacia a change of clothes. Cody, Dan, step outside for a minute. Aurelia, get me a wet washrag." Sarah focused on me, her voice calm and soothing like she was talking to a wild animal. "You're all right."

"Here." Samantha handed Sarah my clothes, and Aurelia held out the wet rag.

Sarah let go of my hands. "Do you need help?"

Shaking my head, I grabbed the washcloth, wiping off my face, neck, hands, and arms. When I tried to pull my shirt off, my hands shook so badly I could barely do it. I pulled on a sweatshirt and sweatpants.

"Do you need anything?" Samantha's voice wavered.

I leaned my head against the wall and shrugged. When I closed my eyes, Draconian sat in front of me, pulling the sword out of his chest.

My eyes sprang open, and I gasped. Cody stood in front of me. He held his hands out and inched toward me. "Please." He stepped closer, and I fought the urge to scramble away. "Let me in."

The pain in his eyes struck something inside me. Holding my hand out, I said, "Help me up?" My voice quivered.

Cody lifted me off the floor, one arm under my legs and one behind my back. He walked over to the chair and sat with me on his lap.

I kept my body rigid. I didn't deserve his tenderness. I didn't deserve kindness. I needed to be locked away where I could never kill anyone else.

"Take my energy," Cody whispered.

His voice startled me, and I jerked back, nearly falling off his lap. He clutched me tighter.

Aurelia knelt beside the chair, grabbed my hand, and her strength flooded into me. *You are not a murderer. You killed him in self-defense, and had you not, you and your friends would be dead or worse, and I would be under his control.*

Her vitality bolstered me, taking the edge off my anguish, and even though her words rang true, I didn't believe them.

When Aurelia let go, I looked at my friends, actually seeing them for the first time since I'd come back. All of them had changed out of their bloody clothes. Samantha's hair was still damp.

"Do you need healed?" I couldn't meet their eyes. I was ashamed for not asking sooner. "Are you all right?"

"We're good," Dan answered. "Arabis healed us."

"I'll probably have nightmares tonight." Samantha shuddered. "I can't believe you sent a dragon to help us. I was scared to death. Luckily, Arion explained before we totally freaked out."

I stared at the floor. "She offered to help, and I needed you safe."

"We were hiding under the trees." Samantha ran her hand along Dan's thigh while she talked. "This gigantic dragon flew at us, but Arion told us it was okay. As she landed, she transformed into a woman with white skin, like sunlight glistening off snow, and white hair. Her eyes were like Aurelia's but purple. She grabbed our hands and teleported back here with us. She healed our wounds and made sure we were safe while we showered. When you ki—" Samantha chewed on her lip. "When, uh, it was over, she left."

I relaxed a little, leaning back into Cody, and rested my head on his shoulder. He ran his hands along my arm and leg.

"How are you doing?" Sarah asked.

"I'm really tired." I yawned to emphasize my point.

She walked over and squeezed my shoulder. "If you need me, my door is open."

"Thanks." I tried to smile but didn't think I managed to pull it off.

"Stay out of trouble," she said as she strode to the door.

"It's not like I go looking for trouble," I mumbled.

Cody raised one eyebrow. "You did." His voice lowered, became somber. "You were saying goodbye."

I nodded.

Sarah turned back. "Cody, Dan, you two can start going back to your room again." She grabbed the doorknob.

"Not tonight," Cody said with no trace of hesitation in his voice.

I tilted my head. He always did what he was told.

"Going to make sure she's nightmare-free first."

"Yes, that's probably a good idea," Sarah said.

Samantha stood, reaching for Dan's hand. "Since we don't have to worry about dragons or Draconian anymore, we're going to dinner. You two can come if you want."

"Thanks"—I stood up—"but I'm staying here."

"Me, too," Cody said.

Samantha hugged me. "Get some rest. You look beat."

I returned her hug, grateful for the opportunity. "I think I'll take a shower, then sleep for a week."

She pulled away and grabbed her purse.

"See you later," Dan said as they headed out.

"I will be across the hall if you need me." Aurelia closed the door behind her.

Cody and I were left alone. "So—" I turned to him "—how are you going to make sure I'm nightmare-free?" I stepped toward him.

"I, uh, thought you could curl up in my arms again." He brushed my hair back and trailed his fingers down my face.

My body hummed in response. "Yeah, I thought we could test that theory, too."

"Once we're married"—his voice softened—"you'll never have to worry about nightmares again."

"That'd be nice."

"Thought I'd lost you." His hands slipped to my shoulders and down my arms. He wrapped them around my waist and pulled my body against his.

With my arms around his neck, I brought his mouth down on mine. He bit my bottom lip. I gasped and closed my eyes.

Draconian lay in front of me. My sword pierced his heart.

I opened my eyes. Cody's hold on me had loosened. My hands were on his chest, pushing him away.

"What?" Cody's face was a mask of confusion.

I lifted my hand to pull it through my hair, but it shook so badly that I stuck it under my armpit instead. "I … I can't right now." I turned away from him and grabbed my bathroom bag. "I need a shower."

Cody beat me to the door. Holding it closed, he said, "Don't shut me out." He dropped his hand to the knob and pulled it open. "I'll be here."

Nodding, I hurried to the bathroom and into the shower. The water rushed over me, but no matter how many times I scrubbed my hands, they never felt clean.

Snuggled against Cody, sleep finally came.

Over and over again, I feel the sword slide between Draconian's ribs, see the shock and pain flash across his face, watch as his eyes dim, and listen when Aurelia decapitates him to make sure his death is final.

The scent of blood fills my nostrils, and bile rises up my throat, coating my mouth with its foul taste.

I woke up, my face wet with tears and dry-heaved into the trashcan. Cody rubbed his hand up and down my back.

He held me while I sobbed. Dark circles surrounded his eyes, and lines etched his face.

Dan and Samantha had opted to stay in Dan's room. For them, it was over. Life could go back to normal, but I didn't know if mine ever would.

Lying on top of Cody with his arms wrapped around me, I felt safe and loved, but as soon as I closed my eyes, horror grabbed hold of me.

Cody, Samantha, and Dan dangle from dragons' claws. Draconian tells Taipan to kill Cody.

Aurelia prowls toward me. Her head lowers. Death flashes through her eyes.

Draconian sneers at me. "You won't use that."

Once again, I plunge the sword through his heart.

I woke with a jolt. My heart hammered in my chest, my breathing ragged.

Are you okay?

I stifled a scream when Aurelia's voice echoed in my head.

I keep killing Draconian, I answered. *I can't turn it off.*

A soft knock sounded at the door. I padded to it, looking out the peephole. Aurelia stood in the hallway in green satin pajamas. Not a hair was out of place.

I felt like a disaster in my t-shirt and athletic shorts. I tugged my hands through my hair, catching on several knots, and opened the door.

"Hey, Aurelia," Cody said from the couch.

"Hello." She focused on me. "I can help you sleep."

"Without dreaming?" I asked as I closed the door.

"I could, however, dreams are a necessity. Without them, the mind cannot get past the terror." She led me to the couch.

"What do I need to do?" I asked.

"Lie down, and do not resist me."

Cody pulled me against him. I used his arm as a pillow.

I nodded at her. "Go ahead."

Aurelia's fingers pressed against my temples. Warmth and comfort flooded my body. My eyelids drooped, and sleep beckoned me closer.

Draconian sits against a tree. His robe is covered in blood. His wounds are horrific, but they're healing.

A redhead stands above him. Sunlight glints off her sword. Prisms dance in the air.

A red dragon swoops at her, and she blasts it with lightning. The beast falls from the sky.

Draconian readies himself to throw a ball of fire at the girl, but she slams the sword through his heart. He slumps forward.

Aurelia takes the sword and turns the girl away. In one swift strike, she removes his head. Blood sprays from his neck. She drops the blade, takes hold of the girl, and disappears.

I watch from the trees. I see the dragons shake their heads as if waking from a deep sleep. They launch into the sky, flying away without a backward glance.

ഈ394ന

Chapter 42

Goodbyes

Tuesday, while the others were in class, I met with Aurelia. We sat in her room. With all the plants surrounding us, I felt like we were in a jungle.

"I am no longer needed here." Aurelia's expression dimmed for a moment.

"Oh." I pulled on my lip with my teeth. "So, you're leaving?"

"Unless you need me." She tilted her head. "Are you having nightmares?"

"No." Heat rushed up my neck and onto my face.

"Are you sure?"

"Uh … yeah." The last two nights, wrapped in Cody's arms, my dreams had been filled with happiness and love. The nightmares held at bay by his embrace. "My dreams have been really good." I shook my head. "You don't think it'll stay that way. Do you?"

"No." She curled her legs on the couch. "The world always needs to be saved from something."

I took a long breath—a breath that said everything I couldn't. "I was afraid you'd say that."

Aurelia looked uneasy for the first time since I'd met her. She shifted on the couch. "It may be years until you are needed, or it might be in a few months or a few days."

I dropped my head into my hands. The room spun around me. "I can't." My stomach heaved. "I can't kill again."

"You will never be free from this obligation." Sorrow flashed across her face. "You may never have to kill again, but now that you have captured Nefarious, freed fifteen dragons, and defeated Draconian, some magical beings may want to test their skills by challenging you. Until you are needed, you can live the life you want."

I rubbed my hands over my face. "I'll do what I can."

"Arion and I will keep an eye on you." She smiled. "When the time comes, we will decide if you need our help again or if you would be better served by someone else."

"I hope it's you." My heart plummeted at the thought of not seeing her again. Looking into her gold eyes, I said, "I'm going to miss you guys. I can count all the real friends I've had on one hand, and you're among them."

"Thank you, Dacia. Arion and I feel the same way." Her shoulders drooped. "Leaving is the hardest part for me."

"There's something else I've been wondering." My stomach twisted at the thought of asking, but I needed to hear her answer.

"You can ask me anything. You have earned that right."

"Well, uh, since you've been a dragon all along—" I looked down at my hands "—how did you feel when I turned into one?"

"I did not like it." Her eyes flashed at the memory. "I spend most of my life in human form, but when I saw you transform into a dragon, the beast within stirred angrily. It took all my control to keep from changing back into a dragon, and that would not have been a pretty sight." She stretched her legs out in front of her. "As a human, I have more empathy. I am able to control myself better. Please, never take that form again. If dragons are in the area, they will not care that you saved so many of us. They will not try to control themselves."

"Thanks for letting me know." I pictured the dragons that had been in the clearing that day. Acacia definitely wouldn't have let me live. It annoyed him enough that I'd freed him. I remembered how Malus Tribulus fought with Aurelia, how he'd nearly killed her, and was certain I wouldn't have walked away. "I might've tried to turn into a dragon when I fought Draconian. With fifteen dragons around … sixteen counting you, I doubt I'd've lived."

"No, that would have been the end of you, as it was in your dreams."

Sitting there, looking into her gold eyes, I realized she wasn't human. I'd known since I met her that she wasn't, but it dawned on me that animals had different instincts, different reactions to things that were perfectly normal for people.

I tilted my head to the side. "So … does it bother you when I look you in the eyes?"

She chuckled. "Years ago, it would have, but I have learned that it is a sign of trust and respect in some cultures and not a challenge."

After a brief pause, she said, "Draconian was dragon-like in one way. He hoarded treasure as we do. You will never have a normal human life. Holding a job will be nearly impossible for somebody in your position."

"I guess Cody will just have to make enough to support us." I heard the despair in my voice. "If I don't manage to run him off by then."

"I want you to have a portion of Draconian's treasure. I can help you convert some of it to currency. There are also a few magical items—like the amulet you wore against Nefarious—that may help you in the future. I know it is not much, but it is the best I can do to help keep you safe."

"It's a lot, Aurelia." Tears pooled in my eyes. "Nobody has ever done anything like this for me, and I'm sincerely grateful."

Aurelia nodded her head. "You have done so much more for me and my kind. This is the least I can do for you."

"Thank you." I swallowed hard, forcing the lump in my throat down. "It's very generous."

She watched me for a few minutes. "Arion would like to see you before we leave. We could meet you and your friends at Falcon Lake tonight if you would like."

"Yes, I'd love to see him again." My heart sank, knowing it might be one of the last times. "I'm sure Samantha'd love to see Arion again, too. She really likes him, and well, now that I don't have to worry about dragons attacking me, I wouldn't mind flying with him again."

"I am sure he would like that, too." She looked out the window, and I wondered if she was communicating with him. "Arion has a deep respect for you. He does not show himself often. He does not have a lot to do with people. He really took to you."

"Why don't you stay until the end of the semester?" I suggested. "It's only a couple more weeks. Then you'll know if my nightmares come back, and you can also show me how to keep people from sensing my presence."

"I can probably do that, but if I am needed elsewhere, I will have to go."

"I understand."

Chapter 43

Cherished Moments

Falcon Lake was all but deserted. Not a lot of students were there since it was Tuesday night. Cody and Dan piled logs in the fire ring. A blue flame ignited in the palm of my hand, spreading warmth to my fingertips. I tossed the fireball onto the logs, then sat next to Cody on our blanket.

Samantha giggled at something Dan said, and the flickering light danced over her face. It was nice to see them laughing and joking.

Pink and orange stained the sky, reflecting on Falcon Lake, and tinting the snow on the mountain peaks. The shadows cast by the pine trees stretched across the rocky shore, reaching for the water.

A twig snapped. The hair on my neck rose. My heartbeat drummed in my ears, blocking out all other sound. I clenched Cody's hand and slowly turned to look over my shoulder.

My breathing calmed, and my muscles loosened as Aurelia's tranquil aura settled over me. She strode toward us, her steps graceful. Her hands were tucked into the pockets of her jeans. Her gold hair was pulled into a high ponytail.

She was the same person I'd known all summer, but I saw her in a new light now. She was still my friend, but she was also something more.

"Hello." She sat on the beach.

"So … uh, you're a dragon?" Dan crossed his arms over his chest and tapped his foot against the ground.

She laughed, easing some of the tension. "Yes, I am."

"Are you usually in human form?"

Aurelia was right about curiosity. That was a question I hadn't even considered, and looking into Dan's face, I was sure he had more to ask.

"I spend most of my time like this." She swept her hand from her head to her feet. "As a human, I am able to rationalize more and be less instinctual. I spend most of my life trying to right wrongs. As a human, I am better able to determine proper justice. However, when I am alone in my lair, I prefer to be a dragon."

It surprised me that she was so candid with him. When I'd been the one asking questions, she'd always been evasive.

"Cool." Dan looked fascinated. "So, why … Oh, do you mind me asking you questions?"

"No, like I told Dacia, humans are very curious."

"Why didn't you tell Dacia you were a dragon? Wouldn't it have been helpful for her to know she had a dragon on her side?"

"No, Dan." I shook my head and smiled at Aurelia. Then I focused on Dan. "The only dragons I met before Aurelia were trying to kill me. I wouldn't have trusted her, and she knew that. When she transformed into a dragon in front of me, I was terrified. Then I was convinced she thought I was going to die because she'd promised to let me know what she was before I died. Then, after all of that, I realized that dragon or not, she was my friend." Staring into the fire, I said, "I wouldn't be here without her or Arion."

"Speaking of Arion"—Samantha turned her head, scanning the beach and trees—"is he here?"

Aurelia turned toward the forest behind her. "Arion, I think it is dark enough that you can show yourself."

He landed on the beach down from us. Reflecting the firelight, his wings shimmered more brilliantly than any star. Folding them against his body, he cantered toward us.

Meeting him halfway, I threw my arms around his neck and whispered, "Thank you for everything you did. I couldn't have done it without you and Aurelia."

"It was my privilege." The rich timbre of his voice soothed me. "You are an asset to your race, Dacia." He bowed down before me, lowering his muzzle until it hovered just above the ground. "I am honored to have met somebody like you."

My cheeks burned with embarrassment. "Thank you." My words caught in my throat, coming out choked.

Arion lifted his head. "I hear you would like to fly with me."

"I would love to." I pressed my hand to my chest.

He knelt next to me, and I climbed onto his back. As soon as I was situated, he galloped down the beach. With a leap, he spread his wings, flapping them to gain altitude.

The wind blew my hair back, and my joyous laughter filled the air.

Arion flew into the star-filled sky, soaring toward the waning moon, and for the first time since Saturday, I didn't feel like I bore Atlas' punishment.

I spread my arms out wide, threw my head back, and whooped with delight. Dropping my hands, I petted Arion's neck. His fur was softer than a chinchilla's. *Is that okay?* He wasn't a horse. Maybe he didn't like being treated like one.

He nickered. *Yes.*

Running my fingers over his silken feathers, I thought to him, *Will I see you again?*

Someday. Aurelia and I are very close. I go where she goes, and she believes we are destined to see you again.

I'm glad. Curiosity got the best of me. *How did you meet Aurelia? A dragon and a pegasus seem like a strange pairing.*

When I was a young colt, she saved me. It was a beautiful spring day, and I was grazing in a mountain meadow. Wildflowers were in full bloom. I had never seen anything like it before. I wasn't paying attention, and a griffon attacked me—pegasus is their favorite food. Aurelia saved me, and we have been together since.

Oh, wow.

Arion began his descent. The air smelled like burgers and campfire smoke.

I patted his neck again. *I'm going to miss you two. It won't be the same here without you.*

We will miss you also. I know very few humans and even fewer I am fond of. Your courageousness and compassion have earned my friendship.

"Thank you," I whispered. A lump formed in my throat. I was honored and humbled.

While I ate my burger, Samantha's excited screams filled the night sky. When Arion landed, Samantha looked like somebody had roped the moon for her. She wrapped her arms around his neck. "Thank you so much!"

Dan and Cody each took a turn soaring through the sky on Arion's back. While Samantha's face had lit up like the sun, theirs shone more like the full moon.

We sat around the campfire, roasting marshmallows and talking. I snuggled up against Cody. These were the times I needed to cherish. Who knew how long I'd have before my life was filled with turmoil again?

Chapter 44

Going Home

Two months ago, I sat in front of my closet packing. Then Draconian and his dragons happened, so there I sat doing it again. Whether demons, dragons, or boogeymen attacked, I had to go home. There was no alternative this time.

I shoved the last of my clothes into my duffle, zipped it up, and stood beside Samantha. I was going to miss this place. The white walls and lavender carpet had become home, but I wouldn't miss it as much as I would Samantha.

Turning away from the room, I looked at her. Her brown eyes were misty. "I'm so glad you got stuck with me," I said.

She chuckled and shook her head. "Yeah, me, too, but I'd've gotten a lot more sleep with another roommate."

"Sorry about that." I resituated my bag.

She grinned, pulled the door shut, and we walked down the hall. "But I'd've missed out on so much more."

Her parents had arrived before the sun crawled above the horizon. They'd loaded everything into their SUV. Then Wayne had taken Deana by the hand and led her away, telling Samantha they'd meet us in Althea for lunch.

I threw my bag into my truck and pulled the tonneau cover down. Then we went to Dracaena Hall to see if Dan and Cody needed help.

We bounded up the three flights of stairs and down the white and green hallway. When Dan opened the door, Cody stood across the room, pulling a white t-shirt over his head.

"Just finished." Cody's words lifted my gaze away from his abs.

"Do you need me to throw anything in my truck?" I asked, making my way over the green carpet to his side.

"That'd be great."

"We'll meet you in Althea," Dan said as he and Samantha stepped into the hall.

"Sure." Cody waved before the door clicked shut.

Wrapping my arms around him, I said, "At least we live in the same town. They're barely going to see each other."

Cody's hands slid over my arms. "Won't be the same."

"No." I sighed. "I can't imagine our parents would be okay with us sleeping in the same bed, fully clothed or not."

He tilted my chin up. "Not all I meant. Will you be okay?"

"I hope so." I rested my palms on his chest, feeling his heartbeat through his shirt. Neither of us knew if my nightmares had been held at bay by his presence or because nothing evil was waiting to descend upon me. "I'm not ready for more monsters."

Leaning his forehead against mine, he said, "Six weeks."

Deana looked around the table at Rocky's Bar and Grille. Her soft brown eyes met each of ours before moving on. "This is so wonderful." A smile lit up her whole face. "I'm so glad Sammi made such good friends. You'll have to get together before next semester. You're all welcome to stay at our house."

Wayne clasped his hand over hers and shook his head. I couldn't help but smile at them. I loved how Wayne's tranquilness balanced Deana's enthusiasm.

Cody and Dan ate peanuts, tossing the shells on the floor. I felt sorry for the poor sucker that had to clean up the mess. Country music filled the spaces between conversations. Dan and Samantha held hands under the table, leaning in toward each other. Samantha barely touched her food.

Lunch finished too soon. We all stood on the boardwalk out front. Butterflies fluttered to the baskets of petunias. A soft breeze ruffled my hair. Deana gave everyone a hug. Then Wayne dragged her off to their SUV. I gave Dan a quick hug but drew out Samantha's.

"I want to know if anything happens," Samantha said. "Anything."

"Promise." I pulled away. Her face blurred. I wiped my eyes and smiled. "I'll miss you."

She hugged me again. "I'll miss you, too."

Cody and I stood, holding hands while Samantha and Dan walked away. They stopped in a grassy area behind the restaurant. Sobs shook Samantha's shoulders. Dan held her, his arms around her waist and his head resting on hers.

"Ready?" Cody asked.

I lifted my shoulders. "Not really."

He turned me around. "I'm only a coupla miles away."

I hugged him, too tightly, not wanting to let go. His lips brushed my forehead. My eyes. My cheek. Then pressed against my mouth.

The kiss started tender. Cody held my face, his lips moving slowly over mine. He slid one hand down my back, clutching me against him. His other one tangled in my hair.

I slid my hands into his back pockets, and the kiss became searing, urgent.

Somebody bumped into me. Only Cody's hands kept me from toppling over.

"Take it somewhere else," the culprit said.

Heat flooded my neck and face, and I stepped back from Cody.

His fingers lingered against my face. "I'll follow you home."

I pulled my truck's door shut and felt a pang of loneliness spear my stomach. Cody would be close by, but Samantha lived three hours away.

Aurelia and Arion disappeared three days ago. She'd left me a note that said, "Duty calls," the keys to several safety deposit boxes, and a suitcase brimming with magical items and treasure.

I cranked the radio and rolled the windows down. With the wind whipping my hair around my face, I drove home, singing at the top of my lungs.

Chapter 45

Nice Kitty

Walking home from Cody's house, lightning bugs flash through the trees. Crickets chirp, owls hoot, and bugs hum, filling the night with their chorus. Stars sprinkle the obsidian sky. A crescent moon hangs low over the horizon, smiling down at me.

A slight wind stirs the Aspen trees. The leaves tremble, filling the air with their unique song. Warmth spreads through me.

Suddenly, everything quiets. I stop walking, searching the trees for the source of this silence.

Fiery eyes glare at me from the cover of the forest.

Inching backward, gravel crunches under my foot.

The beast growls. Stalking toward me, a massive black panther emerges from the woods. Sinewy muscles ripple beneath onyx fur. Flames burn in its eyes.

I glance over my shoulder thinking there must be a blazing inferno behind me, but nothing is alight.

Turning back, the beast is nearly upon me. Its shoulders are even with my waist.

The panther's lips pull back, revealing fangs as long as my fingers.

My heart races, but I stand, mesmerized by its eyes.

The creature prowls closer. I lift my arm, and sparks dance over my fingertips. Flinging my hand out, a lightning bolt blasts into the beast's hide and disappears.

The panther pounces, knocking me to the ground. My breath whooshes from my lungs. The creature's weight presses down on me.

It lowers its head. Red, orange, and yellow flames undulate in its eyes. Its low growl is menacing.

Fear twists my stomach. The panther's hot breath wafts over my face. Its head whips forward, and its teeth sink into my neck.

Pain flashes, bright and intense before dulling to nothing. Blood gushes over my skin onto the ground. Darkness surrounds me.

Sunlight streamed in through the window. My pink sheers do little to stop the brightness. *I'm gonna have to remember to pull the blinds tonight.*

Stretching, I tossed the covers to the side and rolled out of bed. My pillowcase was soaked in blood.

Visions from my nightmare crashed into me. I slumped to the ground and held my head in my hands.

So much for a peaceful summer.

The End

The best thing that you can do to support an author,
especially an indie author, is to leave a review.

Not only do your reviews help new readers find us,
they help the algorithms guide more people to our books.
In turn, that makes it possible for us to keep writing.

Positive reviews bring a bright spot to our day,
and reviews with constructive criticism help
us figure out how to make our books better.

Acknowledgments

I think writing the acknowledgments is the hardest part of writing a book. There are so many people who helped along the way, and I'm afraid I might leave someone out.

First I'd like to thank everyone who read my first book. It was scary to publish it. I was terrified that nobody would enjoy reading it. You've given me the courage to continue publishing my books and to continue writing.

I would like to thank my cats: Bella, Westley, Galadriel, and Merida. They offer their support and "help" daily. In all honesty, though, they do help relieve my stress and give me some inspiration for characters.

Once again, I'd like to thank all the critters at Critique Circle who helped me improve my writing: Kathryn Sparrow, Stone Jeffers, Travis Sullivan, Nadine Ducca, and Astrea Taylor. There were many more who weren't mentioned because I couldn't contact them to get their real names or permission to include them here. I'd also like to thank all the other people who helped me along the way: Marva Mitchell, Berni Stevens, Cheryl Gage, Tammy King, Eileen Sharp, Linda Hirscher (RIP), Curtis A. Cooper, and Peggylou Beazley.

Thanks to all the people at 20BooksTo50K® for the wonderful information and the encouragement. Without them, I'd feel even more lost in this self-publishing wilderness.

Most of all, I would like to thank Jeff, Jami, and Jesse for their support and their love. My life would be incomplete without them.

I would also like to thank God for leading me down this path and helping me when I couldn't do it on my own.

A special thank you to Rob Thomas, Lifehouse, and Daughtry for providing much of the music I listened to while writing my books.

And, of course, Go Cubs!

If you liked this story, you can join my mailing list.
Drop by my website <u>MandiOyster.com</u>
or if you have any comments,
shoot me a note at mandi@mandioyster.com.
I am always happy to hear from people who've read my work.
I try to answer every email I receive.

If you liked the story, please write a short review for me.
I greatly appreciate any kind words, even one or two
sentences go a long way. The number of reviews a
book receives improves how well a book does.

Facebook: <u>https://www.facebook.com/MandiOysterAuthor</u>
Instagram: <u>https://www.instagram.com/mandioyster/</u>
My web page: MandiOyster.com

About the Author

Mandi Oyster lives in Southwest Iowa in the middle of an enchanted forest where unicorns, fairies, and dragons abound. At least, that's what she assumes when she looks out into the trees. Her husband, two kids (when they're not away at college), four cats, and two chinchillas share the house with her. 

Besides being an author, she also runs her own editing business and works full-time as a digital prepress technician for a local printshop.

You can find her online at:
https://www.MandiOyster.com
https://www.facebook.com/MandiOysterAuthor
https://instagram.com/MandiOyster/